Also by Emily Giffin

Something Borrowed
Something Blue
Baby Proof
Love the One You're With
Heart of the Matter
Where We Belong

EMILY GIFFIN

The One & Only

HODDER

First published in the United States of America in 2014 by
Ballantine Books
An imprint of Random House
A division of Random House LLC
A Penguin Random House Company, New York

First published in Great Britain in 2014 by Hodder & Stoughton
An Hachette UK Company

This paperback edition published 2015

I

A CIP catalogue record for this title is
available from the British Library.

B-format Paperback ISBN 978 1 444 79901 9
A-format Paperback ISBN 978 1 473 61301 0
Ebook ISBN 978 1 444 79900 2

Typeset in Plantin Light by Palimpsest Book Production Limited,
Falkirk, Stirlingshire
Printed and bound by Clays Ltd, St Ives plc

Hodder & Stoughton policy is to use papers that are
natural, renewable and recyclable products and made from
wood grown in sustainable forests. The logging and
manufacturing processes are expected to conform to the
environmental regulations of the country of origin.

Hodder & Stoughton Ltd
338 Euston Road
London NW1 3BH

www.hodder.co.uk

For my uncle, Doug Elgin,
who inspired my love of college sports . . . and
taught me that it's more than just a game

The One & Only

I

I should have been thinking about God. Or the meaning of life. Or simply grieving the fact that my best friend was now motherless and my own mother without her best friend. Instead, I found myself gazing into the sleek mahogany coffin lined with generous folds of ivory silk, silently critiquing Mrs Carr's lipstick, a magenta with blue undertones that subtly clashed with her coral dress, the same one she had worn to Lucy's wedding nearly five years ago.

More problematic than the shade of lipstick, though, was the application. Someone, clearly low on the beauty-industry totem pole, had colored just outside the lines as if to create fuller lips. It was an optical illusion that never fooled anyone and seemed wholly unnecessary given the circumstances. After all, there would be no photos taken today. No professional albums filled with various combinations of family and friends, posing with Mrs Carr, horizontal but front and center. In fact, the entire custom of fancying up a corpse for an open-casket funeral seemed suddenly ridiculous. Cremation was definitely the way to go. It was the way *I* wanted to go, rather than risk the possibility of going out on a bad-hair day. Without a husband or sibling, I made a mental note to convey my final wishes to Lucy after some time had passed. She was really the only person it made sense to tell. Besides, Lucy got shit done. She was like a decisive committee with no dissenting members. At least none who dared speak up.

'Do you need anything?' I whispered to her now, breaking into the endless line of friends, family, and virtual strangers offering condolences. I had never seen so many people at a funeral, and, combined with everyone who had come to the wake the night before, it seemed that most of our small town had made an appearance.

'A Kleenex,' she whispered. In contrast to the past three days, she was dry-eyed, but looked to be on the verge of a fresh breakdown, her blue eyes glassy and round. I handed her a tissue from my purse, once again conjuring her wedding, when I had vigilantly shadowed her with mints and a compact of powder.

'Anything else? Water?' I asked, thinking that it felt good to be needed for once, and it was a shame that it took a major rite of passage to turn the tables on our usual dynamic.

Lucy shook her head as I returned to the second pew, where she had instructed me to sit, along with my parents. She had all the details covered – from the seating to the hymn selection to the white orchids on the altar – which was why it was so surprising that she hadn't noticed her mother's lipstick last night at the wake, when there was still an opportunity to fix it. At least I *hoped* she hadn't noticed it, because as a corollary to her efficiency, Lucy was cursed with the crippling capacity to dwell on even the most trivial matters for weeks, sometimes years. Like the grudge she was sure to hold against Angel, her mother's hairdresser, who dared to be away this week, on a Caribbean cruise no less. If not to return to do her mother's hair, Lucy had ranted, then at least to pay her respects to her best client. Secretly, I thought Angel should have been afforded some slack; surely her vacation had been planned for months, and logistically it must be pretty tough to get off a ship on such short notice. But it wasn't Lucy's style to cut anyone slack, especially when it came to a slight to her family, whether perceived or real. As her oldest and closest friend, I was also a beneficiary of her extreme loyalty and had long since memorized her bright-line rules. There was no gray area and no second chances, even when I could muster up my own forgiveness or indifference. That didn't matter to Lucy, who stood by her creed: *You're dead to me.*

There it was again. *Dead.* I shivered at the finality of it all, cursing the cancer that took Mrs Carr's life in ten months flat, not a single symptom until it was too late. Recognizing that praying wasn't at all like riding a bicycle, I bowed my head and formed silent, clumsy words, doing my best not to question God's existence while I asked Him for favors. *Please help Lucy find a way to be happy without her mother.* It felt like an impossible request, and the fact that she had her own daughter, just-turned-four-year-old Caroline, who was too young to attend the funeral or one day remember her Gigi, seemed to heighten all the emotions of loss. A new generation was a constant reminder of everything Mrs Carr was going to miss. Birthdays, benchmarks, all of life's momentous *firsts* stretched ahead without her.

I turned my gaze and prayers to Lawton, Lucy's brother, a carefree bachelor but still a mama's boy to the core. He was standing beside his sister, mopping his face with a handkerchief, likely one Mrs Carr had pressed for him in anticipation of this day. She had made a flurry of arrangements and plans over the past few months, including a morphine-induced request for Lawton and me to marry. *Kill two birds with one stone,* she had said, not exactly a flattering or hopeful description. That wasn't going to happen – Lawton wasn't my type and I was even less his – but I had smiled and told her I'd work on it, while Lucy made a joke about every couple needing at least one grown-up. I looked up at the sun streaming through the stained glass behind the altar, wondering if Mrs Carr was somewhere up there watching us. And if so, could she read my mind? Just in case, I said a final goodbye to her, my throat tight and dry. Then I closed my eyes and mouthed *Amen,* aware of the glaring omission in my prayer: *Coach Carr.*

When I looked up again, he was directly in my line of vision, walking from the opposite end of the casket toward the pew in front of me, his hands clasped behind his back, the way he paced the sidelines of a game. I heard him exhale as he took his seat, close enough for me to touch his shoulder if I only extended my hand and leaned forward a few inches. But I couldn't so much as look at him, hadn't been able to in weeks, even when I dropped by the house with store-bought casseroles and six-packs of Shiner Bock. I knew he was devastated, and the mere notion that I might glimpse him in a vulnerable moment was unbearable, like looking at those award-winning photos of soldiers or firemen, holding babies, weeping after a catastrophe. I firmly believed that it was always harder to be the one left behind, especially if you thought you were on your way to happily ever after.

Coach and Connie Carr's story fittingly began at Walker University, the school with the same name as our small town in North Texas, where he was the star quarterback and she the prettiest cheerleader. Except for the one season he played for the Colts, just after Lucy and I were born, the Carrs never left Walker, as he worked his way up the coaching ladder from quarterbacks' coach to offensive coordinator to the youngest – and now the winningest – head coach in Bronco history.

Coach Carr was something of a deity in our town, throughout the state of Texas, and in the world of college football, which happened to be the only world I truly cared about, and Connie had been royalty in her own right. She was more than the elegant coach's wife, though. She worked tirelessly behind the scenes, as the ultimate fund-raiser, administrator, social chair, therapist, surrogate mother. She sat with injured players in the hospital, wined and dined boosters, cajoled crotchety faculty, and soothed feelings on all sides. She made it look so easy, with her surplus of charm and kindness, but I knew how demanding and lonely her job could be. When Coach wasn't physically gone – on road games or out recruiting – he was often mentally absent, obsessed with his team. Still, Mrs Carr had never wavered in her support of her husband, and I honestly didn't know what he would do without her.

I took a deep breath, catching a whiff of Coach Carr's familiar Pinaud Clubman aftershave, a few airborne molecules triggering rapid-fire memories. Lucy and me sitting on his office floor, playing board games while he drew up depth charts and play diagrams. The three of us riding in the front seat of his truck, my hand out the window, as we listened to country music and sports radio. Sneaking into the locker room with Lucy, not to glimpse the shirtless boys (although we did that, too) but to hear Coach's passionate postgame speeches, thrillingly peppered with cusswords. Much like the one he gave me in his living room when I was seventeen, right after the cops decided not to arrest me for drinking and driving – and instead dropped me off at the Carrs'. *Coach, you got this one?* I could still remember the look he gave me – worse than spending the night in jail.

I allowed myself a fleeting glimpse of his profile now, afraid of what I would find, but comforted that he appeared as strong and rugged as ever. Not at all like a widower. He was a fit fifty-five, but looked a decade younger thanks to a full head of hair, olive skin, and a strong bone structure. It wasn't fair, I had thought for years, whenever I saw Lucy's parents together. Mrs Carr was beautiful, fighting age almost as viciously as she fought death, but her husband just kept getting better-looking, the way it was for a lot of men. And now. Now it *really* wasn't fair. It was a proper funeral musing – the inequities of life and death – and I felt relieved to be maintaining an appropriate train of thought, if not actual prayer.

But in the next second, the pendulum swung in the opposite direction, as I thought of football. Lucy said it was all I *ever* thought about, which was pretty close to true, at least before Mrs Carr got sick. Even afterward, I found myself escaping to the game I loved, and I knew Coach did the same. It upset Lucy because she didn't understand it. She would ask me, through tears, how he could care so much about signing a recruit or winning a game. Didn't he see how little it mattered? I tried to explain that his job was a distraction, the one thing he could still control. Football was our touchstone. A constant. Something to hold on to as a bright light burned out in Walker, Texas, our little version of Camelot.

A few seconds later, Lucy and Lawton sat down, flanking their father, and the sight of three of them, instead of four, was more than I could take. My throat tightened as the organ began to play. Loud, mournful notes filled the church. I could hear my mother softly weeping between chords, and could see Lawton and Lucy wiping their eyes. I glanced around so I wouldn't cry, anything to distract me in that final lull before the service began.

I spotted my boyfriend, Miller, who had played for Coach years ago, during my faded era, standing with a few former teammates in the far aisle. They all looked lost in their ill-fitting suits and shined-up shoes, unaccustomed to Walker gatherings that weren't celebratory in nature – pep rallies, parades, and booster dinners. Miller gave me a two-finger wave with a half smile as he fanned himself with his program. I looked away, pretending not to see him. Partly because I knew Lucy didn't approve of him. Partly because I still felt a knot of guilt for having been in bed with him when she called with the final news, my ringer accidentally turned off. But mostly because it just wasn't the time to be waving at your boyfriend, especially one you weren't sure you really loved.

'No riffraff at the house,' Lucy declared immediately after the burial as she marched down the grassy embankment toward Neil's freshly washed Tahoe. I'd known it was only a matter of time before her sadness turned to anger – and was actually surprised that she had held out this long. Coach had once joked that Lucy had only two gears – happy and angry.

'Define *riffraff*,' I asked – because I really wasn't sure what she meant other than that she cast a wider net than I did when it came to such categories.

'Boosters. Fans. All players, past or present. Except Ryan. Mom loved Ryan,' she finished decisively, tightening the belt of her long black trench coat.

Mrs Carr *did* love Ryan James, who happened to be Walker's only Heisman Trophy winner, but she had also adored every sorry benchwarmer and earnest walk-on ever to come through the program. I exchanged an anxious glance with Neil, who calmly said his wife's name.

'Don't "Luce" me,' she snapped under her breath. 'I mean it. I've had enough. Family and close friends only.'

'How do you plan on enforcing that?' Neil asked, glancing around at the droves of acquaintances making their way to the circular drive surrounding the Carr family plot. He pushed his retro oversize glasses – the kind you could only pull off when you were as boyishly cute as Neil – up on his nose and said, 'Half the town's on the way over there now.'

'I don't care. They weren't even supposed to be at the cemetery. What part of *private* don't they get? And they aren't coming to the house. They aren't. Tell them, Lawton,' she said, turning to look at her brother.

'Tell who what?' Lawton asked, appearing completely disoriented, useless as ever.

'Tell Shea and Neil that it's time for family and close friends only,' she replied, for our benefit more than his. She reached up to make sure that no loose strands of hair had escaped her tight, low bun. They hadn't, of course.

'But they think they *are* family, Lucy,' I said and could hear Mrs Carr saying it now, referring to virtual strangers as part of 'the Walker family.'

'Well, it's offensive,' Lucy said, stumbling a bit as her heels sank into the fresh sod. Neil slipped one arm around her, catching her, and I contemplated how much worse this would be if she were in my shoes, alone. 'I'm sick of these people acting like this is a tailgate at a damn bowl game. And if I see one more teal tie . . . Who wears teal to a funeral?' Her voice cracked just as Miller, in his teal and gold striped tie, loped toward us with an expression that neared jovial. I made eye contact with him and shook my head, but the gesture was far too nuanced for him.

'Yo. Shea. Wait up,' he called out as I noticed that he not only had donned his school colors but also had a 'Class of

2001' Broncos pin centered on his lapel. How he'd managed to keep track of that thing for over a decade was beyond me, especially given that he'd lost his wallet twice since we'd been dating.

Lucy pivoted, squaring her slight frame to all six feet, four inches of Miller. 'I'm sorry, Miller,' she said, her chin quivering. 'Did you want to sing the fight song for us? Or just relive the glory days when you were . . . relevant?'

'Whoa, whoa, girl. What'd I ever do to you?' Miller said, his emotional instincts on par with his sartorial sense. 'Why you gotta call me unrelevant?'

'*Ir*relevant, Miller. Not to be confused with *irregardless*, which, by the way, also is not a word. And I'm calling you *irrelevant* because you *are*.' Lucy's long, delicate fingers made artistic flourishes in the air.

'Fine, then,' Miller said, his cheeks even ruddier than usual, his curly sideburns damp with sweat despite the brisk February day. I had told him twice to get a haircut, but he hadn't listened.

'I just wanted to tell you I'm sorry. Very sorry. For your family. For your loss. I really liked your mom. She was an awesome lady.'

The speech was heartfelt, I could tell, but Lucy refused to cave. I braced myself as she crossed her arms and said, 'Oh, puh-lease, Miller. The only loss you ever cared about was the one to Nebraska when you fumbled on the four-yard line because you were so coked up.'

'I wasn't *coked up*,' Miller said. 'I just . . . dropped the damn ball. *Jesus*.'

I bit my lower lip, shocked that Lucy recollected the play, even the yardage. But she got the rest wrong. It was T. C. Jones who failed the drug test after the game, not Miller, who never really did coke, vastly preferring the mellowing effect of marijuana. In fact, based on his glassier than normal expression, there was a distinct possibility that he had smoked this morning. Maybe even on the car ride over.

'Luce,' Neil said, sliding his grip from her elbow to her

forearm and gently guiding her to his car. A child psychiatrist, he had a calming effect on the most high-strung children – and the rare ability to soothe Lucy. 'Come on now. Let's go, honey.'

She didn't reply, just gracefully climbed into the car, crossed her slender legs, and waited for Neil to close the door. As Lawton collapsed into the backseat, Lucy stared down at the pearl bracelet that once belonged to her mother.

'Are you coming with us?' Neil asked me. 'Or going with your parents?'

I glanced back toward my mom and dad, walking toward her car. Although long divorced, they had managed to be civil to each other through this ordeal, and, to my relief and surprise, my dad had left his wife back in Manhattan.

Lucy answered for me through her half-open window. 'Neither,' she said. 'I want her to ride with Daddy. He shouldn't be driving alone. He's being so stubborn.' She stared at me. 'Okay, Shea?'

I hesitated.

'Just do it. And make sure he wears his seat belt. One death in the family is plenty,' she said as I looked up the hill, finding Coach Carr in a cluster of dark suits.

'But don't you think he'd rather be alone?' I asked. 'I'm sure he doesn't want to make conversation—'

'Well, you're different,' she said, cutting me off. 'He actually *likes* talking to you.'

2

I waited, squinting in the winter sun and watching as Coach Carr talked to the last few graveside stragglers. Lucy was right. They really *were* insensitive, as everyone knew he didn't like to talk after losses, and if you didn't know this, you probably shouldn't have been there in the first place.

He finally broke free and walked toward me. My mind raced, wondering how I was going to tell him he had an assigned chaperone back to his house.

'Hi, Coach,' I said when he was directly in front of me. We made fleeting eye contact before I stared back down at the ground.

'Hi, girl,' he said, sounding weary. 'You need a ride?'

'Um . . . Lucy wanted me to go with you . . . to make sure you wear your seat belt,' I stammered.

I looked up as he shot me a sideways glance. 'All right . . . But am I allowed to dip?'

'I thought you quit?'

Some of his Levi's still had a telltale imprint of a Copenhagen tin on his back right pocket, but it had been years since I had seen him take a dip. His quitting tobacco was all Mrs Carr wanted one Christmas. That and a Cotton Bowl victory – both of which she got, along with a diamond tennis bracelet she hadn't asked for.

'I did quit. I was joking,' he said.

'Oh,' I said, forcing a smile, realizing that the circumstances had dampened my keen radar for his brand of humor.

He gestured toward his car as if granting permission to ride with him but, to my relief, didn't open the door as he usually did for me. For *any* woman, including and especially his wife of thirty-plus years. *Every single time,* Lucy once said when I pointed out the spousal chivalry. I remember the cute way she had smiled, prouder of this fact than she was of any of her father's on-the-field accomplishments. It was the only thing Lucy had that I ever felt genuinely envious of, my own parents being unified only in their hatred of each other. Only now, bizarrely, I was the lucky one. Because divorce was better than death.

Coach Carr went around to the driver's side of his old Ford Explorer, and we got in and closed our doors in unison. He started the engine and did an efficient three-point turn while I calculated that we were about four miles from the Carrs' house. Ten minutes at most, but an eternity when I couldn't think of a single thing to say. Asking him how he was doing didn't seem like my place, and telling him I was sorry felt like too much of a mammoth understatement. So I said nothing, just watched out of the corner of my eye as he reached for his silver Walker thermos, the same one I had seen Mrs Carr fill with freshly brewed coffee at least a hundred times over the years. Probably more than that. I wondered who had made his coffee this morning and if he even knew how to work their fancy European machine. Befuddled by modern gadgetry, he was the least handy man I knew in the state of Texas. He still had a flip phone and did without a computer, insisting that it was the only way to avoid all the Monday morning quarterbacks who would inevitably track down his email address. He took a sip of coffee and made a face, replacing the thermos in the cup holder near the dashboard.

When I could no longer bear the silence, I cleared my throat and imitated what I had heard others say between the ceremony and burial. That the service was really nice. That Lucy did a great job with the eulogy.

'Yeah. She sure did. I'm proud of her.' His voice cracked, and, for a few seconds, I held my breath and looked away, terrified that he was finally going to break down.

But when he spoke again, I realized it was all in my head. He was still composed, in complete control. 'Lawton said you helped Lucy write it?'

'I just helped a little,' I said, which wasn't exactly true. They were all Lucy's ideas and feelings, of course, but I had rewritten and rearranged whole sections because she said her own words didn't sufficiently honor her mother.

'Please make it better,' she had pleaded until I broke out my highlighter and red pen. Lucy was probably smarter than I was and had always done better in school, but writing was my thing.

Coach gave me a look that said he didn't quite believe me. 'Well. I think Connie would have been pleased.'

I caught that he said *would have* – instead of *was* – a clue that he wasn't one hundred percent sure about God these days either, and I felt a stab of despair followed by a more dire emptiness. At that moment, I desperately wanted Coach Carr to have real, enduring faith, although I wasn't sure why that mattered to me so much.

As we turned out of the cemetery onto Baines Avenue, the main thoroughfare bisecting Walker from east to west, I worked up the courage to speak again. 'Coach Carr?'

'Yeah, girl?' he asked, waiting.

'Could you . . . uh . . . put on your seat belt?'

It was the first time I had ever told him what to do – unless you count 'pass the salt' – and I added a *please* to soften it.

He smiled his easy smile, crinkle lines appearing around his eyes as he strapped the belt over his shoulder. 'There. We good now?'

'Yes,' I replied, one syllable closer to absolutely nothing left to say.

'All righty then,' he said, his voice changing again, only this time in the opposite direction – loud, normal, almost cheerful. It suddenly became clear to me what he was doing. He was faking it, trying to put me at ease, which made me feel even guiltier for being in the car, next to him. In *her* place. He finished his sentence with 'Should we talk Signing Day?'

He was referring, of course, to the big day last week, always the first Wednesday in February, and the first day that a high school senior could sign a binding letter of intent, committing to play for a particular college or university. It was one of the most important days of the year in Texas. This year, Walker had made a big splash by landing one of the top recruits in the country, Reggie Rhodes, an explosive, game-breaking tailback from Louisville, beating out Texas, Alabama, and Ohio State. It was impossible to be too excited about the news, given Mrs Carr's death the very same week, but it was something of a salve, and Coach's mention of football now filled me with relief.

'Sure,' I said, feeling my shoulders relax a little as I glanced at him.

He reached out and turned on the radio, bypassing his usual country stations and punching the dial up to AM 1310, The Ticket, tuning in to an animated conversation about Rhodes and how disappointed everyone was in Austin. 'Bronco fans are already rubbing their hands together for the first Saturday in December, when they will have the chance to avenge last season's bitterly close loss to the Longhorns,' Bob Sturm mused.

'Sure hope so,' Coach talked back to the radio.

'With Rhodes on the field and Mrs Carr up there on our case . . . we *can't* lose.'

'Yeah. It's the least the big guy upstairs can do for us,' he said, as I pictured Mrs Carr, waving her teal pom-poms up in heaven.

The first photograph ever taken of Lucy and me together features the two of us lying side by side in a playpen, staring up at the ceiling with cross-eyed, blank baby expressions. We can't be any older than two or three months, just two blobs – one with blond fuzz and blue eyes turned red by the flash (Lucy), the other with a thatch of dark hair and eyes (me). We were wearing matching onesies with the vintage Walker logo, a cursive *W* ensconced in a horseshoe. I couldn't find the negative, and the only surviving copy was yellowed and ribbed from the sticky pages of one of my mother's cheap albums that predated acid-free scrapbooking. So I carefully excavated it, took it to a specialty photography store, and had it restored, then framed – one for me, one for Lucy. I put mine on the mantel over the faux fireplace in my apartment, along with a handful of other momentous photos, and gave Lucy hers for her thirtieth birthday, a few weeks after mine. For a year or so, she kept hers in an equally prominent spot in the family room of the three-bedroom bungalow she and Neil had bought together. But I recently noticed that the frame had been demoted to a dresser in her guest bedroom and, more troublesome, our photo replaced by a professional shot of Caroline, standing alongside a white picket fence, wearing a pink monogrammed sundress.

When I called Lucy out on the unsentimental swap, she looked sheepish, a rare emotion for her. 'We have far better pictures together. Like that one,' she said, pointing to a shot of the two of us, arm in arm, sporting buns and voluminous yellow tutus from our first ballet recital. 'Besides,' she said, 'don't you hate the way they used us as props like that?'

By *they* I knew she meant my mother and her parents, all Walker grads and close friends during their school days. My father had even adopted the Broncos, because Williams, his alma mater, didn't have much of a football team. As Lucy reassembled the frame, our photo on top again, she said, 'I will never foist that rah-rah crap onto Caroline. Don't you ever feel . . . brain-washed? Just sick of it all? The same thing – year in and year out?'

'No,' I said, thinking that summed it up, really. Lucy was absolutely correct in saying that our mothers used us as yet another way to highlight their love for Walker – right along with the flags and banners that they raised over their front porches on game day. But I could never understand why she had always seemed to resent our shared heritage, the way our friend Aubrey seemed to resent the red hair and freckles she inherited from her father's side, and Pastor Wilson's sons balked at Bible camp. Football was *our* religion, the very fabric of our home-town and state, and praying for the Broncos should have been effortless for her, a joyous experience from her sweet box seats on the fifty-yard line. She cared about her father's team, of course, hoping that they'd win, disappointed when they didn't. But she never truly devoted herself to it. Never became one of the faithful.

Coach Carr once explained it this way: I was born on February 22, 1980, within the very hour that the U.S. Olympic hockey team defeated the Soviet Union in the semifinals of the Winter Olympics in Lake Placid, in the game dubbed the Miracle on Ice. It would have been more fitting if it had been an epic football game, Coach said, but the fact that it is widely considered one of the greatest moments in sports still seemed noteworthy – a foreshadowing of my destiny. And then there was Lucy, born in March, on the night J.R. was shot on *Dallas,* the greatest prime-time soap of all time. In other words, Lucy emerged into the world on a rare night when nobody in Texas was thinking much about sports. I told Coach it would have been a better analogy if Lucy had become an actress instead of the owner of the only upscale clothing boutique in Walker. But still, his point was funny.

In any event, maybe Lucy was right about our mothers' attempt to brainwash us. But right out of the gate, I willingly drank the Kool-Aid. As a little girl, I dressed up as a Walker cheerleader virtually every Halloween (except for the few times that I donned pads and a helmet and went as a player). I painted my face with little horseshoes before games, belting out our fight song after every touchdown. I collected autographs and hung team posters in my room with hearts around the cute players just as Lucy did with Keanu Reeves and Leonardo DiCaprio.

As I grew older, my obsession only became more intense and focused. I pored over Walker media guides, studying details of every player, learning their numbers and positions, hometowns and majors, heights and weights. I memorized useless trivia and endless stats and scores, rattling off players' rushing and receiving yards, sacks and interceptions, to anyone who'd listen, including some of Walker's biggest boosters, who could never get enough of my party trick at the Carrs' social gatherings.

'Ask her about the Texas game on Thanksgiving 'seventy-eight,' Coach Carr would say, grinning, as I regaled them with the epic battle that predated my birth. Play by play, I knew it all.

By the time I got to junior high, I was a serious student of the game, subscribing to *The Sporting News,* traveling to any road game that didn't require a flight, and hanging around the fields after my own school day ended. I became a fixture at practice, an honorary mascot of sorts, and did my best to make myself useful, lest someone decide to send me home. Some days, I'd help the equipment managers pass out Gatorade, or collect balls that were kicked over the chain-link fence separating our main practice field from the wheat fields beyond. Other times I'd man the cumbersome video camera or fold towels or time sprints using the stopwatch Coach Carr gave me for my twelfth birthday. But mostly I'd just sit in the stands, watch, and listen. Get my fix. Feed my addiction. Quite simply, I was in love with football, every aspect of it. The smell of the freshly cut grass, the sight of the tight huddle against a backdrop of postcard-blue sky, the sound of the quarterback bellowing out the plays I knew by heart, one even named Shea 80 after me and my year of birth – a play action screen to the fullback. Most of all, I loved the inspiring sight of Coach Carr pacing the sidelines with his clipboard and whistle, throwing out his trademark quips and colorful colloquialisms, often under his breath, cracking everyone up even when he wasn't trying to be funny. Asking linebackers not to take the scenic route to the ball. Telling receivers to pretend that they were going after a Happy Meal, maybe they'd catch it. Informing the line that they looked like dying calves in a hailstorm. And reminding our quarterback that, in the words of one of his own coaching heroes, Darrell Royal, only three things could happen when he threw the ball, and two of them weren't good.

In high school, I grew tall, pretty, and slightly less tomboyish, getting something of my own life apart from Walker. Lucy led the charge for those four years, our priorities more in sync than they'd been in junior high. She was a cheerleader while I played soccer and ran track, but we hung with the same crowd, took the same classes, and both went a little boy crazy. The most popular girl in our class, Lucy had her pick of any guy from any clique, but she tended to reject those who were too impressed with her famous father, passing them off to me. For two years, we dated best friends, both baseball players named Scott, and the four of us became inseparable (until our joint breakup, when Lucy declared us Scott-free). Even amid all the boisterous normalcy of adolescence, though, I remained dedicated to the game of football, working as the sports editor of our paper. I covered our high school's poorly coached and perpetually losing team, but also convinced our journalism teacher to let me write pieces on Walker – straight reporting of the games as well as lengthy features. I was the only high school reporter with press credentials and direct access to Coach Carr, peppering my pieces with insider nuggets on projected lineups or next year's recruiting class. Lucy often tagged along on my assignments, even though the details bored her, explaining that it was the only real way to spend quality time with her dad.

When it came time to apply to college, there was never a question where I'd go, even when my grades slipped to a low B average. My parents pretended to be concerned, reminding me that Walker was practically Ivy League when it came to academic standards, but I knew that, short of a felony, it would only take one thirty-second phone call from our closest family friend to get me in. Fortunately, I didn't have to resort to that, at least as far as I knew, my admissions essay about my passion for Walker football overshadowing my lackluster transcript. There was even a handwritten note on my acceptance letter that said: *Go Broncos!*

Then there was Lucy, who didn't even *apply* to Walker, not even as a backstop. I was shocked at her decision to go to the University of Texas, our blood rival, and remember asking her how she could be so unsentimental. 'I mean . . . you're Coach Carr's *daughter*!'

'It's precisely *because* I'm Coach Carr's daughter,' she tried to explain. 'It's like I don't even have a say in the matter. You do.'

'Well, clearly you do, too,' I retorted. 'You're going to UT.'

'Oh, Lord. Get *over* it already,' she said, explaining for the fiftieth time that she'd picked her school because she wanted a break from our town. She said not everything revolved around football in Austin. She called it *refreshing*.

I told her I was over it, but I wasn't really. Nor would I ever understand how she could have made such a traitorous choice – both to abandon me for four years and, more important, to align herself with our archenemy. Coach Carr was supportive, insisting that he wanted Lucy to live her life, but he also warned her that he better never hear the words *Hook 'em, Horns* from his daughter's lips, or see her make that dreaded hand signal. And orange and white were banned colors in his zip code. Lucy said the rules were easy, but one day when we were both home from school for the weekend, she forgot to change out of a Texas T-shirt, a fairly harmless infraction but for the fact that we'd just lost to them the week before. I winced when I saw it, but it was her mother who made her change before her father came home. He had a thick skin – you couldn't coach without one – but sometimes little things set him off. A stupid call on his radio show. ('Well, Jim from North County, maybe you should come down and call some plays next week?') Or an insensitive question from the press. ('Am I disappointed? We lost on a fluke play and a phantom clip and our quarterback left the field on a damn stretcher. Nah, I'm not disappointed. I'm elated.') And anytime he had to question someone's loyalty. ('You're either in or out. No fair-weather fans allowed.')

In fact, if Lucy had any regrets on this terrible day – I thought, as her dad and I finally reached Myrtle Street, lined on both sides with cars – surely going to the University of Texas had to be it.

Once inside the Carrs' three-story brick colonial, Coach headed straight for his office while I found Lucy in the kitchen, pushing potato salad across her plate. I knew she wasn't going to eat – she hadn't in days, losing pounds she couldn't afford to lose, but it was progress at least to see a fork in her hand.

'How're you doing?' I asked her as she stepped away from several ladies from her mother's garden club who were busy arranging platters. There was more food than Coach could ever hope to eat, and I made a mental note to drop off a few casseroles at the homeless shelter where Mrs Carr had volunteered.

'A little better,' she said. 'I'm sorry about earlier. Losing my temper with Miller. I know he's harmless enough.'

I shook my head, dismissing the apology as unnecessary. It took a lot for me to get upset at Lucy, and I'd always accepted her critiques of my life and boyfriends, both because she always had my best interests at heart and because she was usually right. She had a free pass, good for life.

'Thanks for going with Daddy,' she said, putting down her plate and leaning on the counter. She looked pale, but relaxed, and I suspected that she had popped one of the little white pills her doctor had prescribed 'to get through the next few days.'

'No problem,' I said, suddenly wishing I had one to take myself.

'How do you think he's doing?' she asked. 'How was he on the drive over?'

I shrugged and told her I wasn't sure. 'We didn't really talk about anything . . . Except for . . . you know . . . football.'

Lucy's eyes filled with tears, her chin trembling.

'Oh. Luce . . . I'm sorry, honey,' I said, wondering if I'd said the wrong thing, or if it was just another sickening wave of realization that her mother was gone. I put my arms around her, then led her to the privacy of the laundry room. 'I shouldn't be talking about football,' I said, thinking that I finally saw her point. That there was something about life going on, business as usual, that seemed so wrong. Mrs Carr wasn't my mother, but even I had the irrational sense that the whole world – or at least the state of Texas – should take a respectful time-out to grieve her.

Lucy shook her head. 'No. It's not that. It's fine. Football's fine,' she said, and then added a heartbreaking footnote. 'I'm just glad Daddy still has something to love.'

That night, after everyone but my mother and I had gone home, we sat around the kitchen table and talked about Connie. We laughed about how she couldn't drive on the interstate or read maps, how competitive she was when it came to her pecan pie, widely considered the best in Walker. She had even won bake-offs in Dallas, but always voted for others because, in her mind, casting a ballot for her own pie seemed gauche. We talked about how much she loved her 'stories' – taping soap operas and giving updates on the characters as if they were family members we all should know. We talked about how consistently she bungled song lyrics, our favorite being Bob Dylan's 'The ants are my friends, they're blowin' in the wind.' We laughed and cried until we were too drained to share any more memories.

At which point, they all ganged up on me. Or, more accurately, they ganged up on Miller, who was no longer there to defend himself. It was my mom, Lucy, and Neil versus Miller – hardly a fair matchup – all of them saying, in various ways, that Miller wasn't good enough for me. Even Lawton put in his two cents – and I wasn't sure he was qualified to have an opinion, as he had never been in a relationship longer than three months. Only Coach Carr kept mum on the subject, having moved to the family room, sunk in his easy chair. He was close enough to hear our conversation but seemed focused on watching college basketball, flipping between channels, the television on mute. I hated having my love life dissected, especially in mixed company, but I played along, as it occurred to me that it provided a nice distraction for everyone.

'She really needs to cut him loose,' Lucy said as she transferred her chardonnay from one of the plastic stemmed glasses the caterer had brought to a crystal one from the china cabinet, then sat down again at the expansive farmhouse table that Mrs Carr had stripped and stained herself.

Except for a platter of sugar cookies from Star Provisions, our town's famed bakery, the food was all put away, the kitchen tidy.

'Miller's not that bad,' I said, just as my phone rang in my purse.

'Speak of the devil?' my mom asked.

'Oh, now he's the devil?' I said, resisting the urge to check it. I was pretty sure it was Miller, though, as he had mouthed *I'll call you* upon his departure.

'He *is* that bad,' Lucy said. 'He's thoughtless. He's devoid of ambition. He's a pothead. He has shitty grammar.'

'Thoughtless?' I said, because that was the most serious charge. And because he was actually pretty sweet in his own clueless way.

'Well, he *did* forget your birthday last year,' Neil chimed in, referring to a dinner he and Lucy had hosted when Miller had showed up empty-handed.

'It just slipped his mind. No biggie. Besides, thirty-two was nothing much to celebrate,' I said.

Lucy made a scoffing sound.

'He gave me a present . . . later,' I said, thinking of the bottle of Coco Mademoiselle he'd given me the following day.

Lawton raised his eyebrows. 'Ha. I'm sure he did.'

'Perfume, dummy,' I said, my face burning.

'He's still a pothead gym teacher,' Lucy said.

Knowing how ridiculous I sounded, I mumbled Miller's standard drug defenses – pot was actually better for you than alcohol and he smoked for his chronic back pain.

'Wow. You're really going the marijuana-is-medicinal route here?' Lucy asked.

My mom shook her head and said my name in a concerned tone.

Lucy fired again. 'Does he use poor grammar to help his back, too?'

'Yeah. Even *I* know his grammar is for shit,' Lawton said.

'Okay. Now, *that* . . . I can't really defend. He does have a few pronoun problems,' I said. 'But we're working on it.'

'See? You sound like his mother. Do you give him an allowance, too?' Lucy asked. 'When he does his chores?'

I rolled my eyes, but couldn't help thinking about how often I picked up the check, and that Miller *was* usually broke.

'He *is* cute, though,' my mom said. 'Those eyes. That body.'

'C'mon, Mom. Gross,' I whispered. 'Don't be such a cougar.'

'He's a dumb jock,' Lucy said, turning to look at her father. 'Right, Dad? What was his GPA?'

Coach Carr didn't miss a beat. 'I have no idea what the boy's GPA was.' His eyes were glued to the television, but clearly he was listening to every word of our conversation.

'Ballpark it,' Lucy demanded.

'Well, it wasn't stellar,' Coach Carr said, flipping channels. 'But I think Miller's getting a bit of a bad rap here. He's a nice guy. And,' he said, wagging his finger at Lucy, 'there's nothing wrong with teaching physical education.'

'Exactly. His kids love him . . . He's a great *coach*,' I said, realizing that I said it in the awed voice that most people would use to refer to neurosurgeons.

'For *junior high* football,' Lucy said, taking another long sip of her wine.

'Someone's gotta coach junior high . . . Not everyone can be your dad,' I said.

'Yeah. They don't just magically materialize as college players,' Coach said. 'They gotta have good coaches along the way.'

'Shea, honey,' my mother said. 'I think Lucy's right. He's not marriage material.'

'Who said anything about getting married?' I said, reminding everyone that I was in no hurry for all of that, unlike most of my friends and acquaintances, who had married in their twenties, many straight out of college. It was something I wanted eventually, probably, although I wasn't sure about children, which took a lot of pressure off the quest. Still, I had to admit that the thought of marrying Miller had crossed my mind recently. He wasn't the sharpest tool in the shed, but Coach was right, he *was* a good guy – and I honestly wasn't sure that I could do much better in the shrinking pool of eligible men.

'You're wasting precious time with him,' Lucy said as my phone buzzed again. This time I couldn't resist checking it.

Sure enough, it was a text from Miller. *Left my jacket. U still there? Will swing by.*

Before I could text back that I'd deliver it to him, there was a knock at the door and I had no choice but to fess up. 'I think it's Miller,' I said. 'He forgot his jacket.'

''Course he did. This will be amusing,' Lucy said, perking up. She stood and headed for the foyer.

'Don't you dare,' I called after her, but I knew there was nothing that could stop Lucy once she had an idea in her head.

She returned with a crumpled Miller, in dire need of Visine. 'Look who it is!' she announced. Then she issued a quick apology for her earlier rant and said, 'Sit. Sit. Join us.'

I gave him a look of warning and shook my head. For once, he took the hint. 'Thanks, Lucy, but I can't stay.'

'Why? What do you have to do tonight?'

I answered for him. 'Some of the out-of-town guys are crashing at his place. Robert Siler and Myles Savage.'

'Yeah. And . . . I just came to get my jacket.'

'Your jacket or Shea?' Lucy asked.

Miller smiled and said, 'Well, both. If she's ready.'

'Sure,' I said, standing and hoping to make a getaway. It was better than sticking around for more abuse, or getting a ride and an additional lecture from my mother about how I really needed to seize my thirties lest I end up 'forty and alone.' Like Lucy, she believed she only had my best interests at heart, but she couldn't help making everything about herself. What *she* wanted for me. Namely, for me to be a pampered stay-at-home mother married to a doctor or lawyer or, in her exact words, 'even a vet or a dentist.'

'No. Stay. I insist,' Lucy said, guiding Miller into the chair across from her. 'We were actually just talking about you. And your relationship. With Shea.'

'Lucy,' I said in my harshest tone.

This time, Miller took the bait. 'Right on,' he said, grinning.

'So, Miller, do you think you and Shea are compatible?' Lucy asked.

'Hot seat, bro,' Lawton said. 'Look out!'

Miller reached for my hand, and I reluctantly gave it to him. 'Yeah,' he said. 'We go perfect together.'

'Perfect*ly*,' I said under my breath.

'Perfect, huh?' Lucy said. 'And why do you say that?'

'Well, for one, we both love football,' Miller said. 'Right, Coach?'

Coach Carr raised one fist in the air.

Lucy crossed her arms. 'Well, that means Shea would be good with just about any man in the state of Texas. Except Neil, who isn't totally obsessed.'

I had always maintained that it was one of the things Lucy liked most about her husband. He wasn't the type to spend his days in front of the television watching games. Still, the comment seemed vaguely emasculating, at least in the company of his coaching legend father-in-law, and Neil said, 'Hey, now. I like football. I *love* football.'

'It's more than football,' Miller said. 'She's good for me. She makes me better.'

'And what do you do for her?' Lucy asked, unmoved.

My mother was literally on the edge of her seat, waiting.

'Well. I make her laugh.'

I let out a nervous giggle, and Miller pointed at me and said, 'See?'

'It's late,' I said, standing and gesturing to Miller. 'Where's your jacket? I'll get it.'

He pointed down the hall, toward the master bedroom. 'It's back there on the bed,' he said.

I hesitated, but it was really too late to retract my offer, so I kept going, right past Coach. When I walked into the room, I spotted Miller's jacket strewn on Coach Carr's side of the bed, closer to the window, which I only knew based on the fact that Mrs Carr had spent much of her last few weeks on the side nearest the bathroom. A wave of sick grief washed over me as I quickly walked to the foot of the bed and reached out to scoop up the jacket. Then I marched back to the kitchen and announced to Miller that now it really *was* time to go.

3

February made me shiver. The line from Don McLean's 'American Pie' replayed in my head that whole month, a grim soundtrack on an endless loop. It had always been one of Coach Carr's favorite songs, but I never much cared for it, partly because of its tendency to stick with you long after you wanted to be rid of it, and also because it was just so depressing, all that talk about widowed brides and Satan laughing and dirges in the dark. Now it also reminded me of our collective grief over Mrs Carr's death, along with a host of other emotions nagging at me.

For one, I felt guilty. Guilt for not being as sad as Lucy, my mom, and Coach. Guilt for being able to go a stretch of hours without thinking about Mrs Carr at all. In my most selfish moments, I even felt impatient, longing for things to return to normal. I found myself praying for spring to come quickly to Texas, believing that the change of seasons would help, along with the start of spring practices held every March and all the hope that came with the annual rebirth of our team. In other words, football when we needed it most. With a solid previous season, most of our starters returning, and the addition of Reggie Rhodes and a great recruiting class, there was little doubt in anyone's mind that we were going to be good this year. *Really* good and potentially great. It would be bittersweet without Mrs Carr to share it, but bittersweet was better than plain bitter.

But football could only distract me from the grief and the guilt so much, and in the aftermath of Mrs Carr's death, I found myself reflecting on my own life in a way that I had previously avoided. I couldn't fight the knot of dissatisfaction with the status quo, all the things that had always felt comfortable, good enough. My unexceptional relationship with Miller. My crappy car and apartment, which I refused to see as measuring sticks of anyone's life, let alone my own, but clearly more appropriate for a girl in her twenties than for a woman approaching her mid-thirties. At least I had a decent wardrobe, clothes all chosen by Lucy and purchased at a deep discount from her shop, but most hung in my closet with no occasion to wear them. They were way too nice for my job at Walker – which was something else I started to think about. I was the assistant sports inform-ation director, which meant I worked behind the scenes in the athletic department, attending endless games and matches, recording stats, and reporting them to the media. It was the only real job I'd ever had since my student intern days working in the same office, and the one thing I had always taken pride in – really the sole source of my identity. But suddenly even the job I loved seemed small and unimportant, especially all the parts that didn't involve football. I knew that it was a reach to say I was following my passion – an argument I tried to make to justify my meager salary. Yes, football was my passion, and Walker my home, but deep down I knew that I was there because it felt safe and easy – not because it was exactly right.

I knew that I really should have been *writing* about sports – which had been my plan when I majored in journalism. Yet somehow, that dream had never materialized. I'm not sure why, but probably because it would have required leaving the cocoon of Walker University. Leaving Coach Carr. And that was the final – and perhaps biggest – thing I had to confront in the weeks after Mrs Carr died.

It was hard to say when my infatuation really began, because from a very young age, I adored Coach Carr. I put him on a pedestal the way a lot of little girls do with their fathers – the way I might have done with my own dad if my earliest memor-ies weren't of him and my mother fighting. My mother's voice was always the one I heard in the middle of the night, but it was those angry accusations that formed my first impressions of my father: *cheating, lying son-of-a-bitch.* I was too young to understand anything about infidelity or affairs, but would later piece together the sordid chronology. Namely, that my parents met when my mom was fresh out of college, employed by a brokerage firm in Dallas, and my dad was an investment banker, in town working on a deal. They were an unlikely match, but she fell hard and fast for the hotshot Wall Streeter with slicked-back hair and custom pin-striped suits, and he was equally dazzled by the sassy, bodacious girl he called his 'yellow rose of Texas.' The only problem with their passionate, long-distance, whirlwind romance that yielded the surprise of me (my mother maintains it was an accident, but I've always had my doubts) was that my father was already married with another baby on the way. *Oops.* My mother won the pregnant-lady showdown, lassoing my dad, even getting him to relocate from New York to Texas after her three-month trial run in Manhattan proved 'too overwhelming' for her. (Fortunately my mother brought a box of Dallas dirt with her to the Upper East Side hospital where I was born, putting it under the delivery table so that, quite technically, I'd be born on Texas soil.)

For a few years after their move back to Dallas, my parents were happy, at least according to my mother. Until, in the ultimate case of *what goes around comes around,* he did it again, cheating on my mother with his first wife, ultimately choosing her and my half sister, Bronwyn. Divorce always hurts, but it stung especially hard to lose like that, to another little girl exactly my age who openly viewed my early child-hood as nothing more than a nuisance and an interruption of her own sacred autobiography. When we were kids, Bronwyn told the story every chance she got, how *her* father came to his senses and begged *her* mother to take him back after his disastrously poor judgment with *my* mother. And then, the part of the fairy tale she loved the most: how she walked into the brownstone on Madison Avenue, following rose petals up three flights of stairs into a posh pink bedroom, eyeing the canopy bed with its custom linens as my father anointed it her new bedroom.

'With you or Mom?' Bronwyn allegedly asked as they stood behind her, beaming, hands lovingly clasped.

'With both of us,' they announced. 'We're getting married. *Again.*'

As lore has it, the three of them then scooped up the petals and tossed them around the room, promptly commencing planning for a wedding in Tuscany that I was forced to attend. It was an ass-backwards, twisted version of Cinderella – and Bronwyn never seemed to grasp that I was an innocent party in my dad's first affair. That I had suffered her exact fate, only with no happy ending.

But the worst part of the divorce wasn't losing my dad; it was how my mother completely fell apart in the aftermath of Astrid and Bronwyn's victory tour. I can still remember coming home from school to find her in bed, blinds drawn, the room reeking of cigarette smoke. Jerry Springer would be blaring on television, as if my mother's only solace was listening to people who had more depressing lives than her own. Years later, I discovered that she had suffered something of a nervous break-down, one that required a Connie Carr intervention followed by a six-week stay at a treatment center masquerading as a five-star spa in Austin.

At the time, I only knew what Mrs Carr had told me: that my mother was sick and needed to go away for a little while to get better, and that Lucy and I were going to share a bedroom and be like real sisters. I missed my mother, but was relieved to be in a happy home where there was always someone to play with and grown-ups acted like grown-ups. I loved how orderly everything was – supper served promptly at seven, prayers said aloud at night, beds made every morning. I loved the way Mrs Carr was always in a good mood, singing in her sweet, high soprano while she did housework. Most of all, I loved how football imbued everyday life, elevating the ordinary, making everything feel important and vivid. I was already a big football fan, but it was during that time that I really learned the ins and outs of the game, going to practice with Coach, watching games with him, studying his play diagrams, even learning to draw the Xs and Os of the easier ones myself: the end-around, the Hail Mary, the blitz, the triple option.

As time passed, and my mother returned to her old self, my childhood adoration of Coach Carr morphed into a different kind of reverence. I still mostly saw him as Lucy's dad and a close family friend, really the only man in my life, except for my mom's occasional boyfriend. But at times, especially during the football season, my affection for him verged on hero worship.

When I got to college, I was shocked to discover that Coach Carr had groupies – some of them *my* age. Girls would talk about how hot he was and literally tremble when he passed us on campus, swooning as he stopped to ask me how everything was going and if I'd heard from Lucy. Although he seemed not to notice the adulation, their giddiness still annoyed me. I chalked it up to the usual disdain I felt for silly sorority girls, but, deep down, I think I felt a little territorial about my long-time idol.

After graduation, when I went to work for my alma mater, I no longer gave the subject much thought. I took for granted that Coach was the sun, and that everyone else, myself included, orbited around him. It's just the way it was in Walker, Texas.

Then, about three years ago, *Sports Illustrated* did a big cover story on Coach Carr titled 'The Little School That Could: How Walker Runs With – and Beats – the Big Dogs of College Football.' In the piece, Alex Wolff talked about our quiet and quaint campus, our small and homogenous student body. Considering that we had the fourth smallest student body of any Division I school – ahead of only Tulsa, Rice, and Wake Forest, none of which were synonymous with football – Wolff marveled at our ability to land players from lower-income areas around the country, given our high academic standards, preppy students, and location in a sleepy town with more churches than bars, halfway between Waco and Dallas. He threw out some of the usual theories about our huge endowment, state-of-the-art facilities, and idyllic red-brick campus, but ultimately chalked it up to Coach Carr's charisma and recruiting 'wizardry.'

I knew from watching Coach in action that he actually embraced our Achilles' heel, finding a way to spin the negative into a positive with parents of his recruits, especially the mothers, who in most cases made the final decisions about where their sons would play. It was a central part of his pitch. After charming everyone in the living room – and often the entire neighborhood – he'd explain, usually once the kid was out of earshot, that there was plenty of fun to be had, but not so much that a kid could get himself in trouble. He'd then highlight Walker's staggeringly high graduation rate and the fact that it was virtually unheard of for any of his players to end up on *SportsCenter* for anything other than football. In Coach's entire tenure as head coach, there'd been no scandals – only a smattering of honor code violations, a couple of pranks gone wrong, and a few DUIs. Walker was a squeaky-clean program where Coach Carr turned good kids into even better men. And he did all of this while winning, season after glorious season. As Wolff so eloquently explained: *If a kid signs with Walker, odds are he is going to leave with a diploma, some bowl-game hardware, and more than a fair look from scouts, an irresistible combination from Clive Carr, the beloved coach straight out of central casting. The Knute Rockne of our generation, as rugged as Clint Eastwood, eloquent as Perry Mason, and handsome as George Clooney.*

I remember reading that paragraph, then staring down at the photos of Coach Carr – a candid shot of him standing stoically on the sidelines with his headset and hat, and another more styled, staged portrait of him on the Magnolia Quad – and thought, *Oh, please.*

Everything Wolff wrote was true, but I still felt a familiar stab of annoyance that I had to share my idol, *my* coach, with the masses. I remember rolling my eyes, then shoving that magazine into a drawer, along with coupons and paper clips and wedding invitations I'd forgotten to RSVP to.

Right before I slammed the drawer shut, I spotted Miller's number on a cocktail napkin that he'd given me the week before, on *another* drunken night out. I'd blown him off after Lucy labeled him a loser, and I decided she was probably right. But that morning, right after I ate a bowl of grits and a greasy biscuit, I picked up the phone and called him. He answered on the first ring, we went out that night, and we'd been dating ever since.

Only now, with Mrs Carr's death as a wake-up call, I realized just how stuck I'd become, how much of a rut I was in. Something really had to be done. I had to find a way to mix things up. Move forward.

I was thinking about all of this one afternoon as I took a long walk around the Walker grounds. Although I was on campus virtually every day including the weekends, I typically only passed between my office in the old field house and the student union center, where I picked up my lunch. In fact, I couldn't remember the last time I had strolled without purpose, maybe since I had been a student myself a dozen years before. I did an entire loop around the tree-lined grounds, from Wait Chapel on the quad, down to the dorms, over to the science and business centers on the banks of the Brazos River, then past the pillared mansions on Greek Row. I walked and walked, thinking about Mrs Carr and Coach and Miller, my job and my life.

Then, right when I got back to my office, I saw a note on my desk: *Coach Carr would like to see you.* I stared at it for a few nervous seconds, wondering what he wanted. Likely he just wanted to talk about the small feature Lucy had asked me to write on her mother's life for our hometown paper. I had given Coach a very polished draft a few days ago, with a note that said, *Let me know what you think. Happy to make any changes.* That had to be why he wanted to see me, I decided, as I got up and made my way to the other end of the field house, out the back door, and across the parking lot to the modern, gleaming new football complex. Crossing the marble lobby, I took the spiral staircase up three flights, admiring the shrine to the Broncos, glass cases filled with trophies and banners and photos, then entered the security code to open the doors leading to the coaches' wing.

When I arrived at the huge corner office, I found Mrs Heflin, Coach's longtime secretary and gatekeeper, manning her post. 'Go on in, hon,' she said, jovial as ever.

I glanced uneasily at the closed door, usually a sign that he didn't want to be disturbed.

'Don't worry. He's expecting you,' Mrs Heflin said.

I nodded, but still knocked quietly, tensing as I heard his familiar bellow to come in. I pushed the door open to find Coach sitting at his desk, listening to Trace Adkins's 'This Ain't No Love Song.'

'Come on in, girl!' he said, looking up from a depth chart, the starting players listed at the top, the secondary players' names handwritten below. 'Have a seat.'

I sat on the brown leather sofa facing his desk and glanced around at all the framed photos, newspaper articles, and inspirational messages decorating his office. I never got tired of looking at them.

'Morning,' he said, as Brad Paisley started singing 'She's Everything.' I loved Coach's taste in music, and loved that he still listened to the radio rather than the iPod filled with country songs that Lucy had recently given him, explaining that he liked being surprised by what came on next.

'Good morning,' I said, avoiding his eyes as Brad sang, *She's everything to me*.

'So. I read your piece,' he said, pulling it out of a drawer.

The copy was clean, with no marks that I could see, but his expression was blank enough for me to question the direction I had taken. Was it too quirky or colorful? Coach Carr liked things simple and to the point. No bells and whistles, he always said.

'I can change it. It was just my first draft,' I fibbed. 'So if there's anything you don't like . . .'

He cut me off. 'No changes. It was perfect.'

I lowered my head and thanked him, my cheeks warming.

'Walker is lucky to have you. So am I.'

I smiled, but noticed that, although his words were promising, his expression was somber, troublesome. It was the way he looked at a player who was about to lose his starting spot.

'Thanks, Coach,' I mumbled.

'When J.J. retires, you'll be poised to be one of the youngest sports information directors at a major football school in the country,' he said. 'It's a great position for a lot of folks.'

'Coach,' I said. 'Why do I feel like you're getting ready to fire me?'

He laughed and told me not to be ridiculous. 'And besides, I can't fire you. You don't report to me.'

I refrained from pointing out that he could pretty much do anything he wanted – that our athletic director might technically be in charge, but everyone knew Coach held all the power around here. Instead I said, 'Is there a *but*?'

He smiled, then paused and said, 'But . . . is this really . . . your passion?'

'It's a great job,' I said. But I knew what he was getting at. It was almost as if he had read my mind.

'No doubt. It's a hell of a job. And for some, the perfect calling. J.J. loves juggling all the balls . . . He's an administrator who loves sports. *All* sports . . . But is this really what you were born to do?'

'What do you mean? I love football,' I blurted out, realizing my error immediately. Football was such a small part of what I worked on, as Walker had fifteen other sports.

'Right,' he said. 'And I know you love writing, too. But your job really isn't about football or writing. It's about keeping stats. Going to men's cross country meets and women's volleyball games. Drafting routine press releases, churning out media guides. At the end of the day, it's a PR job, not a writing job.'

'I get to write sometimes. I loved writing this,' I said softly, gazing down at my hands.

'I know, girl. I know,' he said. 'That's my point.'

I nodded, but still couldn't look at him.

'You should be writing,' he said.

'I do write,' I said.

'Writing *full-time*. You wrote more in high school and college than you do now.'

'Yeah. Silly pieces for the school newspaper,' I said, fixing my eyes directly above his head at a shelf filled with photos that had come from our department, various action shots from over the years, including one from my senior year, of Ryan James, standing on the sidelines with one finger thrust in the air, his arm around his beloved coach.

'They were professional-caliber pieces, Shea. Unlike any student work I've ever seen.'

I felt a chill as I dropped my eyes to meet his. 'Thank you,' I said, forcing myself not to look away.

'And besides . . . You shouldn't limit yourself to Walker. There's a big world outside this place.'

It was an odd statement coming from a man whose entire life revolved around Walker, and I was unable to resist making the point, a bold one for me. 'What about you? You turned down the Bills.'

As soon as the words were out, I realized that the comparison was ridiculous. He was the head football coach. He *was* Walker.

He shrugged and said, 'I could never live in Buffalo. Too damn cold. And I love the *college* game.'

'Well, I love Walker,' I said.

He stared me down. Then, just when I couldn't bear it another second, he removed a folded slip of paper from his top drawer and reached across the desk to hand it to me. I unfolded it and stared down at a 214 phone number and, below it, a name. Frank Smiley.

'You know him, right?' Coach said.

I nodded. I had only talked to Smiley a few times, in passing at press conferences, but I knew exactly who he was – the sports editor of *The Dallas Post*, the only major newspaper left in Texas with a legitimate sports section, covering sports like they covered hard news. Smiley was a brash curmudgeon of an old-timey reporter who openly pined for the good ol' days. Back when guys didn't showboat, and college athletes actually went to class and graduated after four years, and boosters didn't buy sports cars, and networks didn't call the shots, and money didn't drive the conferences, and rivalries really meant something, and players stayed with a franchise for life, and coaches stayed put, too. His pressroom demeanor was legendary, as he always knew how to get a coach to *really* say something by asking just the right question in just the right tone. Somehow you liked the guy even when he was pissing you off, and you wanted to give him something because you couldn't be bland around a guy that colorful. He was a pro, no doubt.

'He's looking for a reporter,' Coach said.

'For which beat?' I asked, folding my arms across my chest, thinking that I was pretty sure Smiley was not looking for a female reporter with no experience.

'I don't know,' Coach said. 'I didn't get the details. He just mentioned that he lost two guys to ESPN and another to some sports website . . .'

'I can hear the rant now.'

Coach smiled, then imitated him perfectly. 'Doesn't anyone get their hands dirty in the morning anymore?' he said, referring, of course, to the ink on papers.

'I do,' I said, holding up my hands, palms out.

Coach winked at me, then pointed to the stack of newspapers on his desk. 'Anyway. Smiley asked if I knew anyone.' He looked at me purposefully.

'Well?' I stonewalled. 'Do you?'

'I sure do.'

'And who's that?' I asked, playing dumb while I panicked inside.

'You.'

I didn't hesitate. 'I *have* a job.'

'Right,' Coach said. 'But this one is better. And if you get it, you should take it. Even if that means you have to say a few nice things about other programs.'

I smiled and said, 'No way. That's a deal breaker.'

'Shea,' he said, his face all business. 'Call Smiley. This could be a great opportunity for you.'

I had the feeling he was thinking about Connie, probably something about the brevity of life, the importance of seizing the day, all the things that I'd been obsessing over lately. I nodded, knowing that he was right, and there wasn't a chance in hell I could refuse this interview. Or anything Coach Carr asked me to do.

'Okay,' I said. 'I'll call him.'

'Good,' he said, leaning back in his chair with a satisfied expression. 'Oh. And another thing?'

'Yeah?' I said, as Kenny Chesney crooned *Come over, come over, come over* in the background.

'How do you *really* feel about Miller?'

I shrugged, my answer clear.

'Yeah. That's what I thought . . . And between you and me, Lucy's right . . . you're too good for that boy.'

I stared at him, shocked, as he held my gaze and winked. 'Didn't expect that one, did you?'

'No, Coach,' I finally said. 'I certainly didn't.'

I smiled at him and shook my head, touched by his concern but inexplicably embarrassed. After all these years, the hero worship still surfaced at unexpected moments, flustering me.

'Good enough, then.' He gave me a close-lipped smile, then looked back down at his depth chart, signaling that our meeting was over.

I stood up and silently excused myself, not wanting to break his concentration or waste a second more of his time. As I walked past Mrs Heflin, then back over to my office, I thought about what I should wear to my first real interview. And, more pressing, how exactly I was going to break the news to Miller.

4

Over the next week or so, I could feel the dissatisfaction with my life mounting, as I became more certain of the changes I needed to make. Yet I kept stalling, feeling stuck. I didn't call about the job with the *Post,* and I continued to spend time with Miller. All the while, I did my best to avoid Coach, lest he confront me about my lack of progress.

I don't know what I was so afraid of – failure, rejection, or being alone – but something was holding me back. Keeping me in limbo.

Then, the following Friday night, Miller and I went to see an action flick, sharing popcorn, Twizzlers, and a jumbo Coke for dinner, a typical date night for us. Afterward, he drove me back to my place, his seat reclined, one hand on the steering wheel, some stoner band blaring on the radio. I hated Miller's music and silently put it on the list of 'Why We Aren't Good Together' that had been lingering in my head since the indictment in Coach's office. As I turned down the music, I randomly asked Miller if he was glad he went to Walker. I'm not sure what made me ask the question, other than the hope of baiting him into a wrong answer. If he said anything disloyal about our school, I'd have something else to put on my list. If his answer was too curt or uninteresting, I could put that on my list, too: *poor conversationalist.*

'Sure,' Miller said, his head bobbing to the bass. 'Why wouldn't I be?'

'Oh, I don't know. Sometimes I think it was a little small,' I said, leading the witness.

'Maybe,' Miller said noncommittally.

'Was there anything you didn't like about it?'

'The foreign language requirement,' he said. 'That was some real *mierda*.'

'*Mierda*?' I said. 'I took German.'

'Shit,' he translated, pushing the sleeve up on his plaid flannel shirt, pretty much the staple of his wardrobe, in addition to T-shirts and jeans. To look at him, you'd never know that he once played college ball or currently coached. With shaggy hair to match his grunge clothes, he looked more musician than athlete.

'Well . . . how did you feel about playing for Coach Carr?' I asked.

'Wait. Are you writing some article about former players?' Miller asked.

Delusions of grandeur, I thought, as I shook my head and said, 'No, Miller. I was just . . . wondering.'

'Oh,' he said. 'Well, I didn't like losing my starting spot to Ryan James . . . But I'd rather play backup QB for Coach than start for some jackass.'

I laughed, realizing that my strategy was backfiring. Miller really did crack me up, even when he wasn't trying. He was so easy to be around. In over three years, we hadn't had a single fight, although I knew that said as much about my personality as about his. I avoided conflict at pretty much any cost.

'And I got *this*,' Miller said, pointing down to his hulking Cotton Bowl ring. He winked. 'Works wonders with the ladies.'

I rolled my eyes, and, although I never cared much for jewelry of any kind on a man, I did love how big his hands were and that he could still throw a football fifty yards from his knees.

'What about you?' he asked. 'You glad you went to Walker?'

'Yes. Best decision I ever made,' I said, thinking that it might be the *only* big decision I'd ever made. Everything else just sort of happened *to* me.

'Better than going out with me?' Miller grinned.

I smiled back at him, but my insides were in knots as we pulled into the lot of my condo, next to my ancient Honda Accord, with a substantial dent on the driver side where I had sideswiped a concrete pillar in a parking garage months before. Miller started to open his door, but, when I didn't make a move, he looked at me and said, 'Wait. Did you want to get a bite to eat or something?'

I turned in my seat and said, 'Miller. We need to talk.'

'What's up?' he said.

I took a deep breath, digging down for courage – or at least a little gumption. 'I don't think we should keep seeing each other.'

His face fell. 'Are you serious?'

I nodded. My heart hurt, but the words still felt right, and there was suddenly no doubt in my mind that I was doing the right thing.

'Why?' he asked, a question that is never really productive when someone is trying to break up with you.

'I just don't think it's . . . right.'

'Is this because of Lucy?'

'No. I swear,' I said, knowing how terrible Miller would feel if he knew who it really came from. 'It just doesn't . . . feel right anymore. I think we're both just stalling . . . hanging out because there isn't anything better.'

'But I think you *are* the best,' Miller said, so sweetly. I could tell he meant it, and I asked myself if maybe that wasn't good enough. For one of the two of us to feel the right way. But I knew the answer, so I pressed on.

'That's really nice, Miller,' I said.

'Are you seeing someone else?' he asked.

I said no as vehemently as I could, hoping that this made it better. Then again, what I was really saying was that being *alone* was better than being with him.

'Okay,' he finally said. 'We can break up . . . if that's really what you want . . . But can we still do it? You know – friends with benefits?'

'No,' I said, thinking that the question, along with his earnest delivery, confirmed my decision. 'We can't still *do* it.'

'C'mon. One more time?' Miller asked, reaching out to put his hand on my thigh.

I felt myself weakening, the way I did when a waiter asked if I'd saved room for dessert. But no, I had to rip off the Band-Aid. *Just do it*, in sports speak.

'I want to,' I said.

'Well, then, come on. Let's go,' he said, his face clearing, like that of a child who just wore down his mother to watch another thirty minutes of television.

'I can't . . . Miller . . . I'm sorry,' I said, pushing his hand off my knee. Then I leaned across the front seat, planting a small but decisive kiss on his unshaven cheek, and said, 'See you around?'

'Yep. See you 'round the way,' Miller said, as I pictured him out at the bars with surgically enhanced, twenty-something blondes. I felt a pang of jealousy, but not enough to reverse the tide. I got out of the car and closed the door, unsure of whether I felt more relieved that it had been so easy or hurt by how quickly he threw in the towel. I told myself not to take it personally. It was just the way Miller was. Laid-back, easy-going, taking things in stride. I watched him now, flashing me a peace sign through his car window, then backing out of my complex, the radio cranked up, undoubtedly already plotting his next booty call.

A few minutes later, I walked into my apartment, pushing the clean clothes I had yet to fold to one side of my sofa, clearing a place to sit. I reached for the remote control and turned on my new flat-screen, the one I had prioritized over fixing my car. The ESPN Friday Night Fight was just ending. Tyson Fury was kicking someone's ass – an unknown from Brazil. I watched for a few seconds, then flipped channels. All I wanted to do was call Coach Carr and tell him that I'd taken his advice. But, of course, there was no way I'd ever do such a thing. I had his cell but had never called him and instead left messages with Mrs Heflin. There was nothing so pressing that it warranted bothering him at home – and breaking up with Miller hardly constituted 'pressing' to anyone but me. Apparently including Miller.

Instead I picked up the phone and called Lucy, even though I knew that anti-Miller sentiment was inevitable and wasn't really in the mood to hear him bashed. I needed to talk to my best friend – my 'bosom friend,' as she had called us since reading *Anne of Green Gables* in grade school, even writing a quote from the book in calligraphy and giving it to me for Christmas one year: *A really kindred spirit to whom I can confide my inmost soul.*

Although there was one thing I'd never confide in her, the quote was true, always had been. It didn't matter that we weren't much alike on paper. That I thought the best of people, and she often assumed the worst. That I was an introvert, and she could work a room like nobody I'd ever seen but her mother. That I was even-tempered, and she was moody and dramatic. That I was no frills, and she was all frills. That I loved football, and she simply tolerated it. The list of differences was endless, but, in the end, none of them mattered. What mattered was that we completely accepted each other. That I had her back, and she had mine. That we shared a common history, going all the way back to our mothers' collegiate friendship. Lucy had always been more like a sister than a friend, especially in a crisis, and I needed her now.

'I just ended things with Miller,' I said after she answered.

'Good for you,' she said, as if I'd given her a weather report. 'Long overdue.'

'C'mon, Lucy,' I said. 'I'm really sad. I'm going to miss him . . . It's not like there are many other options around here.'

'You're right. I'm sorry. But, Shea, you totally did the right thing.'

'It still hurts,' I said, thinking that in some ways it hurt more than being dumped because there was no anger to distract me.

'I know. I'm sorry,' she said as I thought of the many times Lucy had soothed me after a breakup over the years.

'Do you want to come over?' she asked me now. 'Open a bottle of wine?'

I considered this, but decided sleep was what I needed most. 'Thanks, but I'll probably turn in.'

'Okay. I'm headed home, too. Call me if you need me.'

'Where are you now?' I said.

'At my dad's. Wow, that sounds so weird.'

'Maybe we should keep calling it your parents' house. I mean, your mother made it a *home*. And . . .' I struggled to find the right words to comfort my best friend. 'It will always be hers.'

'Thank you, Shea,' Lucy said. 'I hope you're right.'

'I *am* right,' I said. 'Everyone knows that your mother is irreplaceable.'

5

About a week later, I agreed to meet Lucy at her parents'
house. My mother was joining us as well, with the plan to
go through Connie's closet, a task I couldn't possibly dread more.

'Any word from Miller?' Lucy asked as we waited for my
mother, late as usual.

'No,' I said, watching her mix up a fresh batch of sweet tea,
heaping in the sugar just the way Coach Carr liked it. 'Probably
easier that way.'

Lucy nodded in agreement as we heard the garage door
rumble. 'Daddy's home,' she said.

I instinctively stood up a little straighter, then reached up
to fluff my hair.

Lucy narrowed her eyes and gave me a funny look. 'Did
you just fix your *hair*?' she said, staring at me.

'No. Of course not,' I said, feeling embarrassed though I
wasn't sure why.

'Okay. 'Cause it looked like you did that thing you do in
bars when a hot guy walks in.'

'What thing?'

She imitated me perfectly.

'I didn't do that,' I said, feeling certain I was telling the truth.
Maybe I *had* fixed my hair – but not in *that* way.

'Good. Because if you did, that would be really . . . *weird*.'

'*You're* weird,' I said, reverting to my little-girl self the way
I often did around Lucy, and she with me.

A second later the side door opened and Coach appeared
in a Walker warm-up and baseball cap. I looked away as Lucy
kissed him hello and reminded him why we were over.

'Well, thanks, girls,' Coach said, his voice gruff and gentle at once. 'I think it's time . . .'

We all stood there for an awkward, sad beat until the doorbell rang and Lucy said, 'That must be your mom.' She went to the foyer, leaving Coach and me alone.

He spoke first. 'Did you call Smiley?'

'Yes,' I said, relieved that I'd finally placed the call that morning. 'And I broke up with Miller, too.'

Coach raised his eyebrows and whistled.

'Impressed?'

'Very,' he said. 'How do you feel?'

I hesitated, then said, 'Hopeful . . . Although right now I'm just thinking about Lucy.'

He cleared his throat and poured a glass of tea. 'You know, I don't want to remove all traces of Connie – but I don't think it's good to keep a museum either. And, in the end, they're just *things*. Stuff. Nice stuff that should be used and enjoyed. Connie would want it that way.'

'Of course,' I said, dropping my gaze to the counter, wondering what was taking Lucy and my mom so long. I hesitated, then worked up the courage to ask, 'And how are *you*?'

He looked surprised by the question, then exhaled and said, 'I'm okay. Mornings are tough. That's when Connie and I always talked the most . . . The whole thing is just really hard to believe. It's like . . .' He shook his head, searching for words. 'It's like an out of the body experience . . . I'm just ready for the season to start. Football really helps. It's a distraction. Get busy living, you know?'

'Yes, I know . . . I'm sorry, Coach,' I said, grief expanding in my chest. 'I don't know if I've really said that to you yet . . . but I am so . . . sorry.'

'I know you are, girl,' he said, reaching out to cover my hand with his. 'Thank you for asking.'

His hand moved back to his side of the counter as my mother and Lucy walked into the kitchen.

'Hellooo, Clive,' my mom said. She was the only person I

ever heard call Coach by his first name. Even Connie had called him *Poppins* – although I didn't know why. I once asked Lucy the story behind the nickname, and she said she couldn't remember it – which boggled my mind.

'Hello, Marie,' Coach said, kissing her cheek.

'How are you?' she said, making the same question sound about as different as possible from the one I'd just asked. Whereas mine had been tentative, hers was bold, borderline condescending, going right along with the Tupperware containers of soup I had spotted in the fridge, all labeled with her handwriting and descriptions, such as 'Basil tomato to warm your heart' and 'Cream of mushroom for cozy nights in front of the television.'

'Doing well. Hanging in there,' Coach said briskly. I could tell by his tone and body language that she got on his nerves, something I had observed for years. But I also knew he appreciated her loyalty, the fact that, unlike many, her love of him and his family wasn't tied to winning football games.

'Well, I'll be in my office,' he said to all of us. 'If you need me.'

'Okay, Daddy,' Lucy said.

'How do you think he's *really* doing?' my mom whispered after Coach had walked out of the room.

Lucy shrugged, frowned, and whispered back, 'It's hard to tell. He won't *talk* about it.'

Two long, draining hours later we had gone through only a fraction of Mrs Carr's closet, sorting her clothes, scarves, belts, and purses into three piles: *take to Goodwill, save in the attic,* and *transfer to Lucy's closet.* My mother and I sat cross-legged on the bedroom floor as we waited for Lucy to emerge with a fresh handful of items, at which point we'd discuss and help Lucy make her designation. It was excruciating, every item unearthing memories, sometimes from three different perspectives. It occurred to me that few things tell the story of a woman's life like her closet, as we pieced together a whole chronology and biography, a composite of good days and bad, big occasions and quiet moments. In the end, the second pile was by far the largest, Lucy deeming item after item too sacred either to give away or to wear herself.

'Oh, Lucy, you should have this one,' my mom said, picking up one of Connie's favorite jewel-toned Hermès scarves.

'I could never wear that,' Lucy said, rubbing it between her fingers, her upper lip quivering. 'It's just so . . . *her.*'

'But sweetie, it's you, *too,*' my mom said – which really was the truth. As we got older, I could see Lucy dressing more and more like her mother. She had always been chic, but her look was becoming less trendy and more sophisticated, timeless. Even her shop was beginning to shift toward a slightly more mature demographic.

Lucy wrapped the silk scarf around her neck and whispered okay, moving on to a long-sleeved pink poplin blouse.

'Oh, that one brings back good memories,' my mom said.

Lucy frowned and said she didn't remember ever seeing it.

'I was with your mom when she bought it. At Neiman's. She wore it to her last garden club meeting. The one at Lynn Odom's house. That was a good day.'

'Will you take it?' Lucy asked. 'I hate the idea of anything going to strangers.'

Blinking back tears, my mother said, 'Okay, sweetie. I'll take it . . . I can't promise that I can bring myself to wear it, but I'd love to just have it.' My mother removed a monogrammed handkerchief she kept in her purse, a practice she'd picked up from Connie.

Lucy motioned toward the Goodwill pile. 'Anything else? Please?' she said, looking lost, her voice small and pitiful. Everything about her seemed fragile – in such contrast to her usual big personality. 'I'd so much rather you have these things. Shea, you, too.'

I hesitated. I really didn't feel right taking any of Connie's things, but desperately wanted to comfort Lucy, the way she so often did for me.

My mother responded for us, stroking Lucy's hair. 'Listen, honey. How about I just take this whole Goodwill pile home with me for now? That way you could have some more time to decide . . . I will keep it safe for you. For now.'

'Thank you, Marie,' Lucy said, giving my mom a long hug. The two had always been close, perhaps closer than I had been to Connie because their personalities were more similar. But it was clear in the past few months that they were becoming even closer – and that my mother was a great source of comfort to Lucy. A maternal figure, but also a real friend.

'One more item and then we're done for tonight,' Lucy said, pulling a shoe box and receipt out of a black Saks bag adorned with snowflakes. She checked the date and said, 'December of last year. Right before she got the news . . .'

I held my breath as Lucy lifted the lid, revealing a gorgeous pair of black suede sling-backs. She removed the tissue wedged into one of the pointed toes, then flipped the shoe over, running her fingers across the pristine sole. I felt a lump in my throat. There was just something so tragic about that pretty pair of unworn shoes. I pictured Mrs Carr trying them on, strolling along the plush carpet of the shoe department, debating whether to buy them. My mother must have been thinking the same thing because she said, 'Maybe you could still return them?'

Lucy's face fell. 'Oh, I couldn't.'

My mother realized her mistake immediately. 'I know, sweetie. You're right. Of course you couldn't.'

'Shea, you take them,' Lucy said. 'They're your size.'

I shook my head, wishing I could come up with an excuse.

'Why not?' Lucy said, still looking hurt. 'Don't you like them?'

It was a no-win question, as I couldn't very well insult her mother's taste. 'I do – but . . . they're not really *me*.'

'What do you mean they're not you? They're beautiful, classic heels. How could they not be you? And why won't you take anything of my mom's?' Lucy said right as Coach Carr appeared in the doorway of his bedroom.

'How's it going, ladies?' he asked.

'Fine,' Lucy said, blowing her nose and looking anything but fine. 'Do you need your room? We're finished . . . for now.'

'Take your time,' Coach said, glancing at the silk scarf still around Lucy's neck.

Lucy took it off and swirled it in the air, then watched it flutter to the floor. 'Do you remember this one, Daddy?' she asked, looking forlorn.

'Of course. Mom wore it a lot.' His voice was sad and very far away.

'Daddy?' Lucy said. 'Are you sure you're ready . . . for this? Is this too soon?'

Coach swallowed and said, 'It was too soon for her to leave us . . . but she did. So we gotta keep going.' His gaze shifted from the scarf to the box of shoes splayed open between us.

'Daddy, shouldn't Shea take these?' Lucy lifted both shoes out of the box, hooking the heels over her pinkies. 'They're her size. Don't you think Mom would want her to have them?'

I watched him process the question before slowly nodding. 'Yes, Lucy. I do believe she would.'

'So. Here,' Lucy said, dropping the shoes onto my lap, the matter settled.

'Thank you,' I said, looking down at them, then carefully putting them back in the box. I still couldn't imagine ever wearing them, but I would keep them in my closet, tucked neatly away.

6

After the closet cleanout, the next big hurdle was Lucy's birthday. Her grief surfaced at unexpected moments, whether at the grocery store or in church or playing with Caroline in the park, but I knew that special occasions were going to be especially difficult, given that Mrs Carr had always been so over-the-top about holidays and birthdays. She had thrown lavish parties for milestone birthdays, and, for all others, there had been extravagant presents, fancy dinners out in Dallas, homemade cakes (Mrs Carr had taken both a pastry class *and* a cake decorating class over the years), floral arrangements sent to Lucy's shop, and balloons tied to her mailbox first thing in the morning. Because of Mrs Carr's diligence and enthusiasm, Coach had always been able to mentally check out of birthday prep, as he did with so much else, knowing that his wife would make things perfect for their children. Even Neil let his mother-in-law take charge; his only duties included buying Lucy a piece of jewelry and bringing her breakfast in bed (a tradition that Mrs Carr had begun years ago).

But obviously this year – and every year that stretched ahead of us – was going to be different, and a mild panic set in among Lucy's inner circle the week before she turned thirty-three. We all knew we couldn't begin to fill her mother's shoes, but we wanted to at least try to get things right.

Lucy, however, was adamant that she didn't want to celebrate this birthday. When I pushed back, she pointed out that I hadn't wanted a fuss this year either. I refrained from enumerating some key differences, including the fact that I had *never* been big on birthdays, and that she had about five times more close friends than I did, including all the girls at her shop, her sorority sisters from UT, the wives of Neil's friends, and her fellow mommy friends. Instead I said, 'We at least went to lunch for my birthday. And you gave me beautiful gifts – even though I told you not to get me anything this year.'

'Gifts from my shop. Unwrapped. That hardly counts.'

'Of course it *counts*. I *love* that wrap dress – and the chandelier earrings are gorgeous.' Buying clothes for a friend was usually a risky proposition, but Lucy nailed it every time. 'Can't I at least take you to lunch?' I asked.

Lucy shook her head and said she just wanted to forget her birthday altogether this year; that it didn't even feel like a birthday without her mother, the person who had given *birth* to her. At that point, I acquiesced, but, later that afternoon, I had second thoughts and called Neil, both of us worrying about the same thing. Even though Lucy thought she was telling us the truth and giving us the right instructions, what if she felt differently on the actual day when nothing special was planned?

'Do you think we should call Coach and ask him?' Neil said.

'I don't think so,' I said. 'I think we should just inform him of the plan, or lack thereof . . . I don't want to bother him . . .'

'Because of the *spring game*?' Neil said with the slightest trace of disgust. 'It's not even the real season, Shea. And this is his only daughter's birthday.'

He had read my mind, of course. The game was *precisely* the reason I thought we shouldn't bother Coach, but I could tell how trivial Neil thought the whole thing was, at least in the context of Lucy's first birthday without her mother, and I felt slightly ashamed as I tried to cover up.

'No. It's not the *game* per se,' I said. 'He's just overwhelmed right now . . . and sad enough without having to make these sorts of judgment calls. Besides, guys don't really get these nuances. Other than you . . . Anyway, I say we have something small. A casual dinner?'

'I agree,' Neil said. 'Just family, you, and your mother. I'll barbecue some ribs . . . Just keep it really simple.'

'Perfect,' I said, selfishly relieved that we didn't have to include Lucy's gaggle of friends, and told Neil that my mom and I would handle the cake and all side dishes.

'And the party hats?' Neil said, only half kidding.

'And the party hats,' I said, smiling. "Cause we all know how much Lucy loves a good party hat.'

On the evening of March 21, thirty-three years after J.R. was shot on *Dallas,* I drove to Lucy and Neil's house with a custom two-tiered birthday cake, Lucy's gift (a coffee table book on runway fashion), and a half dozen party hats. I arrived about thirty minutes late, finding Lawton's and my mom's cars parked in the driveway. There was no sign of Coach.

When I walked in the front door, balancing the cake on Lucy's present, Caroline greeted me in red leggings and a clashing pink glitter top. It was a far cry from the traditional prissy way Lucy usually dressed her child, and I could tell in an instant that it hadn't been a good day over here.

'Hey, Care Bear,' I said, as she clamored for a peek of the cake, which I granted, and a taste, which I denied.

Then, just as I feared, Caroline announced in her high, squeaky voice and oddly clear diction for a four-year-old, 'Mama's crying because Poppy forgot her birthday, and she misses Gigi. Because Gigi was better on birthdays than Poppy.'

She was referring, of course, to Coach, and my heart sank.

'What do you mean Poppy *forgot* her birthday? Isn't he coming tonight?' I asked as Lucy emerged from upstairs in faded yoga pants, a spandex workout tank, and a lifeless pony-tail. She wasn't wearing any makeup or jewelry except for her watch – and not even the nice watch that Neil gave her last Christmas. A *digital* one. It was worse than I thought.

'He's on his way,' Lucy said, trying to take the cake from me. I turned my shoulders so she couldn't get a glimpse of it before it was time to blow out the candles.

'So, then! He didn't forget!' I said brightly.

'Neil had to *call and remind him.*'

Speechless, I glanced down the hallway to see Lawton, Neil, and my mother in the kitchen, huddled together, looking somber.

'It's okay,' Lucy said. 'I get it. He has a lot on his mind, with spring practice and all that . . . *shit.*'

No matter how many times she had alluded to football being 'just a game,' this was the first time she had overtly called it *shit* – and I saw a flash of anger in her eyes that alarmed me.

'Are you sure he forgot?' I said, wishing that I had called to remind him this morning. It had actually crossed my mind to do so, but I'd decided against it, thinking that it might come across as presumptuous or insulting.

'Well, he never called. Not once, all day,' she said. 'I checked my voice mail ten times, thinking maybe I'd just missed it. But no. There were three sweet messages from you and about thirty other messages from other friends and random acquaintances. Including . . .' She ticked off the list on her left hand – her old ballet teacher, our favorite bartender from the Third Rail, and a handful of ladies from her mother's Sunday School class.

'Mom must have told them to call me,' Lucy said, getting choked up. 'On her deathbed . . . They had all these wonderful things to say about her – and how proud she was of me and Caroline . . .'

'Wow,' I said, getting chills, marveling at how Mrs Carr had thought of everything, even as she stared down death.

Lucy seemed to chase away her tears with another wave of anger. She shook her head, her mouth becoming a hard line. 'A bunch of Sunday School ladies. But nothing from my own father.'

I opened my mouth to try to find an explanation, but Lucy interrupted. 'Look. Just forget it. It's no big deal. I said I didn't want any fuss . . . so . . . there you go. No fuss.'

She forced a tight, fake smile, then turned and walked into the kitchen. I followed her, putting the cake and gift and hats on the island, and saying hello to everyone. My mother whispered, 'This isn't good,' as I noticed the pink and white peonies I had sent this morning, a cheerful note amid the heaviness of the room. I had used Mrs Carr's flower shop, and even looked up her order history. After debating with the owner whether it seemed morbid or moving, I opted to send the same arrangement that Mrs Carr had chosen for Lucy last year – the two hues of peonies with sparse greenery in a square vase. The detail wasn't missed on Lucy, who gestured toward them and said, 'At least I have you. I can't believe how sweet you are to send . . . the *same* flowers . . .' Lucy's voice cracked again just as Coach burst through the front door.

'Hello, everyone!' he yelled, barreling into the kitchen, clearly straight from practice. He was wearing gray sweats, a film of dust over his white baseball cap, his whistle still around his neck, and a crumpled gift bag in his hands with a sorry little curled ribbon around the handle. With all of us watching, he deposited the bag on the table next to my flowers, along with his keys, then gave Lucy a big, one-armed hug, kissing the top of her head, and said, 'Happy birthday, Lu. Thirty-three.' He whistled for effect, but I could tell he was flustered, not a common state for him.

'Thanks, Daddy,' she said, as the rest of us watched uncomfortably.

Out of the corner of my eye, I could see him adjust the bill of his cap, a nervous twitch. 'I'm sorry the day got away from me . . . Crazy day. *Crazy.*'

'You forgot Mommy's birthday!' Caroline chimed in after wedging herself in the space between her mother and grandfather and looking up sweetly at both their faces.

'No, I *didn't,* honey,' Coach said, gesturing toward his gift bag. He stooped down and picked her up. 'I was coming. Of course I was coming.'

'Mommy said you forgot,' Caroline insisted as Lucy turned her back on both of them and began setting the table with her everyday flatware, simple plates, and paper napkins.

'Caroline,' Neil said in a reprimanding tone, which we all knew would only make her entrench more. 'Don't contradict your grandfather.'

'But she did,' Caroline replied as I realized that I was

literally holding my breath, in agony over the fact that Lucy looked so upset, and Coach so guilty.

I exhaled as Coach cleared his throat and defended himself. 'Sweetie pie, I most certainly did not forget your mama's birthday. I was just . . . busy until now.' He glanced toward the rest of us and said under his breath, 'Lawton, help me out here.'

'He was just busy,' Lawton echoed. 'Until now.'

Coach cast him a frustrated look that said, *That's the best you can do?*

Lawton shrugged as Caroline pressed on. 'Busy coaching football?'

'Yeah, he was busy coaching football,' Neil said, pulling her out of Coach's arms and tossing her in the air.

She giggled and forgot the debate for a few seconds, as Coach addressed no one in particular. 'Okay, then. No more football talk for the night,' he said.

'Until tomorrow?' Caroline asked, glancing his way with judgment and mischief. It was almost as if Lucy had given her child a script and a course in twisting the knife.

'Until tomorrow, yes, sweetie,' Coach said, pretending to be relaxed. I wondered who else could see through his act, as he looked at my mother and me. 'Hello, Marie. Hey, Shea. How's everyone doing?'

We both murmured that we were fine, then transitioned to breezy small talk. At one point, Coach asked if I'd heard back from Smiley.

'Not yet,' I said, part of me relieved that I hadn't.

'Call him again,' Coach said. 'You gotta be persistent.'

I nodded, then said, 'So how was practice?'

'It was good,' Coach replied, glancing at Lucy, then giving me a strained smile. 'But no football talk tonight. Remember?'

'It's okay, Daddy,' Lucy said, removing condiments from the refrigerator and handing Caroline a few carrot sticks. 'I mean, whatever else would there be to talk about?'

I don't think Lucy meant the rhetorical question to sound as biting as it did, because she followed it up with a shrug and said, 'I mean, it is the week of the spring game. I get it. It's okay. You can tell Shea – and all of us – about practice.'

'Practice was fine,' he said. 'I just had to deal with some other stuff today . . . It's always something . . .'

'What happened, Dad?' Lawton asked, tossing Caroline over the back of the sofa. She bounced, laughing, then giddily circled around for more.

'Oh, it's a long story,' he said with a sigh. 'Just a little issue with Reggie . . . Probably nothing.'

'Who?' Lucy said.

I think I must have gasped, because Lucy glanced at me and said, 'What? Like I'm supposed to memorize a hundred players?'

'Reggie *Rhodes,* honey,' Neil said. 'You know who he is.'

'He's only the biggest recruit we've had since Ryan James,' Lawton said.

'Oh, *him.* Yeah. I didn't recognize the first name,' Lucy said. 'I know him.'

'Of *course* you know him, dear,' my mother said, tossing her tomato and onion salad.

'So what happened?' Lucy asked. 'Did he get hurt in practice?'

Lawton laughed and shook his head, twisting off the cap of a Bud Light. 'He's not here yet, Luce.'

'What do you mean he's not here?' Lucy snapped back.

'Lawton means . . . that he's still in high school,' Neil said. 'He's coming *next* year.'

'Well, wherever he is . . . He could still get hurt!' my mother said, rushing to Lucy's defense. 'He could have gotten in a car accident. Or . . . had a random slip and fall—'

'On a banana peel?' Lawton quipped.

'What happened, Daddy?' Lucy said, scowling at Lawton.

'Nothing, really . . . Just a little mud in the water . . . It'll be fine.' He shook his head, then shifted into his faux upbeat voice and said, 'So, who's hungry? Neil, let's fire up that grill, son!'

We all agreed that was a very good idea – because everyone knew that there weren't many things in Texas that barbecued ribs couldn't fix.

7

A few days later, Walker played its annual spring game, which also counted as our fifteenth and final NCAA-permitted spring practice. More than thirty thousand fans turned out for the glorified scrimmage, also televised on ESPN2, offering the first glimpse of our team minus the recruits. Technically I was working, making my usual rounds between the press box and the sidelines, ensuring that everything was running smoothly. But because nothing was really on the line, it was more party than game, a two-sided showcase of our offensive and defensive talent. We looked good, more fluid and crisp than I'd ever seen us play in March – a sentiment that I heard paraphrased behind me in a smooth Texas dialect, with just a subtle elongation of vowels. I recognized the accent and voice right away, knew it was Ryan James, Walker's golden child, even before I looked over my shoulder. His voice was that distinct, even if I hadn't just heard it on *SportsCenter* the day before, discussing the Cowboys' upcoming season.

'You boys have to convert here,' he mused aloud. 'Let's get it done, fellas.'

'Hey, Ryan,' I said, as he took two steps forward and stood flush with me, watching the drive.

'Hey, Rigsby,' he said. He crossed his arms as we watched the next play. Second and three, but Mark Everclear, our quarterback, stared down the primary receiver for one beat too long, and took a sack.

'Dammit,' I said, happy that our linebackers were looking good but more disappointed by Mark's hesitation.

'Phil Medlin was *wiiide* open,' Ryan said, reading my mind.

I was impressed that he knew our roster so well – and touched that he still made it a priority to return to Walker for the spring game.

'You would have hit him with your eyes closed,' I said.

He made a modest face, as if to say maybe, maybe not, while I sneaked a quick once-over. Always clean-cut and smartly dressed, Ryan looked especially good tonight, in a navy sport coat with a white polo, dark-washed denim, and brown suede loafers. From a wealthy oil family in Midland, he had always reeked of old money and good taste, even before he turned pro and started raking in his own millions. Both George Bushes had attended Ryan's grandiose wedding to his now ex-wife, Blakeslee Meadows, a gorgeous socialite from Houston who transferred to Walker from SMU, in the opinion of many, so she could marry Ryan. Her plan worked, and the two were engaged just days after the Cowboys drafted him as the first overall pick. Lucy had gone to the wedding, along with her parents, and said she'd never seen anything like it – Blakeslee's family's ranch crawling with Secret Service agents, celebrities, and regular people who were so beautiful that they looked like celebrities. I wasn't invited, which didn't hurt my feelings but surprised me a little, not because Ryan and I were that tight in college but because I would have thought we were friendly enough for me to make a nine-hundred-person cut. Lucy told me to take it as a compliment, that Blakeslee must have seen me as competition. I told her that was preposterous. I might have had a few attributes that certain guys appreciated, but I was no Blakeslee, that was for sure, and Ryan was way out of my league, the biggest man on campus when we were in school, and now an NFL star. Big fish, big pond. I'd even heard a tabloid rumor that Giselle had flirted with him at a party in Hawaii during Pro Bowl weekend last year, which led to an exchange of terse words with Tom Brady. When I thought about it, I was pretty sure Ryan was the only person on the planet who could rile Tom Brady, both on the field and off. It was yet another accomplishment in a long list.

I stepped out of the way as a cameraman turned to get a close-up of Ryan for all the viewers at home. Clearly accustomed to the spotlight, he pretended not to notice the bright lights in his face, and kept right on talking to me as if we were alone.

'I'm sorry we didn't have a chance to speak at Mrs Carr's funeral,' he said under his breath. 'I had to be . . . in and out.'

I nodded, fighting a wave of sadness at the mention of Mrs Carr, then said, 'By the way. Great game against the Steelers a few months back. It's not easy to get a win at Heinz Field.'

He smiled. 'You watched?'

'Of course,' I said. 'That was quite a scramble you had at the end there . . .'

He gave me a funny look and said, 'So, how have you been, Shea?'

'Fine. Good,' I said, thinking that, since college, nothing had really changed in my life. 'You know. Same old . . .'

'You still working with J.J.? In sports information?'

I held up the press pass, dangling around my neck, and smiled. 'Yep.'

'And how's Miller?' he asked. 'Is he here tonight?'

'Probably somewhere. Haven't seen him, though . . . We broke up,' I said, surprised that Ryan even knew we were together in the first place.

'Oh?' Ryan said. 'I'm sorry to hear that . . .' His voice trailed off.

'Yeah. It's okay. It had just . . . run its course . . .'

He nodded and said, 'That happens.'

After an awkward pause, I said, 'I'm sorry about your divorce.'

'Yeah. Thanks. At least we didn't have kids . . . So, you know . . . clean break.'

He smiled, putting me at ease, as I remembered the tabloid story I'd read about Blakeslee getting custody of their three-year-old sheepdog, Sasha. They had fought over her, but Ryan had finally relented, based mostly on his travel schedule. Then, a week after Blakeslee took custody, Sasha ate a poisonous mushroom and died.

I tried to think of something clever to say, but came up blank. 'Well, I better get to the press box. It was great seeing you.'

'You, too,' Ryan said.

As I turned to go, he reached out and touched my arm. 'Do you have a card on you?'

'Sure don't,' I said. Although I was wearing a rather unfortunate and unfeminine outfit – a Walker golf shirt and khakis – I hadn't resorted to wearing a fanny pack or carrying a wallet in my back pocket. Besides, I was sure Ryan was just being polite to a fellow alum.

'Well, here,' he said, reaching for his wallet, covered with embossed, interlocking Gucci Gs. He pulled out a card with the Cowboys logo, an all-caps QUARTERBACK below his name, and said, 'Here's my cell. Call me if you ever want to get together. Grab a bite or something.'

I nodded and took the card, my face frozen with a big, awkward smile. Surely he didn't really mean it.

'Or if you want tickets . . . We start playing again in September.'

'September, huh. Is that when the NFL starts back?' I said, smirking.

'Right,' Ryan said, grinning at me. 'Forgot who I was talking to.'

'He gave you his number?' Lucy shouted.

After the game, I had stopped by her place for a glass of wine. It was nearly nine, but Caroline was wide awake, watching *Finding Nemo* as she nursed a cup full of bright red juice, the kind that is just waiting to be spilled. Lucy ran a loose ship – very unlike the way she grew up and the way you'd imagine she'd mother – and there was something about it that was both surprising and refreshing.

'It wasn't like that,' I said. 'Don't get so excited.'

'What do you mean "it wasn't like that"? Of course it was like that. He gave you his number!'

'He gave me his *card*,' I said.

'Does it have his number on it?'

I nodded, laughing.

'Well, then, same difference! Let me see it,' she said, motioning for it.

I mumbled that she was getting worked up for nothing, but pulled it out of the side pocket of my purse.

She stared at it and then called out for Neil. 'Honey! Come here and help us analyze!'

Neil stepped away from loading the dishwasher as she showed him the card and filled him in. 'Now,' she said to him, 'wouldn't you say he's interested? What other explanation is there?'

He studied the card, looking impressed. 'I'd say he's interested,' he said, looking up at me.

'I'd say you're just agreeing with your wife because you know you have to,' I said.

Lucy ignored this and said, 'You need to call him.'

'Come on, Luce,' I said. 'He can go out with any girl he wants. Models. Actresses. Anyone.'

'He had Blakeslee,' she said. 'And now he wants something different.'

'You mean a big girl?' I said. I wasn't one to get hung up on my weight, but I was definitely big-boned compared to Blakeslee.

'Down-to-earth. Normal. He wants *you*.'

I laughed and said, 'He doesn't *want* me. He just likes me as a friend. Besides, even if he were interested, I can't go out with one of Miller's teammates . . .'

'Why the hell not?' she said as she snatched the card back from Neil.

'Because . . . it's a code.'

'It's not *your* code,' she said. 'It's a *guy* code. And Ryan showed you that he doesn't care about that guy code when he handed you *this*.' She studied the card one more time, then gave it back to me. 'You better call him.'

I threw out a final objection. 'I thought you didn't want me to go out with football players. And I'd be going from one to the next like some . . . groupie.'

'There are football players,' she said, making a face. 'And then there is *Ryan James*. God . . . even *I* would be jealous of you if you could close this deal.' Lucy looked over at Neil. 'No offense, honey.'

'Oh, none taken,' Neil said. 'I'd be jealous of her, too.'

'You both are ridiculous,' I said, but just for the hell of it, and to humor Lucy, I banged out a text to Ryan: *Great to see you tonight. Would love to get a bite sometime. LMK. Shea.*

'There,' I said, holding up my phone and showing her the delivered message. 'Happy now?'

'Yes,' she said. 'But I will be happier once we get access to his private plane and house in Cabo.'

'Ha,' I said. 'Keep dreaming.'

The next morning, I had a response from Ryan, a text that he'd sent at 6:00 A.M.: *Charity function Fri. Need a hot date. You game?*

I must have read it a half dozen times, searching for a 'just friends' angle, if only to guard against disappointment, and concluded that he must have been joking about the 'hot date' part. Because if he *really* saw me as a hot date, he wouldn't *call* me a hot date; he'd just think it. Still. The facts were the facts. Whether or not I qualified as hot, he had a function to attend and was asking me to go with him – and I was absolutely going to accept the invitation, this time without any prodding from Lucy. So I texted back: *I'm in.*

He called only a few seconds after that and said, 'That's what I like about you.' I could tell he was on speaker, and pictured him wearing Ray-Bans in a shiny sports car, driving with one hand low on the steering wheel, the sunroof open.

'What's that?' I said, laughing. 'That I'm easy?'

'Well, frankly, yeah. I mean . . . Not easy in *that* way . . . Just easy. You never do the psycho girlie thing, do you?'

'Depends on what you mean by *psycho girlie*,' I said, thinking

of the napkin covered with Coach Carr's doodles that I had
rescued from the trash after an athletic department meeting
sometime last year. That would probably be considered psycho
by most, especially given the napkin's proximity to a half-eaten
Bunki's donut, which also happened to belong to Coach Carr.
At least I didn't finish it.

Ryan clarified, 'You didn't wait three days to write back.
You didn't ask for all the details before you committed. You
didn't make sure you could schedule a blowout and spray tan
on such late notice. You didn't ask exhaustive questions about
what you had to wear. You just said yes.'

I smiled, thinking that maybe Lucy was right. Maybe Ryan
was looking for a low-maintenance anti-Blakeslee. If so, he had
come to the right girl (although I made a mental note to schedule
a blowout and spray tan since that was what he was clearly
accustomed to).

'Well, now that you mention it. What are the details?' I had
given my only proper gown to a thrift shop because I never
wore it and because Lucy had informed me that it was too
short, that my toes should show only as I took a step forward,
not when standing still. 'Is it black-tie?'

'No. Just cocktail attire. The invite actually says "business
casual," I think. It's a benefit for autism. One of my causes,'
he said. 'But I don't really have to do anything. Just show up
for an hour or two. With a stunning girl on my arm.'

I was pretty sure that he didn't mean to call me stunning any
more than he had meant to call me hot, but I still felt a goofy
grin on my face and was grateful that he couldn't see it. 'Stunning,
huh? That's a tall order.' I spun around in my desk chair, turning
to face the only window in my office, with the perfect view of
a gorgeously symmetrical loblolly magnolia already in full bloom.

'It's not a tall order for you. I saw you on the sidelines,
looking effortlessly fine in that Walker getup,' Ryan said as I
heard his turn signal in the background, confirming that he
was in his car. 'Never seen a chick look that good in khakis.'

I laughed with nervousness and a little bit of excitement.

Was this really happening? Was I really about to go on a date with a star quarterback, famous even to non-football fans? I reminded myself that it was only Ryan James, my old friend, who just happened to be a Dallas Cowboy – and that I was sure it would amount to very little.

'Well, then,' I said. 'That's settled. Business casual it is. I'll wear my game-day khakis.'

'You can wear whatever your little heart desires,' Ryan said, taking the phone off speaker. His voice dropped, low and smooth, as though he were whispering in my ear. 'I have always been a big fan of your collarbone, though . . .'

I stopped in my tracks, a distant memory suddenly unearthed from the spring of our junior year. Ryan and I were at some frat party. I was wearing a white tank top to accentuate my tan (those were the days when I actually went to tanning beds, a.k.a. cancer chambers) and was dancing to 'Brown Eyed Girl' when he came up to me and said, 'Anyone ever tell you that you have a sexy collarbone?'

I wasn't entirely sure where my collarbone was until he ran his finger along it and said, 'There are ass guys . . . leg guys . . . boob guys. But *this* . . . is my spot.' His finger lingered there, long enough for three friends, Lucy included, who was visiting from UT, to inquire about the incident later. I told them it was nothing. I *knew* it was nothing. Nothing more than a drunken frat-party exchange with one of the biggest players on campus. And by *player*, I didn't mean *on* the field.

'Yes. I think you mentioned that once,' I said now. 'A long time ago.'

'I'd love a refresher.'

'Well, then,' I said, grinning into the phone. 'I'll see what I can do for you.'

That night, my mother made me dinner, a gourmet French meal in her dining room, complete with candlelight and white-cloth napkins. But the formal presentation didn't stop her from leaping out of her seat and yelping when I gave her the Ryan update, a contradiction that was *so* my mother. At heart, she was a TV-dinner kind of girl, but she fought hard against her redneck roots, doing everything she could to distance herself from her lower-middle-class upbringing in Odessa. Behind her back, and before Mrs Carr got sick, I called it the *Connie effect,* joking to Lucy that my mom had spent her entire adult life trying to extinguish her inner tacky light and be more like her high-class friend. I actually don't know how Mrs Carr stood all the copycat behavior, but I'm sure it had something to do with her own perfect mother instilling in her the charitable belief that imitation was the most sincere form of flattery.

In other words, my mother had sincerely flattered Connie Carr on a daily basis, especially when it came to matters of taste. When Mrs Carr traded her silver car in for a white one, my mother followed suit (even though she had once told me that she'd never own a white car). When Mrs Carr decided to get a crisp bob one summer, my mother chopped off her hair, too. And on and on. Mrs Carr was my mother's best friend, but also her field guide and barometer of all her decisions, both minor and major, and losing her, I could tell already, was having a disorienting, devastating effect. It was unfathomable to my mother that Connie had actually drawn the short straw, and a source of great guilt. Striving even harder for perfection, Connie Carr–style, seemed to be a way of repenting for being the survivor, and, as always, my mother couldn't separate me from her quest. In this way, Ryan James would be the ultimate salve. If I could land him – heck, even *date* him for a minute – there would be some sort of tangible proof that she had raised me right, been a good mother, overcome her blue-collar roots.

All her life my mother had been scrapping and scheming to defy her familial shortcomings, beginning with her own accept-ance to Walker on a full (albeit need-based) scholarship, then continuing when she befriended Connie, landed my dad (Yankee money was better than no money), joined all the right clubs, and, most of all, aligned our family so closely with the Carrs. There was really nothing more she could have done to set me up for her brand of success and status. Yet, I still managed to let her down, time and again, beginning at a young age when she signed me up for riding lessons only to discover that I had a severe allergic reaction to horses. It was downhill from there. I sucked at ballet. I refused to go out for cheerleading. I spent too much time on football. I wasn't into clothes or makeup or all the things that girls in Texas are raised to care about. I didn't get into the exclusive Camp Waldemar, a sleepaway camp with more stringent admissions than Harvard, or the Hockaday School, the fancy boarding school in Dallas that all the 'best' girls attended (the only notable exception was Lucy because Coach Carr didn't believe in sending children away). I made the Homecoming Court, but skipped the festivities for a regional track meet.

And perhaps the biggest disappointment of my mother's life, at least since her marriage ended, was when I wasn't invited to be a debutante. It was a long shot, as these things were passed down through the generations, but, because of my mother's diligence, and our close affiliation with the Carrs, I still had a shot – until I dated Gregory Hobbs my junior year of high school and eviscerated her efforts in one fell swoop. It didn't matter that Gregory was in the National Honor Society or that his father was an economics professor at Walker or that our romance was short-lived and mostly innocent. What mattered was that Gregory was African-American, and, whether or not anyone admitted it, interracial dating wasn't exactly a fast track into the upper crust of Texas society. My mother had zero tolerance for racism and certainly never discouraged my friendship with Gregory, but I could tell she let the debutante dream die after that, slightly lowering her social ambitions for me.

When Mrs Carr and Lucy began the whole tedious debbing process, my mother's wounds were briefly reopened, and I actually felt a little sorry for her. But I reassured her that it was for the best. I wasn't the slightest bit interested in getting all dolled up to walk down a runway in silly white gloves and bridal wear, especially for a bunch of elitists. Nor was I about to get on my knees and do that ridiculous 'swan' curtsy to the boys I had seen belching and swearing in the cafeteria. The whole thing was a big misogynistic joke, and I told my mother I'd be forfeiting my rights as a strong, independent woman if I got up on that auction block. Hadn't she raised me better than that?

With a dash of feminism somewhere in her blood, she didn't disagree entirely, but she was also a realist and warned me that I would never marry into a 'good' family if I didn't learn to play the game – or at least *pretend* to be a proper Southern lady. She was right, of course. Because I never played the game, never became a proper Southern lady, and never made headway with Texas blue bloods, the kind of boys who stand when a girl comes to the table, tip their hats at the right moments, make you look good when they spin you around the dance floor, and have loads of money, the older the better. Instead, I ended up with guys like Miller who broke all the rules and, in my mother's words, wore boots on all the wrong occasions, namely weddings (you didn't have to be Mrs Carr or Garth Brooks to know that boots have no place at black-tie affairs).

But now, seemingly out of nowhere, my mother sensed a comeback. I told her not to get her hopes up. 'Nobody is courting anybody. And I'm not being wooed either. He is not my beau, nor am I his betrothed,' I said, throwing every old-fashioned term I could think of into the mix.

She laughed in spite of herself, then went in the opposite direction. 'What do you suppose he sees in you, anyway?'

'The good Lord only knows,' I said, pressing my palms together, prayer-style, and staring up at the ceiling.

She ignored my sarcasm and asked, 'You think it's all that football knowledge? Finally paying off?'

Unlike my true devotion to the game, my mother's love of Walker football was superficial, all about the fanfare. She went to every home game, tailgating with her famous deviled eggs and baby back ribs, but once she got inside the gates, the socializing never stopped. She was way too busy gabbing about how much she would *just die* if Walker lost to actually watch the game.

'Yes. Finally, it has all paid off!' I said, deciding it wasn't worth it to call her out on yet another charge of sexism. It was the same way I bit my tongue whenever I heard people (and remarkably women were the worst offenders) imply that Erin Andrews and Samantha Ponder couldn't possibly add real value to a football telecast, insinuating that they were merely eye candy on the sidelines.

'That has to be it,' my mom said, looking pleased with her theory.

'Yes! All that useless football information! At last! Bearing fruit!' I said, reaching for the bread basket.

'No more carbs,' she said, smacking the roll out of my hand, a sore spot in my childhood. When I was growing up, if I ate too much bread, sugar, or, God forbid, French fries, my mother would make me go out in the backyard and do calisthenics until I'd 'worked it off.' It was a wonder I'd never developed an eating disorder.

I scowled at her, thinking that if Ryan was going to like me, he was going to like *me*. Then I picked up the roll, smeared on the butter, and took a big, defiant bite.

8

A couple days later, after I'd forced myself to make a follow-up call to Frank Smiley, as per Coach's advice, I finally heard back from his assistant, receiving a curt invitation to meet him for lunch at Bob's Chop and Steak House on the same day as Ryan's event. The woman on the phone did not offer me alternate times or days, and seemed put out by even delivering the message, so I quickly agreed, then hung up and called Coach Carr with the news.

'I'm meeting Smiley at Bob's Steak House,' I told him. 'I assume it's an interview?'

'It's a damn coup is what it is,' Coach said. 'You're meeting the best sports editor in Texas for lunch. At his favorite restaurant. Guy might as well have a typewriter set up in one of those booths . . . Yeah, I'd say it's an interview.'

'He still uses a typewriter?' I said, intrigued. I knew he still brought yellow tablets and mechanical pencils to the pressroom, unlike just about everyone else, who used laptops, but a typewriter was even cooler.

'I wouldn't be surprised . . . People call me "old school." I'm new age compared to Smiley.'

'Doesn't sound like the kind of guy who wants some girl on his staff,' I said, having already done my due diligence and confirmed that there were currently no women on the sports staff at the *Post*.

Coach didn't deny this; he just said, 'You're not *some* girl.'

I smiled into the phone.

'So anyway . . . order the rib eye. Or the porterhouse. No salad – unless it's the chopped to start.'

I wasn't sure whether he was giving me his personal recommendations or some sort of boys' club interview tip, but either way, I said, 'Got it.'

'And be ready to talk baseball,' Coach said. 'Frank's a first-rate baseball snob. You know the type.'

I laughed and said I did, remembering a conversation Coach and I once had about baseball diehards. We concluded that they were a strange blend of snob and nerd, like a cross between an opera aficionado and a computer geek. They really seemed to believe that they were more evolved, with higher IQs than your average football fan. My mother might have been right about my reservoir of useless statistics, but it was nothing compared to the database that was the brain of a rabid baseball fan.

I told Coach that if Smiley wanted me for a baseball beat, I wouldn't take the job anyway, but, after I hung up, I still spent the next hour nervously surfing my usual sites – ESPN, *SI,* FOX Sports, *Rivals,* Scout, *Deadspin,* and Yardbarker. I brushed up on the latest baseball gossip, as well as happenings in basketball, tennis, golf, soccer, and hockey. I could drink a fifth of whiskey and talk intelligibly about football, both college and the NFL, but otherwise I was a *SportsCenter* highlight reel kind of girl and didn't want to embarrass myself. More important, I didn't want to embarrass Coach. If he had vouched for me, I had to make a good impression.

Two days later I drove to the famed steak house on Lemmon Street, wearing a navy pencil skirt, a white button-down blouse, and low pumps. I skipped all makeup except for a dab of lip gloss and put my hair up in a simple twist. My aim was to look like a serious reporter, without a trace of sex appeal.

Arriving at Bob's twenty minutes early, I checked in with the maître d' and waited for Smiley at the polished bar, sipping a club soda and glancing around the room. The crowd was mostly male and appeared conservative, wealthy, and important – or at least self-important – which, based on dining experiences in New

York with my father, seemed to be a standard steak house phenomenon. The power scene felt exaggerated today, on steroids, the way things often were in my home state. Big was bigger. Loud was louder. Rich was richer. And less was never more. Then again, maybe I was just nervous, out of my collegiate comfort zone, where you could get away with wearing sweats to work if you really wanted to. In ten years on the job, plus the two I had interned in sports information as a student, J.J. had never once reprimanded me. He hardly even felt like my boss most of the time, offering suggestions rather than assignments or deadlines. My life was a regular cakewalk, and although I had doubts lately about the direction it was going in, I didn't understand why so many people seemed to have the philosophy that easy was inversely proportionate to worthwhile. Was it really such a bad thing to phone it in – as long as you were happy and doing clean, honest work? Wasn't there something to be said for working to live, as opposed to living to work?

As I contemplated this question, Frank Smiley walked into the restaurant in a brown corduroy jacket, suede patches at his elbows, a bow tie, and his standard hat – this one more trilby than fedora. His expression was gruffer than usual, and I could nearly read the words in a bubble over his head: *This is a waste of my time*. I took a few deep breaths as the maître d' pointed at me too quickly for me to glance away. I gave Smiley a little wave as he tipped his hat in my direction, then barreled toward me, the bubble changing to *Let's get this shit over with*.

'Shea Rigsby,' he barked when he got to the bar, the hostess standing demurely behind him with two oversize menus. He removed his hat with his left hand and extended his right. Neither of us smiled.

'Yes, sir,' I said, my hand falling into a stranglehold. I squeezed back as hard as I could, our hands pumping up and down three times.

'Pleasure,' he said, looking like it was anything but.

'Nice to meet you, Mr Smiley,' I said, though we had met before, or at least collided, in postgame press conferences.

He did not offer his first name, further unnerving me. I stood, catching my heel on my barstool and stumbling a little. A dash of club soda sloshed onto the bar. The bartender swiped it away almost instantaneously, yet Smiley's eyes stayed critically fixed on the site of the spill.

'Whoops,' I said, righting myself. I smoothed my skirt as the hostess led us to a choice mahogany booth in the corner, obviously reserved for him, as inferior tables were filled around us.

He slid in with his back to the wall and fired off his first question. 'So Coach Carr said you can write?'

'Well, I'm certainly not one to contradict Coach Carr,' I said. In my mind, it was a deft reply – a way to combine modesty, humor, and confidence.

'Do you love it? Writing?'

I hesitated, then gave him the risky truth. 'It's a love-hate relationship. I love the feeling *after* I've finished writing something. But the actual writing? Sometimes not so much.'

Smiley nodded, not disapprovingly, then said, 'Yes. I've always said finishing a column is a lot like leaving the dentist.'

'Or the gym,' I added.

'Oh, I wouldn't know about that,' he said, as a young waiter with perfect hair and posture arrived to offer us beverages.

Smiley made perfunctory eye contact, but looked annoyed by the interruption and said, 'We're ready to order . . . Aren't we?'

'Yes,' I said. Then, without looking at the menu, I told the waiter I'd like the rib eye, medium.

'And for you, Mr Smiley?'

'The usual,' he said.

'And any sides for you today?'

'The usual,' he repeated, with a wave of his hand, practically shooing him away from the table.

When the waiter left, Smiley took off his jacket and rolled up his sleeves. 'So. I know all about your Walker ties.'

'Yes, sir. I have . . . a lot of Walker ties . . .' I stammered, reminding myself to answer as simply as possible. Less likely to screw up that way.

'Could you cover college football? And be fair and objective?'

'Yes, sir,' I said.

He raised his unibrow, and I gave way to the silence.

'Yes. I think I could write very objectively about teams getting their asses handed to them by Walker.'

It was a misfire. Smiley wasn't amused. He stared at me, waiting for my real answer. I looked directly into his eyes and tried again, telling him that I was confident I could.

Smiley nodded. 'Okay, Ms. Rigsby, tell me this. What do you see as the role of a sportswriter?'

My mind went blank as I stalled by answering his question with a question. 'For a traditional news outlet?'

'Yes. A *news*paper. Not glib twits or tweets or whatever the hell they're called, or mamsy-pamsy, whining blogs.'

I took a long sip of water, stalling again, then stammered an awkward reply. 'Well, I think . . . at some basic level . . . it's a reporter's job to keep fans in touch with their favorite sports and teams.'

Smiley stared at me, his eyes glazed. My answer bored him, *pained* him, and maybe even pissed him off.

Panicked, I knew I had to come up with something better – and fast. I cleared my throat, then said, 'But when people read the paper now, they generally know what happened the night before. From television or online articles. Radio. Twitter. And the mamsy-pamsy blogs,' I said with a hint of a smile.

He nodded, somewhat reengaged but still appearing skeptical.

'So it's less about actual, immediate coverage,' I continued, 'and more about adding some level of analysis and insight. Exposing all the underlying emotions. The human element.'

He perked up slightly.

'Bottom line, it's just a game, right? But it's our job to show that it's *not* just a game. It's a metaphor for life. If sports don't matter, then life doesn't matter.'

'Yes,' he said emphatically. 'That's *exactly* it.'

I kept going, with more confidence. 'It's like those little human interest clips they show during the Olympics. They make you care about a random Russian luger like he was your brother . . . Because you know what? He *could* be your brother. He *is* your brother.'

'Yes. *Yes*,' Smiley said. 'And who do you think does that well? Which reporters?'

I fought against the urge to say, 'You, for one,' thinking that obsequious was the wrong route to take with Smiley. Instead, I rattled off a handful of the best sports reporters, a mix of contemporary writers and old-timers: George Plimpton, Roger Angell, Red Smith, John Feinstein, Robert Creamer, Frank Deford, Dan Jenkins, Buster Olney, Peter King, and Rick Reilly.

'You didn't name one female writer,' he said.

'Okay. Mike Lupica,' I said, proud of my quick locker room retort.

He smirked as I said, 'Sally Jenkins. She's great. And Robin Herman.'

'Aren't you too young to know Angell? Half those guys?' he asked.

'I spent my childhood reading that stuff. Old articles. And I collect *Sports Illustrated*s. When I was ten or eleven, Coach Carr gave me hundreds of issues when his wife cleaned out the attic. They make for great rainy day reading. Reliving the "rumble in the jungle" or the 'eighty-six Mets–Sox series or the epic McEnroe–Borg rivalry.'

For the first time since we sat down, Smiley looked impressed. Not just satisfied or curious but affirmatively impressed. I knew the look well. It was the look that guys at bars would give me right after I gave them my game day analysis and right before they'd jokingly say, 'Will you marry me?'

'What pieces stand out for you?' Smiley asked, but this question felt different from the others. This one sounded like something he'd pose to his reporter buddies over beers, not to a chick he was begrudgingly interviewing as a favor to a legendary coach.

'Hmm. Let's see,' I said, thinking. 'Well, John Updike's piece on Ted Williams, for one. Phenomenal.'

Smiley lit up as I continued, 'Roger Angell's piece on Steve Blass.'

He nodded. 'Go on.'

'Gay Talese's "The Silent Season of a Hero" . . . Although it's hard not to be a genius when you're writing about Joe DiMaggio . . . Norman Mailer's story on Muhammad Ali. "Ego" – wasn't that the perfect title? . . . And Frank Deford's "Raised by Women to Conquer Men."'

Smiley wrinkled his brow. 'Which one was that?'

'The Jimmy Connors piece . . . And let's see . . . my favorite football books . . . John Eisenberg's *That First Season* . . . *Boys Will Be Boys* by Jeff Pearlman,' I said, referring to the book on the Dallas Cowboys of the nineties. 'And Jack Cavanaugh's *Giants Among Men*. That book makes me wish I had been alive in the fifties – and a Giants fan . . . and . . . probably my favorite, *Paper Lion*. George Plimpton's a friggin' genius.'

'You have good taste,' he said.

'Thank you,' I said, as our food arrived, and I noted that I actually, finally, had an appetite. No matter what happened on the job front, I had proven to Frank Smiley that I was legit.

'Oh. One more thing,' Smiley said. His voice was casual, but I could see in his eyes that he was about to test me. 'How do you feel about women in the locker room? Think that's okay?'

My pulse quickened, perspiration trickling down my sides as I did the silent calculation. I told myself that I could wear these no-nonsense clothes and forgo makeup. I could order a big slab of meat before noon. And I could pretend that true impartiality was possible in my highly charged, partisan world of college football. But I just couldn't – and wouldn't – give Smiley the answer I knew he was looking for on this one.

So without blinking I said yes. Absolutely.

Smiley raised his overgrown brow. 'Oh?'

'No double standards,' I said, unyielding, firm. 'Whether in the NFL or the WNBA. Locker rooms need to be open to all or closed to all. And closing them isn't the answer. We need to be in there to get the immediate reactions and raw emotion. And, as a practical matter, to file our stories on time.' I noticed that I had switched from the third person to *we* and *our* – and wondered what this reflected about my true desire.

'What about player privacy?' Smiley asked.

'What about it?' I fired back.

'Don't players have the right to it?'

I resisted rolling my eyes and instead told him that players of both genders had plenty of time to shower, change, or at least cover up during the requisite cooling-off period.

'And if they don't want to cover up?'

I shrugged. 'That's on them.'

'Wouldn't that make you . . . uncomfortable? If a male athlete chose not to cover up?'

'I've been in locker rooms, Mr Smiley. I've been in winning locker rooms and losing locker rooms. And they all are the same. They all stink. And they are all full of dirty clothes and sweaty towels and bloody bandages.'

'And naked men,' he shot back.

'Sometimes, yes. Sometimes there are three-hundred-pound naked men with gnarly cuts and hairy backs and bruised hamstrings.'

He didn't seem to get my point, or at least pretended not to, so I kept going, 'Locker rooms aren't lounges of flirtation, Mr Smiley. Not in my experience. Nobody is thinking about sex after a battle. And if women are allowed to be war correspondents, they should be allowed in a locker room after a football game,' I finished, feeling jubilant, as if I had scored one for female journalists everywhere.

He looked at me and nodded, as if quietly acknowledging that I'd won the point. We spoke no more of gender after that, just silently spooned big helpings of hash browns and glazed carrots onto our plates and cut into our steaks, moving on to more general sports banter.

About an hour later, we had finished lunch and were walking out to the parking lot. Arriving at my car first, Smiley eyed my Walker bumper sticker circumspectly and said, 'You're sure you can be objective?'

'Those peel off, you know,' I said, picking at one curling edge of the sticker.

'So that's a yes?'

'Yes,' I said.

'What if I told you the beat was for Texas?' he said.

'Is it?' I swallowed, hoping he was calling my bluff. That the beat was for *any* team but Texas.

'Yes,' he said. 'The proud state university with the color you once called "bile orange".'

I cringed, remembering the piece I had written in college as he continued to quote me. '"The hue of regurgitated beer and burritos." Ring a bell?'

'Well,' I said. 'It *is* a bad color.'

'Is that your final answer?'

'No, sir,' I said. 'I wrote that when I was in college. Writing for the *Walker* paper. That was a different job description. I can be objective. I know I can.'

'Good. Because if a reporter so much as lets out one cheer in the press box, he's done. He – or *she* – is history in this business.'

I nodded and said I understood, surprising myself by how very much I wanted the job, even if it involved a whole lot of bile orange.

9

After lunch, I headed to the Lea Journo Salon, where Lucy had booked me a blowout with her favorite Dallas stylist – a heavily tattooed, ripped gay man named Ricardo.

'Do you want sleek, big, or something in between?' Ricardo asked, as he unharnessed my ponytail and tousled my long hair.

I told him to go big, silently finishing the sentence with Coach's words: *Or go home.*

'Old Hollywood big? Victoria's Secret big? Cindy Crawford–throwback big? Or Miss America big?' Ricardo pressed.

'Whatever you think,' I said. 'Just make me . . . glamorous.'

'Oh, honey, glam is a given in this chair,' he said, turning to tell his mousy, bespectacled assistant that I was ready to be washed – and that we were going to need a truckload of Velcro rollers.

'The purples?' his assistant asked.

'No, girl. The blues! You heard the lady! We're going to make her big! Pow! Shazam!'

A full forty minutes later, after my hair was mostly dried, Ricardo put his turbo dryer down and said, 'Honey, you're making me work. Good gawd, you have *a lot* of hair!'

I smiled, knowing that was a compliment, and thinking that it was nice to have at least one outstanding feature. Two if you counted my collarbone.

'So I take it you have big plans tonight?' Ricardo asked as he began to wrap my hair into the rollers.

'Yeah, I'm going to a charity function at the Ritz,' I said.

'Love that Ritz!' he said. 'A lot of folks swear by the Crescent Court, but it has nothing on the Ritz. Such a classic. And do you know that they have their own nightly guacamologist? How divine is *that*?'

'Quite divine,' I said.

Then, wondering how so many gay men had the knack of making you feel like you were their best friend within an hour, I caved and said, 'So. Guess who I'm going with?'

He took the command seriously by saying, 'Oh, I love guessing games! Tycoon, politician, chef, actor, model, or . . . stylist to the stars?'

I laughed and said, 'None of the above. Athlete. Football player.'

'Gurrrl,' he said. 'Don't even tell me. Don't *even*! That Dallas Cowboy stone cold fox? What's his name? James Ryan?'

'Ryan James,' I said.

I watched Ricardo's assistant perk up slightly and realized that I was doing the very thing that would get me excommunicated by A-listers in *any* field. I was kissing and telling even before I had kissed. So I tried to backtrack, explaining that Ryan and I were just friends. But Ricardo was off to the races, speed-dialing the salon's resident makeup artist and asking her if she could come in on her day off and do a face for his new BFF.

She must have said no because he said, 'Adela! This is a total beauty emergency! She's going on a date with Ryan James . . . Um, *ye-esss. The* Ryan James . . . and what if they fall in love and get married? Don't you want to do their wedding? Hmm? Or do you want to get cut out of the action because you couldn't tear yourself away from Ellen DeGeneres?'

He hung up and said, 'Okay. You so owe me. Adela's on her way. She is a genius and will smoke the hell out of those eyes! Shazam! . . . Now. Let's talk wardrobe. What are we wearing?' he asked, eyeing my shoes with disdain.

'Not these. Don't worry,' I said and explained I had come from a job interview and had stilettos in the car.

'*Gurrl,* I was going to say! Those shoes are just *not* okay.

They might not even be okay for an interview! Unless it was at a convent!' he said, cracking himself up.

Ricardo's assistant said his name under her breath, looking aghast but amused by his blunt assessment of my footwear.

'Shea and I are besties,' he said to her. 'She knows I can't lie. I'm like Abe. Yes, I most certainly did chop down that cherry tree.'

'That was George Washington.' I laughed.

'Whatev. Abe was honest, too. And so am I. And those shoes gots to go!' He laughed and said, 'So tell me about the interview?'

'It was with the *Post*,' I said. 'Covering sports.'

'A newspaper reporter! How quaint. And? Did you get the job?'

'I think so,' I said.

'That's the attitude! Now apply that mentality to Mr-James-if-you're-nasty and you *will* get him, too. Especially with *these* drapes,' he said, puffing my hair. 'He is going to be *all* yours tonight, but, honey, do you even want him?'

'As a matter of fact,' I said, 'I think I do.'

At five o'clock sharp, our designated meeting time, I walked into the lobby bar at the Ritz, with big hair, smoky eyes, heels that put me over six feet, and my little black dress that seemed way littler than it had in the dressing room at Lucy's shop. The effort and money spent seemed worth it, as I decided that it was pretty much the best I was capable of looking, a feeling that was corroborated by the double takes I drew from a few men in nice suits clustered by the entrance of the bar. It even started to cross my mind that I had overdone it, tried a little *too* hard, until I spotted Ryan, dazzling in a charcoal suit and slim silver tie. He was lounging on one of the low leather sofas near the front windows, chatting with an attractive couple about our age. He spotted me almost immediately, his face lighting up as he sprang from his seat and sauntered over to me, his gait easy, cocky, sexy. Even if he didn't play football, it was the kind of walk that made girls go to bed with you, no questions asked.

'You look phenomenal,' he said, leaning down to kiss my cheek, his hand on my back. 'Wow.'

'Thank you. You look great, too,' I said, shaking off my pregame jitters, as he guided me over to the couches and introduced me to his friends, Sandy and Barry, explaining that Barry was on the board of the autism charity, and Sandy was last year's gala chair. I said hello as Barry stood and shook my hand, and Sandy complimented my dress. I told her I loved hers, too, as we all sat down and Barry asked what I wanted to drink. I glanced at the low cocktail table between us, noting that the guys were drinking scotch, Sandy white wine. I hesitated, the way I always did when it came time to order a drink, thinking that, at thirty-three, it was high time I had a go-to signature beverage, like Lucy. 'Belvedere and soda with a twist,' she always said so decisively, prettily. No floundering about or jumping around from beer to wine to tequila.

'Shea drinks whiskey,' Ryan proudly announced.

'How did you know about my whiskey habit?' I said under my breath.

He winked and said, 'That's one of those things you don't forget. Girls who drink whiskey. Girls who pack heat. Girls who go commando. Girls who truly understand the game of football.'

'Good Lord, Ryan,' Sandy said, laughing. 'That's quite a list!'

'Yeah. But I think there's a difference between understanding the wishbone formation and packing heat without panties,' I quipped.

'Nah. I'm with Ryan. Significant overlap,' Barry said.

'I'm wearing underwear,' I said.

'That's too bad,' Ryan whispered in my ear.

I smiled and asked Barry what he was drinking.

'Macallan thirty,' Barry said, holding up his rocks glass. I could tell he knew it would impress me, but it wasn't off-putting.

Not nearly as offensive as those who casually name-drop a vintage.

'*Thirty?*' I said, wondering how much that set him back, and if it could possibly be worth it.

'Yep. It's crazy smooth,' Ryan said, while Sandy quizzed me on how I could stand something so strong. 'It's like drinking . . . nail polish remover.'

I laughed and said it was absolutely *nothing* like nail polish remover – but that I should probably stick with wine tonight. Ryan ignored me and told the waitress that I'd like a double shot of 'this good stuff.'

'On the rocks?' she asked, giving me a once-over.

'No. Neat,' Ryan answered for me, which puzzled me a little since he and Barry were both drinking theirs on ice.

Thinking he had his reasons and I wasn't going to nitpick, I smiled and thanked him, reminding myself to be careful. I had an hour drive home tonight, and ending up on Ryan's couch was out of the question. His bed was even *more* out of the question, which Lucy had taken great pains to remind me of. She had already sent me two texts. One simply said: *Do NOT get wasted;* the other: *Guys like girls they have to work for. Don't be a lobby ho.* I laughed after I read that one, remembering that it was I who had taught her the terminology, coined for the girls in low-cut tops and knee-high boots who sat around in the players' hotels, waiting for them to come down for the team bus.

'So. Ryan tells us you went to college together,' Sandy said as I noticed that her accent was the girl version of Ryan's. High-class all the way. So high-class that she could afford to skip the airs. I decided I liked her.

'Yes,' I said. 'We met in our freshman comp course.'

'But we knew each other through football, too. Shea's best friends with Coach Carr's daughter,' Ryan said.

'And you're from Walker?' Sandy asked.

I said yes, all my life except for the first two months.

'Shea works for Walker now,' Ryan added. 'In the athletic department.'

I nodded, then confided that I had had an interview with the *Post* earlier today. 'And get this,' I said, turning to fix my gaze on Ryan. 'It's for the Longhorn beat.'

Ryan slapped his thigh and belted out, 'Traitor! Damn traitor!' He laughed a big, confident laugh. 'Does Coach Carr know about this?'

I said yes, but didn't tell him that it had been Coach's idea in the first place and instead asked Barry and Sandy where they had gone to school.

'I went to SMU, Barry went to Rice,' Sandy said, adding that they were Walker fans, too, because of Ryan.

I refrained from telling them my opinion: if they were fans of all, they were fans of none. Instead I stuck to safer terrain and asked where they had grown up.

'Right here in Dallas,' Barry said. 'We both went to Highland Park High.'

I smiled and nodded, very familiar with the crowd from Highland Park, the wealthy section of Dallas where my socialite friends from Walker had grown up and returned after college, most with husbands they had known all their lives. In towns like Walker, marrying someone from home had a sense of settling, throwing in the towel because what else were you going to do? In Dallas, though, marrying your high school sweetheart had an aspirational, arranged-marriage feel. And Sandy and Barry seemed to be a prime example of combining family money and good genes.

Our waitress returned with my drink. I thanked her, then Barry, picking up the glass and taking my time before I raised it to my nose. I parted my lips, careful not to inhale too abruptly, having learned that this deadens your sense of taste. I breathed in spicy caramel, then closed my eyes and took a heavenly sip.

'You weren't kidding,' I said, mostly to myself. 'This stuff is good. Damn. It's almost twice as old as the best Macallan I've ever had.'

'And twice as good,' Barry said. 'Worth every cent.'

Ryan raised his glass, and said, 'Life's too short for cheap whiskey.'

I laughed and said, 'Spoken like a Dallas Cowboy. Not sure everyone can afford that philosophy.'

Grinning, Ryan put his arm around me, pulling me closer. I dropped my head to his shoulder for one flirtatious beat, aware that people were watching us. I felt special, lucky, even though I knew that it was all a mirage. I really wasn't *that* girl. It was the hair, the dress, the red lipstick. Or maybe it was just the Ryan effect – his bright light radiating onto everyone in his company. I kept sipping my single-malt scotch, feeling warmer and happier by the second, wishing we didn't have to get up off these couches. But the hour passed quickly, along with another round, and, at six o'clock, Sandy declared that it was time to go raise some money for charity. We all stood, and Ryan took my hand and led me out of the bar. On our way to the elevators, he was stopped twice by strangers, and asked to sign autographs and pose in front of the enormous arrangement of calla lilies displayed on a round table in the middle of the lobby. While Sandy and Barry went to the restroom, I watched at a slight distance for a few seconds, then pulled my phone out of my clutch and took my own surreptitious selfie, with Ryan in the background. I sent the photo off to Lucy, amusing myself with the caption *Ain't nuthin' but a lobby ho.* I smiled when I saw Lucy's response – an all-caps *LOL* – but knew it wasn't *entirely* a joke given my sudden, whiskey-induced judgment that spending the night at Ryan's might not be the end of the world.

The rest of the night was a blur. Talking to couples interchangeable with Barry and Sandy. Posing for professional photos with Ryan. Bidding on silent auction items – laser hair removal, a malachite cuff, a hot-air balloon ride – not because I really wanted them but because they seemed like 'good deals.' Dancing on a slippery parquet dance floor to a doo-wop band. Losing my stilettos, then finding them, then losing them again. And sipping a never-ending glass of pinot noir.

Then my memory skips to watching Ryan disarming his

security system . . . walking through his sleek, contemporary compound . . . making out with him in his sparkling marble kitchen . . . going upstairs to his bedroom. Then nothing . . . until I awoke in his bed, wearing only my underwear and a very large Cowboys T-shirt. I got up, the room spinning as I frantically looked for my clothes and cellphone.

Without lifting his head off the pillow, Ryan's voice came back muffled. 'Morning, babe.'

'What time is it?' I asked, my head pounding.

'Six-thirty,' he said.

'Where's my phone?'

'In my bathroom. You were charging it.'

'I was?'

'Yes.'

'What else did I do?'

Ryan rolled over and looked up at me, smirking. 'You don't remember?'

They were pretty much the worst three words you can hear after a first date, particularly when you're standing in the guy's bedroom, wearing his clothing, with a bad hangover.

'Sort of,' I lied, stumbling over one of his boat-size loafers, looking for the bathroom.

'Other way,' Ryan said, pointing to his side of the bed.

'Right,' I said, following the light to a bathroom larger than my bedroom. I had no recollection of ever seeing the room before, let alone plugging in my phone. I pulled it from the charger. Four missed calls from Lucy and several texts from her, asking what was going on. I took a deep breath and checked my call log, with the sinking dread of what I was going to find. And there it was: two outgoing calls to Coach Carr.

Shit, I said aloud, now vaguely remembering placing the calls.

Ryan heard me and said, 'You okay?'

I walked back to the bed, my phone in hand, and said, 'Did I talk to anyone last night?'

Ryan laughed and said, 'Yeah. You called Coach. You were hilarious.'

'Hilarious how?' I asked, my heart racing as I saw that one call to Coach Carr had lasted nearly eleven minutes. I crossed my fingers that I was funny-hilarious, not foolish-hilarious as I got back in bed and pulled the sheet over me. 'What did I say?'

'On which topic?' Ryan said, sitting up, exposing a torso so cut that it didn't look real. 'Your tirade against the Longhorns? Your stance on women in the locker room? Or your declaration of undying love for him?'

'What?' I said, my voice hoarse. 'I said that?'

'You said he was your favorite person in the world. Something like that.'

'I don't love him in *that* way,' I said.

'Well, no shit. He's an old dude.'

'He's only fifty-five,' I said.

'Well, still. I knew what you meant.'

'But I really said that *to* him?' I said.

'Yup,' Ryan said, seemingly enjoying my misery as he imitated my slurred voice. '"Yermyfaaaavoritepersoninthewholewiiiiideworld."'

'Oh, God. *Why* did you let me call him?' I said, burying my face deeper into the covers, every part of me burning with humiliation.

'There was no stopping you. You were on fire.'

'On fire? What else did I say?' I asked.

'You went through pretty much every Heisman Trophy since Jay Berwanger won the damn thing in 1935 and asked Coach who he thought *really* should have won. You put him on speaker for that segment.'

'Did he . . .?'

'Play along? Oh, yeah. He played your little game. Let's see . . . You both agreed that Herschel Walker should have beat out George Rogers in 'eighty-two.'

''Eighty,' I corrected. 'He *did* win in 'eighty-two.'

'Right. Whatever. But according to you, he *shouldn't* have won that year. Eric Dickerson should have . . . And you thought Chuck Long should have beaten Bo Jackson, but Coach disagreed on that one . . . You said Ki-Jana Carter or McNair should have beaten Salaam, and you both agreed that Peyton Manning should have won in 'ninety-seven.'

'Did we discuss you?' I asked.

'Nope. I was a complete footnote. Until *after* you hung up,' he said, peeling back the covers and kissing the side of my face. His breath was warm in my ear, and I couldn't help feeling aroused even as my focus remained singular.

'What else?' I said. 'What else did I say to Coach?'

'You talked about the job. For the *Post*. Coach told you that you were crazy not to take it. You said you didn't get it yet. He said you would. You said you didn't want to leave Walker. God knows why. He said you could commute back and forth between Walker, Dallas, and Austin. Blah, blah, blah. Then I told you to say goodbye.'

'And did I?'

'Nope. You rambled some more.'

'About?'

'What else?' he said.

'Football?'

He kissed me again, this time on the mouth, then rolled me onto my back. 'You have a one-track mind,' he said, covering my body with his. 'I think you love the game more than I do.'

I kissed him back, my body battling my mind.

'And I think,' he whispered, 'you like football more than sex.'

'So we didn't . . .?' I asked, hopeful.

'Hell, no,' Ryan said. 'You passed out on me. Besides, I'm a gentleman . . . But there's still plenty of time . . .'

He kissed me more urgently, cupping my breast with his large hand. I kissed him back, but mentally pumped my fist, relieved. It was ironic, really – and the way it often was with whiskey. You were never quite sure whether to blame it or give it credit. I'd make that final call after I spoke to Coach.

'You want to now?' Ryan asked.

'Talk football or have sex?' I asked.

'Both,' he said, breathing hard, his voice low. 'I can play your little Heisman game while I'm inside you . . .'

'Oh, yeah?' I said. 'Who won in 'sixty-eight?'

'Is this a test?' he said as I felt him grow hard against my leg.

'Yeah,' I said, pushing back against him, but feeling confident that he'd fail.

'Steve Spurrier,' he said.

'Nope. Try again.'

'Archie Griffin.'

'Way off,' I said, wriggling out from under him. 'The Juice. O.J. Better luck next time.' I laughed and sat up.

'Wait. First the dude murders two people . . . and now he's cock-blocking me?'

I made a face. 'Don't ever use that expression again. But yes.'

Ryan laughed and said, 'You really do, don't you?'

'I really do what?'

'Like football more than sex?'

'Hmm . . . it's about tied,' I said.

Ryan's face lit up. 'That's a hell of an answer,' he said. 'I have a good feeling about you, Shea Rigsby.'

I smiled back at him. 'Oh, yeah?'

'Yeah.'

'Well, good,' I said. 'Because I have a pretty good feeling about you, too, Ryan James.'

10

After a weekend of obsessing and worrying and self-loathing for being such a reckless drunk, I headed straight to Coach Carr's office, first thing Monday morning. Relieved to find Mrs Heflin away from her desk, I took a deep breath and knocked on his door.

'Come in!' his voice boomed.

In agony, I made myself open the door and look into his eyes, noticing that they exactly matched the light blue golf shirt he was wearing.

'Hi,' I said, wishing I had brought something to hold, a notebook, folder, *anything*. 'Good morning.'

'Yes, it is,' he said, smiling. 'How are you today, Shea?'

'Fine,' I said. 'How are you?'

'Not too bad,' he said, motioning for me to come in the whole way.

'Are you sure . . . this is a good time?' I said, almost hoping he'd say no.

Instead, he glanced at his watch and said, 'Yup. I have a few minutes before I head into a meeting.'

I took three tentative steps forward, now standing in the middle of his office. 'How's it looking?' I said, glancing at the play diagram on his desk, covered with Xs and Os.

'We're getting there . . . You gonna have a seat or what?' he said, leaning back in his chair, clasping his hands behind his head. I took another step, then sat down, crossing my legs and staring at my lap.

I waited, hoping he'd mention my phone call first, until he finally said, 'Well, c'mon, don't be bashful *now*.'

'Right . . . So about that . . . I just wanted to apologize . . .' I began, meeting his eyes, then looking at his chin, probably my favorite feature of his. It was the quintessential coach's jaw, strong and square with a cleft in the middle that always reminded me of a decisive, authoritative period. It crossed my mind that if a coach didn't have a good chin, he might as well go ahead and find another profession.

'Apologize? For what?' he said, the corners of his mouth turning up in a slight smile.

'For calling you so late and—'

'I was up. Watching film,' he said.

'Well, then . . . I'm sorry that I interrupted you . . . while you were working,' I said, thinking that the hour of the call or the interruption of his work wasn't really the crux of what I was sorry for, but it was hard to say 'I'm sorry I drunk-dialed you.'

'It was fine. You were fine,' he said, now looking full-on amused. You'd think letting me off the hook would have made me feel better, but my anxiety only increased with every incremental absolution.

He cocked his head to the side and said, 'How much had you had to drink, anyway?'

'Um . . . I don't know . . . Probably a little . . . too much,' I said.

'Well. You have to be careful with that stuff,' he said. 'You always want to be in control.'

'Yes,' I said, nodding, trying to remember when I had dropped the *sir*.

'So you were with Ryan, huh?'

'Yes. We went to a charity function. As *friends*.' I said the last part with emphasis, although I wasn't sure why.

'Well, it's good to have *friends*,' he said teasingly.

'Yes. Friends are good. I mean – take us, for instance,' I babbled, my face heating up again. 'I'm glad we're friends. You and me. At least I think we're friends?'

'Of course we're friends,' he said, smirking. 'And, as we established . . . friends are good.'

'Right,' I said, the tension mounting in my shoulders until I just said it. 'And when I said you were my favorite person in the world and all that . . . I just meant—'

'I know what you meant.'

I exhaled. 'You do?'

'Sure. You meant . . . that I'm your favorite person in the world.' He let out a big laugh, his eyes doing that twinkly thing.

'Right . . . I mean I love how you are . . . as a coach . . . and role model . . . and stuff like that.'

'Right. Role models are like friends. They're both good.'

He was *definitely* mocking me now, and I knew I had to save face and say something of substance. Somehow justify my drunken proclamation.

'I think you're great,' I said, sure that my face was now crimson. 'I mean everyone thinks you're great. But I *really* think you're great. And that's all I meant . . .'

'I think you're great, too, Shea,' he said. 'You're a great girl with a big heart and a good head on your shoulders. Don't waste either, okay?'

I nodded, my heart and mind racing.

'And you have to hang in there with Smiley,' he said. 'I think he might give this Texas beat to another guy . . . with more experience . . . But . . . I have a feeling another beat is opening up soon . . . So just be patient, okay?'

'I will,' I said, feeling a wave of disappointment.

'One more thing,' he said, giving me a coy smile. 'On the subject of our little stiff-armed friend . . .'

'Yeah?' I said, knowing that he was referring to the Heisman Trophy.

'The other night . . . You didn't mention John Huarte. No way in hell he should have beaten out Rhome and Butkus.'

'They were rewarding Coach Parseghian,' I said, conjuring the '64 season that I had only read about. 'For turning around Notre Dame's program.'

'But the award shouldn't have anything to do with coaching,' he said.

'I disagree,' I said. 'The two are inextricably bound.'

Coach adamantly shook his head. 'I could be wrong,' he said. 'But I'm not.'

I smiled at his familiar expression, then stood to go.

'You're wrong about Salaam, too,' he said suddenly. 'He was that rare two-thousand-yard rusher. You gotta give it to him.'

'But Ki-Jana had better stats on fewer carries against Big Ten defenses,' I argued. 'And McNair? C'mon. He was the best in the long run.'

'In the long run? You're viewing it retrospectively. You can't do that. The vote happens at the end of the regular season. Even before bowl games. You have to make these decisions on the facts that you have at the time,' Coach Carr said. 'I might change some decisions if I had more time to evaluate them.'

I stared at him, unable to fathom Coach making a bad decision, at least one of any import. I said as much, adding, 'Even the media thinks you're perfect.'

'Hardly,' he said, then took a breath, as if he was about to say something serious. Instead, he shook his head and simply said, 'I'm *far* from perfect. You know that, girl.'

I nodded, thinking that might be true, but that he came pretty damn close.

Over the next few months, I transformed into an assertive version of myself, determined to make headway in both my professional and my personal life, rather than languish in the stifling Texas heat as I typically did every summer.

When I didn't hear back from Smiley, I dropped him an email, telling him how very much I hoped to join his staff. And I shamelessly pursued Ryan, who had reported to the Cowboys' training camp in Oxnard, California. If anything, the long distance made me bolder, our friendly texting banter quickly turning racy. One night, he wrote to tell me that he couldn't wait to see me again, then detailed everything that was going to happen to me when he did. I typed back that I was more excited about that than the start of the college football season. He shot a smiley face back, saying that those were some mighty big words coming from a girl like me.

He was sure right about that, as I was nothing short of obsessed with football in that final countdown to August and the official start of practice. In addition to my usual duties at Walker, which included preparing our media guide and fielding interview requests from all over the country, I spent my free time reading anything and everything I could find about the upcoming season. I memorized depth charts, devoured blogs with preseason projections, and scoured message boards with posts from other diehards. The consensus was clear: this was Walker's year. And that was just on paper. When you took into account the emotional intangible of losing Mrs Carr, how much the players wanted to win a championship for Coach, there was no getting around the feeling that we were a team of destiny.

Unfortunately, this also made us the team to beat. The team to come gunning for – in more ways than one, I discovered one day when I saw a strange woman emerge from the office of Ernie Galli, our compliance officer. I said hello, but she only gave me an icy gaze back, as I observed her Aqua Net helmet hair, severe suit, and hard briefcase. In short, everything about her screamed 'investigator.'

I headed straight for my boss's office, looked J.J. in the eye, and said, 'Is the NCAA on our campus?'

He leaned back in his desk chair and said, 'Why? What have you heard?'

'Nothing,' I said. 'But I saw that woman. She's with the NCAA, isn't she?'

J.J. nodded, looking grim.

'Are we in trouble?' I asked.

J.J. abandoned his usual punctilious ways and said, 'I hope not, but that broad's definitely out to get us.' He then gave me the scoop – that the NCAA had received reasonably substantial information indicating possible violations and was now conducting a preliminary investigation.

'Investigating us for *what*?'

J.J. shrugged. 'You name it . . . Recruiting allegations, drug allegations, eligibility and academic allegations.'

'Where did these allegations come from? Someone in Austin, no doubt?'

'Exactly,' J.J. said. 'Apparently the most pressing rumor is that some shady real estate guy in Cincinnati came down to Louisville a few weeks before Signing Day and took Rhodes and his friends out on a five-star bender.'

'Can a bender be five-star?' I asked.

'Good point. Maybe not. They went to steak houses and strip clubs. So what's that? Three and a half stars?'

I smiled and said, 'So? Since when are steaks and strippers against the rules?'

'Well, I guess that joker went to Walker for a year or two before dropping out. And he held himself out as a damn . . .' He searched for the right word.

I offered him a quote from *Jerry Maguire*, one of my favorite movies. 'Ambassador of quan?'

J.J. laughed and said, 'Yeah. And then, according to the NCAA, *he showed Reggie the money.*'

'Do you think it's true?' I asked.

'I don't know. But I don't think it's a coincidence that the accusations are flying *this* year,' J.J. said. 'When we're going to be really good.'

'Exactly.' I nodded. 'Have you talked to Coach?'

J.J. shook his head. 'Nope. Far as I know, nobody has discussed it with him yet. Not in depth, anyway.'

'Good. He has enough on his mind without worrying about this bullshit,' I said, thinking that there was no way that Coach was involved in anything shady.

11

On the first weekend of August, right before practice began for the season, Lucy invited my mother and me to Lake LBJ with her, Neil, Caroline, Lawton, and Coach. The Carrs had a beautiful home there, high on a wooded bluff with gorgeous views of the blue-green water. Growing up, Lucy and I had gone there often, spending our summer days sunbathing on their private pier or tooling around in the pontoon boat or reading in the hammock on the screened-in back porch. But I hadn't gone since Mrs Carr got sick, and I was a little surprised to get the invite this year, thinking that their family would want to be alone.

But Lucy insisted that we were family, and then referenced football, making a comment about how she couldn't speak her father's language. Twice since her birthday she had asked me to give her the rundown of our roster, especially our recruits, whom she couldn't seem to keep straight. I had offered to make her flash cards, and she said it wasn't a bad idea, marveling over how her mother had managed to memorize every player. I wanted to tell her football wasn't a chore, and it really wasn't that hard, but she probably felt the same about my inability to keep track of her fashion or foodie parlance.

In any event, my mother and I drove up Saturday morning, giving the Carrs one night alone. When we arrived, Coach and Lawton were walking up from the water with their fishing poles. Wearing matching khaki shorts, Walker T-shirts, and flip-flops, they looked more like father and son than they usually did, Lawton favoring Connie's side of the family with his fine bones, narrow face, and blond hair.

'Hey, girl! Hi, Marie!' Coach said. 'Glad you could join us.'

He looked relaxed and content, which was the way he usually was up here. He often said it was his favorite place, other than our football stadium, and I remember Connie once saying that it was the only spot on Earth where he managed to spend some waking hours *not* thinking about football. At least as far as she knew; I had my doubts about that, although it seemed clear he wasn't troubled by the NCAA investigation, his voice chipper and light.

My mother and I said hello, and we gave Lawton, whom we hadn't seen since the spring game, a big hug. Then we all went inside, where Neil was putting the finishing touches on lunch – his trademark tomato pie, along with a Bibb lettuce and radish salad, and strawberry shortcake.

When we sat down to eat, Coach Carr said a quick prayer, which Lucy told me later was the first time he'd said grace in a long while. 'Dear Lord,' he began. 'We thank you for our many blessings and this place that Connie so loved. We feel her presence with us today and are so grateful for the many wonderful memories we shared. Lord, please watch over us all and keep us safe in your care. Amen. Go Broncos.'

When I opened my eyes, Coach Carr looked calm and strong. He glanced around the table and said, 'It's true. I know she's smiling up there. So happy we're here together. And even happier because . . .' I held my breath, feeling reverent. 'Because she knows that I am going to kick your butts in Trivial Pursuit tonight. Who wants to be on my team?'

'I do,' I blurted out. We had always played games at the lake – backgammon, chess, euchre, Uno, Pictionary. But Trivial Pursuit had been our favorite for two decades, and Coach Carr was right; he almost always won, regardless of his partner. I was the second best player, though, almost never missing in literature and sports.

'No way,' Lucy said. 'You two can't be together. It's not fair. You're both too good.'

'That's what Baylor's saying about Everclear and Rhodes right about now,' I said, glancing at Coach.

'Dad-blame right,' he said, then gave me a high-five.

★   ★   ★

Later that night, after Lucy had put Caroline to bed, and the wine and beer and Trivial Pursuit game board came out, we drew numbers out of Coach's baseball cap to select teams. I mentally crossed my fingers, as Lucy and my mother both got threes, Neil and Lawton drew twos, and Coach and I got the ones.

'Naturally,' Coach said, winking and then whispering loud enough for everyone to hear, 'Number *one*.'

Lucy rolled her eyes as Coach and I, in unison, claimed the blue wheel, closest to Walker teal.

'Omigod, you're the same person! My best friend and father are the *same* person,' Lucy said, shaking her head.

Coach took a sip of beer and said, 'Shea's a little prettier than I am.'

I knew he was kidding but felt myself blush, and I only got more flustered when he switched seats with Lawton to be next to me. I looked down, busying myself with the cards, dividing one box into three stacks. I gave one to Lawton, another to Lucy, and kept the third, then handed Lucy the die and said, 'You go first. You need every advantage.'

'Ha,' Lucy said, as she rolled. After a string of ridiculously easy questions that culminated in the entertainment wedge, my mother and Lucy faltered on 'How many colors are there in a rainbow?' (Answer: 'More than the eye can see').

Then Neil and Lawton were stymied on a World War I question about Austria.

It was our turn, and, right out of the gate, we were kicking butt and taking names, gathering three quick wedges. There was no gloating, though, as we both became laser-focused, just the way Coach is during games, not even smiling when we threw up a total Hail Mary and nailed an answer on the leading world exporter of bananas (Ecuador).

'Y'all are so smug,' Lawton said, our silence almost pissing them off more.

'Don't hate the player,' I said, smirking. 'Or the Coach.'

Coach Carr held up a fist and bumped it against mine.

'Sickening,' Lucy said, shaking her head. 'And good luck getting a pink. You two are clueless when it comes to entertainment.'

'We'll see about that,' Coach Carr said, rolling the die and landing on pink. 'When in doubt, go with Cyndi Lauper,' he said to me.

I smiled as Lawton read the question: 'Who once warned: "Never eat more than you can lift"?' I knew the answer, only because I had gotten it before, years ago, and gave Coach Carr a slight brow raise along with a look that said, *Bingo, baby.*

'You'll never in a million years get this one,' Lawton said, passing the card around to Lucy, then Neil and my mom. They all mugged at the answer, taunting us as Coach and I pretended to brainstorm.

'Must be a really thin movie star,' I said, musing aloud. 'Audrey Hepburn, maybe. Princess Diana . . . Farrah Fawcett?'

Coach Carr played along, murmuring, 'Then again, maybe it's a heavier star? Like Nell Carter or Roseanne Barr?'

'Or maybe . . . *maybe* it's . . . a chubby *puppet.* Or even a *Muppet!* Such as Miss Piggy . . .' I winked at him.

'Miss Piggy?' Coach deadpanned as I nodded. 'Yes. We're going Miss Piggy.'

'You. Dirty. Bastards,' Lawton said, throwing down the card.

Coach and I clinked our bottles of Shiner Bock, followed by another fist bump. Then we rolled and landed on science. Our next question: 'Do porcupines masturbate?'

Coach and I exchanged a look. 'Let's see . . . I bet boy porcupines do,' he said.

I laughed. 'Well, I bet the girls do, too.'

'I bet you're right,' Coach said, turning to my mom. 'Okay. We're going with yes.'

'Is that your final answer?' she said, a rookie tactic that we didn't dignify with a reply.

My mom shook her head and handed us our green wedge. 'Ridiculous.'

'Ridiculous that porcupines masturbate? Or that we're about to win this thing,' he said, glancing at his watch, 'in under an hour?'

I rolled the die again, moving to history. 'What did the first Spanish dog to be fitted with contact lenses not see the day after the fitting?' Lawton read.

'The car that killed 'em,' Coach said. *'Bam.'*

'Oh. It's a pity,' I said.

'What's that, girl?' Coach said.

'That we still need the orange to win,' I said, referring to the sports category.

'Yeah,' Coach said, shaking his head. 'That's going to be really, *really* difficult for us.'

I grinned and rolled as we got two more answers, then landed on orange. Coach looked at Lawton and said, 'Fire away.'

Lawton read to himself, then shook his head and said, 'Unbelievable.'

'Read it,' Coach said. 'And then weep.'

'Who won the Heisman Trophy in 1964?'

Coach gave me a knowing look that made me melt, then said to Lawton, 'Wait. Was the question "Who won the trophy?" Or "Who *should* have won the trophy?"'

Coach nudged my leg under the table, and I got a tingly feeling inside.

'Who *won* it,' Lawton clarified, obviously not getting our inside joke.

Coach picked up an orange wedge. 'Shea? I'm drawing a blank. Do you know this one?'

'Hmm. Was it Butkus? . . . Or maybe Rhome?' I mused aloud. 'Or Brian Piccolo? He graduated in 'sixty-four, didn't he?'

Coach shrugged and said he couldn't for the life of him remember what happened that year.

Lawton looked hopeful until I blurted out, 'Actually . . . I think we'll go with John Huarte.'

'Are you *sure*?' Lawton said, his face falling.

I nodded. 'Yep. Huarte.'

'That's your *final* answer?' my mother chimed in.

'Yes, Marie. You heard my girl,' Coach said. 'Huarte. We're going with Huarte.'

'Dammit. She's right,' Neil said, taking the card from Lawton, then throwing it down.

'Of *course* she is,' Lucy said, getting up to refresh her wine.

'Nothing like a little rout to kick off the season,' Coach said with a wink.

'Plenty more of those to come,' I said, winking back at him.

On the morning of our departure I awoke early, just after sunrise, and came downstairs to find Coach alone on the front porch, drinking coffee and staring out at the water. He looked so peaceful and deep in thought that I quietly retreated. But just before I rounded the corner back to the stairwell, he suddenly turned and looked at me through the open front door and said, 'Morning, girl.'

'Good morning, Coach,' I said.

'You're up early.'

'So are you,' I said, shuffling toward him.

'This is late for me,' he said. 'There's a fresh pot of coffee in the kitchen.'

'I'm good for now,' I said.

He nodded and motioned for me to join him, so I walked out onto the wraparound porch and took a seat on the old wooden swing where Lucy and I had logged hours of conversation as little girls, while frequently reprimanded by Mrs Carr for swinging too high or fast. I slowly rocked back and forth now, gazing at the lake, so still that it looked like a piece of glass, a mirror reflecting sky and trees. Coach and I chatted for a few minutes about how nice it was up here, especially this time of day, before we got back to the only topic on both of our minds. I knew he had to be so sick of the slate of usual questions; he couldn't go anywhere in public without being bombarded by them. But I threw one out anyway, hoping it would be a little different coming from me.

'You ready for practice?' I said, studying his profile.

'Yes,' he said, reaching up to stretch with one arm. 'Let's get the show on the road, you know?'

I nodded, then asked the predictable follow-up. 'How do you think we'll be? As good as everyone's saying?'

'No. Not nearly *that* good,' he said.

I smiled, thinking that he always downplayed how good we were while 'godding up' the opponent. All coaches did it, preferring to be the underdog. Less pressure that way.

'We have the talent, but you never know about the chemistry,' he continued. 'Good thing is – the older guys really like Reggie. For a kid that talented, he's very low-key. Not at all flashy.'

'That *is* a good thing,' I said.

'We'll see . . . You never know . . . There might be some rocky roads ahead for us . . .'

'What do you mean?' I said, hoping he was just talking about the toughest stretch on our schedule: Florida State and Stanford and Texas. But I had a feeling it had more to do with that helmet-hair lady I'd seen strolling the halls.

Looking agitated, Coach bolted up in his chair, as if he'd been given a shot of adrenaline. 'I hate the NCAA. They're shameless, self-serving hypocrites . . . They're *evil*.'

'Evil?' I said, raising my eyebrows. 'Isn't that a little strong? I mean the KKK is evil . . . The Taliban is evil . . .'

'At least the KKK and the Taliban aren't *pretending* to do good,' he interjected. He finished his coffee, putting his mug at his feet.

I looked at him and made myself ask the question. 'Coach? Are we really under investigation?'

He hesitated, then said, 'Yep. Sure looks that way.'

'For what?' I said.

'For winning,' he said. 'Plain and simple. Any program that wins is being investigated in some form or another. It was only a matter of time and our number was up.'

'So you don't think they'll find anything?'

'Oh, I'm sure they will if they poke around long enough.'

'Are they . . . saying anything about you?' I asked, bracing myself.

He shook his head. 'No. Not yet, anyway. Right now it's just charges about a bunch of little stuff you can't control. Tutors writing papers. Boosters wining and dining recruits. Professors giving a kid a better grade than he deserved . . . The NCAA generates all this outrage over petty violations to byzantine bylaws – and uses that to justify what they're doing.'

'And what are they doing, exactly?' I asked.

'Flying on private planes. Taking boondoggles all over the place. Just generally using these kids to make themselves rich. Profiting from the glory of amateur athletics.' He began to speak faster, his voice becoming progressively more bitter. 'This entire lofty idea of amateurism is a joke. A smoke screen. A hoax concocted by the NCAA and signed off on by universities so they can exploit young people for their own gain. A kid can't put scripture or his girlfriend's name or any personal message in his eyeblack . . . but they can make him wear corporate logos on his jersey, helmet visor, wristband, pants, shoes . . . Everyone's getting rich here. You know the SEC made over a billion dollars in athletic receipts last year? A *billion* dollars! And the Big Ten is right behind them. Are you kidding me?'

I stared back at him. I'd obviously heard these arguments before, but never so eloquently. And never from him.

'You know how much CBS Sports and Turner Broadcasting paid the NCAA for television rights for March Madness this year? Something like eight hundred million dollars. Three quarters of a *billion* dollars for unpaid labor by student athletes. These kids generate billions for the NCAA and universities and corporations and even us coaches . . . but they can't make a dime for themselves? And don't give me this crap about scholarships.'

'I wasn't going to,' I mumbled with a smile, but I don't think he heard me.

'Ninety scholarships is a *pittance* compared to the revenue being generated. How is that fair? How is that right? It's exploitive . . . It's . . . It's like colonialism – all these things are done for the quote "good of the student athlete"!'

I nodded, taking it all in, so attracted to his passion on the subject.

'Or how about this? The NCAA sells DVDs of games . . . and rights to videogames that relive classic moments in college sports . . . but the guys who played in those games can't profit, even after they graduate and are no longer amateurs. Wouldn't you think that a player's likeness should belong to him? That if a videogame is made using his face, he should see some of the profits?'

'Well, yeah,' I said. 'Of course.'

Coach shook his head. 'Nope. Not a penny. Remember A. J. Green, the kid from Georgia who sold his jersey from the Independence Bowl so he could go on some spring-break trip with his friends?'

I nodded.

'He got a four-game suspension while the University of Georgia continued to sell replicas of his jersey at forty bucks a pop . . . And look at Ohio State. How do you bring down a coach and penalize a whole program because a couple of kids exchanged some gear for tattoos and a decent man tried to protect them? These are *kids*! By definition, they make mistakes.'

'Yeah. That penalty *was* a little harsh,' I said.

Coach scoffed. 'They ferret out the true cheaters and get some bad guys, but for the most part, they're on a damn witch hunt.' He leaned forward in his chair, staring at me, on a roll now. 'Their enforcement is random and selective – and they violate any notion of due process. Everyone is guilty till proven innocent and there is little to no appeals process. They're despots with absolute power, and we all know what happens with absolute power.'

I looked at him, thinking that *he* had absolute power at Walker and had never abused it. Never used it for personal gain or anything other than the good of his players and the program. Yet as he stood to go refill his coffee, I had the tiniest tug of doubt that things might not be quite as cut-and-dried as I wanted them to be.

12

Forty-eight hours after our return from the lake, my favorite day of the year had finally arrived: the first day of practice and the official start to the college football season. Like everyone at Walker, I was charged up and more hopeful than ever. But, somehow, I didn't feel quite the way I expected to feel.

I told myself it was just a simple case of preseason jitters – always worse when big things were expected of us. Or perhaps I was worried about the investigation. Internal rumors had begun to circulate, and I couldn't stand the thought that the NCAA could unfairly rain on our parade.

Then again, maybe it was something else, something bigger. Maybe it was the same concerns that I'd been experiencing since Mrs Carr passed away. The feeling that I wasn't on the right path. That, despite all my efforts to kick-start a new career and relationship, I was still in the same exact spot. Hanging out at practice or holed up in my little office, fielding endless phone calls from real reporters.

One day after practice, I stopped by Lucy's store, something I often did, whether to shop, or help unpack inventory, or simply say hello. She looked happy to see me, stepping out from behind the counter to give me a hug. 'Hey! What's up? You need to do a little back-to-practice shopping?'

I laughed and said, 'Yeah, right. I didn't know you carried Walker gear now.'

Lucy smiled and said, 'I do have some things on hold for you in the back. Some transitional pieces between summer and fall.'

'Great. Ryan's coming back tomorrow,' I said, feeling a tinge of excitement. 'I'd love to get some new things.'

Lucy gave me a funny look and then returned to her counter, where she pulled out a tabloid magazine from a shelf under the register. 'Did you see this?'

I stared down at the page to see a blurry paparazzo picture of Ryan and Blakeslee, sitting together at an outdoor café. The caption speculated that the two might be reconciling, but I was happy to note that the scene looked anything but romantic. Blakeslee appeared miffed, her arms crossed, and Ryan was staring down at his phone. There was only a bottle of Perrier, with two glasses, on the table between them.

I felt Lucy staring at me, trying to gauge my reaction while I slowly processed it myself. Was I angry? Jealous? Sad?

'Maybe he was texting you at that very moment?' Lucy said hopefully, peering down at his cellphone as if she could make out what was on the screen.

I had been wondering the same thing and asked if we knew when the photo was taken.

'It doesn't say . . . Do you think they could really be getting back together?' she said, worried.

I shrugged, still staring at the magazine. Blakeslee was wearing heavy gladiator sandals, the kind that most women can't begin to pull off, short shorts, and a chic Bohemian blouse. She was tiny and tan and pretty much everything I wasn't. 'They could be,' I said. 'I really don't know.'

'Jesus. What's with people in your life divorcing and then getting back together?' Lucy said, referring, of course, to my dad and Astrid.

'I'd hardly put them in the same category,' I said, thinking that you couldn't compare Ryan and Blakeslee's reunion over sparkling water to my dad's decision to leave me for his first-born and clearly favorite daughter.

'I guess not,' Lucy said, shaking her head. 'But this is *really* irritating. He didn't tell you he was seeing her?'

I shook my head.

Lucy put the magazine down and walked over to a sale table covered with Splendid tank tops, all in bright summer hues that reminded me of sherbet. I followed her, helping her rearrange the piles, separating cool tones from warm.

'Well. I guess we shouldn't assume the worst,' she said.

'I know,' I said, as a young mother walked into the shop with her baby, maneuvering a stroller around a display of J Brand jeans. Lucy warmly greeted her, then offered her assistance. The woman declined any help, then proceeded to inspect *every* pair of jeans, searching for differences among a pile of size 28s, ruining the neat pile. It was one of Lucy's pet peeves – really anyone's pet peeve who has ever worked retail and has spent her day refolding clothing.

'Do you have plans to see him?' Lucy asked.

'Not yet. But maybe we should go ahead and try on those clothes now,' I said as brightly as I could. 'Just in case.'

Lucy smiled at me, looking as proud as she had when Caroline took her first few steps. 'Atta girl,' she said.

As it turned out, I saw Ryan the very first night he was back in town, at his request. We discussed going out, but I knew he'd be tired, so I asked if he wanted to just come over to my place. He said that would be perfect as I gave myself a pep talk. *Don't be embarrassed by your apartment. Don't play the underdog. Be confident. Seize the day. Don't think, or talk about, or, God forbid, get a buzz and call Coach.*

By the time Ryan knocked on the door, I was ready, answering it and beaming up at him. He was even more gorgeous than I remembered, his skin tanned to a golden hue, his blue T-shirt hugging the muscles of his shoulders and arms.

'Hi, Ryan,' I said, excited, maybe even closer to thrilled.

'Hey, you,' he said, bending down to give me a long kiss, pausing only to whisper in my ear. 'It's *so* good to see you.'

I felt goose bumps on my arms as I pulled away and looked in his eyes. 'It's so good to see you, too,' I said, deciding that I was not going to ruin the night by asking about Blakeslee.

Instead, I led him over to my sofa, where we made out for a long time under the only luxurious thing in my living room, a cashmere throw that my father and Astrid had given me for Christmas last year. It was so soft that Ryan actually commented on it, murmuring, 'I'd like to be under this thing naked with you.'

I gave him a coy smile, then, before I lost the nerve, took off my shirt and slid out of my jeans. 'I want you,' I said between urgent, deep kisses.

Ryan whispered. 'I want you, too, sweetie.'

'I like when you call me sweetie,' I said as I ran my fingers through his hair, admiring the texture.

'You *are* my sweetie,' he said – and at that moment, I not only believed him but felt sure that nothing was going on with Blakeslee or any other woman.

I watched as he sat up and took off his T-shirt, exposing his lats, pecs, triceps, and all those other muscles I couldn't name. I shook my head, blown away by his body, and he smiled, because he knew exactly what I was thinking – that he was a sublime male specimen. Wishing I were the female equivalent, I unsnapped the front closure of my bra, then pressed my body against his, nestling deeper into our cocoon on the couch. 'See how soft it is?'

I meant the blanket, but it sounded like I meant my own body, and he said, 'Oh, yes, you are,' which turned me on because I could tell he was turned on.

'And *you* . . . you are a friggin' underwear ad. Your body is so sick that it makes me . . .'

'It makes you what?' he breathed.

'It makes me almost not like you,' I said.

'C'mon, now. Don't say that,' he said, smiling.

'Well, it's intimidating,' I said, covering myself, thinking that I had really outkicked my coverage with Ryan. He was way out of my league. '*You're* intimidating.'

He moved my hand away, then caressed my stomach. 'I love your body, too. Right here,' he whispered.

I believed him so much that I stopped sucking in my stomach as he lifted me up off the couch, blanket and all, and carried me back to the bedroom. It was a first. Other guys, including Miller, had carried me to bed before, but it was the first time I hadn't felt completely awkward, like deadweight, in the process. Ryan made me feel lithe, light, downright graceful in his arms, my hands clasped around his neck. He held my gaze as he effortlessly lowered me to the bed, more muscles flexing in the warm glow of my bedside lamp, just the right amount of light to hide some of my flaws but still illuminate his perfection.

'Do you want music?' I said.

Standing over me, he shook his head slowly, then kneeled on the floor in front of me. I tried to sit up, but he pushed me back with one callused hand, as his other hand made its way up the inside of my thigh, resting between my legs. I didn't resist and instead raised my hips, making it easier for him to remove my black thong. Then I sat up, pulled his shoulders toward me, and said, 'C'mere. I want to feel you over me.'

So he did, lying directly on top of me, his gray boxer briefs our final barrier. I ran my hands over his muscled back, and pulled his underwear down as far as my arms would allow, then wrapped my legs around him, hooking my toe into the elastic waistband and removing them the rest of the way.

'Jesus,' I said, now breathing hard, my hands on his steel-hard ass. 'Jesus.'

He rubbed himself against me, teasing me, asking me if it felt good. I told him it did.

'Are you . . .?'

'On the pill?' I said. 'Yes. Do we need anything else?'

He knew exactly what I was asking, maybe even that I was picturing that long line of Cowboy cheerleaders, and said, 'No, baby. I'm very careful . . .'

I relaxed completely, trusting him, feeling that, even if I was one of many, surely I wasn't one of many he trusted without a condom. Multitasking, Ryan kissed my neck while pulling down my comforter and sheets, then repositioned me forty-five degrees, my head now on a pillow. I looked up at him, but was too close to see anything but his eyes and nose, the exact part of his face you see on television through his blue and white starred helmet. He looked that intense, that focused, as he said, 'You ready for this?'

'*So* ready,' I said. 'Are you?'

'Yes, sweetie. I'm ready, too.'

Then he pushed his way inside me, only a little at first, holding back with exquisite timing and control. I opened my eyes. He opened his, looked at me, then closed them again, all his muscles flexing as he pushed deeper in me until he was the whole way inside. *My God,* I said more than once, along with a lot of other expletives, thinking that it was, hands down, the best purely physical sensation of my entire life. Sort of how I'd imagine it would be to try heroin, the kind of drug that can ruin your life. Instant addiction. Still muttering to myself, I lost all sense of time and space as I let him take charge. His speed changed from slow to fast, then slow again, his rhythm scary good. He turned me over, slid inside me from behind, pressing his chest into my back, holding me down, gently pulling my hair, kissing my ear, saying my name. Then, when I couldn't stand it another second, he flipped me back over, telling me to look into his eyes. My room grew sauna hot, and I kicked off the covers, our bodies slick with sweat. I felt myself start to shake, then heard myself scream his name as we both came together.

Afterward, I fell into a coma. I couldn't move or speak or focus on anything other than my breathing, and the thrilling realization that I'd just had the best sex of my entire life with the gorgeous starting quarterback of the Dallas fucking Cowboys.

The next morning, I opened my eyes from a sound sleep to find Ryan standing over my bed. He was fully dressed and wearing his clothes from the night before, but he looked freshly showered, his dark hair damp and precisely styled. I tried to gather myself, pulling my own tangled hair away from my face and wiping my mouth on the back of my hand.

'Was I drooling?' I asked, thinking that stealth early-morning grooming was the worst kind of unfair advantage over a girl who was already the underdog.

'No. You're a very pretty sleeper,' Ryan said.

'Thanks,' I said. It was actually a compliment I'd heard before.

'You're pretty when you're asleep. Pretty when you're awake. And you're *really* pretty when I'm making love to you.' He whispered the last part, as if sharing a secret only he was lucky enough to know.

Embarrassed, I smiled, then sat up, tucking my comforter under my arms to cover myself. 'Are you headed out?' I said, trying not to sound needy and noting, with relief, that I didn't feel that way. If anything, I was actually happy to get the awkward morning-after stuff over with and send him on his way.

'Yeah. I have to. I wasn't going to wake you,' he said, sitting down on the edge of the bed beside me. 'But I didn't want to leave without saying goodbye either.'

'It's okay. I need to get up anyway,' I said. 'I have to go to work. Women's volleyball today. We're hosting Penn State.'

He nodded, then reached over and cupped my cheek in his hand, a gesture that felt surprisingly intimate given that we'd done a lot more the night before. Of course maybe that's *why* it felt intimate. 'I'd stay and make you breakfast,' he said. 'But I have practice. Then I have a couple of meetings and a four o'clock massage.'

I nodded, wondering why he was telling me his schedule. Did he think I minded that he was leaving so early? Because I didn't. Was he laying the groundwork so he didn't have to call me later? Because I got it, I knew he was busy. Big-time busy.

'Okay. Well. Thanks for coming over,' I said, trying to sound casual, even throwing in a fake yawn along with a stretch. 'It was fun.'

I must have sounded a little *too* nonchalant because Ryan shook his head and said, *'Fun?'*

'You know what I mean,' I said, smiling.

'Fun is playing Xbox. Shooting clay pigeons. Going to the movies,' Ryan said.

'Okay. Let me try again. Last night . . . was amazing . . . mind-blowing . . . satisfying on *every* level.' I smirked and reached out to grab his hand, the covers dropping to my waist.

'That's better. And I agree,' he said, squeezing my hand, his gaze lowering to my breasts, then slowly returning to my eyes. Everything he said and did felt deliberate and smooth, but also sincere.

We smiled at each other for a few more seconds, then his expression grew serious, almost soulful, as he said, 'I really like you, Shea.'

'I really like you, too,' I said.

'I've been looking for a girl like you,' he said. 'And you've been right here. The whole time.'

I held his gaze, all my defense mechanisms firing as I considered that he could get any girl in the world he wanted. Why would he possibly choose me? Then again, why would he lie to me? Especially after I had already slept with him? I felt myself taking a small leap of faith as I said, 'Yes. Here I was. The whole time.' Then I leaned in for a long kiss goodbye.

13

The night before our season opening game against Rice, Lucy called me from her dad's house. She'd been having a rough few days, missing her mother more intensely than usual, but sounded reasonably upbeat now.

'Big day tomorrow!' she chirped into the phone.

'Yep. How's your dad feeling?' I asked, even though I'd seen him a few hours before out on the field and could tell that he was in an optimistic zone.

'He's getting nervous. I just made his strawberry milk shake. Thank God I thought to ask Mom for her exact recipe. I never would have known to put in the malted milk powder. And then they'd never win again.'

I laughed.

'Is he not the most superstitious person you've ever met?' Lucy asked me.

'I'm not superstitious,' I heard Coach say in the background.

'Oh, yeah?' Lucy said. 'Strawberry milk shakes for home games? Those nasty old tube socks from 1994? Mello Yello instead of coffee when you play higher-ranked teams? Big Red gum that has to be purchased from the Parkit Market? Not the E Z Stop. Not the Chevron. Not the 7-Eleven. But the Parkit Market.'

I smiled, thinking of the time, when I was in the third grade, that I threw a pack of Big Red in my mother's cart in the checkout line. The next time I went over to Lucy's to play, I gave it to Coach Carr, and, after thanking me, he offhandedly asked me where I got it. I told him the grocery store, and he nodded, smiled, then kneeled down and lowered his voice to a near whisper. 'Let you in on a little secret.'

'What?' I said, leaning in, starry-eyed.

'Big Red is my favorite gum and I will enjoy every last piece of this pack . . . But if you want the very best, luckiest Big Red that money can buy, you need to go to the Parkit Market.'

'Why?' I asked, thinking that surely it all came from the same factories, like the one my grandparents had worked at when my mom was little.

'Because the Parkit Big Red helped us beat Texas in 1985, the year you and Lucy started kindergarten.'

'But we've beaten them since then,' I said.

'I know,' he said, nodding gravely. 'And every last time, I had Parkit Market Big Red with me.' He stood up and patted his front pocket.

I remember thinking that we had *lost* to Texas since then, too. And wondered if that meant he had forgotten his Big Red gum for those games. Somehow I knew that wasn't the case, and it didn't work that way. We might not win *with* the gum. But we *definitely* were going to lose without it. And, in any event, we weren't going to test the theory.

I tuned back into the banter between Lucy and her dad as she said, 'Shea. Get a load of this. Daddy just said, "Those aren't superstitions. They're rituals."' She imitated him, getting his accent and cadence exactly right, though her pitch was way too high.

I laughed and said, 'Did he catch his cricket yet?'

This practice began early in his career when he couldn't sleep one night before a big game, blaming it on a big, noisy cricket outside his bedroom window – which he promptly got up and captured in a Mason jar. The next day Walker won, thus cementing the superstition for the duration of his coaching career.

'Oh, right! I forgot about the *ritualistic* capturing of the cricket! You got him yet, Daddy? Jailed in some jar in the garage?'

'Not yet,' I heard Coach say. 'That comes *after* the milk shake.'

I smiled, as Lucy argued that anything that involved more than thirty minutes of your time, lots of cursing, and a flashlight was more than a ritual. 'Right, Shea?' Lucy asked me.

'Yeah. Think I agree with you on this one,' I said. 'Tell Coach I said . . .'

I hesitated as Lucy finished my sentence, 'Good luck . . . I will.'

'No. Not good luck,' I said, knowing he didn't like to be told 'good luck' before a game and wondering how Lucy could have missed that nuance.

'Tell him what, then?' she said. And then – 'Oh. Just tell him yourself.'

She handed him the phone, and suddenly he was there, in my ear. 'Hey, girl.'

'Hey, Coach,' I said, my hand tightly gripping the phone.

'What do you got for me?' he said.

'Catch a big cricket,' I said, my heart skipping a beat.

'I'll do my best,' he said, and I could tell he was smiling. 'See you tomorrow, Shea.'

'See you tomorrow, Coach,' I said.

The following night I got to Bronco Stadium early, long before the gates opened or before I really had to be there, along with the equipment managers, security guards, and grounds-keepers. It had been *my* routine for years, and the first glimpse of the empty, still stadium always thrilled me. Ours wasn't the biggest, newest, or prettiest in college football (although plans were in the works for a major renovation), but, like Coach, it was still my favorite place in the world. The setting itself was picturesque enough. Horseshoe-shaped, the red-brick façade rose out of acres of grass fields with a scenic view of the Brazos River at its open end. Once you walked inside, it was a different story – the view stark and ugly – but the stadium's aesthetic shortcomings only made me love it more. I loved the dank underbelly with its cinder-block tunnels leading to the locker rooms, the mammoth steel girders covered in layer upon layer of industrial gray paint, and the faded interior signage that dated back to the fifties. I knew every square inch of it, and it all felt like sacred ground.

Maybe it was sacrilegious to admit that I felt closer to God inside that stadium than in church on Christmas Eve, but it was the truth, and I told myself it was no different from people who find their deepest spirituality in the woods or by the sea. Yes, God made those trees and that water, unlike the steel eyesore erected in 1938 and haphazardly added on to over the decades, but I still felt Him there – especially on that night, as I found myself praying for a season to remember. A national championship season.

It was something I had been dreaming about for nearly thirty years, and, although we'd come close many times and won lots of big bowl games, it wasn't the same as winning a national championship. Being number *one*. I couldn't remember a time when I'd thrown a penny in a fountain or blown out candles on a birthday cake without making that singular, simple wish. But it was different now, the stakes even greater. We were now playing for a higher purpose, I thought, as I squinted at the blanched-white sky and thought of Connie and Coach. The sun beat down on the freshly cut field, but as I wiped sweat from my hairline, a merciful wisp of a breeze kicked up, giving the early evening a certain sweet serenity. The calm before the storm.

I walked along the painted white sideline, then crossed back over to the tunnel and headed for the ancient elevator, taking it up to the press box in search of J.J. It was time to get ready for the onslaught of reporters; in other words, it was time to stop dreaming and start working, the best medicine to ward off pregame jitters. I wasn't *that* nervous, though. Not like I usually was. Maybe because nobody really questioned that we were going to beat Rice into submission, if not utter humiliation. Maybe because a winning season really *did* feel preordained.

A short time later, the gates opened, and all the students

and fans poured in, the night unfolding exactly the way it always did. Our team took the field for old-school warm-ups. Walker's flamboyant marching band geared up, playing their big, bold brass notes. The cheerleaders unfurled their enormous teal *W* banner and built pyramids to the football gods. Meanwhile the minutes and seconds ticked off the scoreboard in a final, dramatic countdown to the fireworks and the national anthem and the coin toss and the kickoff and the *season*. Like New Year's Eve in August.

Our first possession was quick and decisive, reminding me of the famed Battle of San Jacinto, only much less bloody. Crisp completion after crisp completion, followed by a gorgeous touchdown. Then, after a sloppy Rice turnover, we had the ball again. On our second down, Reggie Rhodes touched the ball for the first time in a college game, making an impossible catch, then streaking down the field. We all watched, mesmerized, as ten yards turned into twenty, then forty, then sixty. It was an exclamation point of a play, a wake-up call to anybody left in the country who was still calling him overrated. Even the press box got a little rowdy, seasoned reporters chortling with approval. *Kid's got wheels . . . The real deal . . . Playmaker.*

Midway through the first half, the sun finally drifted behind the stadium, turning the sky a brilliant pink and violet. Touchdowns aside, it was always my favorite moment of a night game, that dramatic crescendo as the velvet curtain fell, and Bo Phelps, our longtime electrician, flipped on the final few breakers, all the auxiliary lights switched to their highest setting. It was soul-soaring, seeing those fifty-two thousand people in full, glowing teal Technicolor. I looked down to the sidelines to find Coach, the only one *not* yet smiling.

But when I saw him outside our locker room after the game, the 41–zip score in the books, he finally looked happy.

'Must have caught a big cricket,' I said.

Coach smiled, his sideburns and the front of his shirt damp with sweat. 'Sure did,' he said. 'Now I can let him go. Lucky fella.'

I laughed. 'And if we *hadn't* won?'

'Fishing bait,' he said, winking.

'Ahh,' I said. 'I didn't know *that*.'

I knew I had already taken up too much of his time, and that I needed to get back to the press box to hand out stat sheets, but I couldn't resist another quick comment. 'That's one down,' I said.

'Yup. And twelve to go,' he said – which I knew included the eleven games left on our schedule, plus what we all hoped would be the national championship game. 'A *very* long way.'

I nodded. But for now, in this moment, I felt certain of our destiny. Positive that God was up there, picking favorites.

Coach caught a cricket the following week, too, and we massacred UTEP to open our season at 2–0 and earn a number 11 AP ranking. But early wins were not only expected but planned that way on the schedule, and our first true test was Texas A&M. I hated the University of Texas the most, but in some ways, I feared the Aggies more. Year in and year out, they just seemed to have our number, this infuriating way of playing their very best game of the season just to spoil ours, often in a come-from-behind, improbable win.

This game seemed to follow that same sickening story line, the Aggies playing way better than they should have to keep the game tied at seven all the way to the final minute. I was frantic. Everyone in the entire stadium was frantic. Because we all knew that, without a win tonight, it could be only a good season. Not a great one. Then, on the very last play of the game, with Reggie smothered in maroon jerseys, Everclear managed to complete a miracle pass to another freshman in the end zone. It was a thing of beauty, but more of an intense relief than a source of joy. We were 3–0, still in the hunt.

In the pressroom after the game, as we all waited for Coach Carr to arrive, I ran into Frank Smiley. 'Good game,' he said. 'Doesn't get much closer than that.'

'I prefer blowouts to good games,' I said, thinking that

assistant sports information directors had that luxury. We didn't have to write about it; we just had to celebrate it. 'Did you get a stat sheet?' I held a stack in my hands, hot off the presses.

He took one, said thanks.

'Did you see the longest run we gave up was seven yards?' I asked.

'I did. Some very impressive defensive stats,' he said.

'It all starts up front,' I said. 'When you can control the line of scrimmage like that, it really allows you so much on the back end.'

I was making idle pressroom conversation but was also making a point: I knew this game, inside and out. And he should have hired me.

'So. If this were your beat, Ms. Rigsby, what would you ask Coach Carr?'

I looked at him, thinking that it was some real bullshit, his asking me a pseudo-interview question while I was working. But I played along. 'I don't know,' I said. 'I guess I might ask him about trusting a true freshman with the ball on the final play.'

'Hmm, yes,' he said, nodding. 'And what do you think Coach's answer would be?'

I exhaled, put the stat sheets on a table next to two ESPN reporters, and said, 'The answer is . . . Patrick Elgin might be a true freshman, but we've repped that play a hundred times in practice. So he was ready for it. It's not as much of a gamble as you'd think.'

Smiley nodded but looked dubious. It irked me enough to say, 'I'd also ask something about how often he dropped eight into coverage and went with three down linemen when we're used to seeing him bring more pressure to passing teams.'

Smiley adjusted his cap and said, 'And *that* answer would be . . .?'

'Well, *my* answer is that the Aggies have a very strong receiving corps. So it was a simple matter of matching coverages and having to drop out of our nickel package. That's why you saw three down linemen more frequently today.' I stared at him. 'But that's *my* answer. If you want Coach Carr's answer, I guess you need to ask him yourself. I don't ask questions – I pass out stat sheets.' I almost softened my statement with a smile, but decided against it.

Smiley gave me a long stare, then handed me a business-size envelope with my name typed on the front. 'Ms. Rigsby, here is a formal offer letter to join my staff. You don't have the requisite experience, but you know this game and you're a good writer. Not great, but good. I'm taking a big chance on you. Please let me know by Monday morning.'

Before I could reply, he walked briskly back to his usual folding chair in the front row, left corner, next to Kenny Stone, his longtime reporter on the Walker beat. I looked down at the envelope, shook my head, and allowed myself a small, jubilant smile. Meanwhile, Coach Carr entered the room with Rhodes and Everclear, the three of them walking stoically and in single file up to the skirted table covered with microphones. The room quieted and the cameras rolled as Coach addressed the media, making his standard post-win remarks. *Our boys showed up today. I'm proud of them. The Aggies gave us a tough fight. They're a great team. But things went our way, and I'm pleased with that.* Then he opened it up for questions, and Smiley's hand shot up. Coach called on him, and Smiley's gruff voice fired back. 'Coach. Can you tell us why we saw so many situations with three down linemen tonight?'

I was surprised to hear my question, a little less so when Coach's answer also followed my script. I watched as Smiley furiously scribbled, then turned, looked over his shoulder at me, and gave me a covert and shocking thumbs-up. Against all odds, I was finally in the club.

14

After the game, I met up with Lucy and Neil at the Third Rail, a little hole-in-the-wall bar on North Potomac known for its amazing wings and great jukebox filled with both old and new country, everything from Merle Haggard and Johnny Cash to Taylor Swift and Sugarland. It had been our go-to spot for years, and I considered it a small miracle and one of life's simple joys that it had never been hijacked by drunken coeds, redneck townies, or cougars on the prowl, the three groups that seemed to overrun every other halfway-decent bar or restaurant in town. Miller and I had once brainstormed theories on the subject, concluding that the Third Rail had a series of small strikes against it: bad parking, its proximity to the police station, and an Arkansas-alum owner named Chuck, who steadfastly refused to change the channel on the lone television near the bar if his team was playing. The flaws served us well, though, as even on home game weekends, the bar was never packed and always had a chill vibe. It also happened to be Coach Carr's favorite spot, likely because Chuck and Coach were tight, and Chuck had given Coach a permanent table on reserve in the back room. Someone had even etched a CCC – for Coach Clive Carr – into the grainy wood with a pocketknife.

That night was slightly livelier than usual, a handful of twenty-somethings sprinkled in with the older regulars. Sara Evans was singing 'A Little Bit Stronger' on the jukebox, the Arkansas game was just wrapping up, and there was, to my relief, no sign of Miller or his friends. In the six or so months since we broke up, I'd yet to run into him, which was a small miracle in a town this size. I bought a Blue Moon on tap, spotting Lucy and Neil in the back corner playing pool. As I approached them, I paused to watch Lucy take her turn, amused by her awkward stance, her elbows jutted out at weird angles. I had tried to offer her tips in the past, but she steadfastly refused to acknowledge basic geometry. It was almost as if she sucked on purpose, believing that prowess in both pool and darts was inversely proportional to femininity. A second later, she completely whiffed an easy shot.

'What are we playing?' I quipped, walking up behind her. 'Loser takes all?'

'Lazy Shea-zy!' Lucy spun around and exclaimed, my ancient nickname earned by sitting on the couch and watching football all day long. She threw her arms around my neck and squealed that she was so happy to see me. Lucy was a complete light-weight drinker and could get buzzed from one beer, but I estimated that she was further in than that. They had definitely been here for a while. She handed me her cue and said, 'Will you take over for me? I suck at this sport.'

I glanced at the table, assessing the situation, and laughed. 'It's a game, not a sport. And no, thanks,' I said, tossing the stick back to her as Neil hugged me hello then knocked in his last two stripes, followed by the eight ball, finishing Lucy off.

'So how long have y'all been here?' I asked casually, trying not to look judgmental about them missing the end of the game.

She winced, then put an index finger to her lips. 'Shhh. Since halftime,' Lucy said. 'Give or take.'

I shook my head. 'Did Chuck even let you turn the channel?'

'A couple times. Don't tell Daddy! It's just that we only have a babysitter once a week and we really needed some alone time,' she said, taking off her cropped teal cardigan and exposing a black silk tank underneath. I noticed that she had gained a little weight back since the funeral and was starting to look healthy again.

'Which is why you invited me here?' I said. 'This place is called the Third Rail, not the Third Wheel.'

Neil laughed and said, 'Yeah, but Lucy tells me you have a boyfriend now.'

'I didn't call him that,' I said, looking at Lucy. I had, of course, told her that we had slept together for the first time, then again after the Silver and Blue Debut, the Cowboys' public practice and dress rehearsal before their first game. I had gone at Ryan's request, even mingling with a few of the other wives and girlfriends, which made Lucy positively giddy. I turned the subject back to the Walker game, telling them I'd nearly had a heart attack. 'Like literally. Symptoms of angina. I honestly don't know how your dad does it.'

'I know,' Lucy said. 'I don't either.'

'He had a great press conference. He was on fire. Really relaxed and funny . . .'

'Did he tell anyone off?' Neil asked. 'I love when he does that.'

'He doesn't do that after wins,' I said.

'Omigod! Your boy just walked in!' Lucy said, staring behind me. I followed her gaze and saw Ryan sauntering toward us, in jeans, a just-fitted-enough white T-shirt, and a black Under Armour baseball cap. A five o'clock shadow and dog tags completed the Texas-meets-Malibu look. In short, he was ridiculously hot. Everyone in the bar, of both genders and all ages, stared, his presence causing an immediate, palpable ripple, much less subtle than the impact he'd had at the Ritz, where people knew to play it cool.

'Did you know he was coming?' she asked.

I shook my head, smiling. I had told him I was going to be here, but never imagined that he'd show up. He made his way over to us, high-fiving two guys in his path. When he reached our pool table, he paused for dramatic effect, his hands out to the sides, as if waiting for an embrace. I laughed and shook my head, not wanting to appear overly eager.

'Wow. Nothing? I drive an hour to see you and get no love?' Ryan said with a seductive grin before leaning down to kiss me, the bill of his cap obscuring the exact placement of his lips on mine.

Lucy said hello to Ryan, then sidled in to give him a hug as she introduced Neil. The two shook hands and exchanged manly pleasantries. Meanwhile, a curvy young waitress in black Lycra and stonewashed jean shorts scurried over to us. Beaming and flustered, she reminded me of a kid who finally gets to the front of a line to meet the mall Santa Claus, only to forget what she wants for Christmas.

'Um, hello, Mr James, can I get you something to drink?' she asked him. 'Or some wings or nachos or . . . anything?'

'Call me Ryan,' he said with a grin so charming that I couldn't help thinking that it undermined any look of affection he'd ever given me. 'Ladies first,' he said, gesturing my way.

I held up my beer and said, 'I'm good, thanks.'

The waitress giggled for no apparent reason.

'I'll have a Jack and Diet,' Ryan said. 'But make sure you cut me off after my second.'

'Right. Don't you have a big game tomorrow?' she asked, biting her lower lip in an overtly sensual way, then giggling again.

'Monday,' I mouthed to Lucy, as Ryan told her, no, he had two more days to get ready.

'Oh. Right. *Monday Night Football*!' she said with more nervous tittering and a promise to hold him to his limit.

Ryan winked his thanks, then turned back to Lucy, who began bombarding him with questions, seemingly riveted by every response, no matter how bland. It reminded me of how she used to act in high school around boys, even those she had no interest in whatsoever, giving them all the impression that they were *the* most witty and brilliant and fascinating creatures she'd ever encountered. Of course they'd fall hard and fast in love with her, which really just meant that they were in love with themselves, and she always pretended to be completely floored by the result, explaining that she hadn't been flirting; she was only trying to be nice. Tonight, though, I was pretty sure her motivation was different and that she was only trying to compensate for my apathetic reaction to Ryan's cameo, a hunch that was confirmed when she dragged me to the bathroom and gave me a stern lecture.

'What in the world is your problem?' she demanded as I put on a fresh coat of lip gloss. 'I thought things were going well with you two?' She lowered her voice and said, 'You're *sleeping* with him, for goodness' sakes.'

I shushed her, glancing under the stall doors, checking for feet, then said, 'Everything's fine. Going well.'

'Well, then, what's with the chip on your shoulder? Could you act any less happy to see him? *Gawd.*'

'What do you want me to do?' I said. 'Turn cartwheels? Maybe do a couple round-offs?'

'Hell, *yeah,* you should be turning cartwheels. Ryan James is the most eligible bachelor in all of Texas, maybe the entire country. He is famous, funny, wealthy, athletic, tall, and *painfully* beautiful.'

'Tall?' I said. 'Really? That's on your list? Miller was *tall.*'

'C'mon. What doesn't he have? A Ph.D.? Royal blood? You still looking for a baron or a duke?' she said, mocking my brief teenage crush on Prince Harry.

'I don't know, Luce. The whole thing is just . . . embarrassing. Everyone is staring at us,' I said, my insecurity returning.

'Since when do you care what people think?' Lucy said.

'I don't,' I said, shrugging. 'Not *that* much.'

'Well, then, stop that shit. *Now.* And rise to the occasion, would you?'

'Okay, okay,' I said. 'I'll do better. I promise.'

'Good,' Lucy said. 'Because this is your *life.*'

'I got it,' I said, as we left the bathroom.

When we got back out to the bar, Ryan and Neil had moved from the pool table to a booth. They both did a half stand as we sat down, and Lucy gave me a look that said, *Add chivalrous to the list.*

'So I was just telling Neil about your Heisman Trophy Rain Man thing you got going on. Quiz her. She'll get it. Any year.'

I glanced at Lucy, thinking this was tricky terrain, as I'd never told her that I called her dad that night.

'Nineteen sixty-five,' Neil said, pointing at me.

I knew it was Mike Garrett but played dumb, hoping they'd change the subject. It was the wrong strategy because Ryan said, 'Oh, c'mon. You were on fire that night talking to Coach! 'Sixty-five. You got this!'

'Mike Garrett. USC,' I mumbled.

'What night?' Lucy said, never missing a trick.

'The night of that charity thing in Dallas,' Ryan said.

'Daddy was there?' Lucy looked confused.

'No. Shea called him,' Ryan said in a loud voice as the waitress brought his second drink.

'Called him? On the phone?' She looked at Ryan, then me.

Ryan answered for me, 'Yeah. To discuss Heisman Trophy winners. Classic.'

Lucy gave me a look that I couldn't read, and for a second I was worried. But then she smiled and said, 'You are so sweet, Shea . . . Neil, isn't Shea the sweetest?'

Neil nodded while Lucy continued. 'That is so sweet of you to call Daddy to play a Heisman Trophy trivia game when you know he's lonely. You're the *best.*'

I smiled, then made my big announcement, desperate to change the subject. 'So guess what? I got the job. At *The Dallas Post,*' I said, pulling the sealed envelope out of my purse.

'Omigod. Congratulations!' Lucy said. 'That's *amazing* news! Why didn't you say anything before now?'

I shrugged and told her I was waiting for the right moment, as Ryan squeezed my leg and congratulated me and Neil tapped his mug of beer against mine.

'For which beat? Texas?' Ryan said, finishing his Jack and Coke with one easy tilt of his head. 'Are you going Benedict Arnold on us?'

I said I didn't know as I opened the envelope, unfolded the letter, read it, then reread it, sure that I'd gotten it wrong the first time. But no, it was clear. I felt myself grinning so wide that my cheeks hurt. If Lucy wanted giddy, she was about to get a freaking lap dance from her best friend.

'What's it say?' Lucy asked. 'Is the pay good?'

'Not really,' I said, noting that I'd actually have to take a thousand-dollar pay cut from my current measly salary.

'Then what?' Lucy said, grabbing for the letter.

I held it out of her reach, relishing the final few seconds when I was the only one to know the fabulous news.

'Dammit, Shea! Tell us!' Lucy said.

'Guess who the *Post* just hired to cover . . . *yoooour* verrry own . . . Walker Bron-coooos!' My voice escalated, imitating Mac MacDonald, the voice of the Broncos, then finished off with a yelp, no longer caring who was watching us as I stood and held up the letter like a newspaper boy on V-J Day.

Then I looked at Lucy and said, 'Was this what you were looking for?' Gauging the space between the booth and pool table, I put my hands straight up over my head, pointed my left toe, and busted out my very best cartwheel.

It didn't occur to me until much later, after I'd gone home with Ryan, then had sex with him for the third time, then woken up the next day, then had sex with him for the fourth time, that this could be a setup. An ambush. A sick joke Smiley was playing on the girl from Walker. I hadn't read one printed word about Walker being in trouble with the NCAA, and was sure it would amount to nothing, but maybe Smiley had heard some of the rumblings. Maybe he wanted a reporter with an inside scoop when the dirt really started to hit the fan. I told myself I was just being paranoid. That even if the story did come to light, our name would be cleared – and I'd be the reporter to do it. I told myself that this was my big break. That my life was finally coming together.

15

On Monday morning, I called Smiley and formally accepted his offer of employment, thanking him so profusely that he sputtered, 'Don't ever thank me again. This isn't a gift. It's a job.' Then, to emphasize the point, he went on to explain that Kenny Stone, the guy I was replacing, had sold out to ESPN. 'Another one bites the dust to the network that puts entertainment ahead of sports,' he said.

'Okay,' I said. 'I won't thank you again. But, seriously, this is my dream job. And the salary is a little lower than what I make now, but I'm fine – *happy* – with it.'

Smiley made a scoffing sound and said, 'For the love of Christmas. Let's hope your reporting skills are sharper than your negotiating tactics.'

'Yes, sir. They are. Thank you *so* much,' I said.

'When can you start?'

'When do you need me to start?'

'The sooner the better.'

'I'll give notice today.'

'You do that. And remember—'

He paused, and I said, 'What's that, sir?'

'No more *rah-rah* shit. You're a reporter now.'

'Yes, sir,' I said, squeezing the little teal Walker Nerf ball on my desk before tossing it in the air and catching it with one hand.

Later that day, I found Coach Carr in his office, his door wide open.

'Congratulations,' he said when he saw me, taking a bite of a bagel, then sweeping stray sesame seeds into his trash can.

I smiled my thanks and said, 'Smiley told you?'

'Yep. So I guess he thinks you can be objective.'

'Do you think I can?'

'We'll find out,' he said, taking another bite.

'Maybe we won't.'

'Oh? How do you figure?'

I swallowed, feeling bold as I lifted one eyebrow and said, 'Because you and your program are perfect.'

'That's a good point,' he said, laughing. 'You know that's not true, though, right? I've made a few mistakes along the way.'

'Such as?'

He put his bagel on his napkin, then pushed it aside. 'Are you asking me as a reporter or my friend?'

'Um. Reporter.'

'Well, then I plead the Fifth,' he said.

'Okay. And as your friend?' I asked, leaning toward him.

'What's the question again?'

'Are you as perfect as you seem?'

'Is the pope a bear?' he said, one of his stock expressions.

I smiled. 'He must be.'

Coach laughed a big laugh. 'So, girl. What are you doing tonight?'

'Um, watching the Cowboys,' I said, leaving out the part about watching the game in person with Ryan's tickets that were awaiting me at will call at AT&T Stadium. 'Why? What are *you* doing tonight?'

'Same,' he said. 'Would you like to watch it together? I'll go on record for you.'

'On record? About what?' I said, feeling an odd little rush of emotion that only he gave me.

'Oh, I don't know. The season so far. Injuries. Recruiting. Strategy. Upcoming games. Conference realignments. Your call, girl. Consider it a congratulations-you-got-the-job gift. What do you say? Meet at the Third Rail at eight?'

'Sure,' I said.

'Good. Very good.' Coach Carr smiled his approval. 'See you tonight.'

'See you tonight,' I said.

I waited until late afternoon to send Ryan a text, keeping it as simple as possible: *So sorry can't make it tonight. Have to work. Talk soon and good luck!*

Very technically it was the truth, but I felt a trace of guilt that caused me to tack on an *xo* in a separate text. It was silly, really, because I felt certain that Ryan would care remarkably little about my last-minute cancellation, especially given that it was game day, and was surprised and a little flattered when he wrote back: *That sucks. Call me afterward. Miss my girl.*

I told myself I'd make it up to him later – and that I couldn't turn down the chance to talk to Coach Carr on record. If I was going to be a successful reporter, I had to take these opportunities when they presented themselves. It was as simple as that.

A few hours later I walked into the Third Rail to find Coach already at his table.

'You look nice,' he said.

I thanked him, but felt suddenly overdressed in one of Lucy's ensembles, especially given that he was in the same casual clothes he had been wearing earlier. 'You been here long?' I asked, sitting across from him.

'Long enough to order this,' Coach said, taking a sip of beer. 'Are you hungry?'

I nodded.

'Wings?'

I nodded again, then said, 'So. This is quite an honor.'

'An honor? C'mon, now, girl,' he said, batting away my comment with his hand, making me feel slightly foolish.

'I just meant . . . thanks for suggesting this. It means a lot to spend time with you. And I know you don't like to go out during the season.' I paused as the same waitress from the other night came by to check on us. She seemed not to remember me, apparently *that* blinded by Ryan, and it annoyed me that she was markedly less impressed with Coach. I asked for a Blue Moon, and she departed briskly.

'You don't have to thank me, Shea,' he said. 'And I don't mind coming out to quiet spots like this.'

Our waitress returned with my beer and asked if we wanted to order anything to eat. Coach told her wings and specified spicy, as I knew he would. 'If that's okay with you?' he said, looking my way. I nodded and said that was the way to go as ESPN began its telecast.

'Too bad Faith Hill doesn't do *Monday Night Football*,' I said, musing aloud about how great her legs were.

Coach raised his brows and nodded with appreciation so acute that I felt a pang of irrational jealousy. But the comment also made me feel close to him. Like we were on the same page. Coach and reporter bonding over beers and wings and Faith Hill's killer wheels.

I took a sip of beer, then looked at Coach. *Really* looked at him, trying to pinpoint that certain quality that made him different from other men. There was just something so solid about him. He had a way of taking up the space around him with such quiet dignity. It was almost as if there were an invisible barrier around him that you knew you couldn't penetrate with the usual congratulatory small talk about the last game. Coach was always warm and gracious, even to strangers, yet he remained walled off, self-contained, almost mysterious in a way that had always captivated me.

'What's on your mind?' he suddenly asked.

I shook my head, as if to say nothing at all, as we both turned our attention to Jon Gruden, informing us that Dallas had won the toss and had elected to receive.

'Good,' Coach said. 'Better for Ryan to establish an early rhythm. Calms him down. I don't like him on the sidelines at the beginning of the game.'

Coach Carr and I both nursed our beers as the Giants kicked off for a touchback.

'I like the matchup in the secondary,' Coach mumbled as Ryan handed off. 'If they can protect him up front, he's going to have a good game.'

The series didn't prove fruitful, though, as Dallas went a quick three and out.

'So, Coach? Are you a big Cowboys fan?' I said. It sounded like a throwaway question – a total given for any Texas native, especially one who had once coached the current starting quarterback, but I could tell he understood that the question was more nuanced than that. I was asking about his passion, and, in my mind, it was difficult, if not downright impossible, to have more than one passion in life. In other words, *I know you pull for the Cowboys, but do you truly love them?*

He gave me a very lackluster *yeah,* confirming my hunch.

'Don't sound so enthusiastic,' I said.

He laughed. 'Well, I'm definitely a fan, but growing up . . .' He paused, glanced around the room, then peered up at the ceiling as if searching for hidden cameras before leaning in to share his secret. 'Growing up I was a Green Bay fan. Still am sort of. But that is *way* off the record,' he said with a deep, gravelly chuckle.

'*Green* Bay? Why?' I asked, intrigued.

'Because of my old man. And Vince Lombardi . . . My dad loved Lombardi as much as—' He struggled to finish his sentence as I thought, *As much as all of Walker, Texas, loves you?*

Coach gave me a funny look, as if reading my mind, but said, 'One of his own. I don't know how a man born and raised in Fort Worth came to that – but he passed it on to me. You know how that works . . .'

I nodded, thinking that fandom was one of the rare instances when parental (or even grandparental) allegiances trumped geography or whatever it was your friends were doing.

'Anyway,' he said. 'Are you familiar with the Ice Bowl?'

'Yeah,' I said, then proved it. 'Packers–Cowboys, New Year's Eve 1967. The NFL championship game, but it was known as the Ice Bowl because of the subzero temperatures in Wisconsin.'

'Yep. Minus thirteen at Lambeau that night,' he said, shivering at the mere thought of it. 'I was there with my old man. He got me tickets for Christmas and we drove twenty hours to get there, leaving my sisters and mother behind.'

'How old were you?' I asked, trying to do the math in my head.

'Nine,' he said. 'But I remember it like it was yesterday, especially that final play. Sixteen seconds. Packers down by three. Third and goal inside the Dallas one.'

'And what happened? The Cowboys lost, didn't they?'

'Yep. Bart Starr called a thirty-one wedge but kept the ball. Poetry in motion . . . Later, when I read everything there was to read about Lombardi, I learned that Lombardi let Starr call that one. He just said, "Run what you want and let's get the hell out of here." I sometimes think about that in tense situations and try to take a page from the all-time great. You have your strategy in place . . . but sometimes you can't micromanage. You gotta trust your guys to read the field and make the right play . . .' Coach said. His eyes were on the television, but I could tell he was back in time.

I made no pretense of watching the game. 'How happy were you and your dad after that game?'

'Very. Nearly frostbitten – couldn't feel my earlobes for days – but damn, were we happy. We headed back to Texas that same night, but not before we made a pact never to tell anyone that we'd pulled for the Cowboys' demise. My old man was good – should have been an actor and not a shoe salesman – going on and on to all his friends about what a waste it was to go all that way and lose. How pissed off he was.' Coach shook his head and laughed. 'Never confessed that to anyone. Until now.'

I felt sure that he meant that he'd never confessed to anyone except Mrs Carr, but I still felt special as I asked him another question. 'So when did you know you wanted to be a coach?'

'Oh, I don't know, girl. Not until I stopped playing the game,' he said. 'I don't think anyone grows up dreaming of being a coach. I just think the game gets in your blood and you can't bear to think of your life without it. That's the way it was for me, anyway.'

'Well, I can't bear to think of my life without it either,' I said.

Coach smiled at me, and I smiled back, both of us missing the first score of the game – a Giants thirty-six-yard field goal.

'Maybe we should actually try and watch this game,' Coach said as our wings arrived.

I nodded happily as we spent the rest of the half focused on the television and our food, and an occasional hello from a fan brave enough to cross into the semiprivate area of the bar. Our conversation remained light and easy and never strayed far from the play at hand while Ryan appeared on-screen every thirty seconds. I kept waiting for Coach to ask about him or talk about him, but, to my relief, he didn't – except as it related to the game.

Right at the start of the second half, Coach looked toward the door and said, 'Well, well. Look what the cat dragged in.'

'Who?' I said, not wanting to take my eyes off Coach.

A second later, I heard Miller's voice behind me. 'Hey, Coach. Hey, Shea. What's up?'

I felt a jolt of nostalgia, but no real emotional stirrings, as I turned to say hello to my ex.

'Miller time!' Coach said, breaking the ice. 'Wanna join us?'

Miller grinned without a trace of the awkwardness that you'd expect after a breakup, then pulled up a stool and said, 'Don't mind if I do.'

I kept my eyes on the television, but must have looked disappointed by the interruption because Miller said, 'What's wrong? Are the boys losing?'

'Nope. We're up seven,' I said, forcing a smile as I asked him how he'd been doing.

'Not too bad,' he said, giving me a bland, rambling update about his job and family, then asking what was new with me.

I told him about my job, in as few words as possible, then explained that that was why Coach and I were here together.

Miller congratulated me and said, 'What else is goin' on?'

'Not much.'

'Not what *I heard*,' he said in a singsongy playground taunt.

I knew that he had to be referring to Ryan, but I just shrugged, hoping it would end the discussion.

But it didn't, of course – because Miller had the maturity of the eighth-grade students he taught.

'You and Ryan,' he said, shaking his head, laughing. 'Gotta say. That really stings. I mean, did you have to go for such an obvious upgrade? The guy who took my starting spot?' He put his hand over his heart, a gesture that someone would only employ if his heart weren't the slightest bit hurt.

'We're just friends,' I said, wondering why I was downplaying our relationship with an outright lie. Was it to spare Miller's feelings?

Miller laughed. 'Yeah, right. Ryan isn't *friends* with girls. Is he, Coach? Least not hot girls.'

Coach Carr cleared his throat and said, 'There are exceptions to every rule.'

Miller slapped his thigh and said, 'Oh, man. You used to tell us that in practice! *Flashback!*' Then he changed the subject to an even more awkward topic. 'So is the rumor true, Coach? About the NCAA investigating us?' he asked. It was a question I had avoided all evening, somewhat irresponsibly given my new job.

My instinct was proven right as Coach visibly bristled and said, 'Where'd you hear that, son?'

'From Nan Buxbaum,' Miller said. By the cocky grin on his face, it was pretty clear in what capacity Miller knew Nan.

'Who?' Coach said.

'A professor in the sociology department,' Miller said, leaving out that she was gorgeous. If Nan didn't get tenure, lingerie model wasn't out of the question. 'We've been hanging out since Shea here dumped me.'

'I didn't *dump* you,' I said, objecting to the ruthless nature of the verb.

'The hell!' he said as our waitress stopped by and took Miller's PBR order.

'What did she say?' Coach asked, his expression becoming increasingly agitated.

'She said an investigator is crawling up their asses. You know, since we all major in sociology,' Miller said, still referring to himself as a player. 'They seem to be implying that Walker skates athletes through the department. I think that's the gist. I bet they confiscate Ebert's computer.'

Professor Ebert, widely known as Easy Ebert, had been around forever. He was a huge football fan, and athletes had always clamored to take his classes. But, to be fair, so had all the regular students. If Ebert was the problem, the NCAA's case seemed rather flimsy.

'It's a non-story, Miller,' I said, quoting Coach. 'So don't go spreading rumors.'

'I'm not spreading rumors,' he said. 'About the NCAA or you and Ryan James. I'm just callin' 'em like I see 'em. Gotta be real. Right, Coach?'

'Right, Miller,' Coach said, abruptly standing. Clearly, he'd had enough. 'If you'll excuse me a moment . . .'

I watched him walk away from the table and head for the men's room, then turned back to face Miller. 'Look. Coach is clearly upset about this NCAA stuff,' I said. 'You might not want to talk about it so . . . casually.'

'Yeah. My bad,' Miller said, as I tried to think of a tactful way to get rid of him completely. But short of telling him to please go away, I came up empty-handed, and a couple minutes of babble later, Coach rejoined us and announced that it was time for him to go home and hit the hay.

'Shea, I settled up at the bar. So we're good,' he said, zipping up his fleece jacket.

'Thank you,' I said, my heart sinking.

'You're welcome,' he replied, holding my gaze. I got the sense that he was as irritated by Miller's interruption as I was.

'You sure you don't want to stay? You're going to miss the

end of the game . . . And I know how much you love the Cowboys . . .'

'Nah. Ryan's got this one in the bag,' Coach said.

'Your boyfriend,' Miller said, pointing at me, thoroughly amused with himself.

'Shut up,' I breathed back as we all watched Ryan complete an impossible thirty-yard pass through a forest of red, white, and blue into the end zone. He took off his helmet and thrust one finger up in the air as I read his lips: *Fuck yeah.*

Miller happily chortled, clearly not really jealous of *anyone*, as Coach said, 'See? I know these things. Game over.'

I laughed. 'Would you call it over if you were coaching the Giants?' I said. 'There are still three and a half minutes to play.'

'No,' he said. 'But I also wouldn't have put a block on and roughed the kicker with that much time on the clock.'

I nodded, basking in his final brilliant analysis, as he clapped Miller on the back and said, 'All right, then . . . Good to see you, son. Y'all be safe getting home.'

We promised that we would as he turned to me, hesitating, as if debating whether to give me a handshake or hug or similar backslap. Instead, he put his hand over mine, lowered his voice, and said, 'Enjoyed talking football with you, girl.'

16

It was raining when I walked out of the bar, a light mist that would have felt romantic if I were holding someone's hand, but instead made me feel more wistful and lonesome than I had in a long time. Lonesome enough to text Ryan when I got in my car, congratulating him on a great game. Before I pulled out of my parking spot, he had written back: *Thanks. I think you should come tell me in person.* ;)

'Done,' I said aloud. And, a few minutes later, I was on I-35, headed toward Dallas, my thoughts jumbled and racing, yet returning, again and again, to Coach. Our conversation, his eyes, the way I felt sitting near him, whether in his office or back in that bar. It was different from the way I felt with anyone else. He gave me butterflies in my stomach, and, although I'd always chalked it up to nervousness from being so close to greatness, I was starting to worry that it was something more than that. As I drove, a queasy feeling overcame me. I was finally calling my own bluff – and I hated that I couldn't turn it off, shut it down.

I turned up the radio, shook my head, tightened my grip on the steering wheel, and came up with a battery of excuses. I told myself that I was only confusing my love of football and Walker with an attraction to the head of our program. That, sure, Coach was hot – even a male *Sports Illustrated* writer had acknowledged as much – and a beautiful man could fluster any woman, even one in a committed, satisfying relationship. That everyone and her *sister* loved Coach Carr, and I was hardly unique in Walker, Texas. That having a little crush was just the grown-up version of childhood hero worship.

But the more I tried to convince myself, the more the wall

of denial crumbled. And this time, there was no stopping the realization that hit me hard in the gut, halfway between Walker and Dallas: I had a thing for Lucy's dad. A real, undeniable, heart-thudding, romantic *thing*.

I drove faster, forcing Coach from my mind, focusing on Ryan. How much I *truly* liked him. How perfect he was. How happy he made me.

I told myself I needed to get a grip – and fast. Coach Carr was the last person in the world I had any business having feelings for. He was too old for me. He had just lost the love of his life. He was my best friend's *father*. It was insanity.

The rain fell harder, pelting my windshield, my wipers unable to keep up, the road ahead barely visible. I finally gave up and pulled over to the side of the road, waiting, breathing, denying that I was actually *missing* him, doing everything in my power not to think of him. But that strategy backfired, as it always does, and it didn't help matters when Bonnie Raitt's 'I Can't Make You Love Me,' the most exquisitely sad song ever recorded, came on the radio. *Morning will come, and I'll do what's right . . .*

At some point after the rain had slowed, I got back on the road. And by the time Ryan buzzed me through his iron gate, I had pulled it together. I smiled when I saw him standing in his doorway in slippers and a black robe open at the chest.

'Hello, beautiful,' he said, as I got out of the car.

'Hi, Ryan,' I said, walking to him.

He stepped off his porch, took my hand, and pulled me out of the light rain.

'What're you doing here?' he said coyly, kissing my neck.

'I came to congratulate you in person.'

'Why, thank you,' he said, wrapping his strong arms around me and kissing me again, this time on my mouth. I closed my eyes and focused on the feel of his lips and tongue and large hands drawing me closer. Then I let him lead me upstairs to his bedroom, where he made slow, passionate love to me.

* * *

Just before sunrise, I awoke in Ryan's arms, wanting him again. I gently untangled myself so that I could watch him sleep, stare at his gorgeous face.

At some point, his eyes fluttered open, and he gave me a half smile before reaching for me. 'C'mere,' he whispered, pulling me closer and kissing the top of my head.

'You were really great last night,' I said.

'Well, I can do better,' he said, running his hand along my hip, now fully awake.

'I meant in the game,' I said with a laugh, then described one of his prettiest plays.

'Wait. Wasn't that the first quarter?' he asked, becoming more alert.

'Yes. It was pretty early on.'

'But I thought you had to work?' he said as he rolled onto his side and propped himself up on one elbow.

'I did,' I said, then gave him a choppy explanation about watching the game with Coach, in reporter mode. 'A journalist can't turn down that kind of opportunity.'

I moved toward him, putting my cheek on his chest, my right leg and arm clutching him like a koala bear. It was an intimate maneuver, but really had more to do with wanting to escape his eyes.

'Did you tell him about us?' he asked.

'No. Not exactly.'

'Why not?'

'I don't know. What would I have told him? That we're having sex?' I said, trying to be playful, and perhaps fishing a little.

'Jeez. I think it's a little more than that,' Ryan said, his fingers combing through my hair.

I smiled to myself and asked a shameless follow-up. 'Oh? Is it?'

'Yes. You know it is,' Ryan whispered.

After a stretch of silence, he said, 'So you watched that whole game with him and never mentioned that we are seeing each other?'

Flustered, I said, 'Well . . . he definitely knows about us.'

'How do you know?'

'Because Miller showed up,' I said. 'Of all people. And he told him.'

Ryan bolted upright, one of his many hard body parts clipping my chin as he switched on the light and said, 'You saw Miller last night?' His eyes were intense; his whiskers seemed much darker than they'd looked just a few hours before.

I looked up at him, my eyes adjusting to the light as I tried to interpret what was happening, why he seemed to be so upset. Could he actually be bothered that I had seen Miller? Was he jealous? It seemed far-fetched, but because I had no other explanation, I said, 'Yeah. He showed up out of the blue. It was actually pretty annoying. Coach and I were having a serious conversation about—'

'How long did he stay? Did Coach leave first?' His voice became strained and loud as he crossed his arms, muscles flexing in his chest and arms. He was definitely pissed.

'Ryan . . . C'mon. You can't be jealous of Miller.'

'Of course I'm not *jealous* of Miller,' he snapped. 'That guy is a stoner loser.' The indictment sounded so much worse coming from him than from Lucy, and I felt an odd surge of protectiveness.

'That's harsh,' I said.

'Wow. You're still sleeping with him,' Ryan said. 'Aren't you?'

'What are you *talking* about?' I asked. 'Of *course* I'm not still sleeping with him.'

'Do you still care about him?'

'As a friend. That's it. Look. I can't control who walks into the Third Rail . . . And Coach invited him to sit down. It was no big deal. The three of us sat around watching *you* play. We were all happy for you. *Miller* was happy for you.'

'Yeah, *right*.'

It had been a long time since I had inspired jealousy in anyone, and I found it incredible to believe that Ryan and I were actually having this conversation. It was flattering, but also unsettling.

'It was no big deal. I'm over him. He's over me. He's got a girlfriend,' I said, rambling about Nan Buxbaum, then adding a gratuitous footnote. 'I bet they get engaged soon.'

Ryan stared at me for a few beats longer. 'Okay,' he finally said, turning off the lamp and putting his head back on the pillow. 'I'm sorry.'

I told him he had nothing to be sorry for.

After a long beat, he said, 'Can you just promise me one thing?'

'Sure. What's that?' I said, wanting to make him happy.

'Promise me that you won't see anyone else,' he said. 'Because I know I can be old-fashioned . . . But I believe in monogamy. And I want you all to myself.'

'I promise,' I said, surprised by how quickly things were moving.

'I promise, too,' he said, then sealed our pact with a long, intense kiss – the kind that always leads to more.

17

A week later, after we drummed Oklahoma State on the road to move up three spots in the polls, J.J. and his wife, Mary Ann, threw me a going-away party, even though I'd been insisting that I wasn't really 'going' any-where and that everyone would see me just as often. I dreaded being the center of atten-tion, and hoped that once things got under way, it would feel like a generic party with the usual athletic department suspects. But when I pulled up to the Justuses' house and spotted Ryan's black Porsche, I knew there would be nothing generic about the evening. Nothing ever was when Ryan was involved. I couldn't help feeling a jolt of annoyance that he was here when I had specifically *not* mentioned the party to him or told anyone at work we were dating. I decided that Lucy had to have orchestrated the appearance of Walker's golden child, as low-key was never her default position.

I got out of my car and walked inside the house, finding Ryan in the foyer, handing Mary Ann a bottle of wine as she gushed about how thrilled she was to see him, how wonderfully he had been playing, how proud we all were of him. As they both spotted me and turned to say hello, I managed to change my attitude, shifting into grateful mode. I might not like this sort of thing, but it was really nice of everyone, Ryan included. He walked the few steps over to me, slid his arm around my waist, and kissed me on the lips, leaving little doubt about the nature of our relationship, while Mary Ann complimented my teal dress.

'I got it at Lucy's. Thank you. And thank you so much for tonight,' I said as the three of us moved toward the living room, which was already filled with voices and laughter.

'Surprised?' Ryan whispered to me in the hall, his arm now casually draped across my shoulder.

'Yes. Very. Thank you for coming,' I said, smiling up at him, bracing myself for our grand entrance.

'Of course, babe. I wouldn't have missed it,' he said. Then he kissed me once more, this time in plain view of Scott Street, our head trainer, and Tim Seymour, the academic counselor whom Coach jokingly referred to as 'the grim reaper' because he only came knocking with bad news. Scott and Tim both looked surprised to see Ryan, and it occurred to me that my relationship would trump my new job, the former being the more impressive accomplishment in most everyone's eyes.

Trying to act as natural as possible, I began my round of hellos and hugs, observing, as I frequently did at such gatherings, how eclectic the group was, just about as diverse as it could be given that we all worked at a small private college in Texas. Gay and straight, black and white, young and old. It was one of the things I loved about sports: all the built-in diversity and intense bonding that came with having one huge thing in common. We really were like a tight-knit family, as Mrs Carr had always said. Although our patriarch had not yet arrived, Lucy was already working the room, with Neil at her side. Wearing a gorgeous coral pantsuit with several long strands of pearls, she glowed. Even her hair had been freshly highlighted with wide streaks of golden blond. She rushed over to give me a big hug. Her mood was infectious, and I instantly absolved her from her ensuing admission that she and Ryan were indeed in cahoots.

'I know you don't like surprises, but . . .'

'But what?' I said, smiling but trying to prove a point.

'But . . . sur-*prise*!' she said, high-fiving Ryan as if they'd just completed a tactical military invasion. Meanwhile, Coach Carr made his understated but still grand entrance, in a polo and khakis, strolling over to us just as Ryan headed to the makeshift bar to get me a glass of champagne.

'Hello, girls. You both look so pretty,' he said, reminding

me of how he talked to us when we were teenagers, before a dance or party.

'Hi, Daddy,' Lucy said, kissing her father's cheek.

'Hi, Coach,' I said, feeling the warmth of being near him, while doing my best to push away my recent unsettling epiphany. 'How was practice?'

'Other than the fact that our o-line is as useless as a screen door on a submarine?'

I burst out laughing, then recalled another recent colorful colloquialism slamming our linemen. 'Slightly less damning than being an ashtray on a motorcycle?'

He raised his brow and said, 'Maybe not. Least smoking on a bike won't kill you.'

I smiled as Ryan returned with two glasses of champagne. He handed me one, then gave Coach a hearty, manly hug and told him it was great to see him.

Coach smiled and said, 'You, too, son. Hell of a game last Monday night.'

'Yes, I heard you watched with Shea. And Miller,' Ryan said, with a calculated grimace.

Fortunately I had told Lucy about the odd Miller exchange with Ryan, so she was quick to defend me. 'Yeah. Shea said it was annoying the way he just showed up out of the blue and glommed on to her conversation with Daddy.'

I looked at her, thinking that hadn't been what I'd said at *all*, but I knew what she was doing and appreciated her effort on my behalf. I still felt compelled to throw Miller a bone, though. 'He means well,' I said, glancing at Coach, who nodded his agreement.

Ryan wasn't going to let it go so easily. 'He's a mess.'

Lucy nodded. '"Mess" is an understatement.'

I changed the subject back to football, as Coach covertly checked his watch, confirming my suspicion that he had only shown up to be nice and was biding his time until he could leave. Sure enough, about thirty minutes later, after we'd both drifted into different conversations, he found me again, tapped me on the shoulder, and said he really needed to go prep for the next game.

I nodded and told him I understood.

'I brought you a little something. It's in my car. Want to come out with me and grab it?' he asked.

'Okay,' I said, feeling happier than I should have.

'I meant to give you this thing the other night,' he said as we walked to the foyer. 'But then Miller showed up . . . and I forgot.'

I nodded, both of us falling silent as we walked outside, then over to his car. I stood in the grass, watching as he opened the passenger door, reached down on the floor, and grabbed a flat, rectangular package, wrapped in brown paper.

He handed it to me and said, 'Consider it a congratulations and good-luck gift rolled into one.'

Relieved that he hadn't called it a 'goodbye' gift, I took it from him and said, 'I don't know what to say . . . Thanks, Coach.'

'You're welcome, girl,' he said, his eyes switching on, becoming all twinkly. 'I'm real proud of you.' He bit his lower lip on the right side and said, 'Now go back in there and enjoy yourself. And don't let Ryan steal all your thunder.'

'Thanks, Coach,' I said again and very nearly hugged him.

I didn't, though, just stood there as he got in his car and drove away. Feeling light-headed, I went back inside, hoping nobody had missed me. But as I stowed the package in the foyer, Lucy emerged from the hall powder room, her quick mind processing every detail.

'Where were you? What's that?' she said, staring down at my gift.

'Outside,' I said. 'Your dad gave me something.'

'What did he give you?'

I shrugged and said I didn't know.

'Well, open it!'

'Later.'

'No. Now. I'm so curious to see what he came up with without my mother's help!'

Her delivery was straightforward, but I knew her well enough to know what she was thinking. That he had gone to a lot of trouble for me, just months after he had completely forgotten her birthday. I felt a guilty pang as she scooped up the package and walked back toward the party.

'Look, Neil!' she announced as everyone paused and watched her. 'My dad got Shea a present! Wasn't that sweet of him?'

Neil nodded and smiled, but something in his eyes confirmed my hunch. It was fleeting, but I could see the look of sympathy or consolation. I was suddenly sure that they had discussed my friendship with her dad – and equally certain that she had confessed her feelings of jealousy – or at least frustration that she and her father seemed to have such trouble connecting when it was so effortless for him and me.

Ryan and a half dozen other guests followed her over to the sofa, where she instructed me to sit and open it. My cheeks burned as I carefully peeled back the paper to reveal a matted and framed newspaper article. I recognized it immediately as the first full-length feature I had written for my high school newspaper, nearly twenty years ago. It was a rambling ode titled 'Why We Love Walker' along with a photo I had snapped myself of Coach Carr at practice, and another one of Walker's then quarterback, Adam Gipe, dropping back in the pocket, his arm cocked, ready for a bullet pass. Next to my byline, in a patch of white space, Coach Carr had scrawled with a Sharpie: *'We love you, too, girl. Knew you could do it! Coach C.'*

As everyone processed what it was, there was a chorus of oohs and aahs as J.J. seized the moment to hand me a teal fountain pen and a Walker lamp, both of which I recognized from the school store. 'This is from everyone here,' J.J. said, his voice turning formal. 'To thank you for two decades of diligent service.'

'Two decades?' I said. 'It hasn't been that long.'

J.J. reminded me of the volunteer work I had done as a kid, detailing some of the more mundane tasks. I smiled, as Roxann Moody, our equipment manager, cupped her hand around her mouth and yelled, 'Speech! Speech!'

Flanked by Lucy and Ryan, I bit the bullet and thanked everyone for coming, telling them how much I appreciated the gifts, then giving a special thanks to J.J. and Mary Ann, followed by a reminder that I'd still see everyone often. I closed by raising my glass and saying, 'Go Broncos.' Everyone clapped and whistled, and I thought I was in the clear. But then Ryan quieted the crowd again and said, 'I'd like to say something.'

I had no idea what he had up his sleeve, but I thought of what Coach had told me in the driveway. He definitely knew his former quarterback well. The room was absolutely silent, pure adoration on everyone's face as Ryan continued. 'I'd like to thank J.J. and Mary Ann as well for including me tonight,' he said, expertly pausing. 'As always, it's great to be back home, especially now that I'm with Shea. I just wanted to thank her for being the girl she is. And all of you for being so good to her. It makes me proud as hell to be a Bronco.'

Everyone swooned while I sweated, fanning myself with my hand, making desperate eye contact with Lucy, who knew exactly what I was thinking. *Make it all end.* Then, just when I thought it couldn't get more uncomfortable, Ryan reached into his pocket and handed me a small wrapped box.

'Open it!' Lucy demanded, and I knew there was no stopping the tide now, so I tore off the wrapping paper as quickly as I could, discovering a gray velvet box, the kind that houses expensive jewelry. Holding my breath, I opened the hinged lid, the room now completely silent as we all gazed down at two huge sparkling diamond studs.

'Congratulations, Shea,' he said, a cue for feverish applause and a few whistles.

'Holy shit,' Lucy gasped.

'These are . . . way too much,' I said to Ryan.

He shook his head. 'No. They're not.'

'Put them on,' Lucy said.

I froze. All I wanted to do was give them back to Ryan, but I knew that wasn't an option, at least not now, so I took off my ordinary gold hoops and replaced them with the only real diamonds I'd ever owned.

Speechless, I looked at Ryan and shook my head, while everyone kept grinning and gawking. At me, at him, at the huge rocks now adorning my lobes. I made myself smile, trying to piece together how this had happened, how we got to this so fast, from sex to jealousy to diamonds.

I reached up to touch one of the stones, almost hoping that they weren't real. Or maybe they were real, but Ryan was so wealthy that it was like a regular guy giving a girl flowers. Then again, maybe things really were getting serious.

Whatever was happening, I had no idea what to say or how to act or, most important, how to extricate myself from the spotlight. So I just kept my eyes down, staring at Coach's framed article lying on the coffee table, and his sloppy, half-printed, half-cursive message: *We love you, too, girl.*

That night, I tried to give back the earrings. Ryan refused, then got agitated. 'They were a gift,' he said. 'Do you always try to return gifts?'

'They're too expensive,' I said for the third time.

'Not for me,' he said. 'I can afford them.'

'But—'

He cut me off with a kiss and said, 'Seriously, Shea. You're going to piss me off if you keep this up. I bought them for you. I *want* you to have them. Now shut up.'

'Okay,' I said, nodding and kissing him back. Then I pulled my hair into a makeshift bun, turning my head from side to side. 'How do they look?'

'Gorgeous,' he said. 'Like you.'

'So are we really together . . . like this?' I blurted out.

'Like what?'

'Like diamond-stud-earring together?'

He laughed and said, 'It's looking that way, yeah.'

'Don't you think it feels . . . fast?' I said.

'Yeah. A little,' he said, which made me feel better. At least he wasn't pretending that this pace was normal. 'But if you think about it – we've known each other forever. It's not like we just met . . .'

'That's true,' I said.

'And I'm very decisive. I know what I want.'

I smiled. 'And what's that?'

'You, baby,' he said, leaning down to kiss me.

I kissed him back, feeling like the luckiest girl in the world.

18

The following Monday, two days after a decisive win over Arkansas, I began my job as a sports reporter. Smiley didn't give me a start time, but I left my apartment at six in the morning so that I could beat rush-hour traffic and arrive at the Bank of America Plaza in Dallas by seven. His assistant, an older lady channeling the sixties with her teased hair and cat-eye glasses, met me in the lobby and humorlessly escorted me to his office.

'Good morning, Ms. Rigsby,' Smiley said, glancing up from a completed *New York Times* crossword. His office reeked of cigars, though there was no sign of ashtrays or smoke. There was, however, a half-empty bottle of scotch on the corner of his desk.

'Good morning,' I said.

Smiley cleared his throat, as if on the brink of issuing a proper welcome, but thought better of it. 'C'mon. I'll show you around,' he said instead.

He then embarked on a tour of the newsroom, consisting mostly of a maze of cubicles under drab fluorescent lighting. Smiley made a few introductions in what he referred to as the 'sports corner' of the floor, but only when he absolutely couldn't avoid it, often omitting the names of his colleagues while making me sound as uninteresting and green as he possibly could. 'This is Shea Rigsby. Kenny Stone's replacement. She comes from sports information at Walker, but contends she can be objective,' he said once, mumbling a footnote: 'We'll see about that.'

He pointed out the assignment desk, where two phones were currently manned, explaining that it was a command center where various leads were phoned in on hard news stories. 'Doesn't really apply to us,' he said. 'Our stories aren't generally a surprise. Although these days you never know what athletes are going to do . . . If someone shoots his girlfriend or tortures dogs, it'll be phoned in right there.'

I nodded as we stuck our heads into a bare-bones break room with a microwave and refrigerator, then an even more dismal room housing a watercooler and a copier adorned with a sign that said: ANOTHER DAMN PAPER JAM. He concluded our tour with my very own cubicle, located just outside his office. Lucky me. The whole floor was much quieter and less glamorous than I'd imagined, and I felt a dash of disappointment as I reminded myself that this wasn't the Woodward and Bernstein era of journalism and most writers probably worked from home.

'So that's it,' he said curtly. 'Any questions?'

I shook my head.

'Okay, then. Your first assignment. We need a pregame piece on the Walker–Baylor matchup. Give me eight hundred, not a word more because space is tight. Damn advertisers,' he grumbled. 'As for angles – maybe focus on the running back situation. Maybe look at the rash of injuries that squad has suffered . . . Find out if any of the assistant coaches hate each other. And I need it by eight A.M. tomorrow. Not a minute later.'

Before I could so much as nod, Smiley turned and headed for his office as the guy one cubicle over glanced my way and said, 'And you caught him on a good day.'

I smiled, and he reached over the partition and shook my hand. 'Gordon Chambers.'

'Shea Rigsby,' I said, feeling an instant rapport with this new colleague, as much for his comment as for his face. Everything about it was warm – from his honey-brown skin, to his full lips, to the dimples in his rounded cheeks that remained even when he stopped smiling. 'What's your beat?'

'Dallas Cowboys.'

I must have looked impressed because he said, 'The low man on that totem pole. I do social media. Smiley's necessary

evil. And I cover injuries. Pulled hamstrings? I'm your guy.'
His grin grew wider, his dimples deeper.

I smiled, wondering if he had ever talked to Ryan, as I put
down my bag, then did a cursory exploration of my cubicle. I
opened and closed a few drawers cluttered with stray rubber
bands, paper clips, and a package of saltines that another reporter
had left behind. Then I adjusted my chair, and inspected the
ancient desktop computer, trying to figure out how to power it
on.

'I wouldn't bother with that piece of shit,' Gordon said as
I noticed that he was typing on a big silver Mac.

'Right,' I said, fishing my laptop out of my bag and plugging
it in, then staring at my ESPN home screen for a few shell-
shocked seconds, wondering where to begin.

'Wow. You better get off that page before Smiley sees it,'
Gordon said as he passed by my cubicle with his empty coffee
mug. 'Don't you know that's the network that puts entertainment ahead of sports? Get it? *ESPN*.'

'Right. Thanks,' I said, shutting down the browser, then
pulling up a blank document and typing *Baylor–Walker* at the
top of the screen. It was an inauspicious start to say the least,
especially when coupled with the utter blankness in my brain.
It was as if I'd never read a pregame piece in my life. The
escalating din around me didn't do much to quell my nerves,
as the few writers on the news end of the floor seemed to be
typing away with great caffeinated efficiency, but I took a few
deep breaths and told myself that they probably weren't penning
Pulitzers. They were just diligently doing their job, covering
mundane events – funerals and fires and fairs. Or, in our corner
of the sports cube farm, pulled hamstrings. With that in mind,
I took another deep breath, then went to Baylor's official athletic
site, clicked on the football tab, and got to work. *Just write
what you know,* I told myself. *You were born to do this job.*

The day passed quickly, but, by two o'clock, I had yet to eat
lunch and had written only four sentences, none of them keepers.

The only really productive thing I did, other than fill out a bunch of forms for human resources, was schedule a phone interview with the Baylor sports information director for that evening. I had also brainstormed a few basic questions to ask him, which was pretty easy to do given the number of times I had heard J.J. on the receiving end of such interviews. Meanwhile, I eavesdropped on Smiley lecturing Gordon for overusing adverbs and, apparently an even greater transgression, synonyms for *said*.

'He *said*, she *said*, they *said*,' Smiley shouted, socking one fist into the other open palm. 'That's the only attribution you should use in here. Keep it invisible. We want to hear what the guy said, not *how* he said it. Should I hang a sign in your cubicle?'

I couldn't hear Gordon's reply, only Smiley droning on. 'So I don't want to hear your sources comment, claim, assert, suggest, state, disclose, imply, admit, concur, argue, or remark. And they sure as hell better not guffaw, chuckle, or chortle either.'

As he dismissed Gordon, he caught me looking at him and barked, 'Did you get that, Rigsby?'

I nodded, resisting the urge to tell him that I heard what he *said*.

Later that afternoon, I headed back to Walker for football practice. It was like high school all over again, with Coach granting me access that he didn't give other reporters. I caught him afterward, as he was walking back up to the football complex, and asked if had a few minutes to talk about the Baylor game. He glanced at his watch and said he needed to get home to meet his handyman, something about a problem gutter, but could talk later.

'When's a good time?' I said.

'For you? Anytime,' he said, patting my shoulder.

Around eight o'clock that evening, I worked up the nerve to send him a tentative text: *Is now a good time to chat?*

He wrote back: *Not alone. Can you text me the questions?*

Okay, I typed, then specified that we were on the record before asking him to confirm our starting backfield.

He texted back: *They can all play. Who do YOU think I should start?*

I laughed, then typed: *Ha. If I pick your lineup, will you write my piece?*

I stared at my phone, waiting, knowing that he was a slow one-finger typist: *I don't think your readers would appreciate my third-grade writing style.*

I smiled and wrote: *Don't try to play the dumb jock with me. I know better.*

And the conversation continued from there, the screen filling with our banter:

CCC: *Really. And what else do you know?*

Me: *I know you're sitting in that big armchair, with the TV on mute.*

CCC: *Ha. You got me.*

Me: *Probably with a Shiner Bock on your drink stand next to the remote.*

CCC: *Where's the hidden camera? How many fingers am I holding up?*

Me: *One. As in: number one. Which is how we'll finish the year.*

CCC: *You give me way too much credit. Always have.*

Me: *Nope. Not possible. But back to the story. What do you think of Lache?*

CCC: *That kid can run like small-town gossip.*

Me: *Can I quote you on that?*

CCC: *Yes.*

Me: *What else can I quote you on?*

CCC: *Tell 'em it's going to be a flesh-on-flesh, in-the-trench battle.*

Me: *And your strategy?*

CCC: *Hold on to the ball and score more points than they do.*

Me: *Sounds simple enough.*

CCC: *Yes. But don't be fooled. The best things in life only seem simple.*

I smiled down at my phone, thinking just how true that was.

★   ★   ★

The next morning, at 7:58, I filed my first story with *The Dallas Post.* Twenty minutes later, Smiley stormed over to my cubicle, barking at me to call it up on my screen. I did as I was told, discovering that he – or someone at the copydesk – had already heavily edited the piece.

'Not awful,' he said, which felt like high praise. 'But you need to tighten it up, lose some of that flowery description, and cut down on the quotes. I get it. They're down a lot of men. Say it once.' He pointed over my shoulder as I tried to follow all the electronic changes made in red in the margins.

I nodded and said I understood.

Then, as if he knew how long the first draft had taken me, he added, 'And I need it back ASAP. Ten minutes ago.'

As he returned to his office, I noticed that the only sentence without a single edit was my lead, lifted directly from my cell-phone: *According to Walker University's Coach Clive Carr, Saturday's contest against Baylor is going to be 'a flesh-on-flesh, in-the-trench battle.'*

Later that day, after I had refiled my first story and worked on the next, I met Lucy at the practice field, like old times. She brought us gourmet sandwiches from her favorite deli, and we sat in the bleachers, talking and watching practice. At least *I* was watching practice, while she did most of the talking.

'How's Ryan?' Lucy asked as she handed me half of a portobello mushroom, mozzarella, and red pepper sandwich. It was her favorite topic these days, and I was happy to give her a good report.

'He's great,' I said, watching a weak-shoulder run drill in progress. Coach was holding a shield at the fifteen-yard line, while his running backs lined up across from him and pressed his outside shoulder to get back up the field. Somehow he managed to look sexy in the process, right down to the way he blew his whistle and bellowed instructions, his voice a little hoarse. I looked away from the field, back at Lucy, telling myself to get a grip. Stop looking at her father like *that*.

'Could I get a little more than "great"?' Lucy said.

I smiled, thinking that my vague answer was the kind I'd hate if I were doing the interview, and said, 'I'm staying over a lot lately. It really is convenient to work.'

'The ol' convenience factor, huh? That's the best you can say about it?'

I laughed and said, 'Um. I can also say I *love* his house.'

'So, proximity to work and luxurious accommodations? Sounds like the perfect relationship.'

I took a sip of Snapple lemonade and said, 'What do you want me to say?'

'I want you to say that you're in love.'

I gave her a close-lipped smile and shook my head.

'Headed in that direction? Falling ever so slightly?'

'Maybe,' I said, reaching up to touch one of my diamond earrings as Coach blew his whistle then asked Barry Canty if he planned on breaking a sweat anytime soon.

I laughed.

Lucy looked at me and said, 'What?'

'Your dad,' I said. 'He's so funny.'

'Oh. Yeah.' She put down her sandwich and said, 'So. I want to talk to you about something else.' I knew the look on her face. Something was wrong.

'What?' I said, a knot of worry in my chest.

'It's about Daddy. I think he might be seeing someone.'

My stomach dropped as I asked her why she thought that, picturing an attractive lady, in her mid-forties, perhaps a widow.

'Because I was over at his house, and he was on his phone. Texting someone,' she said, as Coach transitioned the backs into a pass protection drill.

'When?' I said.

'Last night,' she said. 'Around eight.'

I felt a rush of relief, then guilt, knowing that he was texting me – and made the split-second decision not to tell her.

'It was weird,' she continued. 'I asked who he was talking to and he said nobody. I mean, *nobody*?'

'Maybe he was surfing the Net?' I said, hating myself for lying to my best friend and confused about why I was doing it. We'd been doing an interview; it was all legit.

'No. He was definitely texting. I saw his screen. And when I tried to look over his shoulder, he flipped it over.'

'Maybe he was texting his coaches,' I said, biting my lower lip. 'You know, top secret stuff about the game.'

She gave me a look. 'Top secret stuff? He's a *coach*, not an FBI agent.'

Having run out of all plausible explanations – other than the truth – I shrugged.

'Do you think he could be seeing someone?' she asked.

I said no, then asked, 'How would you feel if he were?'

'Are you serious?' she asked, as if it were the most ridiculous question in the world.

'I mean – I know you'd be upset, but would you be . . . mad?'

She sighed, putting her sandwich down. 'Well, how could I be mad?'

'You just could,' I said, thinking that the fact that she *shouldn't* be angry had never stopped Lucy before. On any topic. It was amazing how different we were – yet how much we still loved each other.

'Well, no, I don't think I would be *mad*. But I think he should wait at least a year before he even *thinks* about talking to another woman. Isn't that the rule?'

I shrugged, thinking of Mrs Carr. How she had little rules for everything. *No linen or seersucker after Labor Day. Never be early to depart a party, but good heavens, don't be the last to leave. Gift registries are gauche and so is writing 'no gifts, please' on an invitation.* And my favorite – *manners trump etiquette.* In other words, you shouldn't put your elbows on the table, but it is far worse to point it out.

'I don't think there's a rule about this, Luce . . . I think it depends on a lot of things . . .' I said, my voice trailing off.

'I know. And I really want him to be happy,' she said. 'But,

God, I don't know if I could bear it . . . Do you know someone recently asked me about *your* mother?'

'What about her?' I said.

'Whether I thought she and my dad would get together. You don't think she'd ever be interested in him, do you?' Lucy asked.

'No,' I said as quickly as possible.

'Out of respect for my mom?'

I shook my head and said, 'I just can't see them together. He'd never go for her. And she likes the slick, suit-and-tie type. Speaking of which,' I said, trying to change the subject, 'my dad's coming down for Thanksgiving.'

'Solo?'

'Of course not. He's bringing Bronwyn and Ass Face,' I said, my nickname for Astrid.

Lucy laughed. 'Did you tell them about Ryan yet?'

'Not yet. And I must confess, I can't wait,' I said, smiling.

'Yeah. That will be so satisfying,' Lucy said.

I looked down the field at Coach, as he blew his whistle and shouted, 'Dammit, Sanders! If I tell you a duck can pull a truck, then shut up and hook the sucker up.'

I laughed and wrote the quote down. I knew I probably wouldn't use it, and certainly not without Coach's okay, but I still wanted a record of it to read later, along with our texts that I had yet to delete.

19

In a game that was even more ugly than the one Coach predicted, we barely escaped with a win in Waco, beating Baylor 21–20. Other than the final score, pretty much everything went wrong for us. We dropped the ball, missed field goals, and got a lot of stupid penalties. I knew from experience that Coach was going to be terse in the press conference, more frustrated with his team for their mental lapses and lack of discipline than happy to come away with a victory.

Sure enough, he came out surly, barking at reporters and barely acknowledging me when I raised my hand. Instead of calling my name, he simply pointed at me and said, 'Yep. Question right there.'

'Coach Carr,' I began nervously, 'what did you see in the play where Rhodes fumbled? At the end of the first half?'

'What did I see?' He squinted, as if confused, then replied, 'I saw the official call a fumble. That's what I saw.' His voice was gravelly from yelling over fifty thousand fans – and probably at his team afterward.

I felt my face turn red but pressed on. 'Have you seen the replay? It looked very close as to whether he was down or not.'

'Yeah. I saw the replay.'

'And? Do you think the right call was made?' I asked, flustered, not able to articulate what I really wanted to know – which was how he felt about his team collapsing after such a pivotal call.

'It was the official's call. And, as you well know, I had already used my challenge on an earlier play. So. They ruled it a turnover, and that was that. It really doesn't make any difference what I think.'

I looked at him, thinking it made *every* difference what he thought about that call, the game, and everything else, too. He stared back at me, waiting, as I forced myself to ask one final question. 'Do you think that changed the tide of the game for . . .' In the nick of time, I stopped myself from saying 'us' and finished the sentence with 'you.'

Coach crossed his arms and heaved a weary sigh. 'There were a lot of plays in this football game. A lot of things we could have done better. Bottom line, we were lucky to get a win. *Damn* lucky. Okay. That's all.'

He got up abruptly and, without another word, walked off the platform and out the side door, back to the visitors' locker room.

That night, I was in a mood as foul as Coach Carr's and ignored the phone when it rang, not picking up for Lucy, or for Ryan, who was at the Four Seasons in St. Louis, preparing for the Rams game tomorrow. The only person I wanted to talk to was Coach, but I didn't dare call him, knowing the last thing he wanted to do was hear from a reporter who asked him annoying questions. At some point, though, after I had filed my story, I broke down and decided one little text wouldn't hurt. After drafting and deleting at least a dozen versions, I wrote: *Sorry about the game and also for the dumb question.*

I didn't expect to hear back from him at all, and certainly not right away, but he replied almost instantaneously: *It's ok. I'm sorry for snapping at you.*

Then, before I could respond, the phone rang. It was him. Shocked, I fumbled it Rhodes-style, then scrambled to scoop it up and answer before it went to voice mail.

'Hey,' Coach said. 'How are you?'

'Probably the same as you,' I said, though my frustration over the game was suddenly supplanted by relief that he wasn't angry at *me*.

'That was one hell of a hollow win,' Coach said.

'It was still a win,' I said.

Coach made a disgusted sound, then said, 'I'd rather play well and lose.'

I wasn't sure if I believed him, and I know I didn't subscribe to the notion, especially during a year like this one, but I still murmured my agreement, adding, 'That *was* a terrible call, though.'

'Even shittier on the replay. That ref is a joke. And yes, to answer your question, I think that was a game changer. It definitely changed things for those boys. Got in their heads. We do that against a better team, and we're done for.'

'Yeah,' I said, letting him vent.

'Beyond the painfully obvious fact that we couldn't establish our run,' he said, 'we just missed a lot of opportunities. What were we in the red zone?'

'O for three.'

'You can't win many football games when you're O for three in the red zone.'

I murmured in agreement, surprised that Coach was discussing the game with me, when he typically didn't even talk to his staff immediately after poor performances.

'So what are you doing?' he asked suddenly.

'Right now?' I asked.

'Yeah. Now.'

'Nothing. Why? What are you doing?' I asked, wondering why I was so nervous.

'About to go for a run,' he said.

'At eight-thirty?'

'If that's what time it is . . . then yes. Wanna join me?'

Stunned by the invite, I said okay, my heart beginning to race.

'Good enough. Meet you at the track over at school in fifteen?'

'Okay,' I said again, marveling that I could feel this good, this *happy*, so soon after a bad game.

Fifteen minutes later, I pulled into the lot closest to the track, adjacent to the tennis courts and our original field house. I was wearing gray sweats, a standard issue from the equipment room, and an ancient Walker baseball cap, my long ponytail threaded through the back. A pale light shone on the track, a mix of moonlight and halogen, but a fog had rolled in, and at first I didn't see the lone figure stretching near a high stack of pole-vault mats. It was Coach, and my heart stopped for a second as I stood at the top of the brick staircase and watched him. When I finally descended the steps toward the entrance, he looked up through a curtain of mist and gave me a half wave, half salute. I took a few deep breaths, trying to calm myself down as I entered the security code and unlatched the squeaky metal gate. Then I slowly crossed the spongy red track, walking onto the turf. I stopped a few yards away from Coach, overcome with a rush of pure joy. We were completely alone on a beautiful night, and I simply couldn't imagine anything more exhilarating.

'Hi, girl,' he said, giving me a half smile.

'Hi, Coach,' I said, wishing I could read his mind. There was no way to tell what he was thinking, his face expressionless.

'Little chilly,' he said, pulling the drawstring on his gray sweatshirt, a hooded version of mine.

'I know. I like it,' I said, nervously bending over to tighten my laces.

'Me, too,' he said, lightly jogging in place and stretching.

'Do you always run after games?' I asked, thinking it was easier to speak when he wasn't looking at me.

'When we play like shit,' he said, sitting down to stretch more thoroughly.

I nodded, watching him.

'So did you get your story in?' he said, glancing up at me.

'Yeah,' I said.

'And?'

I wasn't sure what he was asking so I said, 'And . . . it's done.'

'You happy with it?'

'As happy as I can be when I'm writing about a game . . . like that one,' I said.

Coach nodded, only his eyes smiling at me. 'Don't you need to stretch?'

I shrugged and reluctantly sat next to him, spreading my legs in a V-shape, imitating his form. I touched my toes a couple of times in a jerking, bouncing motion – the way they always tell you not to stretch – then stood up, murmuring that I was good to go.

'Youth,' Coach said. 'If I stretched like that, I'd tear something.'

'We're only, like, twenty years apart,' I said, feeling myself tense inside.

'*Only* twenty? That's not the best reference tonight.'

I looked at him, confused, then remembered that was how many points our defense gave up.

'Oops,' I said. I waited for him to smile, and, when he did, I followed suit, as we walked a few steps over to the track, then began a slow counterclockwise jog. Coach started out on the inside but then moved to my right shoulder, two lanes over from me. The adjustment felt chivalrous, almost romantic, but I told myself to stop thinking such crazy, delusional thoughts. He probably just preferred an outside lane.

After one straightaway and two curves of the track, not quite a quarter-mile warm-up, I was already sucking wind, my thighs burning. Coach clearly was in better shape than I was, and I vowed to start hitting the gym with some regularity. You'd think dating a professional football player would have motivated me, but there was actually something about Ryan's ridiculous physique that made me want to blow it off altogether. Running with Coach was a different matter.

After another couple of silent laps, Coach said, 'Warmed up? Ready to go?'

'Yeah. Sure,' I said as he opened up his stride. Struggling to keep up with him, I said, 'Damn. You're fast. What's your mile pace?'

'When I'm tired?' he said. 'Because that's the real question. Not your personal best, but how fast you can go when you're tired. Down and out.'

'Are you tired now?' I gasped.

Coach shook his head. 'Nope. But I *am* down and out,' he said. I caught him smiling again, and it occurred to me that I was making him feel better, at least a little. I felt emboldened by that notion, enough to increase my speed, hang in there with him.

We fell silent after that, as I lost track of our laps. But somewhere around the three-mile mark, he turned to me and, breathing hard, asked, 'So how's Ryan?'

Ryan was the last thing I wanted to think about now, and I was too winded for a long answer anyway, so I just panted, 'He's fine. Rams tomorrow.'

'Heard about the earrings,' he said, glancing at my ears, although I wasn't wearing them now.

'Yeah,' I said, rubbing my left side where a cramp was beginning to form. 'I tried to give them back . . . but—'

'I'm sure that didn't go over,' Coach said, slowing a bit.

'No. He acted like they were a little something out of a gumball machine.'

Coach laughed, then stopped running altogether, leaning down to grab on to his knees. 'Yeah,' he panted. 'That boy's so rich he buys a new boat when he gets the other one wet.'

I laughed, making my cramp worse. I felt a little guilty, talking about Ryan behind his back, but told myself that it wasn't disloyal given that Coach cared about him as much as I did.

'Please tell me we're done,' I said, wincing.

'Yeah. We're done,' he said.

After walking another half a lap in silence, we walked through the gate, then up the staircase to the parking lot.

Only when we reached our cars did he finally speak. 'Well, thank you, Shea. I feel better now.'

'Thank *you*, Coach,' I said, feeling light-headed even before I met his gaze. 'That was . . . nice.'

'Yes. It was,' he said, our eyes still locked. He gave me a slow smile, and I could tell he was talking about my company as much as the running.

I hesitated, overcoming another small wave of guilt over Ryan, telling myself that my attraction to Coach would never be reciprocated. It was safe, feeling this way about something that was never going to happen. Frustrating, and a little sad, but also very safe. I looked back down at the ground and said, 'I hope we can do it again.'

'Didn't I tell you I only come out here and run when we play like shit?' he said.

'Oh, yeah,' I said. 'Well, then I hope we *never* do it again.'

'Me, too,' Coach said. 'And you'll be happy to know . . .'

'What?'

'That I eat chocolate cake after we play well.' He gave me a little wink.

'Excellent,' I said. 'Because I'm not much of a runner. But I'm *really* good at eating cake.'

20

The week leading up to the LSU game, Smiley gave me my first feature assignment: a three-thousand-word piece on Reggie Rhodes. He gave me very little guidance, just told me he wanted 'a lot of flavor on the guy.' His background. His adjustment to the college game. All the hype and whether or not he was living up to it. I breathed a sigh of relief when he ended the meeting abruptly, with no mention of any recruiting violation rumors. I was starting to think that Walker might be out of the woods and I, as a reporter, off the hook. Of course, I'd subscribed to the don't-ask, don't-tell philosophy, intentionally avoiding the subject with anyone at Walker.

When I called J.J. to ask for access to Reggie, the two of us danced around the obvious, focusing only on one fact: that I was the first reporter to get the plum interview, the only one Coach trusted to interview his young star in anything other than a postgame press conference.

For two days, I prepared for my conversation with Reggie, reaching out to various people from his life. I talked to his high school coach and principal, his parents, and, of course, Coach. Everyone said variations of the same thing. That Reggie was a rarity. A superstar without Twitter. Tim Tebow without all the ostentatious religion. A good kid. The real deal.

On Tuesday night, I met Reggie at the plush academic counseling center as his tutor wrapped up an American lit session.

'Hey, Miss Rigsby,' he said, standing to shake my hand. He had a soft voice and a friendly gap between his front teeth.

'Hi, Reggie,' I said, surprised that he remembered me,

although we'd talked a few times during my old job. 'What are you working on?' I pointed down at his notebook.

'*Huckleberry Finn*,' he said, smiling as he shut his books and slid them into a nylon messenger bag at his feet.

'You like it?' I said.

'The CliffsNotes are real good,' he said, nodding seriously before breaking into a big grin. 'Nah. I'm just playin'. I do like it. We were just discussing that scene where Huck plays the trick on Jim with the leaves on the raft. You know, making him think he was dreaming everything?'

I nodded although I only vaguely recalled the scene.

'And then Jim says that part about how trash is what people are who put dirt on the heads of their friends and make them feel ashamed?' Reggie shook his head. 'And then Huck works himself up to go apologize, humble himself to a . . . excuse my language . . . nigger?'

I flinched, hearing the vile word spoken aloud, but was able to maintain eye contact, transfixed by Reggie's take on the scene and impressed by his ability to engage an adult, talk about literature instead of himself. I nodded, waiting for him to continue.

He whistled and said, '*Man*. That's some powerful stuff right there. Powerful. You can see how Twain humanizes Jim. It's *so* good.'

I smiled, thinking that we were just a few minutes in and I could understand why everyone liked Reggie. He was so easy to talk to – and so humble.

'So,' I said. 'Can we talk about you for a bit? Your experience so far at Walker?'

He nodded and said sure.

'Let's start with why you chose to come to college here. You had a lot of choices . . . So why Walker?'

His face became somber as he gave me the answer that I wanted. 'I came to Walker for a lot of reasons. The education. How nice everyone was to me. How pretty the campus is. All that stuff . . . But I ain't gonna lie, I mostly came to Walker so I could play for Coach Carr. He's the *man*. Always keeps it a hundred percent real. For me, it really came down to that, ya know?'

'Yes,' I said. 'I know.'

The day after my interview with Rhodes, as I was putting the finishing touches on the story, Smiley called me into his office. I was all jazzed up, on the verge of telling him about all the great stuff I got, when he gave me a long, accusatory look. Then he whipped off his reading glasses, tossed them onto his desk, and said, 'Have you heard anything about Walker being in trouble with the NCAA?'

I opened my mouth, choosing my words carefully. 'I've heard . . . rumblings.'

'Rumblings?' Smiley demanded, slapping his desk. 'Define *rumblings*.'

'You know . . . rumors.'

'Rumors from rednecks at your local bar or rumors from the inside down there at Walker?'

'Um. Both, I guess,' I hedged.

'And? You didn't think that was something to discuss with your editor?' Smiley was now shouting, and I could see beads of sweat on his upper lip.

'I guess I should have,' I said, looking down at my lap.

Smiley nodded, now pacing. He was hot. Hotter than I'd ever seen him. 'Yes. You should have. Your ass should have been all over that story. And you better hope that we run something on it before anyone else does!'

'Yes, sir,' I said, deflated, and a little worried about my job. 'I mean – I have, sort of, stayed on top of it . . .'

'And? What's the status?'

'Well . . . I'm not sure *exactly*.'

'You're not *sure*?' he said, rolling up one sleeve. 'That's your definition of "staying on top of it"?'

'Not ordinarily. No, sir. You're right—'

Smiley cut me off. 'Who have you talked to? What sources have you lined up?'

'Well. I've, um,' I stuttered. 'I've talked to our enforcement guy. Ernie Galli.'

'*Our?*' Smiley roared, rolling up his other sleeve.

'Walker's,' I said, correcting myself. 'I meant Walker's . . .'

'Look, Shea. We need a story,' he fumed. 'Because this *is* a story. You have twenty-four hours to get me something. Got it?'

I nodded briskly and said I'd get right on it, as if it was the easiest thing in the world to report bad news about *my* school. I walked out of his office, remembering something Coach Carr said to me a long time ago. It was in the context of another school, a different set of problems, but I never forgot it. 'When the local media turns its guns on you,' he had said, 'you're toast.'

Some of my earliest and most vivid college football memories have nothing to do with loving Walker or hating Texas but with being mesmerized by the scandal of the highest order at SMU, my introduction to the corruption in the sport I loved. I was still in diapers when Eric Dickerson and Craig James, a.k.a. the Pony Express, galloped onto the scene, becoming one of the most prolific backfields in history. And I certainly was too young to remember Ron Meyer, with his long sideburns and slick suits, in anything other than old footage. But by the time Lucy and I were in the first grade, I was paying attention, and it was absolutely clear to me that the Mustangs were in trouble. *Big* trouble. It was all grown-ups seemed to talk about, whether at neighborhood block parties, or the country club, or church. I didn't fully grasp the ins and outs of NCAA rules and regulations, but I knew they were big-time cheaters. During one of Coach Carr's first tutorials on the subject, he likened SMU's brazen rule breaking to Lawton playing banker in Monopoly and stealing the orange five-hundred-dollar bills, willy-nilly. He explained that there were wealthy boosters involved, the kind who swaggered around in mink cowboy hats, bragging about Saturday's game as if they had played in it themselves, and giving players loads of cash to play for their school. I heard the outlandish stories about the cars and jewelry, livestock and *houses,* that these men, known as the Naughty Nine, bought for players and their families. Coach shook his head and said things about SMU such as 'They're the best team money can buy' and 'They have no shame.'

Then, just three days after my seventh birthday, on February 25, 1987, the hammer fell. I was home sick from school, or at least I was pretending to be sick so I could watch the televised press conference. David Berst, the director of enforcement of the NCAA, announced that SMU was guilty under the 'repeat violator' provision and would get the most severe punishment allowed. The *death* penalty. No scholarships, no practice, no games for a whole *year*. The entire program shut down. Even though everyone knew they were guilty as hell, it was still shocking. So shocking that Berst himself fainted right on television.

Later that night, I heard Coach Carr tell my dad, who was in town visiting me, 'We shouldn't be so surprised. Everyone knows . . . we *do* execute people in this state. If you ask me, it's a lot easier to follow the rules.' My dad, of course, replied something along the lines of 'Yeah. If you're going to cheat, you better be damn good at it.'

Now fast-forward twenty-six years, and Walker was in possible trouble. Not of the SMU magnitude, but trouble nonetheless. And in an unsettling twist of fate, I was no longer watching it on television. Rather, it was *my* job to report it. My job to write a story that could, potentially, damage Walker football. I told myself that it would all be fine. Because Coach Carr was still the good man he'd always been.

That evening, after talking to J.J. and Galli, I went over to Ryan's and told him about the NCAA story Smiley was making me write.

'Do you think there is any truth to it?' I asked him, after filling him in on everything.

'Probably,' Ryan said, hitting a golf ball across a putting green in his basement. 'Where there's smoke, there's fire.'

'What's that supposed to mean?' I said, taken aback by his answer.

'I mean . . . if you're consistently winning at this level, you're probably cheating along the line somewhere,' Ryan said. 'And even if you're losing, and you're trying to win, you're probably still cheating. At least on the margins.'

'Coach Carr does *not* cheat,' I said. A statement of absolute fact.

Ryan gave me an infuriating smirk, then knocked the ball into the hole. 'Okay, then.'

'He doesn't,' I said, a little pissed off.

He shrugged, then squared his shoulders for another shot. 'I know you think he's the second coming of Christ, but the man isn't perfect. He may not be bankrolling his players, but I'm pretty sure he looks the other way now and then. He has to.'

'No, he doesn't.'

'Sure he does! He's the CEO of a major corporation and his employees are a bunch of dumb kids. He *has* to look the other way. It's a matter of survival.'

'Give me one example,' I said. 'Of Coach looking the other way.'

'Okay. Do you remember Cedric Washington's Cadillac Escalade?' Ryan asked.

'Yes. No. Not really. But whatever. Go on,' I said. Cedric had been a wide receiver during our era, a year behind Ryan, and almost as heralded, leaving school a year early to enter the draft.

'Ever wonder how he got a truck that nice? With tinted windows, spinning rims, that booming bass sound system playing Dr Dre all over town?'

'No,' I said. 'Never gave it a thought.'

'Well, you're the only one . . . There's no *way* Cedric could afford a truck like that. C'mon. He was from the *projects.*'

'Okay,' I said, giving Ryan a blank stare.

'Okay? Well. Someone gave him that thing. And it wasn't anyone in his family. And guess what? Coach looked the other way. He ignored it. Willed it to go away. And it did.' He snapped his fingers. 'Just like that. That's what winners do. They make things go down like they want them to go down.'

'Is that what *you* do, Ryan?' I said. I was pissed and felt myself start to lash out at him. 'You're a big-time quarterback. Do you cheat?'

He leaned his putter against the wall and cracked his knuckles. 'No. I don't, actually.'

'So if you could steal another team's signals and not get caught . . .?'

'You mean like Tom Brady filming the Jets?'

'Yeah. Like that.'

'Or *Greg* Brady stealing the playbook?' He laughed. 'Did you ever see that episode?'

I smiled in spite of myself. 'Of course. I've seen every *Brady Bunch* episode. And it was Jerry Rogers who tried to steal the playbook from Greg. Greg would never do something like that. Now answer the question.'

'I did answer it. I said no. I don't cheat because I don't need to cheat. I'm *that* good. But if I had to . . .'

'Have you ever cheated on a girlfriend?' I pressed, now looking for any excuse to be mad at him.

He cracked the knuckles on his other hand and looked me right in the eye. 'Never,' he said.

It seemed impossible, given the opportunities he must have had over the years, but he didn't flinch or even blink.

'Okay,' I said, deciding to believe him.

'Look, Shea. All I'm saying is – sometimes you just gotta do what you gotta do.' He picked up his club and knocked in another easy putt.

The next morning, and another few phone calls later, including one to the NCAA, I emailed Smiley my measly three-hundred-word story, relieved that there were no smoking guns, only a couple of quotes, including one from a not very credible UT insider. In other words, it was the best I could have hoped for when I started poking around.

NCAA PROBES BRONCOS
BY SHEA RIGSBY

Walker University's football program is officially under NCAA investigation, having received a notice of inquiry in late July, says a source with knowledge of the case. The specific nature of the alleged violations was not disclosed, but one source, speaking on the condition of anonymity, described the transgressions as 'mostly minor but potentially more major and wide-ranging in nature,' including concerns about several past and current players' eligibility and academic misconduct, as well as 'extra benefits and possible recruiting violations.' Another source close to the University of Texas athletic department specifically named Walker freshman running back Reggie Rhodes, claiming he was 'inappropriately entertained by a Walker booster.'

According to the NCAA's legislative database, this is the first investigation during Coach Clive Carr's tenure at Walker, a school known for its squeaky-clean reputation. NCAA senior spokeswoman Emma Potts said: 'We can't comment on current, pending, or potential investigations.'

According to Scott Galovan, Walker's senior vice president for public affairs, the school is cooperating and collaborating with the NCAA as part of the ongoing inquiry but, as a private university, is not subject to Freedom of Information requests to reveal the notice of inquiry. The notice is sent to schools as formal notification that an investigation is being conducted. If violations become substantiated, the next step in the NCAA process would be a notice of allegations, which would spell out detailed violations.

Walker University athletics director Stuart Sherrill issued the following statement: 'The focus of our coaches and student athletes is solely on preparing for LSU this Saturday. As such, I have instructed Coach Carr, his staff, and our student athletes to refrain from commenting on or answering questions regarding the status of this investigation.'

Within seconds of filing my story, my phone lit up with Smiley's name. 'A school known for being *squeaky clean*? Oh, *really,* now?' His voice was dripping with sarcasm.

'Well. It is.'

'That's *your* opinion, Ms. Rigsby.'

I resisted the temptation to argue that it was actually closer to fact than opinion, sort of like saying: *Most people describe the sky as blue.*

'Except for that bit of covert propaganda, it's fine,' Smiley said. 'We'll run it tomorrow.'

That evening after practice, I stopped Coach on his way back to his office and asked if he had a minute.

'For you? Sure,' he said, adjusting his cap with an easy half smile.

I smiled back at him and said, 'You feeling good about LSU?'

'Yeah. I am. But don't print that.'

'Obviously. I'm not that much of a rookie.' Then I took a deep breath and said, 'But . . . I just wanted you to know that we . . . I have to run another story tomorrow.'

'Oh, yeah?' he said.

'Yeah. About the investigation.'

He stared at me for a second, then gave me a brisk nod. 'Okay.'

'I'm sorry,' I said. 'I know how much you hate distractions.'

'It's fine,' he said. 'I don't listen to what people say and write about this program. There are fifty-two thousand people yelling at me in this stadium every time we play. I learned a long time ago to tune out the noise.'

I nodded and said, 'I hope you can tune it out. I hope Reggie can tune it out, too. He's named in the story.'

'I hope *you* can tune it out, girl. Don't let this get you down.'

We were in that golden hour of dusk, the setting sun reflecting in his eyes, and he shifted his gaze to something in the distance.

'I'll try,' I said. 'I just hate having to write a story like this.'

'It's your job,' he said. 'You don't have a choice.'

I nodded, hoping for more, perhaps an adamant denial of any wrongdoing. I got something almost as good, as I watched him switch gears into his philosophical coaching mode.

'It's like this,' he said, and I prepared myself for a good nugget. 'You know in your heart when you're doing the right thing and when you're not. And you just have to do everything you can to stay the course.'

'Right,' I said.

'Keep your eyes on the prize.'

21

The story ran the next morning, and by noon I had over fifty texts and emails, most from alarmed friends and former colleagues. They were surprised by the story, but more surprised that my name was attached to it. A lot of people asked if I was okay. No death threats yet, I told them, although the hate mail was beginning to trickle in from a few Walker crazies.

That night, my mother came over in a panic and demanded to know what was going on, why I hadn't told her anything, and whether Coach was mad at me.

'No, he's not mad at *me*,' I said.

'Is he okay?'

'Yes, Mom. He's fine. He's a head coach. He's just focusing on our next game. One day at a time.'

'Well, is it true?' she said.

To anyone else, I would have said a flat no. That the reports came from jealous boosters at a rival school. A bitter transfer. Someone with a beef or a chip on his shoulder. But there was something about my mother, always so extreme in her views, that made me say, 'Probably some parts of it. Otherwise, there wouldn't be an official notice and a full-blown investigation.'

She shook her head and said, 'No way. I don't believe it.'

At that moment, I heard and saw myself in her, my blind allegiance to Coach Carr and anything related to Walker, and it made me a little sick.

'It's not that black and white,' I said. 'This isn't SMU in the eighties. But, yeah, we probably looked the other way . . .'

My mother shook her head adamantly. 'Cheating *is* black

and white,' she said. I could tell she was talking about my father, and I marveled at how she always forgot that she was once a cheater, too. That that's how it all began. How I came to be. 'Bottom line, Coach Carr would *never* knowingly cheat,' she finished.

With this, I had to agree – and did, aloud.

'Do you know, in all those years of marriage, he was always true to Connie? Always. Do you know how few coaches at his level can say that? Connie told me stories you wouldn't believe . . . Brazen, rampant serial cheating by so many coaches. I think they're worse than investment bankers.'

My heart skipped at the mention of Connie and Coach and their marriage. I loved the affirmation of his strong character, but my heart filled with something else, too. Maybe guilt, maybe a dash of envy. Which in turn confused me and made me feel even more guilty.

'So they were really happy, huh?' I said, lowering my eyes.

'Yes,' she said, but then hesitated as if considering whether to say more. 'They had a very happy marriage, but it wasn't easy . . . It's tough being married to a coach. She was lonely a lot. Sometimes she said she felt like a single mother. Especially around the holidays. She loved him so much, but . . .' Her voice trailed off.

'But what?' I said.

'But I think she had to give up a lot of her own dreams to be with Clive.'

'What dreams did she have?' I said.

'Connie could have been on Broadway. She really could have. With her looks and that voice . . . she could have been a star . . .'

I nodded, remembering how beautiful her voice was. How she used to play the piano and sing during more intimate family gatherings. 'Did she want that?' I said, unable to picture her in anything other than a supporting role.

'Oh, I think so, yes. When your dad left us and moved back to New York, she made a comment that always stuck with me.

She said she was jealous of him . . . Not that he had left his family, but that he was getting out of Walker. Out of Texas. Connie was more layered than most people knew . . . She followed all the Southern conventions and was always the perfect wife and mother . . . But deep down, she was a dreamer. A head-in-the-clouds dreamer . . . She chose Coach over all of that and never looked back. But . . .' My mother paused, as if to fight a wave of emotion.

'But what?' I said gently, feeling so sorry for her, unable to imagine losing my own best friend.

'But I think she was waiting for her turn. Someday. There was so much that she wanted to do when Clive retired . . . See the world. Live abroad. She talked about Vienna a lot. She loved Vienna.'

'Why Vienna?' I asked.

'She lived there for a few years growing up, when her father was in the service . . .' My mother's frown turned to a faint smile. 'Can you imagine Coach in Vienna?'

'Do they get ESPN there?' I said, smiling back at her.

'Exactly,' she said.

My phone buzzed, and I looked down to see a text from Coach: *Shea, Don't sweat this story. Stay the course. Onward.*

'What is it?' my mom said as I stared down at my phone.

'Nothing,' I said. 'But I do have to go pack now. I have an early flight to Baton Rouge.'

'What's in Baton Rouge?' my mom said, looking confused.

'Um. LSU,' I said. 'We have a football game to play. Remember?'

Then, as I shooed my mother out of my apartment, I wrote back: *Thanks, Coach. Onward.*

The next day we hit LSU right in the gut. Three yards and a cloud of dust all day long. But the 27–3 victory in the blazing hot sun seemed only to add fuel to the media fire, and I could sense that every major paper, sports website, and blog was poised to run some variation of my story, rather than the highlights of our domination over the Tigers. Still, the win felt good, better than most, and I could see in Coach's eyes a renewed determination to make this our year. Despite the investigation, and maybe *because* of the investigation, this really could be our season to remember. After all, winning was the ultimate *fuck you* – everyone in sports knew that much.

'Onward,' I whispered to Coach as he was heading into the press conference with Rhodes and Everclear.

He gave me a quick wink in return, then said, 'You got it, girl.'

A few minutes later, the Q & A began, the first question predictably directed at Reggie about the investigation. Reggie, whose performance was nothing short of outstanding, leaned into the microphone with complete poise as he said, 'Um. Yeah. I'm just gonna talk about football today.'

Undeterred, the reporter pressed, 'Do you know Raymond Matthews?'

I knew from my investigative digging that this was the name of the Cincy booster in question, and could tell by the look on Reggie's face that he knew the name, too.

Coach barked into his mic, rushing to Reggie's aid. 'You heard Mr Rhodes. Now we're gonna end this thing real quickly if y'all don't keep your questions on the game today.'

I bit my lip and looked down at my laptop, typing up the quote, and thinking that there was pretty much nothing sexier in the world than a fired-up Coach Carr.

22

The following week, Smiley finally ran my piece on Rhodes, which only threw fuel on the NCAA-investigation fire, bringing out all the haters who couldn't stand how good we were, now ranked fifth in the country. At 7–0, we were just past the midway point of our schedule. It was something of a surprise every year, to find ourselves with more games played than remaining, perhaps because fall has a way of sneaking up on you in Texas, deceiving you with its balmy weather. The Saturdays roll along at a steady clip until you're astounded to realize that November is just around the corner. This season was passing especially quickly, with no losses to break up our forward momentum.

Meanwhile, the Dallas Cowboys were looking strong, too, which put Ryan in a mood as upbeat as mine, and the two of us fell into a comfortable, cozy rhythm with several sleepovers a week. I still hadn't attended any of his games, which he had pointed out more than once, but I couldn't help feeling paranoid that Smiley would somehow find fault with our relationship and hold it up as another example of my unbreakable bias. Ryan was a Cowboy, but he'd always be a Bronco, too.

Ryan and I managed to make progress in other ways, though, a set of feminine toiletries taking root in his bathroom, a few articles of clothing hanging in his custom walk-in closet. I even decided to cook for him, a big step. I had stalled on the notion for weeks, partly because he had a personal chef, partly because I hated having him at my place and didn't feel comfortable taking over his fancy gourmet kitchen, but mostly because I didn't want to give credence to my mother's old-fashioned contention that it was critical to cook in a courtship. I had the sense that she just might be right, though, after Ryan made an offhanded remark about Blakeslee's inability to boil water or make toast – and the fact that he 'should have known then that things weren't going to work out.' In the long run, I didn't think our relationship would come down to my domestic abilities (or lack thereof), but I couldn't help wanting him to like me as much as I liked him. Which was becoming quite a lot.

So one morning before we both left his house for work, I casually mentioned that I'd love to make him my yellow squash and hominy casserole. 'It's almost as famous as you,' I quipped.

'Well, all right! I'll give Tre the night off,' he said. 'My place?'

'Yes. Come home hungry,' I said.

He gave me a seductive look and said that was a given, he was always hungry around me. I smiled as he pulled keys from his pocket, removed one from the chain, and handed it to me. 'Here. I've been meaning to give you this anyway.'

'You sure?' I said, trying to be cool even though I knew I was going to speed-dial Lucy the second I was alone. 'You might want to try my casserole first.'

Later that day, after I'd gone to the grocery store and bought all the ingredients for my casserole, along with chicken to fry, corn bread, and a chocolate mousse pie, I drove to Ryan's house, let myself in the back door, and got to work. By the time he returned from practice, most of the chopping and prep work was done and his kitchen restored to order (another thing my mother had always preached and probably a nugget she got from Connie – no dirty dishes on counters or dirty underwear on the floor, at least until you have the ring on your finger).

'Wow. I'm already impressed,' Ryan said, as I handed him a glass of a pinot noir I'd just opened from his wine refrigerator.

'I hope this isn't too nice of a bottle?'

'The best bottles are in the wine cellar. But nothing's too nice for you,' he said with a gallant smile.

'Thank you,' I said. Then I raised my glass and said, 'To our winning streaks.'

'And to the chef,' he said, raising his glass.

'And to your kitchen,' I said, laughing.

Our glasses touched and our eyes locked before we both took a sip. He nodded approvingly, then leaned down to kiss me.

'How was practice?' I asked when we separated, glancing at the diced onion softening in the heavy iron skillet behind me.

'Not too bad,' he said, sitting on a barstool at his counter while I returned to the stove. 'Knee's feeling much better.' His left knee had been banged up in the Bears game, nothing out of the ordinary, except that every bump became significant to a quarterback in his thirties. He extended it now, then bent it again, wincing. 'MRI came back fine. Just a bad bruise.'

'Good,' I said, feeling like the nurturing girlfriend and relieved to realize that it was sincere, not an act. I really did worry about him. His knee, his reputation, his surprisingly fragile ego, *all* of him.

I added the sliced squash, bell peppers, jalapeño, pickling liquid, and oregano to the pan. The mixture sizzled, and, aware that he was watching me, I stood up straighter, stirring for a few seconds before adding the milk, reducing the heat slightly, and covering the pan.

'You really know what you're doing, don't you?' Ryan said, taking another sip of wine, as I rolled the chicken legs and thighs in my specialty batter one last time. 'It's hot.'

I decided not to tell him this was pretty much the only meal I had mastered. Instead, I cocked my head to the side, smiled, and said, 'Frying chicken is hot?'

'Yes,' he said. 'Especially if you took off those clothes and put on a frilly little apron and some stilettos.'

'Don't hold your breath on that one. I'll cook for you, but I don't role-play or dress up.'

He laughed and said, 'Not even as a Dallas Cowboy cheerleader?'

'*Especially* not as a Dallas Cowboy cheerleader,' I said.

Ryan stood, walked over to the stove, and put his arms around my waist. 'I'll be back,' he said after planting a kiss on the top of my head. 'I want to change into something more comfortable – and make a few quick calls. That okay?'

'Sure,' I said, happy to be able to concentrate on frying my chicken. Ryan left the room, cellphone in hand, scrolling through his texts as he walked. I had the fleeting, unsettling thought that he might be scrolling through texts from girls, but I told myself not to be paranoid as I transferred the vegetables into a casserole dish, alternating layers of the mixture with grated cheese, then finished with a topping of crushed chips. I slid the whole dish into the preheated oven, glancing at the kitchen clock, then set the table with china, crystal, and real silver.

About thirty minutes later, just as I was putting the casserole on the table, Ryan reappeared in what could only be described as loungewear. The matching set was heather gray and the drawstring pants so beautifully cut that they looked custom-made. I gave him a quick onceover, smirked, and said, 'That's a pretty sweet getup you got there.'

'Getup?' He laughed as I walked over to him and ran my hand down one ultrasoft sleeve, resting for a moment on his shoulder.

'Designer cashmere sweats?' I teased.

'Cashmere-*cotton* blend,' he said, smirking. 'With maybe a hint of Lycra. Wears better than straight cashmere.'

It sounded *exactly* like something Lucy would say; in fact, I was pretty sure she had uttered the exact words to me before. I shook my head and said I'd keep that in mind, although I could count on one hand the number of garments in my closet that contained *any* cashmere.

'So are you ready to eat?' I asked, gesturing toward the banquette at the other end of his kitchen, where I had set the table. I had the feeling that we were playing house as he told me how wonderful everything looked and smelled.

'Let's hope it tastes good, too,' I said.

'I know it will,' he said, then stopped me on the way to our table and grabbed my hands. 'Shea?'

'Yeah,' I said, looking up into his face. His expression was earnest and loving.

'I just . . . wanted to thank you,' he said after a thoughtful beat.

'For what?' I said.

'For making me dinner.' Still holding both my hands, he looked in my eyes and said, 'This was really sweet of you. I appreciate it. A lot.'

I found his gratitude touching, especially considering that he had gourmet dinners prepared for him pretty much every night of the week except for the days he had a four-star training table awaiting him.

'You're welcome,' I said, overcome with a feeling of true affection. Perhaps the strongest I'd ever felt for him.

As we sat down to the table, the satisfied feeling lingered, and expanded until I realized what it was. I was happy. Really in-the-*moment* happy, which has always seemed a completely different animal than retrospectively recognizing that you *had been* happy, the usual case with me. I could tell Ryan was conscious of the mood, too, because he kept smiling at me, and touching my arm as we talked. Our conversation wasn't particularly deep, but it was easy and intimate, and, every few moments he'd sprinkle in a compliment on my dinner. I could hear my mother – *the way to a man's heart is through his stomach* – and felt proud in spite of myself, knowing that I had definitely nailed my first meal. Ryan heaped seconds of casserole onto his plate, calling it 'simple yet soulful,' while I drank most of our bottle of wine by myself. By the time we finished, I had a strong buzz.

'So,' he said, after he cleared our plates and settled back into his seat. 'What are you doing for Thanksgiving?'

'Same thing you're doing,' I said, thinking that I didn't measure the end of the year the way other people did – in terms of holidays. Instead I thought of it as rivalry weekend versus Texas, followed by bowl season.

'You're playing football?' he asked, smiling, stroking my arm again.

'Ha. No. I'm *watching* you play on television,' I said, thinking that I couldn't remember a Thanksgiving that didn't include the Cowboys. 'With my dad. He's coming down with Bronwyn and Astrid.' I rolled my eyes, then made a face. I hadn't told Ryan much about my father, other than the basic but bizarre chronology of his three marriages to two women – and a little about my smug half sister. How condescending she was about all things Texas, calling everything 'quaint' or 'rustic' and buying cowboy boots as if they were exotic souvenirs from a foreign country.

'Well. Would y'all like to watch the game *in person*? Instead of on television?' he said. 'In a suite with my parents? You could invite your mom, too . . .'

'That'd be great,' I said, as the full weight of the invite sunk in. Not only was he asking to meet my parents, but he was introducing me to his, and our parents to one another. After a short pause, my voice turned coy. 'So you want me to meet your parents, do you?'

'Yes, I *do*,' he said the way he made a lot of statements. Definitively and with the utmost confidence.

'Well, okay, then,' I said. For one second, Coach flitted into my head, the fact that we often saw the Carrs on Thanksgiving, and how Ryan's plan would certainly preclude that tradition. But I forced him from my thoughts, telling myself to *focus*, reminding myself that, if I played my cards right, this could be, in Lucy's words, a friggin' fairy tale.

Over the next few weeks, as Walker racked up two more wins over Iowa and West Virginia, Ryan and I stayed in our heightened happy zone, meeting for lunch, going to dinner, staying connected. At some point, things stopped feeling tenuous and started to feel real. So much so that I dropped my defense mechanism of downplaying our relationship to Lucy and my mother – and told them that things were getting serious.

My mom was giddy when I told her that Ryan had included her in his Thanksgiving invite.

'Have you told your dad about Ryan yet?' she asked, practically rubbing her hands together. I knew what she was thinking – that Bronwyn might be married off to a rich guy, but that a famed NFL quarterback trumped a venture capitalist any day of the week.

'No. Not yet,' I said, although I was relishing the moment. As much as I saw Ryan for Ryan, there were times when I was acutely aware of his fame. Whenever his face appeared on television, or we garnered a double take in public, I felt validated, proud. To Lucy's dismay, the news had yet to hit the tabloids other than a tiny blurb on the autism gala in the Dallas social pages, and nobody outside the Walker bubble really knew we were together. I hadn't even told Gordon, my only friend at work, because every time I found a casual opening, it still felt like name-dropping. Bottom line, there was no getting around the fact that Ryan was a feather in my cap, a gold star on my helmet. And I was as excited as my mother to break the news to my father.

'Well, what are you waiting for? Tell him!' she said, her brown eyes shining.

'Do you want to listen on speaker?' I asked. 'Maybe we could get Astrid on speaker, too?'

'Oh, that would be perfect!' she said. 'Could we?'

'No, Mom,' I said, shaking my head. 'We cannot. It was a joke.'

She looked momentarily deflated but not defeated, as she began to brainstorm what she should wear to the game. 'Blue, of course,' she mused. 'Or should it be teal for Walker?'

'Any blue would be great,' I said, throwing her a bone, and imagining just how out of control she'd be if Ryan and I ever, one day in the very faraway future, had a *real* event to plan.

The next day, I decided to practice telling my dad about Ryan during an intercubicle conversation with Gordon about NFL quarterbacks.

'I would get pistol-whipped in this town, *but*—' Gordon began in a loud whisper, after I asked him to rank them.

I laughed, knowing where he was headed with his preamble. Born and raised in Philly, Gordon loved the Eagles and had no use for the Cowboys outside of his paycheck. In other words, he was a true professional, while I often felt like I was *playing* a reporter.

He continued, 'I go Aaron Rodgers first, Peyton Manning second, Tom Brady third, then Ryan James.'

I felt a pang of loyalty but tried to be objective. 'I'll give you Aaron Rodgers. *Maybe*,' I said. 'But I put Ryan ahead of Peyton. And he's *way* ahead of Brady.'

Gordon made his arguments, the whole 'stats are one thing but it really comes down to winning big games,' then had the audacity to suggest that maybe even Brees should be put before Ryan. 'That guy can *execute* like nobody else,' he said.

'You think Ryan doesn't execute? *Really?* He's a *total* executioner,' I began, then strategically added, 'Of course, I'm biased.'

'Everyone in this state is biased,' Gordon said. 'Especially you Walker alums.'

'Yes,' I said. 'But I'm *really* biased . . . We're actually . . . kind of . . . dating.'

Gordon laughed and kept on typing.

'No. We are. I didn't want to say anything at first . . . Because you work on that beat . . . And I don't know,' I blathered, 'it still sort of feels like name-dropping. And for all I know Smiley has some kind of policy against it . . . Since Ryan went to Walker and all.' I glanced in Smiley's direction, then returned my gaze to Gordon. I had his attention, finally, but he looked incredulous, waiting for the punch line.

'You serious?'

'Yeah. We're dating. We have been for a couple of months . . .'

Gordon nodded, finally believing me, then said, 'Well, cool. That's awesome.'

'Yeah. I guess,' I said. And then, 'I really like him.'

Gordon laughed and said, 'Well, I guess you do. Damn. What's not to like? And I say that as a very straight dude.'

I smiled and said, 'Well, I'll be sure to tell him that, if you were gay, you'd go for Brees, Brady, Rodgers, and Manning over him.'

Gordon grinned and said, 'No. If I were gay, I'd actually go for Ryan. Better hair. And you can tell him I said that.'

My dry run completed, I called my dad that night and, after some awkward small talk, used the same 'Who's the best NFL quarterback?' line as my opener.

'Oh, Ryan James. For sure,' my dad said, following the sweetest of scripts. Even better, Astrid was chattering in the background as usual. It was one of my biggest pet peeves – she was *always* right there in his ear, chiming in on our conversations. If I ever wrote a book on divorces, one of my first suggestions to parents would be: Get rid of the second (or third) wife in the background when you're talking to your child – at least *some* of the time. And good *Lord*, don't put her on the phone. As in 'Here, Shea. Say hello to Astrid.'

But this time, I loved it.

'What *about* Ryan James?' I heard her ask.

My father repeated the question verbatim, and Astrid agreed that Ryan was the best, then added that she loved Tom Brady, too. I would bet my earrings that those were the *only* two football players she could name.

'Tell her we're not talking about who has the most tabloid press,' I said with as much disdain as I could without being outright rude.

My dad laughed, then asked about my job. 'I've been reading some of your stuff here and there. It's really good.'

I made a face at the phone, thinking that these were the first and only three words of feedback or praise my father had offered on my fledgling career in journalism.

'Thanks, Dad,' I said. 'It's been fun.'

'I bet,' he said. 'Like a dream job for you.'

'*Like* a dream job?' I said. 'It *is* my dream job.'

'Right, right,' he said. 'That's what I meant.'

'And speaking of dreams,' I said, making an awkward but still satisfying transition. 'I'm sort of dating the dream guy, too.'

'Oh?' my dad said as I heard Astrid clamoring in the background: *What'd she say? What'd she say?*

My father didn't even try to mute the phone or cover the receiver. *She said she's dating her dream guy.*

'Yeah,' I said. 'I'm actually dating the best quarterback in the NFL.'

'Come again?' my dad said.

'Ryan James,' I said, smirking to myself. I could practically hear the drum roll. 'I'm dating Ryan James.'

Silence.

'He wants to meet you when you come down. He invited us to sit in his box with his parents for the game. On Thanksgiving.'

More silence except for Astrid, peppering him with questions.

'Dad? Did you hear me?'

'Are you joking?'

'No, Dad. It's not a joke. He's my boyfriend. He gave me diamond earrings. Big ones. We're pretty serious.'

By now, I was fist-pumping, and Astrid was frenzied. I heard him relay everything to her, down to the size of my studs. *Big diamonds.*

Astrid suddenly was speaking directly in my ear, obviously having ripped the phone away from my dad. 'Are you really dating Ryan James?' she said.

'Yes, Astrid. I am, in fact.'

Her voice became higher, more stilted than usual. 'Well, tell us! How did this happen? Where did you meet?'

'We went to school together, Astrid,' I said. I liked punctuating my statements with her name, and the weary effect it created.

'And he gave you diamond earrings?'

'Yes, Astrid. They're gorgeous.'

'Send us a photo. Wow,' she said, but her voice was flat. She was either in shock or jealous – both, I hoped.

'Sure, Astrid. I'll do that, Astrid,' I said, savoring the moment, thinking *I win*. No matter what happened in the long run, for one moment in time, my mother's daughter was *finally* winning.

23

When things seem too good to be true, they usually are. It was yet another of Coach Carr's favorite statements – a sentiment that seemed pretty on the money as we cruised past our bye weekend and geared up for Florida State, Stanford, and Texas – our final three, and by far toughest, opponents of the regular season.

So I shouldn't have been surprised when Ryan said, out of the blue one night, as I was on the verge of falling asleep, 'I just want you to know that you might be hearing some things about me and they aren't true.'

'What *things*?' I said, now wide awake, though my eyes were still shut.

'Blakeslee knows I'm seeing you,' he said. His face was so close to mine that I could feel his breath on my cheek. 'And I'm worried that she might lash out.'

'Lash out? At me?' I asked, my eyes snapping open. I blinked, adjusting to the dark, waiting, thinking of that picture in the magazine that I had never asked him about.

'Not at you. At *me*,' he said. 'I think she's upset. And she can do stupid shit when she's upset.'

'Why is she upset?' I said, thinking that she had no right to be upset when they were divorced. Of course I knew emotions – and divorces – didn't always work that way, and that sometimes there was no such thing as closure.

'She heard about your earrings,' he said.

'How?' I said, increasingly uneasy. 'Who could have *possibly* told her about my earrings?'

'Well . . . I did.'

I tried to process this information, piece together what the conversation might have sounded like, as he offered a flimsy, unprompted explanation. 'We still talk occasionally.'

'Oh,' I said, a knot growing in my chest. 'Yeah, I saw that picture of the two of you. This summer.' I suddenly felt foolish for never asking about it.

'That was nothing,' he answered, almost too quickly. 'She was in California for work. And we had lunch. That was it.'

'Uh-huh,' I said. 'So how often do you talk to her?'

'Not often at all,' he said. 'I swear.'

'I believe you,' I said, although I wasn't sure that I did.

'But we did speak a few days ago . . . And she asked me if I was seeing anyone. I told her about you . . . and it sort of deteriorated after that.'

I still couldn't quite figure out how my earrings factored into the whole conversation, but I just nodded, taking it all in.

'Are you mad?' he said.

'No,' I said, although I was irritated by Ryan's double standard. Why was it all right for him to stay in touch with Blakeslee, when I couldn't talk to Miller?

Thirty seconds or so passed before he said, 'Are you sure you aren't mad?'

I rolled over, fumbling for the ChapStick I kept in the nightstand next to his bed, taking off the top, and applying it as I mumbled that I wasn't mad. But I didn't sound convincing. I didn't even *try* to sound convincing.

I glanced at Ryan, making out his face in the dark. His expression looked vaguely disappointed, corroborating a theory I've always had – the more jealous a person is, the more he wants you to feel the same. In fact, maybe that was why he'd told Blakeslee about the earrings in the first place. Maybe she was seeing someone new and it bothered him enough to want to make *her* jealous.

I said I was exhausted and that we both needed to get some sleep. He agreed, but after a few more minutes said my name again.

'Yes?' I said, waiting, staring up at the ceiling.

'I only want to be with you,' he finally said.

'Good. I only want to be with you, too,' I said.

But before I fell asleep for good, it occurred to me that it wasn't the kind of thing you said if it was completely true – and maybe we were both trying to convince ourselves as much as each other.

The next morning, Ryan surprised me with breakfast in bed. Scrambled eggs, wheat toast, and mixed berries on a black lacquered tray. There was even a sprig of parsley on my plate.

'Thank you,' I said, although I've always thought breakfast in bed was far better in theory than in practice, especially when the meal is sprung on you seconds after waking. As I sat up, Ryan positioned the tray over my lap, then stretched out beside me. I had no appetite, probably because I was still thinking about Blakeslee, but took a bite of the eggs and told him they were delicious.

'Did you already eat?' I asked.

'Just a protein shake and oatmeal,' he said. I could feel him staring at me and had the feeling he was thinking about Blakeslee, too. The mood was definitely subdued, if not down-right awkward.

I took a dainty bite of toast, trying not to make crumbs in his bed, thinking how much I needed to go to the bathroom but didn't want to go through all the upheaval of moving the tray.

'What are you doing today?' he asked me.

'Remember that little kid with brain cancer I told you about?' I said. 'The one obsessed with Walker football?'

Ryan nodded. 'Yeah. Isn't his name Max?'

'Yes,' I said, noting once again what a good listener he was. It was as if he was never *not* paying attention – highly unusual for a man. 'Coach invited him to be on the sidelines with the team against Stanford. So Smiley wants me to do a feel-good story on him . . .'

'Smiley wants feel-good?' Ryan said, laughing a little too hard, clearly trying to lighten the mood.

'I know, right?' I said, running my hand over a crystal goblet filled with freshly squeezed orange juice, refusing to laugh.

'What are you thinking, babe?' he said.

So I told him exactly what I'd been thinking. 'I was wondering whether this was a wedding gift,' I said, tapping on the glass.

Ryan hesitated, then nodded gravely, as if making a somber admission.

I picked up the silver fork in an ornate pattern. 'And this?' He nodded again, then sat up.

'Why did *you* keep them?' I said, more curious than anything else. 'Doesn't the girl usually keep this stuff?'

He shrugged and told me Blakeslee didn't want them.

'Why not?'

'I don't know. She just didn't.' His forehead went from smooth to furrowed. 'Her taste changed, I guess.'

'In one year? Her taste changed in *one* year?'

'She changed her mind about the marriage. So why not the crystal and silver?'

It was a fair point, but I still felt confused, agitated. I said nothing, a trick of good reporting. Silence keeps them talking.

It worked, as Ryan offered up more information. 'I picked most of this stuff out anyway.'

'You handled the registry?'

'Well, we went together. But she let me pick most of the stuff.'

'Huh,' I said, thinking: *That's weird.*

'And besides . . . things ended badly . . . So she said the gifts were tainted . . .'

'I thought you said you were still friends?'

'We are. Now. Sort of.'

'Even though it ended badly?' I tried to sound breezy but spoke too quickly, giving the question a cross-examination feel.

He gave me a circumspect look and said, 'I knew it. You *are* pissed.'

'No,' I said with a purposeful shrug. 'I'm really not.'

'It seems like you are.'

'It seems like you want me to be.'

A chilly standoff ensued, each of us staring at the other, neither speaking until he said, 'Look. Let's not talk about her anymore, okay?'

'Okay,' I said, thinking that it would be just fine if I never heard her name again.

No such luck. Because later that morning, just as I finally got Blakeslee out of my mind, the phone in my cubicle rang, an unknown Houston number on the screen.

'Shea Rigsby, *Dallas Post*,' I answered, thinking that it hadn't worn off yet. Every time I said my title, I felt a little thrill.

'Hi, Shea,' a woman's voice on the other end of the line said. I tried to place it, but it didn't sound familiar. 'This is Blakeslee Meadows. I don't know if you remember me?'

'Yes,' I said, my heart pounding. 'How are you?'

'I'm well,' she said. 'How are you?'

'I'm fine,' I said, as it occurred to me that we had never actually had a conversation, only a few passing hellos in college. She had always made it clear that I was beneath her – and I wondered if she felt the same now.

'It's been a while, hasn't it?'

I murmured my agreement, trying to anticipate where she'd possibly go from here just as she said, 'I'm sure you're wondering why I'm calling you.' Her voice was soft and hesitant, and didn't match my memories, her polished photos, or her confident public persona.

'It's about Ryan,' she continued.

'Yeah. I figured,' I said, lowering my voice and glancing at the cubicles surrounding mine. Murphy's law had quieted the floor down in the one moment that I needed privacy.

'He told me he was seeing you,' she said.

'Yeah. He told me that he . . . told you,' I stammered as Gordon glanced my way. Ever since I'd told him about

Ryan, I had the feeling he was more interested in my conversations.

'Right. Well. I debated calling you . . . And I know your relationship is none of my business.'

I said nothing, thinking this was a pretty major understatement.

'But I just . . . I had to . . .' Her voice cracked, making her sound both sad and desperate, and I felt an unexpected stab of sympathy. In one instant, she was no longer competition, just a girl who had lost her husband, perhaps the one man she'd ever loved. Maybe she still loved him. Maybe that's what this was about. Her trying to get him back. Maybe she was actually manipulating me.

'Are you okay?' I asked, feeling disoriented.

'Yes. Thank you, Shea. I'm fine . . .' I heard her take a few deep breaths, and, when she started speaking again, I had the feeling she was reading from a script. 'As you know, Ryan and I got divorced about a year ago. It was really hard and very, very sad. I loved him a lot . . . and we both really wanted things to work. But they just didn't. They couldn't.'

'I'm sorry,' I said, waiting for her to continue.

'Thank you . . . So anyway . . . I know that he started seeing you this summer . . . And again, I know your relationship is none of my business . . . But . . . God . . . this is a really hard thing to say . . . And I feel really shitty for telling you this . . .'

'You can tell me,' I said, feeling certain that she was about to confess that he'd cheated on me with her.

Instead she said, 'What I'm saying is that Ryan has a really bad temper. Like . . . really bad.'

'Okay,' I said as calmly as I could, mentally switching gears.

'Our divorce is sealed . . . confidential . . . for privacy . . . and I don't want to spread rumors about him, especially since I know you work for a paper now. I would hate for this to get out and hurt his career or reputation or endorsements . . . Or even what he has going with you . . . But I just had to tell you . . .'

I nodded, now in full-on reporter mode. 'Wait. Let's back

up,' I said slowly. 'When you say temper . . . what exactly do you mean?'

'Most of the time he's a great guy. Really sweet and . . . wonderful,' she said, clearly evading the question. 'But . . . he has a temper.'

I waited.

'He gets it from his father,' she continued. 'Not that that's an excuse. But . . . have you met his dad?'

'No. Not yet,' I said, thinking of our Thanksgiving plans.

'When you do, watch how Mr James talks to Ryan's mom. Really to all women,' she said. 'He's a classic misogynist and a horrible father. He put crazy pressure on Ryan when it came to football. If Ryan had a bad game, he'd chew him out. Throw his cleats in the dumpster behind the school. Make Ryan walk home. Five miles in one-hundred-degree heat . . . And that was the least of it . . . Have you ever asked him about that scar he has on his forehead?'

I knew exactly the one she was talking about. 'The one he got the night of the high school state championship. His senior year,' I said, showing her how much I knew about him, how close we were.

'Oh, he *did* get it that night,' Blakeslee said. 'Because they lost the game. And his father thought the quarterback was to blame.'

'*Shit,*' I said under my breath, feeling sure that she was telling the truth about at least this part of the story.

'And so . . . and so it's not *all* his fault that he is the way he is,' she concluded.

'What way is that?' I said, needing her to spell it out for me.

Blakeslee was so quiet I thought we had gotten cut off. But when I said her name, she said, 'When he gets angry, he can be really mean. And violent. And scary.'

Mean, violent, scary. The words swirled around my head as I reminded myself that Ryan was innocent until proven guilty. I clung to the hope that she wasn't really saying what I thought she was saying, but there wasn't a lot of wiggle room with that lineup of adjectives.

After a long pause, she said, 'Has he shoved you yet? Grabbed you too hard?'

'No,' I quickly replied. 'Never.'

'Well,' Blakeslee said quietly. 'Maybe he *has* changed. If you believe that people can. I don't think I believe that, though . . .'

I waited, as she threw out another loaded question. 'Has he asked you to change your clothes? Or gotten upset at you for wearing tight pants or short dresses or low-cut tops?'

'No,' I said, comforted by the question, telling myself that she was only being a drama queen. Trying to stir the pot. Were we really discussing cleavage?

But just as I was dismissing her as crazy, she said, 'Okay. Well, has he gotten crazy, psycho jealous over . . . nothing?'

I thought of Miller, but didn't answer.

'He has, hasn't he?' she said softly.

'Not really. I mean, he can be jealous. But not *psycho* jealous. Nothing like *that*,' I said.

'Well, be careful, Shea. Because that's how it starts . . . You know . . . I thought it was me for a long time. Because I wasn't perfect either. I got really jealous over all the girls who are always after him. And sometimes, at first, I tried to make him jealous back . . . I told myself that it was my fault for starting trouble. And if I tried harder to be more secure . . . or more tolerant . . . or just the perfect wife, I could keep him from getting mad. But it didn't work that way. And I know now that it wasn't my fault. And it isn't his dad's fault. It isn't anyone's fault but his own. And I can't believe I'm the only one he's done it to.'

Done what to? I wanted to ask. But I didn't because the question felt too personal, the answer too obvious. Instead I said, 'Well, thank you for calling and telling me this.'

'You're welcome.'

Silence. And this time she outwaited me as I babbled, 'I . . . I guess I don't know what to say . . .'

'You don't have to say anything,' she said. 'And please believe that I'm not trying to hurt your relationship. This is about helping you. *And* him.'

'Okay,' I said, now desperate to get off the phone.

'Can I ask you for one favor?' she said.

'Okay,' I said again.

'Please don't tell him I called you.'

'I won't,' I said, even though I didn't owe her my allegiance, especially not over Ryan. Yet I had the feeling that I was going to keep her secret – and didn't have a good feeling about what that meant.

'I just want to move on with my life . . . But I had to tell you. I wish his girlfriend before me had said something . . . You know?'

I said I did, picturing Tish Termini, Ryan's first serious college girlfriend, a petite Italian girl who was as beautiful as Blakeslee but in a slightly trashy way. I remembered her well, flaunting her toned, tanned body around campus, wearing colorful push-up bras under white tank tops, and Daisy Dukes paired with cowboy boots. Everyone knew they had a turbulent, on-again, off-again relationship, but I'd never heard a single word about him *hitting* her. I put it in the column of evidence suggesting that Blakeslee might be lying or exaggerating, realizing that, no matter what, I was going to feel guilty. Either guilty for denigrating Ryan without a chance to defend himself, or guilty for thinking that any woman would lie about something so serious.

'Well. Thank you again for calling, Blakeslee,' I finally said.

'You're welcome,' she said. And then – 'I'm so sorry.'

I said goodbye and hung up, thinking about her last words: *I'm so sorry.* There was something about them that was both poignant and telling. She really *did* sound sorry, although I wasn't sure if she felt sorry for me, herself, or Ryan.

That afternoon, I went to Lucy's shop to give her the update. I did not editorialize, reporting only the facts of the conversation. What Ryan said. What Blakeslee said. What I said.

The first question she asked cut right to the crux of the matter: 'Do you believe her?'

'I don't know,' I said. 'I don't think so . . . But I wonder . . . I mean, he did get really jealous over Miller.'

'Lots of people get jealous,' Lucy said. 'Especially at the beginning of a relationship, when people are at their most insecure. Neil used to get *so* jealous. We look back and laugh about it now. It was ridiculous . . .'

'I know. But this was different,' I said, remembering the look on Ryan's face when he made me promise not to see anyone but him.

'Are you sure you're not just saying that now that you heard all this mess from Blakeslee?' Lucy asked.

'Maybe,' I said.

'You have to remember . . . he's probably been burned before. Girls constantly using him. Liking him for the wrong reasons. Just because he's famous and gorgeous doesn't mean that he hasn't been hurt.'

'True.'

'So if that's true, could you really blame him for being possessive? Or a little insecure? Maybe you should take it as a compliment that he cares.'

I nodded, definitely seeing her point.

'Besides, she really could be making the whole thing up,' Lucy said. 'Don't you have to give him the benefit of the doubt?'

'And assume she's lying?' I said. 'Assume that the woman is lying about domestic violence? That's pretty dangerous terrain, Luce.'

'Well, isn't that what our justice system is based upon? Innocent until proven guilty rather than the other way around?' she said, nailing all the highlights of my internal monologue.

I shrugged, staring out the window onto Main Street, a block I knew by heart, store by store, brick by brick.

'How about this for a plan?' she said, talking slowly in her take-charge voice. 'How about you give him a chance? And

the very first sign, the smallest shove or tiniest hint of a temper
. . . you end things.'

'Okay,' I said, wondering how to define a *hint of temper*.

'Can I discuss this with Neil?' Lucy said. It was a question
she always asked, and one I appreciated, but, at this point, it
wasn't necessary. I always said yes, viewing Neil as an exten-
sion of Lucy in almost all respects.

'Of course,' I said.

'And maybe you should talk to Daddy?' Lucy said. 'Maybe
he has some insight into Ryan.'

'Yeah. I don't think so,' I said. I was all about finding excuses
to talk to Coach, but not about Ryan. And definitely not about
this. I wasn't sure exactly why – if it had more to do with
unfairly casting aspersions against one of his former players or
if I simply didn't want Coach to know the details of our relationship. 'I don't want to spread this stuff around – if it's not
true,' I said.

'Yeah,' Lucy said. 'And I'm sure it's probably not.'

'Me, too,' I said, thinking that so much of how we see the
world is a matter of interpretation. A matter of wishing and
wanting and hoping rather than really deep-down believing.

24

I decided not to worry about Ryan for the time being and focused all my wishing and wanting and hoping on the rest of our season. After beating FSU in Tallahassee, we were so close to reaching the promised land, with only Stanford and Texas in our way. A few days later, we were halfway there, having eked out a 44–41 victory over the Cardinal.

'Great win,' I said to Coach Carr outside our locker room. I was headed to the pressroom but had stalled here on purpose, hoping I'd see him.

'You like that?' he said, angling his shoulder toward me in a thirty-second private sidebar. The favoritism was obvious to anyone even half paying attention, but nobody was. In my peripheral vision, I could see a well-known writer for *Sports Illustrated* barreling toward us, so I kept a stoic expression, nodding, scribbling on my pad as if getting a quote from Coach.

'Call me later,' he said.

'What?' I asked.

'You heard me.'

My heart fluttered. 'You mean tonight?'

'Yes. Tonight.'

I was already warm from the lights and crowds and my hustling move to get down here, but my whole body heated up a few more degrees as I nodded, promising him I would.

Three hours later, after the press conference, and after I had written and filed my story, I called Coach. He didn't answer, and the weight of the disappointment was like a great check and balance to the high of our earlier exchange. To distract myself,

I called Ryan, who had just hunkered down in his hotel room in D.C. I had only seen him a couple times since talking to Blakeslee, both evenings pleasantly uneventful, and Lucy and I were both beginning to believe that, at the very least, Blakeslee had exaggerated his temper. I had decided not to tell him about the conversation, coming up with a bunch of rationalizations, including that I knew he had to stay mentally focused, in the zone, during this part of the season. With this in mind, I asked him about the Redskins game tomorrow, how he was feeling, if he was ready. He informed me that his knee was feeling pretty good, only a little tight, then asked if I'd finished my story. He knew we had won but hadn't caught any of the game, so I filled him in on some of the highlights. Then he told me he missed me, and I said I missed him, too. We still hadn't said I love you, but I could feel it coming soon. For the most part, I was ready.

After we hung up, I watched an hour or so of ESPN before my stomach started to growl, and I remembered that I hadn't eaten dinner. My refrigerator was close to bare, par for the course, so I got in my car to find food, the faster and greasier the better. As I drove through town, my thoughts kept returning to Coach. It bothered me that he hadn't picked up or called me back – but it bothered me more that I cared so much. Then, just as I was pulling into the Taco Bell drive-thru, his name lit up my phone. My heart racing, I pulled out of line, into a parking spot. I simply couldn't do two things at once when one of them involved Coach Carr.

'Sorry I missed your call. I must have been in the shower,' he said.

The update felt intimate, and all I could say was 'Oh.'

'Did you file your story?' he asked.

'Yes . . . And what about you? How much Texas–Nebraska tape have you watched since you got home?' I asked. The game had kicked off about the same time as ours, the score about the same, Texas coming out on top.

'How'd you know?'

'Lucky guess,' I said, feeling my chest rising and falling with excitement. 'Where are you now?'

'My back porch . . .'

'Eating chocolate cake?' I said, thinking of our night on the track, and how much happier he sounded now. The score was just as close, but we had played *so* much better. Probably the best we'd played all year.

He laughed and said, 'That was earlier. For dinner . . . Where are you?'

'Taco Bell,' I said.

'Now, that sounds good,' he said.

'You want me to get you something?' I blurted out before I could think better of it, stop myself from being too forward.

But before I could really regret it, he replied, 'I'd love a couple of beef tacos. And some of those cinnamon things.'

'Okay,' I said, staring at the drugstore across from the Taco Bell.

There was a stretch of silence as I considered the awkward logistics. 'Should I . . . bring them over . . . there?' I finally asked.

'Sure. Unless you think that's a bad idea?' I heard hesitation in his voice as if he, too, registered that a late-night food delivery was a bit unorthodox, if not inappropriate. 'I mean, could you . . . get in trouble with Smiley?'

'For bringing you tacos?' I laughed nervously. 'I don't think so. Besides. No one would know. It's dark.' I shook my head, regretting the comment as soon as it was out. Too shady, conspiratorial.

Then he asked if I'd talked to Lucy tonight, and I realized he was right there with me, thinking the same way I was.

'Yes,' I said.

'And what's she up to?'

'She was going to bed when we last spoke.'

There was a long pause, and then he said, 'Well, just to be on the safe side . . . why don't you park in the garage?'

'Okay,' I said quickly. 'I'll be right over.'

25

The house was completely dark when I arrived, but, as I pulled down the driveway, I could see that the garage door was open, and Coach was standing inside, illuminated by my headlights. He was wearing a Walker warm-up suit and a teal baseball cap, his feet uncharacteristically bare. The turn from the end of the driveway was a tight ninety-degree angle, and the two-car garage felt more like a one-car with all the shovels, rakes, mowers, and old bicycles lining the perimeter. I cut my wheels as hard as I could, inching forward as Coach motioned for me to keep driving, until he finally held up his palm to stop, then gave me a thumbs-up. It occurred to me that, of the hundreds of times I had driven to the Carrs', I had never pulled inside their garage. I nervously offered this observation after he walked around to my door and opened it.

'Yeah, it's not an easy turn,' Coach said.

'Not easy at all,' I said, remembering that Lucy wasn't allowed to go anywhere near the garage when she first got her license. I also recalled that Connie had banged up her car a time or two over the years, but I certainly wasn't going to bring that up now. I reached for our bag of food on the passenger seat and got out of the car. We had yet to make eye contact.

'Speaking of driving . . . You really need to get that thing fixed,' he said, gesturing toward the dent in my fender. I glanced at him, then quickly away. His face was serious, and I could tell he was nervous, too. Maybe even as nervous as I was. I hoped he wasn't regretting the invite and commanded myself not to be awkward. If I could somehow manage to keep things natural, maybe we could make a habit out of spending time together.

'I know,' I said, my voice coming back faint. Embarrassed, I cleared my throat and said the words again, stronger.

'Take it to my guy,' he said, bending over to run his right hand along the metal groove. He patted it twice before standing up and taking the two steps back to my door. 'This thing will start rusting soon if you don't.'

'Who's your guy?' I asked, even though I already knew he went to Lloyd at Performance Auto. Just like I knew where he went to the dentist, where he got his suits cleaned, where he picked up his prescriptions.

'Lloyd Hardy,' he said.

'Looney Lloyd?' I smiled.

'Yeah, ol' Lloyd's missing a few screws for sure,' he said with a laugh. 'But he's the best when it comes to cars. And guns.'

'Does he know football?' I asked. I could tell we were both stalling, neither of us in a hurry to go inside.

'Nope. Just NASCAR. But he likes me pretty well and pretends to care about Walker. Tell him I sent you. He'll give you a deal.'

'I'm sure he will,' I said. Coach reached past me and pushed my car door shut, his arm brushing mine.

'All right, girl. Let's go in,' he said, turning toward the house. I trailed after him, pausing as he hit the button to close the garage door, then following him inside. We walked past the laundry room, where 'You Don't Bring Me Flowers' was playing on his portable radio. The thing was at least as old as Lucy and me, now bound with duct tape, Coach's favorite building material. A roll of tape could often be found in his office or car, along with a wealth of rubber bands in all sizes and colors, the full extent of his handiness.

'Barbra Streisand?' I teased.

'And Neil Diamond,' he said. 'Don't forget Neil.'

'You going soft, Coach?'

He laughed. 'Soft? Is that what you call beating Stanford?'

'Good point,' I said as he ducked into the laundry room and

switched off the radio. A pile of T-shirts and boxers were sloppily folded on the dryer along with one lone tube sock. The sight of his clothes, especially that sock, gave me a stab of intense sadness. I hated the idea of him doing his own laundry, being so alone.

I followed him past the pantry and into the kitchen, noticing details that I normally overlook. The tall baseboards, the slight sheen of the taupe walls, the distinctive smell of this house – a clean, and somehow old-fashioned, white-vinegar and woodsy scent. I caught Coach following my eyes, then misreading my thoughts. 'I know. It's messy. Lorna doesn't come on the weekends.'

'It's not so bad,' I said, though it was pretty messy. Dishes, several piles of mail, and an open box of raisin bran sat on the counter.

'I was just straightening up when you got here,' he said, closing the box of cereal and sweeping a few flakes from the counter into the cupped palm of his hand. He deposited them in the sink as I pulled our food out of the bag, unwrapping our tacos to determine which were his beef and my chicken.

'Want some plates?' he said.

I shrugged and said that wasn't necessary, then thought of how refined Connie was, and changed my answer. 'Actually, plates might be nice,' I said, reaching up and getting two from the cupboard, thinking that no other woman would know where everything was in his house. Except for Lorna and Lucy, and they didn't count. I arranged the tacos as artfully as I could, putting his cinnamon twists aside for later, then grabbing a couple of napkins from a drawer next to the flatware.

'I didn't get drinks,' I said. 'Figured you'd have something here.'

Coach nodded, then pulled two frosted mugs out of the freezer, along with a liter of A&W root beer from the fridge. 'Or would you rather have a real beer?' he said.

I smiled and said, 'Root beer's perfect.'

'Scoop of vanilla ice cream?' he said.

I laughed, shook my head, and said, 'With tacos? No thanks.'

'Vanilla ice cream goes with anything,' he said, pouring the root beer. 'But in light of the chocolate cake and cinnamon twists, I'll skip it, too.'

We both smiled as he carried the glasses over to the family room. He put one glass down on his drink stand, the other on the coffee table, then sat in his usual armchair. I followed him with our plates, handed him his, and sat diagonally next to him on the sofa.

'What a satisfying win,' I said.

He tore open a packet of hot sauce, put it on one taco, and said, 'Yeah. Those boys did a fine job today. Executed the plan to near perfection. Now—'

'—if we can beat Texas,' I finished for him.

He nodded, indicating that I got it right, as he flipped the television from Georgia–LSU on ABC to Cal–Oregon State on ESPN, then back to ABC, the tighter of the two contests.

We chatted about both games and the other scores of the day, spending a good ten minutes on Texas. I had only seen the highlights, but Coach filled in the details on their balanced offensive attack and stingy defense.

'It'll be tough to beat them,' he summarized with a long sigh.

'We'll get 'em,' I said, wondering if Smiley would fire me if he could see and hear me now. Then again, he had known Coach and I were close when he hired me. He had to have realized I wasn't going to flip a switch and become unbiased and estranged from all my former friends. And as long as I wrote objective pieces, and kept up public appearances of being impartial, wasn't this okay? It crossed my mind that Ryan might have the bigger issue with this moment, but I quickly discredited that thought, too. Miller was one thing, but there was no way Ryan would be jealous of his college coach. He loved the man almost as much as I did.

A few minutes later, Coach asked if I'd heard anything more about the investigation.

'Not really,' I said. 'Just the usual chat board rumors and

speculations . . . J.J. and Galli seem hopeful that the case will be closed for lack of evidence.'

'That would be nice,' he said.

'Don't you think this whole thing was cooked up by fans of another team?'

'I do,' Coach replied quickly.

I looked at him, thinking of the alternative theory, and said, 'Ryan thinks that all winners, at some point, cheat.'

'That's ridiculous.'

'That's what I said.'

'Does he cheat?'

I smiled. 'That's what I asked him.'

'And?'

'He said he doesn't have to.'

Coach rolled his eyes, flipped the channel, flipped it back.

I hesitated, feeling a little uneasy as I continued. 'Ryan said that someone bought Cedric Washington that Escalade he drove back in college. He implied that it was a bribe. So that he'd come to Walker . . .'

'*Someone,* huh?' Coach said. 'You mean someone like Ryan's daddy.'

'Are you serious?' I said, feeling my eyes grow wide.

Coach nodded. 'Well, that was the rumor. He wanted a top-notch receiver for his son to throw to.'

'But . . . So . . . You *knew* about that?' I stammered. My heart sank a little, hearing him toss out the theory so casually. Maybe Ryan was right – maybe I was naïve.

'I knew that was the rumor. As I said, I don't know for sure . . . I have no idea where Ced got that truck. I know he didn't buy a damn Escalade from his paper route in the Third Ward,' Coach said, as I remembered Cedric lovingly referring to his neighborhood in Houston as 'the Trey.' Come to think of it, he reminded me of Reggie, with an outgoing personality and an affable way of bridging the gap between the children of privilege at Walker and the blue-collar athletes. Everyone had rooted for him – there was even an impromptu pep rally on the quad the spring of our junior year when the Falcons drafted him as the seventh overall pick. He had done well in the NFL since then, still playing for Atlanta, married with three or four children – and maybe a fleet of Escalades.

'Did you ever ask Cedric about the car?' I pressed. 'Or Mr James?'

Coach Carr seemed a little defensive as he answered. 'I asked Ryan about it. I asked his daddy. They both denied it. I asked Cedric himself . . .'

'What did he say?'

'He said it was his uncle's. The title was in his uncle's name and his uncle was making the payments on it.'

'Did you believe him?' I asked.

'As opposed to calling one of my kids a liar?' he said, putting down his plate. 'What am I gonna do? Confiscate the truck? Trace the title? Strap his uncle to a lie detector? Bottom line, Cedric was a good kid. He worked hard on the field and in the classroom. And you know what?'

Before I could reply, he said, 'I'm *glad* Ced had a nice ride . . . He deserved it. Wherever the damn thing came from. Good for him.'

I digested this, wondering if I had come across as self-righteous or judgmental.

'You're right . . . I didn't mean to . . .' My voice trailed off as I searched for the right verb. I started to say 'accuse' but changed it to 'suggest.'

Coach nodded, but kept his eyes on the television.

'I'm sorry, Coach,' I said, although I wasn't exactly sure what I was apologizing for.

When he finally looked at me, his eyes had softened. 'It's okay. I'm not mad at you, girl . . . I'm just annoyed and frustrated by the whole thing. Here's the deal . . . In a sense, Ryan's right. There's always going to be a little shadiness. Cheating. Whatever you want to call it.'

I stared at him, trying to keep an open mind, though I hated where this was going.

'When I was in school, there was this old guy – Fred Tripp – who used to slide us five if we had a good game . . . We called it *Mr Tripp's handshake*. We'd tell the freshmen . . . "Oh, you played a good one. Get ready for the handshake!"'

'Five hundred? Or five thousand?' I said, shocked by what he was telling me.

'Five. As in – *five* dollars.'

We both laughed. 'Yeah. That's how the freshmen felt when they got home and looked in their envelopes and we all had a good laugh at their expense.'

I smiled.

'But, see, that's the thing. Forget the amount. Some of us took that envelope. And some of us didn't.'

I nodded, afraid to ask what camp he'd been in.

'Regardless of the amount, that five spot was still against NCAA rules. And every kid who accepted Mr Tripp's hand-shake was in violation. Walker was in violation . . . So did Rhodes break the rules? I really don't know. You can ask him – but he's gonna tell you no. Just like Cedric told me no. You understand what I'm trying to say?'

I nodded, but didn't love his answer, which seemed only to be a variation of what Ryan had told me in his basement.

We both turned our attention back to the TV, just as Georgia kicked a long field goal, making it by a hair. Coach clapped once, though I knew he wasn't really invested in the game, just happy for the kicker. Happy to see a good play. Maybe even a little bit happy for the underdog, although it had been a long time since we were in those beleaguered ranks. We both ate for a few seconds, watching Georgia celebrate.

Coach flipped back to the other game as I started chewing on my bottom lip, a nervous habit, and said, 'What do you think of Ryan's parents?'

'His mother is nice but very meek. As for Sherwood . . .' Coach shook his head. 'Brash, arrogant son-of-a-bitch. The do-you-know-who-I-am? kind of guy . . . Ryan's actually turned out pretty good in spite of him.'

I nodded, trying to analyze his choice of words. *Pretty good* wasn't exactly a ringing endorsement, but it could have been just the understated way Coach spoke.

'How are things going with Ryan, anyway?' he asked, just like he had at the track, as if maybe the update would have changed in a few weeks.

'Fine,' I said, shrugging.

'Getting serious?'

'No,' I said so reflexively that it surprised me, and I found myself wondering whether I'd told the truth. Then again, if I were disclaiming my relationship so effortlessly, didn't that mean, by definition, that Ryan and I weren't serious? My head suddenly hurt as I put the ball back in his court. 'What about you?'

'What about me?' Coach finished his taco, folded his napkin twice, then deposited it over his plate.

My palms sweaty, I said, as nonchalantly as possible, 'Do you think you're going to date anyone . . . anytime soon? . . . Or are you . . . not ready?'

'I might be . . . just a little bit . . . ready,' he said, staring into my eyes as my heart really began to race. 'But only for the right woman.'

'Of course,' I whispered.

'Someone who would always respect what I had with Connie. My past . . .'

'Right,' I said, nodding.

'Even better if this woman actually *knew* Connie,' he said, leaning toward me, his voice lowered. 'She has to be intelligent. Strong. With some gumption.'

'Of course,' I said, wondering if I had gumption. At this moment, I wasn't so sure.

'And she definitely has to understand this coaching thing . . . the game of football . . . She has to love football. Has to.'

'Right,' I said, hypnotized by his words and his eyes and the sound of his voice. 'What about physically? Do you have a type?'

'Not really,' he said. 'But I like brown hair. Reddish brown is nice. What do they call that – auburn?' He looked right at my hair as my vision blurred.

'But the hair is just a bonus. A two-point conversion if you will.'

I tried to speak, but couldn't.

He stared right into my eyes and said, 'You know anyone who fits the bill?'

'I might,' I managed to whisper.

'Oh?' he said with as much charm as a man could possibly have without being *too* charming. 'You *might*?'

'Maybe,' I said.

'Well, let me know . . . Because short of that woman, the one I just described . . . I'd rather be alone . . . Just sitting here, alone, watching football.'

He gave me a slow smile, staring even deeper into my eyes. So deep that I suddenly knew. Almost for sure. I held his gaze, paralyzed with fear, excitement, utter shock. Never in a million years had I seen this coming.

'Shea?'

'Yes?' I said, finally breathing, wondering if I'd heard him wrong. If it were only wishful thinking.

'Are you okay?'

I nodded, took a breath, and said, 'So . . . what do you think Lucy and Lawton would say? If you found this . . . woman?'

Waiting for his answer, I pushed Ryan from my mind, telling myself that I hadn't crossed any lines. This was a theoretical conversation. That's all.

'Lawton would be okay . . . I think . . . But Lucy? . . . I don't know. That might be a problem . . . Then again, she wants me to be happy.'

'Of course she does,' I said. 'Do you think . . . you can be? Happy again?'

'I think so . . . I hope so.'

'I hope so, too, Coach,' I said, wondering if you could faint from attraction.

I could hear in the background that someone had just scored, but neither of us looked toward the television. 'But you know what, Shea?'

He rarely used my name, and it caught me off guard. 'What, Coach?'

'I'm already happy. Right here. Right now.'

I smiled and said, 'Well, guess what?'

'What's that?'

'I am, too,' I said.

'Well, good,' he said as we both turned back to watch the game.

The rest of the night was all about football, both of us pretending that we hadn't had the conversation in which he told me, more or less, that my crush was not one-sided after all.

26

The first two times I said I should go, he protested, but just after midnight, when I caught him stifling a yawn, I got up and said it really was time. He walked me back to the garage door and gave me a hug, then a kiss. It was only a friendly peck on the cheek, but still significant, since it was the first ever, at least since I was about ten. I floated home, so dazed that I didn't realize that I had left my purse in his kitchen until the following morning. I waited until nine, in case he was sleeping, then dialed the only number in the world I knew by heart other than my own.

'Yep, you left your pocketbook,' he said before I could ask.

'Pocketbook?' I said, mocking his old-fashioned terminology.

'Yes. You're lucky you didn't get pulled over. How would you have explained that one?'

'Easy. I'd tell the police that you had my license. Drop your name . . . Works every time in this town.'

'Yeah, we already went down that road once,' he said, referring to my teenage drunk-driving episode. 'Remember?'

I shuddered at the memory. 'God, you scared me that night. Worse than the cops.'

'That was the idea,' he said.

'You know, I vowed that night . . .' I started, my voice trailing off.

'What did you vow?' he said.

'Never to let you down again.'

'And you haven't,' he said. 'So. You gonna come get this thing or what?'

'Yes,' I said. 'I'll be right over to get my *pocketbook*.'

* * *

A quick shower later, I was headed back over to Coach's in jeans, an old Cotton Bowl hoodie, and a haphazard ponytail. I was still on a crazy high until I pulled into the driveway and saw Lucy's car. Panicked, I started to back up, until I spotted her in the front seat looking right at me through the back window. She gave me a little wave, then got out of her car in a navy dress, nude pumps, and a double strand of pearls. She reached into the backseat to unleash Caroline from her car seat before they both walked over to my car. My mind raced for an explanation of why I could be here so early on a Sunday morning as I lavished attention on my goddaughter, buying a few seconds of time.

'Hey, honey! Don't you look pretty!' I said as Caroline crawled onto my lap and began playing with the buttons on my dash. 'I love your dress. And your braids.'

'They're *French* braids,' Caroline said. 'Mommy did them!'

'Well, *oui, oui*! She did a great job,' I said, glancing up at Lucy, who gave me a distracted, fast-twitch smile.

Caroline babbled some more random updates about her morning, something about her stuffed bunny named Monkey falling into the sink and getting wet. She then made a rapid transition and asked if I had candy in my car.

'Sure do,' I said, opening my glove compartment and pulling out a roll of cherry Life Savers that I kept there just for her. They were sticky from the sun, having melted into the paper wrapping, but Caroline didn't mind, shoving two into her mouth. One dropped from her mouth and rolled down the front of her white piqué dress, leaving a red trail before falling onto the driveway. Lucy wearily sighed, as Caroline scrambled down from my lap, plucked the candy off the ground, and inserted it back into her mouth.

'Hey, Luce,' I said as nonchalantly as I could, realizing we'd yet to speak directly to each other. 'You going to church?'

'Yeah . . . But who knows if we'll ever make it there,' she said, talking more to herself than to me. She sighed again, looking exhausted. 'What's going on with you?'

Clearly she was asking me what I was doing at her father's house on a Sunday morning, but I shrugged and said, 'Oh. Not much.'

'What are you doing here?' she asked, point-blank.

I glanced up at her through my sunglasses and could see that she looked slightly puzzled but not accusatorial or suspicious. I told myself not to be defensive or, worse, lie, as Caroline scampered toward the house. I could see in my peripheral vision that Coach had emerged from the garage. He bent down to scoop up Caroline, then walked toward my car. Right away, I saw that his wedding ring was now on his right hand, a change since last night, and one that made my heart thump in my chest.

Lucy repeated her question. 'So? What are you doing here? Just checking on Daddy?'

I considered simply saying yes, but forced myself to be truthful, mumbling that I had left my purse here.

'Your purse?' Lucy said, Coach now standing beside us. 'When?'

'Last night,' I said, sneaking a glance at Coach, who looked the way I felt. Uneasy, guilty, totally busted.

'It's in the kitchen. On the counter,' he said without looking at me, as Caroline reached up and played with the bill of his cap. She knocked it off, revealing a head of messy hair – as messy as short, coarse hair could really be.

'Why is your purse—' Lucy began as Coach cut her off.

'Shea was sweet enough to bring me some tacos last night. After the game. Very nice of her.' He looked at me and said, 'Thank you, again.'

'You're welcome,' I said with a lump in my throat.

Lucy studied her father, then me, then her father again, finally saying, 'You don't look ready for church.'

'Was I supposed to be?'

Lucy shook her head and said, 'It's Sunday morning, isn't it?'

'Since when do I go to church on Sunday morning if it's not Easter or Christmas?'

'Since this past Wednesday. When we talked about you

going to church with us and you said you'd make every effort
to go,' she said, as I wondered if she, too, noticed that his ring
had changed hands. Was that part of what she was upset about?
Or was it only that I had come over last night? Or merely that
her father wasn't going to church? 'Ring a bell?'

'Vaguely,' he said.

'So this is your *every effort*? Talking about Taco Bell in those
clothes at . . .' Lucy glanced at her white ceramic watch. 'Nine
forty-five?'

Coach stared sheepishly back at her.

'Ugh. Okay. We have to go,' she said.

'Next week,' he mumbled.

'That's the day after Texas,' I said, the words just slipping
out. My tone of voice saying, *So we all know that ain't happening.*

Caroline ran her hand over her grandfather's whiskered face
and said, 'Ow. Your face hurts!'

'Yes, Care Bear. I need to shave today,' Coach said, then gently
put her down and looked back at Lucy. 'Where's Neil, anyway?'

'He's meeting us there,' she said.

Coach nodded, then glanced at me and said he'd be right
back with my pocketbook. Once he had made his escape, Lucy
stared at me intently, her eyes narrowed. 'So was last night . . .
work-related? For your story?'

I shook my head and admitted that I'd already turned my
story in.

'So you really just stopped by to check on him?'

'And bring him Taco Bell,' I added, hoping I didn't look as
guilty as I felt.

Lucy studied me for a few seconds and finally nodded. 'Y'all
are friends. I get that.'

I said nothing.

'It's sort of weird, though,' Lucy said, doing her toe-pointing
thing left over from years of ballet.

'Weird?' I said, still watching her feet.

'That you're friends. Apart from me. I mean, can you imagine
me hanging out with your dad?'

'*I* don't hang out with my dad,' I said. 'But you're friends with my mom.'

'Not like that. Not like . . . eating Taco Bell together late Saturday night . . . without *you*,' Lucy said. 'But whatever, I *really* gotta go.'

'Me, too,' I said.

'Where are you going?' Lucy said.

'Home,' I said.

'Why?' she asked, a little on the shrill side. 'Don't let me chase you off. He's not going to church. And what do you have to do today?'

'Well, watch the Cowboys,' I said, just as Coach returned with my bag. I took it from him and murmured my thanks.

'What time do they play?' Lucy asked. 'The Cowboys?'

'Kickoff's at three,' I said.

'Well, then? What's the rush?'

'I was only coming to get my purse,' I said.

'Yes. But you're here now. You should stay. Go on in. Have breakfast together.'

Lucy was *definitely* agitated, now boxing us into a corner. To protest any more than we already had would almost look worse than acquiescing, so he finally just looked at me and said, pleasantly, casually, 'Shea. You're welcome to stay. But I really don't have much to eat in the way of breakfast. Other than raisin bran . . .'

'Okay,' I said stiffly. 'I'll come in and have a bowl of raisin bran. Thanks, Coach.'

Lucy nodded with a broad, forced smile, her lips reminding me of how they used to look in braces, stretched across her face. She stooped for a second to retie Caroline's sash, now dragging on the ground, and neaten her French braids. Then she picked her daughter up and headed for her car. 'All right, then,' she said over her shoulder. 'You two enjoy your breakfast together.'

'I want to stay with Poppy and Shea,' Caroline protested.

Lucy shook her head and said, loud enough for us to hear,

'No. They have things to discuss. Football things. You wouldn't be interested.'

She belted Caroline in the backseat as I realized that I had to back up to let her go. So I did, waiting in my car, the engine running, as she drove away a little too quickly.

My stomach and heart hurt as I got out of the car.

Coach shook his head. *'Shit,'* he said under his breath. Then he looked right at me and stated the obvious. 'Well. She's not happy.'

'You don't say . . .'

'You think it's because . . . you were here last night? Or that I'm not ready for church?'

'I don't know,' I said. Even though I did. 'Maybe both?'

'There's no peace in church. Especially during the season,' he said, although I could tell he, too, knew that wasn't the main problem.

'I can imagine. And you *really* can't go next week. C'mon,' I said, referring to Texas again.

He nodded. Then, as I followed him toward the house, he addressed the elephant on the driveway. 'I think maybe our friendship . . . bothers her a little.'

'I know,' I said. 'But she understands—'

'That you and I have more in common,' he said, finishing my sentence.

I wasn't sure if he meant that we had more in common than she and I did or than the two of them did, but, either way, the statement was true.

I returned to safer ground and said, 'I think Sundays are just hard . . .'

Coach nodded and said, 'Yes. You're probably right. And I think I did, maybe, sort of promise her I'd go to church this week.'

I grimaced as we walked inside through the garage, the same pile of clothing remaining on the dryer but the radio back on a country station, Garth Brooks singing 'Shameless.'

'That's better,' I said, pointing at the radio.

'I love this song,' Coach said just as Garth wailed: *But I can't walk away from you.*

He gave me a purposeful look that made me feel exactly the way Garth sounded in that song. Down on my knees and shameless.

Remembering Lucy, I gathered myself and followed Coach into the kitchen, watching as he got out two bowls, two spoons, and two napkins, setting the kitchen table. I got down our glasses, poured orange juice, and brought them to the table.

'Milk,' he said, snapping his fingers. Then shook his head, disgusted. 'Damn. I'm out. I'm sorry.'

'It's okay,' I said. 'I'm not hungry anyway.'

He nodded, looking as conflicted as I felt, and said, 'I know. Me either . . .'

'I really should go,' I said, even though I wanted to stay.

'Okay,' he said so quickly that it hurt my feelings.

Leaving the bowls on the table, we stood and walked right back outside to my car. By the time we got there, I was completely disheartened, sure that we would never be hanging out alone again. That it just wasn't worth all the accompanying angst and guilt and whatever was going on in Lucy's head.

But a few minutes later, just as I pulled into my driveway, a text came in from Coach that said: *Sorry about the milk. Going to the store now. Rain check on the raisin bran?*

Overcome with relief, and pushing Lucy as far from my mind as you could push your best friend, I typed back: *You bet. Anytime.*

Later that afternoon, as I was watching the Cowboys and folding laundry, Lucy came over to my apartment, unannounced and without Caroline. She had changed out of her church clothes into linen drawstring pants and a long-sleeved black T-shirt, but had forgotten to take off her pearls. As I went to the refrigerator to pour us both drinks, I informed her that Dallas was up by a touchdown, but it was clear she hadn't come over to watch the game.

'Daddy moved his wedding ring. To his right hand,' she announced, looking like she might cry.

'He did?' I asked nervously, putting ice in two glasses, then filling both with Coke Zero. I handed her one, forcing myself to look in her eyes.

'Yes,' she said. 'What do you think that means?'

'I don't know,' I said.

'That he's moving on?'

'Not necessarily.'

'Then why would he do that?'

'I don't know, Lucy. Maybe you should ask him,' I said.

She stared at me for several more seconds, then took a dainty sip. 'I can't.'

'Why not?'

'Because we don't talk like that . . .'

Then, before I could respond, she said, 'I'm sorry for being so grumpy this morning.'

I played dumb as I followed her the few steps back to my family room. 'You weren't grumpy. Were you?'

She glanced at the television, then took a seat on the floor, her back to the screen, before continuing, 'I told you I wanted you to help look after Daddy . . . then when you tried to do that . . . I acted . . . difficult.'

'It's okay,' I said as quickly as possible. This was as close as Lucy came to an apology, and it made me uncomfortable given everything that I knew to be true. Bottom line, she really didn't owe me one. 'I get it.'

'Do you?' she asked as I turned the volume down three notches.

'Yeah. I think so. Sure.' I folded a pair of flannel pajama pants from the pile on my sofa, avoiding her hard stare. It was obvious that the conversation, whatever it was she wanted to discuss, was not going away no matter how much I wanted it to.

'It's just that I'm a little bit . . . jealous,' she said.

My pulse quickened and my mouth got dry. 'Jealous of

who?' I said, folding a T-shirt with great care and precision. It was quite possibly the neatest folding job of my life, which is saying a lot given my practice in Lucy's store.

'Jealous of you and Daddy. How close you are,' she said. 'He's my father, but sometimes I think he's closer to you.'

'That's not true,' I said, feeling queasy. I plucked another shirt from the sofa, shook it out, and got to work.

'It is true, though,' she said, taking a sip of Coke, then placing the glass on a pile of *Sports Illustrated* issues on the floor beside her. 'It always has been true.'

'It's just . . . *football*,' I said, although I really didn't believe those two words belonged in the same sentence together. 'We have football in common. That's it.'

'That's like saying that . . . that . . . Ralph Lauren and Calvin Klein only have fashion in common . . . or . . .' She stared up at the ceiling, thinking. Analogies had never been her strong suit.

'I get your point,' I said, smiling, pretending to be amused when I only felt sick.

'Whether it's football or something else . . . you two have always had this connection . . . He talks to you. *Really* talks to you. He doesn't do that with me. I go over there . . . and it's just awkward. It's like he has nothing to say.'

Her description weakened me, but I shook my head and denied it again. 'We don't have a *connection*, Luce,' I said, thinking about the look he gave me last night. 'We just like football. I'm a sportswriter. He's a coach. And we both love you. That's it.'

'But even when you're not talking about football . . . You could be playing Trivial Pursuit . . . and it's like you have all these inside jokes.'

I almost said, *They're not inside jokes – they're simply jokes. You just don't get them.* But I didn't think that would make her feel much better – so I simply said, 'No, we don't.'

Lucy leaned back on her hands and stared at me. 'Okay. Look. I'm curious. Last night? Did he invite you over? Or did you call him?'

I told her it was his idea, and could tell right away that wasn't the answer she wanted. The corners of her mouth drooped slightly, and her forehead scrunched up.

'See? That's what I thought,' she said, although I wasn't sure how this fact made a difference. Wouldn't it be just as bad if I'd initiated?

'Well, wait,' I said, pretending to think over the particulars, then backtracking. 'Actually, come to think of it, I called him. Then he called me back. But I was at Taco Bell . . . and so . . . I offered to bring him something to eat. So, technically, I invited myself over. All he said was yeah, he'd love a taco. See?'

She waved off my explanatory babble and said, 'The fact remains . . . he never calls me like that. He never invites me over like that. And definitely not after a *game.*'

'But you're his *daughter,*' I said. 'It's totally different.'

She asked why, folding her arms across her chest.

'Because fathers don't need to *invite* their daughters over. Daughters just . . . stop by whenever. Like you do all the time.' I thought for a second, remembering my own dad. 'Unless a divorce is involved.'

'Or unless a dead mother is involved,' Lucy snapped back.

I shuddered, perhaps visibly. Or maybe Lucy realized how harsh her statement sounded. In either event, her voice and expression softened markedly as she said, 'Look. It was one thing when my mom was here. She was our go-between. My mom and I talked three, four times a day, and at least one of those times, he was somewhere nearby. In the background. And that worked just fine. We were all happy with that arrangement. But now . . . Everything is different. *Everything* . . .'

Lucy paused, choking up, then dabbed at the corners of her eyes. I wanted to give her a hug, or say something comforting, but couldn't make myself move or speak. A few seconds later, her composure regained, she continued, 'And without my mom . . . my dad and I have to work a little harder at our relationship. We *both* have a responsibility to put in the effort.'

I nodded and said she was right. Because she *was* right.

'Only we're not. At least he's not. Not at all. I'm doing all the work – and it makes me really sad.'

'Maybe . . . he just doesn't want to bother you . . . He knows how busy you are with Neil and Caroline and your shop . . .'

'So he calls *you* instead?' she said, but not in a confrontational way, like before.

I shook my head. 'First of all, he doesn't call me often . . . And secondly, I'm . . . alone.'

'You're hardly alone,' she said, rolling her eyes. 'You're in a *relationship* with *Ryan James*. Remember him?'

'But Ryan was in D.C. last night,' I said, pointing to the screen. 'See?'

She turned around to glance at the TV as he completed a crisp, short pass for a first down. When she faced me again, she looked a little less stressed. 'Jesus. That is so cool you're dating him,' she said, as if it was still surreal to her.

'Yeah,' I said, exhaling hard.

'Okay. Let me ask you this . . .' she said.

I braced myself for another uncomfortable question as I kept my eyes on the game.

'What if he *had* been in town last night?' she said.

'Who? Ryan?' I asked, trying to stay one step ahead of her, determine the direction of her inquisition so I wouldn't say the wrong thing again.

'Yes. Your *boyfriend*,' she said. 'So let's say he *was* in town . . . And my dad called you to come over . . .'

'Lucy,' I said, officially worried. 'What are you driving at here?'

She stared back at me and said, 'It just seems like . . .'

'What?' I said, holding my breath as I saw something flash across her face. It was as if she was processing all the facts. Putting everything together. But in an instant it was gone, and I breathed again.

'Never mind,' she said with a shrug, seemingly talking herself out of her hunch. The notion that her best friend and her father could actually have feelings for each other was absurd, ridiculous.

My head still pounding, I flashed a big smile at Ryan, his face filling the screen, now pumping his fist, whipping his helmet off in all his post-touchdown glory.

'*Niiice*,' I said, even though I'd missed the play entirely.

'Did he just score?' Lucy asked, glancing over her shoulder at the replay.

'Of course he did,' I said as proudly as I could as we both watched the replay – Ryan moving in slow motion, athletic, strong, and graceful at once.

'And that, right *there*,' I informed Lucy and reminded myself, 'is why Ryan James is the best quarterback in the NFL.'

Lucy smiled, appeased.

27

The day before Thanksgiving, my dad and his family descended upon Dallas. Astrid and Bronwyn invited me to go shopping with them, but I said I had to work and would meet up with everyone for drinks.

I had learned through the years the importance of pacing myself, and faking pleasantries over the course of a few hours at a time was far more doable than pretending to like people for multiple days. Vacations of any kind had been ruled out since our disastrous trip to Napa Valley following my graduation from college, originally billed as a cycling trip with my father. Astrid had decided to tag along at the last minute, changing out our bikes for a Jaguar convertible and turning the outdoorsy jaunt into a pretentious showcase of her knowledge of California's finest grapes. By the end of the week, I was so disgusted with the whole scene that I sailed right into a vineyard with a portable cooler packed with Budweisers, announcing that I wasn't much of a wine girl. I don't think she ever got that I was trying to make a point, that I really wasn't *that* much of a redneck, but, regardless, it was infinitely satisfying to crack open a cold one while she threw around her wine adjectives like confetti at a ticker-tape parade. The only saving grace was that my father *did* grasp what I was trying to accomplish, and seemed amused by my antics, later even apologizing, in a roundabout way, that the trip had become so 'one-dimensional.'

But the apology almost made it worse – because he never did anything about it, and he certainly never bothered to give me any quality alone time. It was always a relentless package deal, and that was still the case today.

So by the time five o'clock rolled around, I had worked myself into a resentful lather, and called him to cancel altogether, blaming it on a 'work crisis.' He seemed bummed enough to bring me some sick pleasure, and I couldn't help thinking of that dreary 'Cat's in the Cradle' song – and how many times he had blown me off over the years. Yet the chief difference between the song and my life was that my father was *still* just as busy as he ever was, and I was in a desolate office with no evening plans whatsoever and a familiar holiday melancholy welling inside me. Lucy called it my *Charlie Brown funk,* and had always done her best to force traditional cheer upon me, but obviously she was in worse shape than I was this year and, on top of everything, had made the mistake of offering to host Neil's family from Oklahoma City. What she had thought would be a welcome distraction was turning out to be nothing but an enormous culinary burden. I had already offered to help her a couple of times, at least keep her company while she cooked, but she had declined, insisting that she and Neil had everything under control.

What I really wanted, I realized, as I merged onto I-35 toward Walker, was to spend the night at Ryan's, as much for his company as for the tranquillity of his home, but he had already checked into the Gaylord Texan Resort & Convention Center in Grapevine, where the team was always sequestered before home games to ward against 'unwelcome distractions.'

'Just turn around at the next exit and go to my house,' Ryan offered when I reached him in his room and told him I was stuck in standstill rush-hour traffic. 'You have a key.'

I briefly considered this option, but decided that I didn't want to be there without him. During the day it was fine, but, at night, I found myself picturing gruesome crime scenes. There was something about all the white marble, white linens, white walls, even white carpet and furniture that conjured the splattering of blood. Like giant red psychiatric inkblots.

When I made the mistake of sharing these involuntary images with him now, he gasped and said, 'Good Lord, Shea. You're watching too many horror movies. That's sick.'

As soon as he mentioned movies, I thought of one in particular that haunted me whenever I was alone at his house: *Sleeping with the Enemy,* one of the most disturbing films of all time in my opinion. I told myself that it was only his sleek, cool décor and propensity to be neurotically neat that Ryan shared with the antagonist – nothing else – but couldn't help wondering if Blakeslee's accusations were factoring at all into my sub-conscious, making me imagine things whenever I noticed that a towel was askew in his bathroom.

'I know. I just get a little scared in a house that big,' I said, then gratuitously added, 'Besides. Being there without you would make me miss you more.'

'Aw. That's sweet,' he said. 'I really miss you, too. Wish we didn't have these damn hotel bed checks.'

'Stop lying,' I said in a teasing tone. 'You know you like ten hours of sleep before games.'

He laughed because it was true. Everything Ryan did on the night and in the hours before a game was carefully calcu-lated, designed to maximize his performance, right down to the temperature in his room – the thermostat always set to sixty-eight degrees, apparently the ideal temperature for REM sleep.

'Okay, you got me on that one . . . Here's a fact for you . . . I haven't had sex the night before a game since high school . . .' He laughed.

'Wait. Let me guess. You had sex before the state champion-ship game? And because you lost, you vowed to never do it again?' I said, picturing his high school girlfriend, whom he had described as a half-Pakistani beauty.

'Yep,' Ryan said, but he no longer sounded amused.

I thought of Blakeslee's story and very nearly confessed to him our conversation, but decided against it, once again. If nothing else, the day before a big game and the meeting of potential in-laws wasn't the right time. Instead I said, 'You're as superstitious as Coach, aren't you?'

'Hey, now. I'm not that bad,' he said. 'I just save my legs

for the game . . . It's a question of stamina . . . It's not like I'm out there catching bugs in Tupperware containers.'

'Mason jars,' I said, annoyed at myself for bringing Coach up. It was like an involuntary reflex, and I wondered when Ryan was going to catch on. He was so perceptive, and given his jealous tendencies, I was surprised that he hadn't yet. But the fact that he had not also underscored how far-fetched the whole notion of Coach and me was. I had revisited the look that Coach Carr gave me in his house at least a hundred times and had gone from feeling starry-eyed to foolish. Surely, it had to have been in my head.

I changed the subject as quickly as I could and asked Ryan if he was ready for the game tomorrow. He said yes, then detailed some of the reasons: great practice, sound strategy in place, knee feeling good, Philly's secondary sucks. I never tired of the inside scoop, and never would, but the starstruck feeling had finally, mostly, faded, replaced with the belief that I belonged in his world.

'What are you going to do tonight?' Ryan asked. There was an edge in his voice tipping me off that the Third Rail might be the wrong answer – and that I probably shouldn't confide that I was suddenly craving beer freshly poured from a tap as opposed to one opened from my refrigerator.

So I said, 'Oh, I don't know. Not much. Just laying low.'

'Good girl,' he said in a way that was equal parts condescending and nurturing. I decided to focus on the latter, especially when he asked me for the tenth time if I had my VIP parking pass, and then reminded me that the tickets were under my name at will call.

'Yes. Thank you,' I said.

'Are you sure you don't need a couple more?'

'I'm sure. Thank you,' I said, thinking that, for a pampered star with multiple assistants, housekeepers, personal chefs, trainers, and sports psychologists on his staff, he really could play the caretaker, too.

'You're ready to meet my folks?' he said.

'Yes. I can't wait,' I said. The statement was true, but it had as much to do with curiosity about his father and a sick need for one-upmanship over Astrid and Bronwyn as anything else.

'Good,' Ryan said. 'It'll be a fun day. *If* we win.'

'You will,' I said. 'All right. I better hang up before I rear-end someone. I'll text you before nine.'

'No. Call me,' he said.

'Okay,' I said, bristling just a bit. I told myself that I was being completely unfair to him. He simply wanted to say good night before he went to bed. That was it – and it was sweet. A sign of a good boyfriend. A *great* boyfriend. I told myself to go home and get some rest. That I might not be playing football, but that I had a pretty big day tomorrow, too.

Yet I couldn't resist the magnetic pull of the Third Rail, and forty-five minutes later, I was saddled up to the bar, ordering a Blue Moon on draft with extra oranges. The place was unusually packed, and I knew, or at least recognized, a good dozen people, including several girls from my high school class. In the way of small towns, most had stayed put in Walker after graduation, many not bothering with college at all, so it wasn't unusual to bump into classmates. But around the holidays, there were always a few homecoming surprises – faces you hadn't seen in years.

That night, I spotted Michelle Sheffield, a girl in the class behind me whom I'd always really liked and who now lived in San Francisco. We gave each other a big hug, then exchanged updates. I told her about my job at the *Post*, while she shared that she was practicing patent law. It was refreshing to discuss jobs – rather than mommy updates, which was the typical conversation when I ran into someone from Walker.

I glanced at her bare ring finger and said, 'So you're still single?'

'Yep,' Michelle said.

'Me, too,' I said.

She smirked and said, 'Yes, but I hear you have a boyfriend.'

I nodded.

'So it's true? You really are dating *Ryan James*?'

I tried to smile modestly.

'Wow. That's so cool. How did that happen? Did you meet him through your job?'

'We went to college together,' I said. 'So we've been friends for a while now.'

'What's he like?'

'He's cool . . . He's . . . really nice.'

She stared at me, waiting for more, so I added, 'He's very intense. Competitive. Focused. What you would expect of a quarterback playing at that level.'

'Does he get recognized everywhere you go?'

'Yeah. But we really don't go out that much. He lays pretty low during the season. We mostly just stay in and watch movies. Stuff like that. Although he's pretty outgoing and extroverted . . . Very smart. He's great,' I finished.

'That's soo cool,' Michelle said again. 'Do you think you'll get married?'

I shrugged and said, 'Oh, who knows? He just got divorced – so I can't imagine that that would happen for a long time, if at all . . . Though we *are* doing the whole meet-the-parents thing tomorrow. But enough about Ryan James. You're the one with the glamorous California life.'

Michelle smiled and gave me her updates, as we ordered another round, and then another, playing pool and bumping into various other friends and acquaintances. It was a nice commingling of groups from high school and Walker. At some point, I spotted Miller with a bearded hipster type and went to say hello. Miller introduced me to his friend Lion, explaining that he was an artist, originally from Boston, now teaching a sculpture class at Walker after a gig at UCLA. Clearly Miller had met him through his professor girlfriend, and I thought how amusing it was that someone like Miller had found his way into an academic clique.

'Hey. You're a sculptor, huh? That's cool,' I said, shaking his hand, always grateful for new blood. 'Welcome to Walker.'

'Lion has a kid,' Miller announced, seemingly mystified, as if he'd told me that Lion was once a conjoined twin.

Lion caught it, too, laughing. 'Yeah. Crazy, huh?'

'Forgive him. Miller can't imagine responsibility greater than getting the mail,' I said.

'Shit. I forgot to get the mail again!' Miller said.

Lion laughed and said, 'Well, I couldn't imagine it either . . . I just found out about him four years ago. His mother never told me she was pregnant.'

'Wow. How old is he now?'

'Ten.'

'Damn. You're kidding me,' I said, grateful, not for the first time, to be a woman. It was the one bit of news that could never be sprung on you.

'Nope. But it's all cool now. Charlie's a great kid.'

I nodded, telling him he needed to bring his son to a Walker football game.

'And a Cowboys game,' Miller said, grinning, as Michelle returned from the bathroom. Within seconds, he was working her over, cracking her up.

'Don't you have a girlfriend?' I said, now buzzed.

'Yeah. But she's a freethinker,' Miller said with a wink. 'She'd love Michelle here. If you get my drift.'

I rolled my eyes and muttered, 'Pig.'

'How's your boyfriend? You two engaged yet? I heard you're meeting his parents.'

'I am meeting his parents. But, no, we're not engaged,' I said, thinking it was the worst part about living in a small town – word traveled fast. About *everything*.

'Your dad coming in?' Miller asked.

I nodded. 'He's here already. I'm avoiding him as we speak.'

'Maybe Ryan's going to ask him for your hand.'

'You're an idiot,' I said.

He playfully slapped my ass and said, 'You love it.'

I punched his shoulder as hard as I could but recognized

that I wasn't as offended as I probably should have been. He was harmless – always had been.

'Ow!' Miller yelled, then turned to Lion and Michelle and said, 'Shea dumped me for Ryan. But it's all good. I get it. I'd dump me for Ryan, too. I mean, gym teacher – or pro quarterback?'

Michelle laughed, and I could tell she was into him.

'We broke up because you're an idiot. End of story.' I smiled, and he grinned back at me.

'It's cool,' he said. 'I'm not really the marrying kind.'

Michelle got into the fray after that, trying to psychoanalyze him and, thereby, all bachelors, while I ordered shots of Jack – with beers for chasers. It occurred to me as I started a tab that it wasn't the wisest decision to tie one on the night before meeting my boyfriend's parents, but I was already impaired enough to come up with a handful of rationalizations.

So I kept going, drinking, laughing, playing pool, even dancing, feeling merrier by the minute, full of goodwill toward all, even background players and characters two degrees removed. We all had Walker in common, in one way or another, a point I made over a boisterous, heartfelt toast.

'Do you realize,' I began, feeling much more profound than the words that escaped my lips, 'that we all either come from this town or now live in this town?'

'Whoa,' Miller said, mocking me. 'That is quite an observation. Since we're all getting shitfaced in this shit box of a town.'

'It's not a shit box,' I said. 'It's about to be the home of the best team in college football coached by the most amazing, incredible . . .'

'Aw, *please*!' Miller shouted over me. 'Here we go again!'

'What?' I said, wobbling a little as I looked up at him.

'The hero worship. Fuck. It never ends.'

'Shut up,' I said.

But Miller was as drunk as I was and kept shouting, pontificating to his audience. 'Coach Carr! That's who she's *really* in love with. Not me. Not Ryan. But Coach *Cliiiiive* Carr.'

Michelle gave Miller an incredulous snort and said, 'That's Lucy's *dad*. Her best friend's dad.'

'So?'

'He's way too old for her,' Michelle added.

'Shea doesn't mind,' Miller said, shaking his head. Then he pointed at me and said, 'See? Look at her. Look at her face.'

Whatever had been on my face, I instantly changed to an exaggerated scowl.

'She's in love with Lucy's old man. Always has been. Always will be. I saw them in here one night together.' He looked at me and said, 'You gonna deny that?'

'We were working,' I said. 'I'm a reporter. He coaches the team I cover. We have a *working* relationship.'

'The hell.'

I denied it again, as strenuously as I could, but, in my impaired state, a small part of me loved what Miller was saying about us. So the next words out of my mouth were 'You know what? I'm going to call him now and tell him what you're saying about him.'

Then I walked across the bar and out the door. The crisp night nearly knocked some sense into me, but not enough, apparently, because I dialed Coach's number.

'*Qué pasa?*' he said, his voice chipper.

'I'm at the Third Rail,' I announced. 'You should come over.'

He laughed and said, 'You know I can't do that.'

'Why not?' I said. 'You did it before.'

'That was a Monday night. That was an exception. Probably shouldn't have done it that night.'

'But I want to see you,' I said.

'I want to see you, too,' he said. Plain as that.

Shocked, I said, 'Well, then. Come over.'

'I can't.'

'Then I'll come over there,' I said, staring up at the sky. 'Do you know there's a full moon tonight?'

'It's not full. Not quite,' he said. 'How much have you had to drink?'

'A few . . .'

'Then you can't drive.'

'I'm not. I wouldn't. I'm going to take a cab. To your house.'

'No. You can't do that. People will talk.'

'And why would they talk? Nothing's going on. Is there?' my voice rose in a flirting, leading lilt.

He laughed and said, 'Okay, girl. Stay put. I'm coming to get you.'

'I'm ready,' I said. 'Come and get me.'

'I'll be there in ten. Go around to the Monroe Street side . . . and be careful.'

'What about my car?' I said.

'You can get it tomorrow.'

'Okay.'

'Stay put.'

'Okay . . . Coach?'

'Yeah, girl?'

'Hurry,' I whispered.

Ten minutes later, long enough for me to say goodbye to my friends and lie about calling a cab, Coach pulled onto Monroe, slowed, stopped, and waited for me to open the passenger door. I climbed in, leaned over to pat his arm, and gave him a big, silly grin.

He smiled back at me but then said, 'So, tell me the truth. How much did you *really* have to drink?'

'A few,' I said, putting on my seat belt. 'A lot.'

He shook his head. 'I wish you wouldn't do that. I've told you before – you should always be in control.'

'I am in control.'

He glanced over at me and said, 'Oh? You sure about that?'

'Very sure about that,' I said, suddenly remembering my credit card, still at the bar. I texted Miller and said, *My tab's still running. Have one on me!!*

He wrote back right away. *Will order a round for the whole bar. Cheers!*

'What an ass,' I slurred, smiling.

'Who's that?'

'Miller,' I said. 'But nah . . . he's not so bad.'

'No,' Coach said. 'He's not so bad. Just wasn't right for you.'

'Who is?' I said coyly.

He smiled but didn't answer. When we got to the stoplight on Jefferson, he turned on the radio, found Rascal Flatts singing 'These Days,' and started drumming on the steering wheel. When the light turned green, he went straight instead of turning right toward his house.

'Where are you going?' I asked him.

'I'm taking you home.'

'But I wanted to go to your house.'

Coach shook his head. 'You need to sleep. Besides, we all know what happened last time you came over.'

'What happened?'

'Lucy,' he said. 'Remember?'

'Did you get an earful, too?' I said.

'Oh, yeah. I was interrogated.'

'What did you tell her?'

Coach cracked a smile, glanced at me sideways, and said, 'You really are quite the little reporter, aren't you?'

'I'm not little,' I said, puffing out my chest and running my hands through my hair to make it fuller. 'I'm . . . statuesque.'

He grinned. 'That you are,' he said, glancing down at my legs before returning his eyes to the road.

I reached over and turned up the radio as Carrie Underwood and Brad Paisley's 'Remind Me' came on, announcing how much I loved the song, then joining in, despite my terrible singing voice. 'If you still love me, don't just assume I know!'

A few seconds later, we pulled in to my complex. 'Which unit are you?'

I pointed straight ahead. 'That one.'

He parked in a guest spot but let the song end before he

turned the ignition off, staring straight ahead, his face serious. Then he got out of the car, came around to my door, and opened it. Still sitting, I looked up at him, our eyes locking. 'What?' I asked, without moving, just staring.

He reached down, took my hand, and gently pulled me out of the seat.

'I don't think Luce would like this very much either,' I said.

'Me giving you a safe ride home?'

'No. You taking me by the hand.'

'She'd understand that it's for your own drunk good,' he said, leading me over to the cement path lined with trodden-down white and purple pansies.

'I'm meeting Ryan's parents tomorrow,' I offered, out of the blue. 'And he's meeting mine.'

'And you'll be hungover.'

'Worth it.'

'How do you figure?'

'Because you're here,' I said. 'Holding my hand.'

He smiled but dropped my hand, moving his arm around my waist, guiding me toward the open-air staircase, then up two flights to my door. I fumbled in my purse for my keys, found them, and slowly unlocked the door. Then I walked in, holding the door open, hoping he'd follow me. He did, and, before he could change his mind, I closed it behind him, then dead-bolted it. Amused, he shook his head, then peered around my dark living room, his eyes resting on the framed article he'd given me, leaning on my mantel.

'Looks good,' he said.

'I love it,' I said.

'I'm glad.'

'I love that it's from you.'

Coach nodded. 'Good. Now go to bed.' He pointed down the dark hall toward my bedroom.

'I'm not sleepy,' I said.

'Count sheep.'

I made a face.

'But first drink some water and take a couple Tylenol.'

'Okay,' I said. 'But one question first.'

'One question.'

'Why do you think Lucy doesn't want us to spend time together?'

'I don't know what makes Lucy tick.'

'Take a guess. Or I'm going to ask another question.'

He smirked, looked up at the ceiling, then reached out and took my hand again.

'Because,' he said, squeezing it, taking one step closer to me. 'Because I think she *knows*.'

'She knows *what*?' I said, inhaling his aftershave. My heart swelled, and I felt dizzy – dizzier than I already was – as I imagined how easy it would be for me to lean in and kiss him.

'Nope,' he said, pulling back his hand and shaking his finger at me. At first I thought he meant no, I couldn't kiss him, but then he said, 'You said *one* question. And I answered it. Now. To bed. Go.'

His face was in a shadow, but I heard in his next deep breath that he was feeling *something*. We both stood frozen, staring, waiting, for a long few seconds, before he turned around, undid the dead bolt, and opened the door.

'Goodbye, girl,' he breathed, now standing in the doorway.

'Goodbye, Coach,' I said as the door closed behind him.

I exhaled, pressed my cheek and palm against the metal door, and closed my eyes. His voice came back from the other side. 'Lock the door and go to bed.'

I opened my eyes and smiled, then did what I was told.

28

I *never called Ryan.*

It was the first thought I had when I snapped awake the next morning. Followed by: *How am I going to get my car?* Followed by: *I'm never going to drink again.* I reached up for my phone on the nightstand, my temples throbbing and my heart sinking as I saw six missed calls and seven texts, all from Ryan, each progressively more agitated.

8:30: *Heey babe. Just called u. Hit me back.*

8:42: *Going to bed in a few. Miss u. Call me.*

9:05: *Where are u?? Why aren't you picking up?!*

9:38: *Worried. Hope u r ok?*

10:07: *You must be out. Turning phone off. GN Shea.*

10:43: *Nothing? Wow. Ok . . .*

11:21: *Can't sleep. This sucks. Hope it was worth it.*

I stared at the screen as I tried to form my defense. I was drunk? I lost track of time? I forgot? I fell asleep? Poor cell reception . . . dead battery . . . lost phone? The truth? What was the truth? That he hadn't crossed my mind except to field a few questions about him from old classmates? That Coach had been the one I wanted to call – and *did* call?

I forced myself to dial Ryan's number now, having no idea what I'd say if he answered. It rang once and rolled right to voice mail, as I began my rambling message. *Hey, Ryan. I'm really sorry about last night. Will explain what happened when we talk . . . but obviously I know you're only focusing on the game at this point. Good luck . . . I can't wait to watch with your parents . . . I'm sorry.*

I hung up, awash with mixed feelings. On the one hand, I

really *was* sorry. I'd told Ryan I was going to do something – and I hadn't done it. I had been on the receiving end of such empty promises with Miller and others before him, and knew how frustrating it could be. I also knew how much Ryan liked to control everything that happened on the night before a game, so I was sure his nerves had compounded his irritation. Bottom line, I had been insensitive and thoughtless.

At the same time, though, it all seemed a bit overblown. So I hadn't called him during a two- to three-hour window on one random night? Big deal. Why couldn't he just say good night and go to bed, already? Was it really necessary to leave that many messages? Was it really worth getting that upset?

As the room began to spin, I moved more squarely into the defensive camp. It wasn't like we'd had firm plans that I had blown off. I just forgot to call him. I mean, *seriously,* didn't he have more important things to worry about? Like the Philadelphia Eagles? Get over it, already.

My phone rang, and I scrambled to answer, expecting it to be Ryan and dreading the confrontation. Instead, I saw CCC lighting up my phone. My stomach kept fluttering, but now for a very different reason.

'Hello?' I said, my voice hoarse.

'Well, well, well,' Coach said. 'Someone doesn't sound quite as peppy as she did last night.'

I tried to laugh, but my throat was too dry and it came out a small groan. 'Yeah. I guess not.'

'You feeling okay?'

'Yeah,' I said. 'I'm sorry about last night.'

'Nothing to be sorry about,' Coach said – which somehow made me resent Ryan's guilt trip more. If anything, Coach should be the one annoyed with me. Would Ryan have preferred a nice drunk dial at midnight? 'We just need to get your car.'

'We?' I said, curling into a ball and feeling overcome with that dreamy feeling he always gave me, especially when he used pronouns like *we* and *us.*

'Yes. *We.* That is, if you're okay to drive now?'

'I didn't have *that* much to drink,' I said. 'You must think I'm a total lush . . .'

'Nah. Two benders in eight months does not a lush make.'

'Two?'

'Heisman Trophy night. Was that the last one?'

'Oh, yeah,' I said, no longer embarrassed about that call. 'Yeah. That was the last one.'

'So. Let's schedule the next one for *after* the season. You and me. In January.'

'Okay. Yes. January,' I said, thinking of the national championship game. I reached over and knocked on my wooden nightstand. 'It's a date. Just you and me.'

I could feel his smile coming over the phone, and I beamed back at him.

'Okay,' he said after a few intimate seconds. 'I'll be over around nine.'

'You will?' I said, excited.

'Yeah. Someone has to take you to get your car. Don't you need it today? To get to the game?'

I said yes, sitting up and checking the time. It was nearly 8:30 – which gave me thirty minutes to look presentable.

'Okay. Get up,' he said. 'Get the blood pumping. You've got a big day ahead of you. Big game. Big meeting.'

'Right,' I said, wondering how I was going to get through it all.

Thirty minutes later, after I had showered, thrown on some jeans and a sweatshirt, and half dried my hair, there was a brisk knock at the door. I ran to open it and found Coach, wearing a Walker warm-up suit and a ball cap, holding a large coffee from Bunki's.

'Happy Thanksgiving, girl,' he said, raising the coffee.

'Oh, right. I forgot. Happy Thanksgiving,' I said, taking the hot to-go cup from his outstretched hand. 'Thank you.'

'Figured you needed some coffee but then realized . . . I don't even know how you take it.'

Even. The word suggested that he *should* know, that we had passed that point in our relationship.

'Plain. Black,' I said, which was the way he drank it, too.

'Well, you're in luck . . . I hope I got the donuts right, too,' he said, holding up the bag, then placing them on the small table right inside my door.

'Glazed?' I guessed, knowing that was his favorite.

He winked and patted the bag. 'Yep.'

'Do you wanna come in for a second?' I asked, still feeling forward but not nearly as bold as last night.

'I would, but we need to hurry. You need to be on the road soon for a one o'clock kickoff.'

'I know,' I said, grabbing my keys and purse as we headed out the door. He took my coffee as I locked the door, then handed it back to me as we walked down the flight of stairs, our footsteps echoing in the stairwell. Once on the sidewalk outside my building, he glanced around, then lowered the bill of his cap.

'Are you worried someone will see you?'

'Not really,' he said, giving me a sideways smirk. 'I sort of got over that one last night. Waltzing over here at midnight like I did.'

I smiled and said, 'Right. But . . . we're allowed to be friends.'

He gave me a purposeful look as we reached his car. 'We're allowed to be any damn thing we want to be. Right?' he said, as he opened the door for me.

'Right,' I said, my voice and hands unsteady. I ducked my head to climb inside his car as his hand dropped to my shoulder, guiding me. I had to catch my breath as he went around to his side, got in, and put his key in the ignition. Right before turning it, he looked at me again and said, 'Do you know what's going on here?'

I froze, trying to interpret the question, wishing my head were clearer.

'With us?' I clarified, the word filling the space between us, shrinking it further. I could smell his skin now, see individual whiskers on his face, pick out the few salt among the pepper.

He nodded, holding my gaze. 'Yes,' he said. 'With us.'

'I have an *inkling*,' I said, my pulse quickening further.

He flashed me a full-on, crinkly-eyed smile and said, 'All right. Just checking.'

Then, as he fixed his attention on the road, I looked out my side window, my thoughts racing. We did not speak again, nor did we look at each other, until I directed him to my car, crookedly parallel-parked about fifty feet beyond the bar.

'So,' he said, pulling up behind it. 'Here we are.'

'Yes,' I said. 'Here we are.'

He squared his shoulder to me and reached out for my free hand. I gave it to him, and he squeezed my fingers between his. 'Happy Thanksgiving, girl. Hope your Cowboys get a win,' he said, his hand warm and strong.

'They're not *my* Cowboys,' I said, staring into his eyes. 'I only have one team.'

'Oh, come on,' he said, releasing my hand, then reaching up to adjust his cap. 'You know that's not true.'

'It is true,' I said.

We sat that way for another few seconds, holding on to the moment, whatever it was that was happening between us. I broke the spell by saying, 'Actually, Ryan's pretty ticked at me. So today should be interesting . . .'

'Why's that?'

'I didn't call him last night.'

'Is that mandatory?' he retorted. 'That you check in?'

'Last night it was. He asked me to call him by nine.'

'He gave you a *deadline*?'

'That's when he goes to bed. Before games.'

'I see.' Coach nodded, clearly aware of such practices, as the enforcer of his own rules about sleep before games. His next question was neutral enough. 'So why didn't you?'

'Because,' I said. 'I had other things on my mind.'

'Oh?'

I nodded. 'I wasn't thinking about Ryan. At all.'

'Well . . .' he began, then stopped.

'Well, what?'

'If you broke your promise, then just apologize . . .'

'I already did.'

'You spoke?'

'Voice mail.'

He nodded. 'So that's that. You apologized . . . Don't grovel.'

'I won't.'

'And don't . . .' Coach began, looking down at my hand again. He seemed to be on the verge of holding it again but stopped himself. 'Don't let that boy control you.'

'What do you mean?' I was pretty sure I knew what he meant, but I wanted clarification, as much information as I could gather.

'Ryan is used to getting what he wants. He fully *expects* to get what he wants . . . And, because of that, he usually does.'

I nodded, thinking that it was an excellent summation of Ryan, but was still unsure of where Coach was going with the point until he looked at me and said, 'Just make sure it's what *you* want.'

I stared back at him, my hangover making my thoughts hazy but also emboldening me. It was an odd, scary combination. 'I know what I want,' I said.

Coach held my gaze. 'Good,' he said. 'That's a very good start.'

'Yes. It's a start . . .' I said, then hesitated. I felt disloyal to Ryan saying anything more but managed to overcome that feeling, rationalizing that we were still speaking in generalities. 'I just have to figure out how to get it.'

'Well,' Coach said, a hint of a smile appearing on his lips. 'In my experience . . .'

I raised my brows, waiting for some philosophical gem. But instead, he finished his sentence with 'The Big Red at the Parkit Market never hurts.'

I smiled and said, 'So I've been told.'

Thirty minutes later, after I'd changed into black leather leggings, suede boots, and a Cowboy-blue sweater with a deep

V in the back, I was on the road to Dallas. I checked my phone on and off the whole way, hoping to hear back from Ryan, while obsessing over my last exchange with Coach. When I pulled into the driveway at the Ritz, I was only ten minutes late, a small miracle, and spotted my dad and his family preening by the valet stand. Astrid, Bronwyn, and her husband, Wiley, who reminded me a lot of my dad, were all wearing black or shades of gray and charcoal, a cluster of brunette Manhattanites. Bronwyn and Astrid had the same long, slippery, stick-straight hairstyle but Bronwyn had cut side-swept bangs that I couldn't decide if I liked or hated – or, perhaps most accurately, hated because I actually liked.

I got out of the car and waved, feeling unpolished and sloppy, an effect this group almost always had on me. In their company, no matter how much effort I put into my appearance, my hair always felt too wild, my clothes and lipstick too bright, my body large and graceless. Sort of like Julia Roberts in *Pretty Woman, before* her makeover. But I reminded myself why we were all here today, and that Ryan James had legitimized me just as Richard Gere had done for Julia.

'Hey!' I said, smiling, probably showing too many teeth and wishing I had remembered to spit out my gum in the car. 'Welcome to Dallas!'

Too loud, I thought, adding it to the list as Astrid and Bronwyn gave me stingy finger waves and prim smiles.

'Hello,' Astrid trilled. 'Love the boots. Don't you look fab!'

'Thanks,' I said, the awkward recipient of her double-cheek kiss.

Bronwyn moved in next, but I snubbed her at the last second, turning toward my father, wishing we could have even one moment alone, unobserved by Bronwyn and Astrid.

'Hi, Dad,' I said.

'Happy Thanksgiving, honey,' he said, giving me a big hug.

'You, too,' I said, hugging him back.

I greeted Bronwyn and Wiley next, exchanging cool pleasantries, noting, not for the first time, that they seemed to equate aloofness with refinement. I had to give it to them, though. They *were* refined, with impeccable grooming and etiquette and clothing, right down to the shiny buckles on his Gucci loafers and the black-patent bows on her five-inch pumps. I couldn't imagine either of them ever having a hangover – or drinking too much in the first place.

'Are y'all excited about the game?' I asked, the *y'all* escaping my lips before I could remember to change it to the proper *you all*.

'Yes,' Bronwyn said with a tight, Botoxed smile.

'Certainly,' Wiley chimed in. 'This is wonderful. Thanks for arranging everything, Shea.'

'You're welcome,' I said. 'I didn't do much. Ryan did . . .'

'So *how is* Ryan?' Astrid said, linking arms with me as my father gave the valet his ticket.

'He's fine,' I said, a fresh wave of guilt and worry washing over me. I had yet to hear from him and clearly wasn't going to at this point, with the game kicking off in less than an hour.

'And you're . . . *really* dating him?' she said, about as transparently insulting as a question could be.

I gave her a long look and said as pointedly as I could, 'Yes. Why? Does that surprise you?'

'Of course not,' my dad answered for her, picking up on the nuance. He had to have at least thirty IQ points on her – and so, for that matter, did my mother, a small source of comfort.

Astrid didn't take the hint. 'So it's really getting serious? Or are you just casually seeing each other?' she pressed.

'We're sitting in his parents' box at the game,' my dad said to her with a tinge of irritation that delighted me. 'You do the math, honey.'

'Astrid can't do math,' I said, smiling and quickly adding, 'Just joking!'

'She actually can't, though,' Bronwyn said. The only thing that redeemed my half sister was that she seemed almost as bothered by her mother as I was, and I was reminded of the odd fact that I actually liked Bronwyn more in person than I did in theory. She was infinitely more interesting than Astrid, having inherited my father's intelligence.

The valet pulled up with their rental SUV, and we all piled in, Wiley, Bronwyn, and me in the back, Bronwyn in the middle. I glanced down at her hands, resting on her thighs, noticing her huge diamond ring and fresh manicure. I made two fists, hiding my own ragged cuticles, and did my best to make small talk. How was New York, their work, their new house in the Hamptons? Bronwyn's answers were either succinct or modest, depending on your interpretation, not leaving much room for follow-up, and, to her credit, she tried to turn the conversation back to me, and seemed more interested in my new job than in Ryan.

'Do you like it?' she began. 'Is it what you thought it would be?'

'Yes – and pretty much,' I said as everyone listened to my answer. 'It's tough operating on such tight deadlines, but I really do like it. I like concentrating on one sport, one team.'

Bronwyn nodded, and I could hear respect in her voice when she said, 'How many other women sports reporters are there?'

'At the *Post,* specifically?'

She nodded.

'None,' I said.

I caught my dad's proud smile in the rearview mirror – which pleased me more than it should have.

'Did Ryan help you get the job?' Astrid chimed in.

'No,' I said. 'He had nothing to do with it.'

Wiley asked a few questions about the quickly growing obsolescence of newspapers – and whether I thought we'd be completely online at some point in the near future – until Astrid managed to hijack the conversation and manipulate it in a completely unrecognizable direction. As she blathered on, I reread Ryan's messages, trying to detect aggression in them, relieved not to find any. They were decidedly controlling, high-maintenance, and self-righteous, but I didn't see any of Blakeslee's accusations embedded anywhere. Of course I still hadn't listened to his voice mails, and wondered why this was.

Did I not want to find damning evidence right before meeting his parents? Was I just too exhausted? Or did I simply not care enough? As I stared down at my phone, a new message popped onto the screen. It was from Coach: *Tell your dad I said hi.*

I typed back: *Will do.*

I kept staring at my phone, willing another message to appear. It finally did. *How do you feel? Any better?*

Me: *Yes, much. The coffee and donut helped. Thanks again.*

CCC: *Of course. You at the stadium yet?*

Me: *Almost.*

I looked up from my phone and said, 'Dad. Coach Carr says hi.'

'How is he doing?' Astrid asked with exaggerated sympathy.

'Fine,' I said.

'Is he dating yet?'

I told her no as tersely as I could.

'What about your mother?'

'What about her?' I snapped.

'Do you think they'll get together?'

'God, no.'

'I told her that already,' my dad said.

'Why not? They're close friends – and I have always thought he was so sexy.'

'Astrid. Please stop,' I said.

It only fueled her fire. 'You don't think he's sexy? *Way* sexy – in that rugged Texas football coach way . . . Though that's not really my type.' She patted my dad on the hand.

'Astrid,' my dad said, exasperated. 'Connie just passed away in February.'

'That's plenty of time to move on,' she fired back.

'Drop it,' my dad said.

'What? Are you jealous?' Astrid said, as we approached the stadium. 'Would it bother you if they got together?'

'No,' my dad said. 'I just don't see that happening.'

I glanced back down at the phone as another text from Coach appeared: *Enjoy the game.*

Thanks, I typed. Then paused and added a very bold *I wish I were watching with you.*

CCC: *You and me both . . .*

I grinned down at the phone, lost for a moment, putting images to the ellipses as we pulled into the VIP parking lot at AT&T Stadium.

When we got to the Jameses' suite, Ryan's parents were already there along with a handful of couples about their age. I recognized them right away, both from seeing them in the stands during college and because Ryan looked so much like his father. Mr James made a beeline for me, effusively greeting me with a two-armed bear hug. It wasn't what I expected, and I could tell Bronwyn and Astrid were impressed. If there was any suspicion of exaggeration, Ryan's dad had just dispelled it with one big Texan embrace.

'Honey! Come meet Shea!' he hollered to Mrs James, who approached me with a similar measure of ebullience.

'We've heard so much about you!' she said.

Mr James nodded. 'Ryan just thinks the world of you. He said you know more about football than any girl he's ever met.'

'Well, that's very sweet,' I said, ignoring the obvious sexist undertones and taking the comment in the spirit it was intended. 'I love the game.'

'And he loves you,' Mr James said.

Astrid's mouth literally fell open.

'He's a great guy,' I said, milking the moment for all it was worth, then turning to make the necessary introductions. My father, Mr James, and Wiley all hit it off right away, finding endless business overlaps in their respective financial worlds, while Astrid did her best to impress Mrs James, dropping her own version of important names, labels, locales. Bronwyn kept a lower profile, following me over to the bar area in the suite.

'Want me to make you a drink?' I asked her, eyeing the vodka. 'Bloody Mary?'

'Are you going to have one?' she said.

'Think so,' I said. I wasn't usually a hair-of-the-dog kind of girl but decided that I might need to make an exception – it was going to be a long day and my mother hadn't even shown up yet. And to compound all the social pressure, I was beginning to feel nervousness over the game. I obviously wanted the Cowboys to win as a fan, and as Ryan's girlfriend, but it further crossed my mind that, if he didn't win, last night might be raised as a factor.

I mixed two drinks, handed one to Bronwyn, and confessed that I had overindulged the night before.

'You went out?' she said.

Remembering that I had lied about working, I babbled another cover-up lie about going out *after* I turned in my story, but I could tell she didn't buy it.

'Okay,' I said. 'I didn't really have to work. I was just . . .'

'I get it,' she said. 'I know my mother is tough to take.'

'And so's mine,' I said, just as she made her grand entrance in a powder-blue Chanel suit and patent navy sling-backs. She looked amazing, the best she can look, and decidedly better than Astrid.

'Your mom looks great,' Bronwyn said as my mother sailed straight over to my father and said hello. It was a strong move, adding another tally to our collective score.

'And really happy, too,' Bronwyn added. '*Is* she seeing someone?'

I shook my head and said, 'Not at the moment. And you know? I admire that about her. She doesn't need to be with someone to be happy.'

'Isn't that how you are, too?' she said.

'In a way,' I said. 'I mean everybody wants to find true love . . .' I said as my mother flitted over and kissed me hello. Meanwhile she ignored Bronwyn, who took the hint and rejoined Wiley.

'Mom, you might want to be a little less obvious,' I said.

'Pfft,' she said. 'They don't exist.'

'But Dad does?'

'I *have* to acknowledge him. He's your father.'

'Okay. Whatever,' I said with a shrug as I added a little more vodka to my Bloody Mary, then led my mom to the front of the box, where I introduced her to Ryan's parents.

Although she was slightly less affected than Astrid, she, too, was overeager, trying to impress Mrs James – and thoughtlessly chatty given that their son was about to play. Mrs James seemed not to mind, though, and I wondered if Astrid and my mother were both providing a welcome distraction from maternal worry. I definitely felt anxious myself, more nervous watching him in person, sure that every snap would feel more perilous, every defender more menacing. In any event, the game was about to begin, and it was time to focus. So I settled into the front row of the box, put my blinders on, and tuned out everything but football.

But right away, I had a terrible feeling about the game. Ryan looked emotionless. Then, midway through the first quarter, he threw an egregious interception that was returned for a touchdown so ridiculous it was sure to make the *SportsCenter* highlight reel. The mental errors, sloppy plays, and turnovers continued from there, and, by halftime, Dallas was down by twenty-one, the mood in the suite matching the one on the field. Only my mother and Astrid seemed oblivious, continuing with their chirpy, overly optimistic commentary, which was clearly making Mr James more irate, a tough thing to do. At one point, I pulled my mother aside and said, 'Mom, they don't want to talk. Their son is getting destroyed out there.'

'He is?' my mom asked. 'They're only down three touchdowns.'

'Only?'

'They can come back.'

'But it's not just about the score,' I hissed. 'He's the quarter-back. His stats are atrocious. This is easily the worst game of his professional career.'

'Oh,' my mother said, taking the hint after that, while Astrid continued to pepper Mrs James with small talk about Neiman Marcus's resort wear collection, the new exhibition at MOMA, and her upcoming trip with my father to, of all places, Dubai. Where the shopping, FYI, was *to die* for.

Fortunately, nobody, not even his buddies, attempted conversation with Mr James as he migrated to the rear of the suite with his back to the playing field, watching the game on television. The one time I got near him on the way to the restroom, I could hear him swearing at the screen, a string of expletives directed at his son. As I crept past him on my way back to my seat, he barked my name.

'Yes, sir?' I said.

'Can you believe this game?'

'No. I really cannot,' I said. Then, realizing that I wasn't helping matters, I added, 'But all the greats have games like this . . . Eli Manning does this once or twice a season – and he's a two-time Super Bowl MVP.'

'Yeah. Well, I'd give Ryan some leeway, too, if he had a ring,' Mr James snapped back.

Christ, I thought, grinding my teeth. *You really* are *an asshole.* But instead I said, 'He's only human . . . He'll bounce back.'

Mr James made a grumbling sound while I stood next to him in silence, filled with that sickening, sinking feeling that comes with getting your ass kicked. Only this was even worse because, with every shitty possession, I felt responsible. What if it did come down to Ryan's lack of sleep? What if that threw him off his game, which in turn threw the whole team off? I didn't want to give myself that sort of credit – or blame – but it was hard not to consider the possibility. As FOX went to a commercial, I said to Mr James, 'Do you think maybe he doesn't feel well? Or didn't get a good night's sleep?'

Mr James looked at me and said, 'Hell, he didn't get *something* . . . I haven't seen him look this bad in years.'

I sighed, shifted my weight from foot to foot, then nervously checked my phone, which I'd wedged into my back pocket. There were two new texts, one from Lucy, saying: *Oh noo!!!!*

Terrible game! I'm so sorry!!! ☺ and one from Coach: *Wow. What's going on up there?*

Lost in anxious thought, I must have mumbled something to myself, because Mr James looked at me and said, 'What's that?'

'Nothing,' I said, making uneasy eye contact. 'I just got a text from Coach. That's all.'

He looked at me confused, and I realized that he probably thought of 'Coach' as Coach Garrett now, head coach of the Cowboys. So I said, 'Coach Carr.'

'And? What's he saying? That he can't believe his guy is responsible for such a shit show?'

I shook my head, feeling a swell of anger, and said, 'No. That's not what he's saying at *all*.'

'Well?' he said, staring me down, his voice dripping with disgust. 'What, then?'

'He just said . . . that it's not Ryan's day,' I said, holding my ground, knowing that was what Coach *would* say. He understood the mental component of this game, especially for quarterbacks, and never got pissed at his guys as long as they were doing their best. And it seemed clear to me that Ryan was doing his best. If anything, he seemed to be trying *too* hard. Forcing plays, out of his usual rhythm. Sometimes it just happened – and there wasn't anything you could do about it. I hated Ryan's father for not knowing that – or not giving a damn. All these years of watching his son and he still hadn't figured out that Ryan wasn't a machine.

Then, as if proving that exact statement – that Ryan's body wasn't robotic – we watched him try to field a bad shotgun snap on a third and eighteen. He stumbled and went down, lying on the ground as the Eagles pounced on the ball. I knew even before they showed the replay that it was his knee. His bad left knee, already heavily braced. I felt instantly nauseated, the way I always am when someone gets hurt in a game – especially when knees are involved, the most vulnerable parts of any athlete's body.

I held my breath and prayed as I watched all the color drain from Mr James's tanned face. 'God dammit. No,' he said. The stadium fell as silent as a stadium can be, as Mrs James came scurrying back to her husband in an absolute panic. One sling-back heel slipped off her foot, and she kicked it away, hobbling awkwardly with one shoe until abandoning the second.

'How bad is it?' she said to no one in particular, breathless.

'How the hell should we know?' he snapped at her.

'Did you see the replay? Who hurt him?' she said, her voice shaking.

'Your boy tripped. Nobody touched him,' Mr James said, disgusted.

She ignored his tone and said, 'Shea, what did you see? What happened?'

'I can't tell,' I said, watching the replay for the third time, feeling cold with dread. I babbled some more, explaining that it didn't look too serious, and they were probably using the injury time-out for everyone to get a breather. But what I didn't tell her, and what I also knew to be true, was that even the very smallest movements could result in catastrophic injuries. That knees were funny things that way. But she didn't wait for me to finish my answer, running back to the front of the suite to be just a little closer to her son. I was torn, wanting the closer-up view on the television but also wanting to see him in the flesh.

Then, suddenly, Ryan got up by his own power and limped off the field with the help of only one trainer, to the applause and enormous relief of eighty thousand fans. Except for Ryan's own father, who still seemed more pissed than anything else. I took a few steps away from him, now standing in the middle of the suite, with really no view whatsoever of the field or the television, as another text came in from Coach.

CCC: *It's not torn. He'd be on a stretcher.*

Me: *I know. But Mrs James is freaking out.*

CCC: *And let me guess. Mr James is guns-a-blazing blaming Ryan?*

Me: *Yep.*

CCC: *He's going to demoralize that boy. Worse than he already has.*

Me: *I know. Now I really wish you were here.*

I meant for Ryan's sake, but also for mine, and Coach took it that way, writing back: *Me, too. Miss you, girl.*

I stared down at my phone, hesitating, then slowly typing: *I miss you, too.* Then I put my phone back in my pocket and walked to my seat, avoiding the worried stares from my parents. I don't think I watched another play after that, my eyes fixed on the sidelines, as if staring at the blue number twelve on my boyfriend's back would somehow turn the terrible tide.

29

The Cowboys ended up losing by twenty-eight, their worst defeat ever on Thanksgiving Day. The only ones who stuck around our suite until the very ugly end were the people who had come with me. Mr and Mrs James, along with my mother, hit the road with a couple of minutes left on the clock. There obviously wasn't enough time for Dallas to come back, but it still felt disloyal.

'You ready?' my dad said as both teams cleared the field and disappeared down their respective tunnels.

I shrugged, nursing my third drink of the day, wishing I had an actual buzz, anything to dull the loss and the worry I felt over Ryan's injury – and what he was going to say to me when we finally spoke.

'Really no hurry,' I said. 'Either sit here or in traffic.'

'Okay. Well . . . What's the plan, exactly?' my dad asked as it occurred to me that, for once, I was the one in charge.

'We're meeting at Café on the Green at five-thirty,' I said, having intentionally left our plans vague until this moment.

Unfamiliar with Dallas, Astrid gave me a questioning look as I said, 'Private dining room at the Four Seasons. Relax.'

She smiled and said, 'Perf.'

I couldn't help rolling my eyes at Astrid as Bronwyn said, 'Mom doesn't understand that only teenagers have any business abbreviating adjectives . . . Presh, fab, jeal. And my least favorite – totes.'

'*Totally* isn't an adjective, though, is it?' Wiley said as Astrid laughed, seemingly proud to be compared to a vapid youth.

'It totes isn't,' I said. 'Adverb.'

My phone rang, and I jumped, thinking it might be Ryan, but it was only Gordon shouting hello in a din of testosterone.

'You in the locker room?' I said.

'Headed in now . . . Sorry about the game,' he said, which I appreciated given that he was an Eagles fan. 'Tough day for your boys.'

'Yeah. Sometimes you get the bear . . .' I began, one of Coach's sayings. 'And sometimes the bear gets you.'

'Ha. Right,' Gordon said. 'Well, looks like I'll be talking to your guy in a minute here.'

'Any word so far on his knee?' I asked.

'Nothing official. They won't know for sure until later, but the buzz is that they think it's minor. Have you talked to him?'

'Not yet,' I said. 'You'll probably hear before I do . . . So let me know . . .'

'Will do,' he said.

I hung up, realizing that everyone was staring at me.

'Who was that?' Astrid nosily demanded.

'My colleague,' I said. 'On the Cowboys beat.'

My dad nodded, looking intrigued, then asked a few questions about Gordon's background. I gave him the rundown on his traditional, esteemed journalistic path – NYU, then the Newhouse School at Syracuse for his grad degree, then a string of small-town papers until he landed this gig. My dad seemed to get my implication, saying, 'You really scored big with this job, didn't you?'

'Yes,' I said. 'I feel very lucky.'

'It's not about luck,' my dad said. 'You're good.'

'And I know Coach,' I said. 'That's as good as a grad degree.'

'I'm telling you,' Astrid said, looking straight at me. 'That man is *hot*.'

An hour later, after we had stopped off at the Ritz for Astrid to 'freshen up,' and my mother had called to tell me she would not be joining us for dinner, I had yet to hear from Ryan, even after texting him twice. I couldn't imagine that he'd blow me off altogether, though I was starting to panic that that was a real possibility. But when we arrived at the Four Seasons, I was relieved to see Ryan's Porsche in the primo valet spot, a couple of guys in uniform admiring it. As much as I understood guys and sports, I would never understand their love of cars.

'Ryan's here,' I said. 'That's his car.'

'Wow. Beautiful,' my dad said with a long whistle.

'Is that the Turbo S?' Wiley asked.

'Yep,' my dad said. 'Sure is.'

'How much did *that* cost?' Astrid asked.

'About one seventy-five,' my dad said as we all piled out of the car.

I checked my phone one last time, but there was only a text from Lucy replying to an earlier question, informing me that her dinner was a success and she didn't know how her mother had managed to make it look so easy. I felt a wave of intense guilt, realizing I hadn't said a single word to Lucy about her mom all day long. It was inexcusably self-centered of me, practically putting me in Astrid's camp – and I made a mental note to call her as soon as dinner was over.

A few minutes later, after checking in with the hostess at the restaurant, we were ushered into the private Decanter Room, where Ryan and his parents were already seated. Ryan and Mr James promptly stood when we walked in, but neither smiled. They looked about as miserable as a father-son duo could be, and I had the sense that they had just exchanged heated words. Both their faces were flushed.

I held my breath, bracing myself for a chilly greeting, and the embarrassment that would come with it, but that didn't happen. Instead, Ryan walked over to me, put his arm around my waist, and kissed me, his lips landing just shy of mine.

'Hi, babe,' he said, as if I were the only one in the room.

'Hi,' I said as softly as I could without whispering. 'I'm really sorry . . .'

Ryan nodded, as if accepting my apology, then smoothly

handled the first introduction himself, shaking my dad's hand, his voice becoming robust. 'Mr Rigsby! I'm Ryan James.'

'Walt,' my dad insisted firmly.

'Walt. Okay, then. Good to meet you, sir!' he said, turning to the others. 'And you must be Bronwyn, Wiley, and Astrid.' He pointed as we went, shaking their hands, too. Astrid beamed, then, unbelievably, asked if they could take a photo together before we sat down.

I think I gasped, and Bronwyn looked horrified, as her mother handed me her iPhone. But Ryan handled it well, smiling, posing, even letting Astrid check my work to make sure she liked the photo. Meanwhile, my dad, Bronwyn, and Wiley made small talk with Mr and Mrs James.

'Did I blink?' Ryan asked when I handed Astrid her phone. 'I always blink.'

'No. It's perf,' Astrid said.

'Great!' Ryan said with such jocularity that I wasn't sure if I was impressed or disturbed that he could fake things to this degree.

We sat down as my father grew grave and said, 'We're really sorry about the game, Ryan. How's your knee?'

'It's okay,' Ryan said. 'I just twisted it a little.'

'How'd you do that, anyway?' Mr James said.

'What do you mean?' Ryan said, the tension palpable. 'How does one ever twist one's knee?'

Mr James mumbled something unintelligible as the waiter came in with his spiel about the prix fixe meal and took our drink orders. For a few minutes, the atmosphere lifted, as everyone but Mr James made polite small talk.

But by the time our wine and whiskey arrived, Ryan's dad had picked right back up with his veiled insults. Ryan ignored them until he seemingly couldn't take it another second.

'Dad,' he said, staring ahead, 'can we *please* change the subject?'

'Sure. What would you like to talk about, son?' Mr James said, his voice dripping with sarcasm. 'It's *your* day.'

My father raised one brow and looked at me.

'Anything. But. Football,' Ryan said, his nostrils flaring.

Mr James pushed on. 'Such as?'

'Such as . . . *anything*,' Ryan said, raising his voice slightly.

'Okay. How about this Walker investigation? Shea – I saw your story . . . Anything to that?'

I opened my mouth to answer as Ryan dropped his palm to the table. 'That's football, Dad.'

'But at least it's not about your god-awful game today.'

'Honey. Don't,' Mrs James whispered to her husband as Ryan threw back his whiskey.

'How's the investigation going?' Mr James pressed, not letting me off the hook.

'It's . . . going,' I said as Ryan touched my leg under the table, giving me strength to continue. 'I guess. I really don't know. The NCAA won't comment. Walker won't comment. My sources won't be named . . . Which is actually a relief for me. Means there's nothing to write about.'

'And? Do you think they have anything on us?'

I wanted to tell him he wasn't any part of *us*. I wanted to tell him to shut the hell up. Instead, something inside me snapped and I said, 'Well, I don't know, sir. I did hear that you bought a car for Cedric Washington. Is that true?'

I glanced at Ryan, who gave me a small nod, though I wasn't sure if he was confirming the rumor or giving me moral support.

In any event, Mr James remained perfectly calm as he said, 'What's the statute of limitations on that?'

'I don't know,' I said, then pressed, 'So you did? Buy him a car?'

'I might have,' Mr James said.

'Honey,' Mrs James said again.

'What?' he snapped back at her. 'Shea asked me a question.'

My father started to whistle, a nervous habit, and even Astrid had caught on that the situation was becoming dire, as she began murmuring to herself how much she loved the wine, then turned to ask Wiley what he had ordered. Wiley filled her in on the vintage and vineyard. He'd been there, of course, with Bronwyn, who also chimed in. Ordinarily it was the sort of thing that irritated me, but I could tell everyone was doing their very best to cast a lifeline to Ryan and me. It was almost touching.

'Where did you hear that, Shea? Or do the questions only go one way?' Mr James said with a big, fake laugh.

I smiled and said, 'I can't reveal my sources.'

'C'mon. Did you talk to Ced?'

'It's just a rumor. Just like this entire investigation is built on rumor, conjecture. It's a house of cards. Like everything else the NCAA is doing these days.'

It was the right thing to say because there was a perceptible shift after that. Or maybe the whiskey was just doing the trick.

'Couldn't agree more,' Mr James said, raising his glass.

I didn't like the idea of being on the same side of an argument with him, but I was more intent on getting through the meal without a full-on explosion, so I kept on with my anti-NCAA rant, lifted mostly from Coach. Meanwhile, Ryan retreated into a dark silence, speaking only when spoken to. I couldn't blame him, though, and was sure nobody else held it against him either. If anything, as we muddled through dinner, I felt myself growing ever more protective of him – almost as if he were still a little boy getting bullied by his father.

By the end of dinner, when my father suggested that we all return to the Ritz for a drink, I quickly declined. 'Ryan needs to get home to rest,' I said.

'Yeah. I need to ice this knee,' he said, as conversation hit another major lull, a rarity with that many people at the table.

When the bill came, all the men fought over it. Mr James won, and the other three quickly relented, likely accepting it as repentance for his awful behavior. Then we all got up and made our way back to the valet. They brought Ryan's Porsche first, even though he'd lost his ticket, and Ryan discreetly tipped the valet a twenty. Only then did he turn to me and say, 'What are you doing now?'

'What do you want me to do?' I whispered.

'It's up to you,' he said.

'Do you want to be alone?'

'No,' he said. 'I want you to come over.'

'Okay, then. I'll go get my car at the Ritz and come over.'

Ryan nodded. Then I watched him dig down and scrounge up a last scrap of charm.

'Really great to meet you, sir. And next time,' he said, shaking my dad's hand, 'I'll make sure you guys see a win.'

'At least give 'em a good game,' Mr James said. 'And not a woodshed beating.'

Ryan ignored his dad but kissed his mother, then Astrid and Bronwyn, and went on to shake Wiley's hand. Finally he turned to me. 'See you in a few?'

'Yes,' I said, leaning up and kissing him, partly for effect, partly because I wanted to, but, more than anything else, because I actually felt sorry for the great Ryan James.

30

Within five minutes of arriving at his house, Ryan transformed into a different person than the one I'd kissed goodbye at the Four Seasons. It was as if he'd flipped a switch, going from forlorn and formal to furious. He was angry at himself, angry at his teammates, angry at his coaches, angry at his father. He wasn't animated or upset but caustic and cold, as he launched into one articulate diatribe after the other, like a character in an Aaron Sorkin television show. And he did it all from a reclined position on his white sofa, shirtless, with a bag of ice on his bad left knee while I sat on an armchair across from him.

He saved me for last. 'And where the hell were you last night?' he asked. 'You've conveniently managed to evade that question all day.'

'No, I haven't,' I said, staring at the lines of his oblique muscles, dipping down into his blue mesh shorts. 'This is the first you've asked me that question.'

'Well, I'm asking it now,' he said, as I tried to determine if he had a six- or an eight-pack. I silently counted to eight, while deciding that lying wasn't the way to go.

'I went to the Third Rail,' I said, careful to maintain eye contact.

'So you went out to a bar even though you told me you were going home?'

'I changed my mind,' I said. 'I wanted to see some old friends.'

'Old friends?'

'Yes. From high school. A girl named Michelle. She lives in California. Came home for Thanksgiving.'

'Who else was there?'

'Well, there were a lot of people out . . . You know how it is before holidays . . .'

'No, I'm actually not familiar with that phenomenon . . . since I'm usually locked up in a hotel room.'

'Right,' I said, thinking that it was hardly the jail sentence he was making it out to be.

'So who else?'

'You want me to name names?'

'Was Miller there?'

I shook my head, making a split-second decision to abandon my truth-telling strategy. As I tried to keep my gaze even, it occurred to me that there was an absolute reason that lie detector testing worked so well. Nothing in my body was operating the way it had only seconds ago.

'He wasn't there?'

'No.'

'So you didn't see him?' Ryan pressed, staring at me, making me wonder if he somehow knew the truth. Either way, I had to stick to my story.

'No,' I said. 'He wasn't there, and I didn't see him.'

I should have just ended my reply there, but I kept going, the way liars often do. 'But so what if he was there? Big deal. Ryan, *what* is your obsession with Miller? I'm not obsessed with Blakeslee, and you were *married* to her.'

'Yes,' he said. 'And then I divorced her. That's pretty final.'

'It wasn't final for my father,' I said, the only time in my life I was grateful for Astrid.

'Well. It is for most. It is for me.'

'And I'm just as sure that I'm never getting back with Miller.'

'Is he still with that professor chick?'

'No . . . I don't think so . . . I'm not sure.'

'You're not sure? What does that mean? You either heard that they broke up or you didn't.'

'What are you? A lawyer or a quarterback?'

'I'd probably make a better lawyer.'

'You had *one* bad game. And even today, you made some amazing plays,' I said, hoping to change the subject.

But Ryan wasn't finished. 'Back to Miller,' he said.

'Jesus,' I said under my breath.

'When did you last talk to him?'

'C'mon, Ryan,' I said, trying to avoid another outright lie. 'This is ridiculous. Miller is . . . ancient history.'

'Well, it might seem ridiculous to you. But I couldn't sleep last night because I kept picturing you with him.'

'Why would you do that?'

'Because you didn't call me.'

'Oh, *please*.'

'I couldn't sleep, Shea. And I'm sure I don't have to tell you how important sleep is to performance.'

There it was, out on the table; he was blaming me for his bad game. But just to confirm the accusation, I said, 'Are you saying that . . . today . . . was *my* fault? You threw interceptions because I didn't call you?' The question was a little mean, but so was his implication.

'No,' Ryan said. 'I played like shit on my own. But you not calling last night certainly didn't help.'

'Wow.'

'All you had to do was call me, say good night, do what you promised you'd do. Then you could have gone out, had a big time at the bars. I never would've known about it.'

'C'mon. That's not fair,' I said, my voice starting to rise.

'Neither is breaking your word the night before a big game.'

I heaved a weary sigh, then said, 'I just . . . lost track of time.'

'All night long?'

'By the time I got your messages, it was too late to call.'

'You sure you don't mean that it was too *early* to call? What time did you get in, anyway?'

'Ryan. Please. I'm truly sorry,' I said, for what felt like the hundredth time. 'I had too much to drink . . .'

'What other mistakes do you make when you drink too much?'

'Well, let's see . . . I left my credit card at the bar.'

'You had a tab open?'

'Yes. Is that a problem? Isn't it better to start my own tab than to have guys buying my drinks?'

'What guys were you talking to?'

I crossed my arms, shook my head, and stared him down, refusing to answer another question. Meanwhile, Ryan lifted the bag of ice and examined his knee, his skin red with cold. Then he tossed the bag onto the floor, sat up, and said, 'Look. If you're my girl, I need you to be my girl. And part of being my girl is supporting me the night before a game. I needed you last night. I needed to hear your voice – and you obviously didn't give a shit—'

'Don't say that. You know I care. Very much.'

'It doesn't seem that way. If you cared, you would have called. Period.'

It was the closest he'd come to making a reasonable, calm point – a far cry from Blakeslee's characterizations of his jealous rages. But I still felt unsettled. There was something off about the whole inquisition, and I could only imagine how much worse it would be if he knew Miller really was at the bar.

'You gotta be all in or all out,' Ryan said, one of Coach's lines.

I nodded.

'Well?'

'Well, what? I heard you!'

'And? Are you in? Or out?'

I hesitated, just long enough for Ryan to shake his head, disappointed. 'That's what I thought.'

'I didn't say anything!' I shouted, my frustration building. 'Why are you doing this? I know you had a bad game . . . but that just happens sometimes. You're still one of the best quarterbacks in the entire league! Don't tell me you let your father get in your head.'

'I let *you* get in my head. The fact that you couldn't take a few minutes to call me.'

I stared at him, incredulous that we were really going around in the same circle *again*. 'Okay. Ryan. Once again, I'm *sorry*. I gave you my word and I didn't follow through. You have a right to be irritated. Even mad. I'm sorry I made you feel bad. It won't happen again.'

He stared at me for a long time, then said, 'Shea. I *love* you.'

I stared back at him, shocked, my heart racing. I hadn't seen that coming. Not one little bit.

'Are you sure about that?' I said, stalling, but also thinking that part of loving someone was having faith in them.

'Yes. Do you love *me*?' His voice was quiet, with a needy, insecure edge. It was unfathomable, a complete reversal of anything anyone in the world would imagine was happening between us.

Rather than answer, I stood up and walked over to the sofa, sitting, facing him, one hand on his shoulder, as if the physical contact might suffice as my answer.

It didn't.

'Do. You. Love. Me?' he repeated. 'It's a very easy question.'

'Yes, Ryan. I do love you,' I said, feeling cornered, thinking that it had to be in the running for the least romantic first utterance of *I love you* of all time. And the worst part was, I was pretty sure I had told another lie. A whopper bigger than pretending I hadn't seen Miller the night before. I nervously dropped my gaze to his knee and said, 'Well. Now that we settled that. Do you need more ice?'

He shook his head, then exhaled. 'But I do need *you*, babe. C'mere.' He pulled me closer to him, so that my head was on his chest, my body across his. As I listened to his heart beat, I found myself wondering what exactly he needed from me. Because I could remember to call on the nights before games. And I could avoid the Third Rail and contact with Miller. I could probably even learn to love him. But there was one thing I couldn't change and would never give up. Not now, not ever, and I could feel myself starting to panic with every breath he took.

He finally broke our silence and said, 'So my dad's a real asshole, isn't he?'

I turned my head so I could see his face, at least half of it. 'Yeah,' I said, as there was really no way to sugarcoat it. 'He sure is.'

'And by the way, you were right. He totally bought Cedric's car.'

'I figured,' I said, relieved that he didn't ask me my source. For the first time, I worried about the ethical implications of not chasing the story, no matter how stale it was.

'And he didn't buy it because he wanted to help *Cedric* out.'

'Right,' I said.

'He controls people with his money. It's sick.'

'He can't control you, though. Not anymore,' I said, feeling my loyalty shift back to Ryan. Maybe I *did* love him. At least a little bit.

'Yeah,' Ryan said, with a faint smile. 'I have more money than he does. I think that kills him.'

I rolled over so I could see more of his face, propping myself up with one elbow, my eyes resting on his scar. He caught me looking at it and said, 'What?'

'How'd you get that scar?' I asked.

He swallowed, then said, 'I told you – I got it the night of the state championship. In high school.'

'Right. But *how*?' I said.

He looked at me, and I could tell he was debating whether to tell the truth. Part of me hoped he wouldn't. Because it would make me feel better that I had just lied to him. But I also wanted him to feel better, and I was pretty sure that the truth always brought you closer to peace.

Another few seconds passed before he said, 'My dad threw a cleat at me. After the game.'

'Oh, *Ryan*,' I said.

'I didn't want to tell you before . . . But that's what happened.'

'I'm so sorry, honey,' I said, imagining him that night in the emergency room, getting stitched, lying to the doctor about how it happened, likely with his father right in the room, supervising the whole thing. 'That's awful.'

'Yeah,' he said. 'It's okay . . . I guess I'm lucky he didn't hurl anything at me tonight.' He laughed bitterly.

I reached up to run my finger across his brow, then murmured, 'I first noticed it in college . . . and I always loved it.'

Ryan looked touched. 'Why?' he said.

The real reason, at least at the time, was that I always think a vivid scar on a guy is sexy, especially when he's athletic, because you assume it's a battle scar from a game. But tonight, I liked it for more than that.

'Because,' I said. 'It's part of you. Part of who you are.'

'Yeah,' he said. 'I guess it is.'

He put his hand on my neck, brought my face to his, and gently kissed me. I drew back and looked at him.

'Thank you,' he said. It was as if he got the deeper point I was making, that he was connected to his dad, no matter how much he didn't want to be, just as I was connected to mine and to Astrid and to my mother. Neither of us could help our stories, only what we did with them. 'Thank you for accepting my flaws . . .'

'You don't have to thank me for that,' I said. 'You know, I might actually love you more when you're throwing an interception than a touchdown.'

He smiled but said, 'Don't say that.'

'But I think it's true,' I said.

'Well, that's where we differ,' he said, his smile growing wider. 'Because I love you more when you *don't* drop the ball. So to speak.'

'Got it,' I said. 'No more turnovers.'

My father and his crew were scheduled to depart the following afternoon, and I hadn't planned on seeing them again, having said my formal goodbyes the night before. But the next morning, as Ryan was leaving for his MRI, my dad called and asked if I had time to meet for brunch or coffee. As I opened my mouth to decline, blame it on work again, he added 'Just the two of us.' Pleasantly surprised, I told him that would work out just fine.

Thirty minutes later, I arrived at Buzzbrews Kitchen, his suggestion but one of my favorites, and found him already seated in a corner booth, sipping coffee. He looked up from his menu and smiled as I slid in across from him. 'Hey, Dad,' I said.

'Hi, honey,' he said, taking off his reading glasses and slipping them into the monogrammed pocket of his starched, blue and white checked button-down shirt. 'You hungry?'

'I'm always hungry. I'm your daughter who actually has an appetite. That's how you can tell us apart,' I deadpanned, hoping the comment sounded more self-deprecating than snarky, especially given that I'd actually liked Bronwyn the day before.

My dad laughed, and I observed how different he seemed today, more relaxed and natural. 'There are a few other differences between my daughters,' he said, taking another sip of coffee.

'Yeah. I guess there are,' I said, ticking through some of them in my head, plagued by my standard inferiority complex. Although there was really no concrete evidence to suggest that my father compared the two of us, I was pretty sure he did. Dating an NFL quarterback and writing for an esteemed paper helped make up my usual shortfall, but she still had me beat by a comfortable margin.

A few seconds later, a waitress came by to take our order. I had the menu memorized and went with my usual Blazing Huevos, a single banana nut pancake, and a cup of coffee. My dad pretended to be tempted by my selection, murmuring that it sounded *really* good, but then ordered two scrambled eggs and a side of bacon, no toast or hash browns.

When our waitress departed, I said, 'Are you back on Atkins?'

'Always,' he said. 'As I've said many times, the only way to stay trim is to eat bacon.'

I laughed and said, 'You're still a little bit Texas, aren't you?'

'Definitely,' he said, drumming on the table to the beat of a Vince Gill song playing in the background, as if to tell me that he appreciated country music. He had lived here just long enough for Texas to get in his blood, but not long enough to never want to leave.

'So,' I said. 'Did you have fun yesterday?'

'Yes. I had a very nice time,' my dad said. 'Although it would have been a lot nicer if we'd won.'

I smiled and said, '*We*, huh? Thought you were a Giants fan.'

'Yes. But Dallas is *America's* team, right?' my dad said.

'Right,' I said, even though it was an expression that had always annoyed me. 'So can you believe Mr James? How awful he was about the loss?'

My dad whistled, then shook his head. 'Holy smokes. I really can't . . . I feel sorry for Ryan.'

I nodded, thinking, *Yeah, it's hard to overcome the feeling that your father doesn't love you.*

I told myself to quit with the pity party as my dad asked about Ryan's knee.

'It's really sore, but I don't think it's too bad. He's getting an MRI as we speak.'

'And how are . . . his spirits?' my dad asked as our waitress returned with my coffee and refilled Dad's cup. He added half a packet of Splenda and a dash of milk, then stirred the way he always did, rigorously and noisily, with maximum contact between spoon and cup. It always seemed unexpected when most everything else my father did was so measured and methodical.

'He was really upset,' I said, still trying to make sense of everything that had been said and promised the night before.

My dad looked contemplative. 'And what about you?'

'What about me?'

'Is it tough . . . dating someone so famous?'

I shrugged, uncertain of what he was asking. 'Not really. The media doesn't seem to notice or care,' I said. Then, lest he think this fact disappointed me, I added, 'Which is nice.'

My dad nodded and said, 'Only a matter of time . . .'

'Mom has her fingers crossed,' I said, laughing.

I felt vaguely disloyal for the barb, but he took it in the playful spirit it was intended and said, 'Astrid, too. She's hoping that someone runs a piece on Ryan's girlfriend's stepmother.'

I smiled but said, 'Dad. Please don't call her that. She's your wife, not my stepmother.'

I'd exhibited a very poor attitude many times over the years, particularly when I was forced to go to New York as a child, but this was the closest I'd ever come to directly telling my dad how I felt about the situation. His expression changed so drastically that I almost regretted the remark. I wanted to make a point, but didn't want to hurt his feelings.

'I just mean – she didn't raise me . . .' I said. Using the term was actually sort of insulting to all the stepmothers out there who played an important role in a child's upbringing. As opposed to Astrid, whose only contributions to my childhood were theater tickets over the holidays, an occasional designer handbag, and really great Fifth Avenue haircuts.

'I understand, honey,' he said, sipping his coffee. 'I know she can be . . . overbearing . . . but she means well. She cares about you.'

'I care about her, too,' I lied. 'But sometimes . . .' I stopped, losing my nerve.

'Go on . . . Sometimes what?'

'Well . . . let's just say that I'm glad you asked to see me *alone*. For a change.'

'I know,' he said, his body language and posture earnest, apologetic. 'It's hard to get a word in edgewise around her.'

I just nodded.

'So what else is going on with you?' my dad asked.

I looked at him, wondering what he was getting at.

'Nothing,' I said. 'What do you mean?'

'Well, you have this wonderful job . . . and this incredible, famous boyfriend . . . but . . . are you happy?'

It seemed to be such an odd burst of insightfulness from my

father that I thought surely it must be a coincidence. He obviously knew nothing of the fight Ryan and I'd had the evening before. 'Yes. I'm happy,' I said. 'Why?'

'Oh, I don't know,' he said. 'I just have this feeling . . .' His voice trailed off, but then he cleared his throat and tried again. 'Should I be worried about you?'

I felt confused, then touched, then annoyed at myself for being so easily moved that I actually considered retorting, *Hell, yeah, you should be worried about me. That's what fathers are supposed to be. Perpetually, constantly worried about their offspring.*

Instead I said, 'No, Dad. You shouldn't be.'

Feeling uneasy, I glanced around the restaurant, my eyes resting on a young couple with a toddler. The child was about two, sitting atop a plastic booster seat, eating a crepe, her face covered with chocolate. With blond ringlets and big blue eyes, she was exceptionally cute, and she must have just said something cute, too, because her parents stared at her adoringly, laughed, then held hands across the table. It was the sort of scene that rarely made me wistful, and it didn't now either, although I felt a pang of emotion I couldn't quite place.

My father followed my gaze, then looked back at me, as if trying to read my mind. 'Do you know what you want?' he said. His question was as vague as they come, but his expression seemed purposeful.

'Yes. I'd like to beat Texas and then win a national championship,' I said.

'But what do you want in *life*? In your personal life? Do you want to get married? Have children? Do you think Ryan could be "the one"?'

It was such a peculiar line of questioning coming from my father, who had never seemed particularly perceptive or empathetic. In fact, I'd always been able to absolve him over the years based on my belief that he simply wasn't capable of anything more. So, in a convoluted sense, his compassion at this moment was backfiring, making me feel worse.

'Did Astrid put you up to this?' I asked, thinking that grown men who have been married three times typically don't think in terms of 'the one.'

'I beg your pardon,' my dad said, looking vaguely insulted. 'Give me a *little* credit.'

I smiled to lessen the charge, then said, 'Okay. What do I want *in life*?'

'Yes.'

'I don't know . . . I guess I want what everyone wants . . . To be happy.'

I thought I was artfully dodging the question, but my father didn't let me off the hook. 'And does Ryan make you happy?'

'Happy enough,' I said, before I could think better of it.

My dad lifted his mug, pausing halfway between his mouth and the table, and said, 'Happy *enough*? That's a dangerous proposition, Shea.'

I looked into his steel-gray eyes, feeling a wave of resentment building in my chest. I wanted to say, *Who are we kidding here? Let's stick to small talk, Dad. This is way too little, too late.* Instead, I shifted gears in a radically different direction, thinking, *You want candor? You want a heart-to-heart? I'll give it to you. I'll tell you who I really love.*

My head told me it was a bad idea and that my father hadn't even remotely earned the role of confidant. But something inside me just didn't care. Maybe it was the burning desire to unload my secret. Maybe on some level I wanted to shock him. And maybe I wanted him to feel genuine worry for me. Concern that, due to his absence and the vast paternal void in my life, I was making bad choices, pursuing a wildly inappropriate older man. I didn't believe this, of course, but part of me wanted my father to wonder.

'The truth is, Dad,' I said, now unable to stop myself. 'I really like Ryan . . . But I think I might be in love with someone else.'

No matter how much I had felt this coming on, it still felt strange and startling to say it out loud.

My dad put his mug down, still gripping the handle, and said, 'Your ex? What was his name?'

'Miller,' I said. 'And no. I never loved Miller.'

My dad didn't ask who, likely because he assumed he wouldn't know him anyway, but I opened my mouth, and could feel the words tumbling out of me, almost uncontrollably. 'I think I'm in love with Coach Carr,' I announced, my voice low but steady.

My dad stared across the table at me, clearly in shock, while I tried to overcome my own feeling of vertigo. It was as if I was standing on the edge of a cliff without a guardrail. Or, perhaps more accurately, already in midair, falling. And just like it wouldn't be possible to stop a fall halfway to the ground, I knew it wasn't possible to undo my confession, though it crossed my mind to try, pass the whole thing off as a joke.

'Coach Carr? What?' my dad said, flustered. Floored.

I nodded.

'Are you . . . serious?' he asked, his mouth falling open like a cartoon of a man surprised.

'Dead serious,' I said, now riding a cathartic wave of relief.

'But what about . . . Ryan?' my dad asked, seemingly confounded.

'What about him?' I said. 'C'mon, Dad. You, of all people, know this sort of thing is complicated. Why else would you marry the same person twice?'

'Right,' he said, looking satisfyingly sheepish.

Our waitress arrived with our food, giving us both time to process everything.

When she left, he said, 'And Clive . . .? He feels the same?'

'I think he might feel the same, but it's all under the surface . . . And obviously all of this was well after Connie died. In case you were wondering.'

In other words, *no foul play of the kind you're accustomed to.*

My dad looked slightly relieved, then said, 'Are you sure it's not just . . . football?'

'If it were football, don't you think I'd be just as happy with Ryan?'

He nodded and said, 'Good point.'

'Nobody is like Coach Carr,' I said. 'Nobody is half the man he is.'

It was the way I felt, but it was a bit pointed, too.

I think my dad got it, because he looked down, suddenly remembering his coffee. He took a long swallow, as if gathering his thoughts, then said, 'I just think . . . you've always looked up to him so much. As a father figure . . . You know . . . Since I wasn't around when you were growing up . . .'

'So what you're saying is – Bronwyn would never fall for Coach Carr because she had a father, growing up?' I looked into his eyes, and saw a flicker of regret. Though it occurred to me, not for the first time, that once he shacked up with my mom and had me, he was screwed either way. No matter what, he was going to be abandoning a woman and her daughter.

'No,' my dad said. 'That's not what I'm saying at all . . . I'm just saying . . .' He stopped, then said, 'Okay. Maybe I was saying something like that . . .'

I picked my words as carefully as I could. 'Dad, isn't it possible that I actually just . . . have genuine feelings for him? Apart from anything that happened to me as a child?'

'Yes,' my dad conceded, but he still looked flummoxed. 'That is possible.'

We both pretended to concentrate on our food for a few seconds, until he put down his fork and said, 'Who else knows? Lucy? Your mom?'

I shook my head. 'Nobody but you.'

He gave me a half smile and said, 'Well, I'm honored.'

'You should be,' I said.

'Thank you for trusting me.'

'Yes. Please don't tell Astrid.'

'I would never.'

'I believe you.'

'And Ryan?'

'Ryan will be fine,' I said. 'No matter what happens, Ryan will be just fine.'

'Can I give you some advice?' my dad said.

'Sure.'

'If you know it's wrong with him, end it sooner rather than later.'

I looked at him, wondering if he was speaking from experience, and, if so, was he talking about Astrid or my mom? I considered asking him but decided I really didn't want to know, as he continued. 'Figure out what you want . . . whatever that is . . . and go for it.'

'I will,' I said. 'But for now . . .'

My dad raised his eyebrows, waiting.

'For now, I just want to beat the hell out of the Longhorns.'

My dad laughed and said, 'Yeah. You just might belong with Coach, after all.'

31

O n Saturday morning, the day of the final Walker game of the regular season, I woke up feeling sick to my stomach. My hatred for Texas always compounded my standard nervousness, and this year was even worse, with so much more at stake. If we won, we would be playing for the national championship. If we lost, Texas would forever relish their role as spoiler, and we'd finish the year ranked third or fourth, at best, in some ways more painful than a mediocre season.

I got out of bed, too rattled for coffee, too nauseated to eat, pacing and praying and fidgeting all over my apartment. I listened to music and even did some yoga poses and breathing exercises, but nothing worked. I told myself to get a grip. The game was big – as huge as they come – but there were more important things in life, fates worse than losing to the Longhorns. On this very day, people would get terrible diagnoses. Die in fluke tragic accidents. Others would get fired, lose their homes to the bank, their spouses to divorce, their best friends to petty differences. Beloved pets would be put to sleep. Suicide notes penned. Innocent men arrested. Natural disasters might even strike and topple whole villages in remote corners of the world.

This was *only a game,* I kept telling myself. Not life or death. But no matter how hard I tried to remain philosophical, I couldn't talk myself into that perspective. Into *any* perspective.

And then, a few hours later, I actually puked in a trash can at the stadium.

J.J. busted me, coming up on my left shoulder, laughing.

'Did you just do what I think you did?' His voice echoed in

the cavernous corridor that would later be squeezed with bodies and vendors.

I wiped my mouth with a napkin, took a swig of water from a bottle in my bag, and popped in a piece of gum before turning around to face him.

'Yep,' I said. 'I sure did.'

'And something tells me it wasn't bad fish.'

'Ha. No. It was the emasculated bovines,' I said, my favorite nickname for the Longhorns.

'So much for an impartial media.'

I laughed but quickly sobered up again, J.J.'s face mirroring the way I felt.

'Do you get the feeling that it's now or never?' he asked.

'Yeah,' I said. 'I do. Why do we feel that way?'

'Because,' he said. 'We're *so* close. I can't imagine getting this close again. It could take years. And I'm sixty-one. I don't have that kind of time.'

'I know,' I said. 'You have to be *so* good . . . But so damn lucky, too.' I crossed my fingers, stared up at the ceiling of the atrium, and prayed for the hundredth time since that morning.

'You think we'll pull it off?' he said.

I shrugged, thinking that when it really, truly mattered, I never had a good gut feeling. It wasn't so much that I didn't have faith in my team, but that I maintained the truest fans always reverted to a doomsday position in the same way that parents always worried about tragedy befalling their children. Love made things feel precarious, and, when you got right down to it, everything in life was tenuous and fleeting and ultimately tragic. Yes, someone would win this game, and two teams in the country would go on to play for a championship in January. And someone would win *that* game. And a few seniors at one program in the nation would end their careers on a jubilant high note. But for many, many more, the college football season would end in utter disappointment. Even heartbreak. Just like life.

J.J. slapped me on the back and said, 'When's the last time you tossed your cookies like that before a game?'

'The Cotton Bowl,' I said.

'Well, that's a good sign, no?'

'Yep,' I said, having already thought of that superstitious angle. Because, no matter how pessimistic I was before a big game, I never stopped looking for signs, never stopped praying for the right alignment of stars over the Brazos River.

As it turned out, there was no need to pace, puke, or pray. Because Walker kicked the shit out of Texas. We were faster, sharper, and better on nearly every play. It was an art and a science and a thing of beauty and a glorious act of God, the final scoreboard glowing brighter than the moon: Walker 28, Texas 0.

Buoyant, I sprinted to the press conference, counting down the minutes until I could see Coach, hear him recapping the game with his usual matter-of-fact preamble. When he walked in, he scanned the room as if looking for something or someone. Then he spotted me, standing in the back with a couple of guys from *The Dallas Morning News*. Our eyes locked, and he threw me a wink. My insides melted, and I couldn't help but grin back at him.

'Let me guess,' one of the reporters next to me said in a snide voice. 'You went to Walker.'

'Yep. And let me guess. You went to UT-Austin,' I said, knowing that he had. The *Austin* infuriated Longhorn fans, who liked to think of their school as *the* University of Texas – which his irate expression confirmed.

A few seconds later, the press conference was under way, and I furiously scribbled notes and quotes, waiting until the end to ask my own question.

'Yes? Shea,' Coach said, pointing to me.

'Congratulations on an undefeated regular season,' I began, wanting these to be my first postgame words to him.

'Thank you,' he said, nodding, waiting for the question.

I took a deep breath and said, 'So . . . We all know that you've had an exceptionally difficult year . . . and I was hoping you might say a few words about what this season has meant to you personally.'

Coach nodded, his face somber. 'Yes, this year has been enormously difficult and emotional for me and for my children, Lucy and Lawton . . . My wife, Connie, meant everything to us and this program and community, and there's been a void without her . . .' He stopped, blinked, then looked down, seemingly rattled, and, for a few seconds, I regretted the question. But when he looked up again, he had his composure back and said, 'So to end the regular season this way means a tremendous amount to me . . . and I think it is the ultimate tribute to her.' He cleared his throat and continued, 'I'd like to thank my players, coaches, and the Bronco nation for making today possible. Thank you.'

Then he smiled, stood, and walked off the platform.

The press conference continued with Mack Brown and a couple of his key players, and I stayed, gathering a few quotes. But I already had what I needed for my story, my angle, and I left as soon as possible to rush back to the press box and write. I was getting faster, and that night, words, sentences, whole paragraphs flew from my fingers, the entire piece written in just under ninety minutes – a record. It was factual reporting, but poetic, too – and I was prouder of it than of anything I'd ever written, concluding with Coach's quote about Mrs Carr. I emailed it to Smiley, who wrote back, 'Well done. Congrats.'

I wasn't sure if he was congratulating me on my piece or the game, but I took it as both, and drove straight to the Third Rail, where Lucy, Neil, Lawton, and Ryan were in full celebration, along with dozens of other friends, acquaintances, and former colleagues from Walker. Every bar in town would be jamming tonight, but I couldn't imagine more of a scene than the one here, as I was pretty sure that word had gotten out that this was Ryan's new hangout. We all hugged and kissed and hollered and high-fived. I couldn't remember ever feeling so grateful or euphoric after a ball game. Couldn't remember a night more thrilling.

Until it wasn't.

32

'Well, well,' Ryan said, tendons appearing in his neck as he stared beyond me. 'Look who it is.'

I knew who it was even before I turned around to see Miller, loping toward us, looking as happy as I'd felt only a few seconds before. When he got to the table, I saw the credit card in his hand.

I stood, considering my options. I knew that hugging him hello and whispering in his ear would be problematic, but it was the best chance I had. My only hope.

So I did just that, cutting Ryan off, sidling up to Miller, leaning in and frantically whispering, 'Don't say anything about the other night.'

Of course it backfired, as he was way too dense or drunk to catch on. 'What do ya mean?' he asked in a loud voice. Then, holding it out for the world to see, announced, 'I have your credit card!'

Ryan stood up, chest swelled, like he was ready to throw a punch. But in the next second, he gathered himself in a way that seemed more sinister than your garden-variety bar fight.

'What do you have there?' he asked me as Miller handed me my card.

'My credit card,' I mumbled, wedging it into my back pocket.

At this point, Lucy gave Miller a hug and said, 'Good to see you, Miller. I like you so much more after a big win! Or maybe it's just that you aren't dating Shea anymore.' Her voice was playful.

Miller grinned but said, 'Don't be a bitch, Lucy.'

Lucy made a face, put one hand on her hip, and said, 'Omigod, did y'all hear that? Miller just called me a bitch.'

'No, I didn't,' Miller said, still grinning. 'I just gave you some really good advice. *Don't* be a bitch!' Then he raised his glass, leaned back, and bellowed up at the ceiling, his voice filling the bar, 'Fuck Texas!'

At which point, everyone erupted in a chorus of 'Fuck Texas!' Except for Ryan – who reached out and grabbed my forearm.

'Can you c'mere for a second?' he said, pulling me by my arm toward the restrooms in the back. Clearly it wasn't a question or an invitation; it was a command.

'What are you *doing*?' I said, though I knew exactly what he was doing.

'Care to tell me why Miller has your credit card?' he said as he dragged me along with him.

'I left it at the bar the other night. I told you that,' I said, my heart racing.

'Yeah? So how did he end up with it?'

'I guess he . . . got it from the bar,' I said.

'I thought you said you didn't see him?'

It occurred to me to layer my lie with another lie, tell him that Miller had come in after I'd left, but I knew the jig was up. Ryan was way too savvy and determined not to get to the bottom of things. 'Okay. He was here. I saw him the night before your game.'

'So you *lied* to me?' he said.

'I'm sorry.'

The admission must have both surprised and further outraged Ryan because he shouted, 'You're *what*?' Then he squeezed my arm harder. I tried to pull away, more concerned about a potential scene than anything else, but I couldn't break free.

'I'm sorry. He did come into the bar that night . . . But that was it.' I pulled away again, but like with those Chinese finger traps, the harder I pulled, the tighter his grip became. 'I can't control who walks into a bar!'

He took a step toward me, backing me against a wall. 'You freakin' lied to me!' he yelled, jabbing his finger into my chest.

'I know. And I'm sorry,' I said, cringing as I made eye contact with a girl headed to the ladies' room. She was staring at us, taking it all in.

'You're sorry?' he said, his voice dripping with sarcasm. 'You say that a lot, Shea. Don't you?'

'But I *am* sorry,' I said, feeling pathetic and ashamed. Not for lying but for being trapped like this, in a bar no less.

'Bullshit!' he yelled. 'You're not sorry!'

'I am, Ryan. I really am. I only lied because you were so upset about the game . . . and I didn't want to make it worse. And nothing is going on . . . I just saw him at the bar. And he got my credit card. That was it.' I was talking as fast as I could, but nothing seemed to work.

'You just *saw* him?' he shouted louder as another girl stared, along with the guy she was with.

'I mean we talked . . . in a group . . . that was all.' The more I babbled, the more enraged he became. And, at one point, he grabbed my other arm, our chests inches apart, so I had no choice but to look directly into his face, veins bulging everywhere, his features distorted with rage.

'Yet he got your credit card? Huh. And how, exactly, does that work?'

'I left my card. He got it for me. That was it. Do you really think he'd hand me the card in front of you if something were going on?' I was frantic now, my cheeks on fire.

'Yeah,' Ryan said. 'I think he would. I think he absolutely *loved* disrespecting me in front of everyone.'

'Nobody's disrespecting you,' I said. 'Stop being crazy!'

'Crazy?' he said, ratcheting up his grip another notch.

'Ouch,' I said, wincing. 'Ryan, that hurts. Let go!'

'I'm not crazy, Shea. You're the one who got drunk, left your credit card, and let your ex-boyfriend pick it up for you. You're the one who broke your promise. You're the one who lied to me. What am I supposed to think?'

'You're blowing this out of proportion,' I said, sweat trickling down my sides. 'Let go!'

'No. Answer me. What am I supposed to think?'

My arm hurt too much to struggle, so I stopped and said, 'You're making a scene.'

'Answer the question. What am I supposed to think?'

I said I didn't know, my voice coming out in a whimper.

'Okay. I'll tell you what I think. I think you fucked him. Didn't you? Admit it, Shea. You fucked him.'

'No.'

'Yes, you did,' he yelled, shaking me.

'No, Ryan,' I said, on the verge of tears. 'I didn't. I swear I didn't. Nothing happened.'

At this point, Lucy appeared, taking everything in, her eyes wide, horrified.

'What's going on here?' she said, as Ryan finally released me from his grip.

'Nothing's going on here,' he said. 'I'm out.'

He turned and stormed off, leaving me with Lucy. 'What in the world . . .?' she said. 'What just happened? Is this because Miller walked in?'

I got choked up but managed not to cry as I cobbled the story together, downplaying things.

She looked at the red mark on my arm and winced.

'It doesn't hurt,' I said, wishing I had kept my jacket on.

'Omigod,' Lucy said.

In some kind of shock, I said, 'I can see how bad this looks to him. God, I wish I hadn't lied.'

'That doesn't excuse *this*,' she said. 'There is no excuse for *this*.'

'I know,' I said, although I could hear the rationalizations forming in my mind: *He has big hands. He doesn't know his strength*. And the most pathetic: *It's my fault*.

Lucy's face twisted in anguish. 'Shea, honey . . . I don't like this. I don't like this at all . . . I think maybe Blakeslee was telling the truth about him. On some level.'

Maybe. On some level. I could see and hear that she was qualifying, too, trying to find a way out for Ryan, not wanting to believe what had just happened. Surely Ryan wasn't that person. Surely I wasn't the girl in peril.

'I just want to go home,' I said.

'You can't drive.'

'I'm okay to drive,' I said. 'Honest.'

Lucy nodded reluctantly, then said, 'Okay. Call me when you get home. I'm really worried about you.'

'Don't be. I'll be fine. I promise,' I said. As if that were something I could will to be true.

As I unlocked my apartment door, my cell rang. I expected it to be Lucy, or maybe Ryan, but it was Coach. His voice was filled with joy as he said hello, reminding me of what tonight was supposed to be about: Walker one step closer to the promised land.

'Hey, Coach,' I said, trying to conjure the elation I'd felt only a short time ago.

'Where are you?' he asked.

'Home.'

'Alone?'

'Yes,' I said.

'Well, how 'bout that game, girl?' he said, laughing, giddy. 'How 'bout that *game*?'

'It was great. Awesome. I'm so happy for you. And proud of you,' I said, trying to sound the way I would if I hadn't just been manhandled.

I must not have done a good job, because he said, 'What's wrong?'

'Nothing,' I said, finding my way to the sofa and curling up in a fetal position, the phone pressed to my ear.

'C'mon. What's going on? Talk to me.'

I took a deep breath and said, 'I got into an argument with Ryan. At the Third Rail. That's all.'

'Oh, boy,' Coach said, suddenly somber. 'What about?'

'Same old stuff,' I said. 'He still thinks I have a thing for Miller. Which I don't. *Obviously.*'

'And he got jealous?'

'Yeah. And really angry . . . It was bad.'

'What happened? Do you want to talk about it?'

I didn't really, but I felt that I had to explain, at least in broad strokes. 'We were at the Third Rail with Lucy and Neil . . . celebrating . . . and . . .' My voice cracked, but I kept going. 'Miller walked in and Ryan got mad and things just turned ugly.'

'Ugly?'

'Yeah,' I said, thinking that word summed it up better than any other. 'On Ryan's end. Miller was his usual happy self.'

'What did Ryan do?'

'You know . . . he just . . . lost his temper and acted stupid . . .'

'Are you okay?'

'Yeah,' I said, remembering the way those people in the bar had looked at me. With voyeuristic pity and concern. The opposite of the way people usually looked at me when I was with Ryan. 'I'm fine.'

'Do you want me to come over?'

The answer was both yes and no, so I said, 'I don't know . . .' And then, because I had the feeling that he was just worried about me and trying to do the right thing, I said, 'You don't have to do that. I really am okay.'

'I know I don't *have* to. I *want* to see you,' he said, and, for a few seconds, there seemed to be nothing complicated about our situation. He was simply a man who liked a woman. I could hear it in his voice. I was sure of it, and, despite everything that had happened, I felt a little rush that Coach wanted to share such a special night with me.

'I want to see you, too,' I said.

'All right, then,' he said. 'I just need to make a few phone calls, and I'll be over.'

'Okay,' I said again, frozen in the same position, not even

moving the warm phone from my face for several seconds after Coach said goodbye and hung up. I calculated that, with his calls and the drive over, I had at least twenty minutes, just enough time to take a quick hot shower and pull myself together. Fighting an overwhelming sense of fatigue, I willed myself to sit up, text Lucy that I was home safe, then walk down the hall, into my bedroom, then my bathroom, where I began undressing. When I took off my jeans, the credit card fell from my back pocket onto the tile floor. I stared down at it but left it there, then pulled my sweater over my head, both arms, especially my left, throbbing. Then I took off my underwear, staring at my naked self in the mirror. From a straight-on view, I couldn't see the marks on my arms, which somehow made me feel better. I took a few steps to my shower and turned on the water to the hottest setting, wondering if what had happened in the bar had made me a statistic.

Waiting for the water to get hot, I decided that it was too minor to qualify, then told myself not to be so stupid. Of *course* it counted. It didn't matter, though, because, either way, I was going to end things with Ryan the first chance I got. For a lot of reasons. Because he didn't trust me – and nothing would ever work without trust. Because I didn't really love him, and I knew I never would. But mostly because he had crossed a very clear line.

I stepped into the shower, breathing in the steam, letting the water stream down over my back, then my face, thinking of how many reports and stories I'd read over the years about girls showering after an 'incident.' It had always made sense, but now it *really* made sense. I hadn't been seriously injured, but I still felt violated.

After another few minutes, I turned off the water, stepped out of the shower, and wrapped a towel around my body. I glanced back toward the mirror, but it was too steamed up to show my reflection, and I was grateful for that. I took a few deep breaths, thinking about Coach, then walked back into my bedroom.

And that's when I saw him, sitting there on the edge of my bed.

33

I jumped and made a small gasping sound, the kind I make when I spot a roach in my apartment.

'Your door was unlocked,' Ryan said, holding up his hand as if to calm me. 'So I came in.'

'I see that,' I said, turning my back on him to grab a pair of sweats and a T-shirt from my chest of drawers. I dropped my towel to the floor, dressed as quickly as I could, then faced him again.

'I'm sorry, Shea,' he began, looking docile, distraught. His complete about-face caught me off guard and took the edge off my anger.

'It's fine,' I said, though it wasn't. 'Let's just forget it.'

I knew that neither of us could do that. That he couldn't forget the lie about Miller any more than I could forget what he'd done to me, but I just wanted to get rid of him. Even if Coach weren't on his way over, I'd had enough of him for one night. I searched for the right combination of words as he stood and walked calmly toward me. Without thinking, I held my breath and backed up one step, then another.

His face fell. 'Shea. Baby. Please tell me you aren't scared of me. I would never hurt you. C'mon. You know me. You know that.'

He sounded so sweet, so persuasive that I almost believed him. 'I'm not scared of you,' I said. 'But you *did* hurt me.'

It was a compromise between my head and my gut. I didn't want to let him off the hook completely, but I also didn't want to put myself in the full-blown victim category.

'I didn't mean to hurt you,' he said.

I considered this, deciding that his intent was relevant; maybe he didn't know his own strength. Then I shook my head, flip-flopping again. 'But you *did*,' I said.

He took another step forward, then reached out and gently touched my left arm, exactly where he'd first grabbed me. 'Does it . . . does it really hurt?'

'Yes. It does. And there's going to be a bruise there tomorrow. I guarantee it. You think that's okay?' I said, my voice rising as I spoke more quickly. 'To put your hands on a girl like that? Like you're in a damn football game? It's *not* okay, Ryan. You outweigh me by a hundred pounds. It's not okay.'

He shook his head. 'You're right. I'm sorry, baby.'

'Don't call me *baby*,' I said, feeling a fresh swell of anger. 'I'm not your baby.'

'Shea. I'm sorry . . . Just like you're sorry about Miller.'

I threw my hands in the air, then put one on my hip. 'Don't even put those things in the same category,' I said. 'What I did and what you did. And I'm not sorry about *Miller*. I didn't *do* anything with Miller. I'm sorry I *lied* to you about him. But I lied because I was sick of discussing him. He is a nonissue.' I slapped the back of my hand into my palm for emphasis.

'I believe you,' he said.

'Do you, though?'

'Yes. I do.'

'Good. Thank you,' I said, aware that the seconds were ticking down toward Coach's arrival. Ryan reached out, his long arm encircling my waist, pulling me closer to him as he leaned down to try to kiss me.

I said his name in protest, but he persisted. 'C'mon, babe,' he said. 'Kiss me. Let's make up. Can we? Please?'

I turned my head, suddenly repulsed by his natural scent – one I'd felt neutral about before tonight. 'Can we please just talk about this tomorrow? I'm really tired.'

Ryan's face darkened, his eyes narrowing. 'Why? Are you planning on company? Is Miller on his way over here to comfort you?'

Something inside me snapped as I shouted, 'Dammit, Ryan. Get out! Get out *now!*'

He stared at me calmly, shaking his head. 'So it's like that?'

'Like what?'

'You trying to turn this around. You lie to me like you did. And now this is about me holding your arm a little too hard?' He sneered, then laughed, as if mocking me, and I suddenly hated him.

'Shut up, Ryan. And get the fuck out of my house. This relationship is over.'

'Oh, it's over?' he said, laughing again. 'Because you have a better option?'

'Yes,' I said, *wanting* to hurt him now, with words, my best weapon. 'I do, actually.'

'Okay, then,' he said. 'Go do your thing. Go fuck Miller.'

'Fuck you,' I said, pointing at him, jabbing at his chest with my finger as he'd done to me outside the restroom at the Third Rail. When I got no reaction, I jabbed harder. He blocked me, and I swung. It was as if I wanted him to hit me. To prove Blakeslee's claim true. To justify my decision to end things with the great Ryan James.

But when I got my wish, and he reached out with his crazy-quick reflexes, easily catching both of my wrists in his hands, then pushing me down onto the bed, I regretted it.

'Get off me!' I said, breathing hard, struggling as he held me down with more force than was necessary. And then, suddenly, I was scared. *Really* scared.

'Get off me!' I said again, moving my head from side to side, crying. 'Get off me, Ryan. I mean it!'

He loosened his grip just enough for me to start struggling again, and I might have screamed something, too. I can't recall exactly what happened after that, and have no idea if several seconds or several minutes passed. All I remember is looking up and seeing Coach Carr in the doorway of my bedroom, his silhouette backlit.

I don't know what he saw or heard, but it must have been clear that I wasn't a willing participant in whatever was happening because he then yelled, 'What the hell's going on in here? Get off her!'

Ryan leapt to his feet and headed for the door, but Coach blocked him like a scrappy defensive end, his hand on Ryan's shoulder. 'You're not going anywhere.'

Ryan said, in so many words, that he begged to differ and pushed his way past Coach, toward my living room. I sat up, and Coach looked at me for a beat, as if to determine if I was okay. Then he turned and followed Ryan. I stayed put, frozen on my bed, listening to Coach shouting, 'What the hell were you doing in there? You might as well tell me, because she's going to tell me!'

Ryan said something in response, but I couldn't make it out, other than the word *liar.*

'Shea Rigsby is not a liar. You're the liar, Ryan. And I'd take back that Cotton Bowl championship and sit your ass if I could.'

Ryan said something that sounded like 'Sure you would, Coach.'

Then I heard sounds of two grown men fighting, followed by a loud crash of furniture hitting the wall. That's when I got off the bed and ran down the hall and saw Coach on top of Ryan, pounding him amid an overturned end table and a scatter of magazines. He hit him three times, maybe four, until Ryan said, 'So I guess you're sleeping with her, too?'

Coach popped him once more for good measure.

Ryan didn't throw a punch back. He just laughed, the same way he'd laughed at me in the bedroom, as blood trickled down his face. 'You know what, Coach? It's what I've always thought about you,' he said, sitting up, catching his breath. 'You're a hypocrite. You see what you want to see when you want to see it. It's all terribly convenient, isn't it?'

'You're a disgrace,' Coach said, grabbing his knees to catch his breath. 'An absolute disgrace.'

'Well, maybe I am,' Ryan said, now on his feet and almost to the door. 'Maybe I am. But then what's that say about you? Huh, *Coach*?'

He looked at me over his shoulder, shook his head, and was gone.

34

'Are you okay?' Coach asked after he had righted my table and we'd both found our way to my sofa. He was still winded and disheveled, his shirt untucked, wrinkled, and a little bloodstained.

'Yeah. I'm okay,' I said, staring straight ahead, both hands tucked under my thighs. The only light in the room came from the hallway and the orange glow of a streetlamp working its way through the slatted plastic blinds covering my windows. 'Are you?'

'Yeah,' he said. 'My first fight in thirty-five years. If you can call it that . . .'

'Yeah. I'm pretty sure you can call it that,' I said. I made myself look at him, taking in his shell-shocked expression. It was as if he was still processing everything.

'He never took a swing back at me . . .'

Coach seemed to be talking to himself, but I offered a theory. 'Maybe he was afraid of you.'

He snorted. 'Yeah. I don't think so. An NFL player in his prime? And an old coach?'

'You're not old,' I said reflexively.

'Feel old now,' Coach said under his breath, staring down at his knuckles, a cut on his middle finger.

Several long seconds passed before he spoke again. 'Well. He deserved what he got.'

On the face of things, it was a plain statement of opinion. There was no rise in his voice suggesting a question, but I knew he was asking me something. I could tell he was looking for reassurance that he hadn't overreacted. That he'd done the right thing.

'Yeah. He did deserve it,' I said, hoping that would suffice.

'What exactly happened?' Coach asked. 'Leading up to . . . what I saw? Will you tell me?'

'Yes, I'll tell you,' I said. 'But let me make some tea first . . . do you want some?'

'No, thank you,' he said.

I could feel his eyes on me as I stood and walked to my kitchen, filled my kettle with water, turned on a gas burner, then assembled a mug, a tea bag, and a large spoon because the little ones were all in the dishwasher that I'd forgotten to run. All of this, and I didn't even want tea. I was stalling. The last thing I felt like doing was reliving what had happened back at the bar, much less in my bedroom, but I knew that it could only make Coach feel better to know the truth. He *deserved* to know the truth. So I turned off the stove and went back to the sofa, sitting a little closer to him this time, but still half a cushion away.

'I changed my mind,' I said, glancing at his profile.

'About what?'

'The tea,' I said.

Then I told him everything, uncensored, right down to the call from Blakeslee. When I finished, he reached across the sofa for my hand. I met him halfway, our pinkies grazing.

'Thank you,' I said, realizing I hadn't said it yet.

'Don't thank me. I just did . . . what any man would do. Neil, Miller, anyone.'

'Maybe. But you're not Neil or Miller. You're his *coach*,' I said, the unfathomable part of tonight starting to sink in. I could accept who Ryan was more easily than I could swallow what had happened between the two greatest legends in the Walker program.

Coach covered my hand with his, and I flipped mine over, our palms touching. 'His *former* coach. That was a long time ago.'

'Still. I feel bad for putting you in this position,' I said, processing that we were actually holding hands. It was as if the trauma of the evening had dulled my reaction time, caused a tape delay.

'You didn't do anything wrong . . . And what position do you mean, exactly? The position to defend you? *Shit*.' Coach shook his head. 'You don't know how grateful I am that I walked in when I did.'

'I'm sure nothing terrible would have happened,' I said, thinking that it was a Catch-22. I didn't want Coach to regret hitting Ryan – for *his* sake – but I also didn't want to ex-aggerate what had happened. Ryan was a bully with a terrible temper – but he wasn't a full-blown criminal. Surely he wouldn't have *really* hurt me. Or would he? Why, in the face of violent proof, did I still want to believe that he wasn't *that* bad?

'I can't stand the thought of anything even *remotely* bad ever happening to you,' Coach said, squeezing my hand.

I squeezed back, thinking that, although this thing with Ryan had brought us to the moment we were in, our hands clasped in a darkened room, I also had the unsettling sense that it had eroded something. The romantic undercurrent so clear in the final conversation before he'd entered my unlocked apartment was gone. It was as if the blows he'd dealt Ryan had set us back to the long-standing dynamic I had hoped we could transcend.

I released his hand and turned to face him, sitting sideways, one knee bent against the back of the sofa, the other dangling to the floor. 'Coach, I appreciate what you did tonight. So much. But I don't want to be another person in your life that you have to look out for. Protect.'

He turned toward me, touched my cheek, and said, 'And why's that?'

I struggled to explain, wishing I had gone ahead and made the tea so I had something to do with my hands. 'Because,' I said. 'Because I don't want to be like . . . your daughter.'

'You're nothing like Lucy.'

'You know what I mean. I don't want you to *see* me as your daughter,' I said, calibrating my words. 'Or someone you mentor. Or a journalist on your beat. Or an old family friend. I don't want to be your friend at all . . .'

'You don't want to be my friend?' Coach said with a beseeching half smile. I couldn't tell if he was confused, playing dumb, or simply asking me to give it to him straight.

'Well, I *do* want to be your friend. Of course I want that. But I might . . .' I looked into his eyes, telling myself not to lose my nerve, hearing his voice in a huddle telling his players to *man up*. 'I might want *more* than that, too.'

'You *might*?'

My heart pounded in my ears, my throat burned. 'I *do* want more than that. I *definitely* want more than that. And I'm telling you this now . . . at this moment . . . not because you just burst into my apartment and defended me . . .'

He was staring at me so intently, nodding slightly as I spoke, as if connecting with every word. It emboldened me to keep going even before he said, 'Please. Go on.'

'I'm telling you this right here, right now because . . . I *have* to. I can't stand it another second. No matter what you think – and I really have very little idea about that – I need you to know that I have feelings for you.'

I took a breath so deep that it felt more like a sob, and he gave me another tender nod, permission to continue. 'And maybe it's wrong,' I said. 'Because of Mrs Carr . . . Or because you're too old—'

'Hey, now,' he said, cracking a small smile.

'Too old for *me*. Not too old,' I qualified. 'Although what's a couple of decades in the scheme of life? Not much . . . But the age difference aside, maybe I shouldn't feel this way because you're my best friend's father. Because let's face it – Lucy would freak if she heard this conversation.'

Coach murmured his agreement.

'But I have never been more sure of my feelings. More sure of *anything*. And I had to tell you . . .'

It was the bravest thing I had ever said to anyone, and possibly the dumbest, too, especially given what we'd both just been through, but I felt enormous relief getting it all out. A burden lifted.

'So that's it,' I finished. 'That's all I wanted to say.'

Coach looked rattled but not unhappy.

'Coach? Say something.'

He shook his head, as if at a complete loss, but shifted toward me, closing the gap between us completely, then putting his hand on my shoulder. 'Maybe you should start calling me Clive,' he whispered.

Then he pulled me toward him, wrapping both arms around me. His breath in my ear made me shiver, and he held me closer.

'Okay. Clive,' I said, breathing him in.

'This is crazy,' he said.

'As crazy as you coming over and roughing up your only Heisman Trophy winner?' I murmured.

'Maybe not that crazy,' he said. 'But still crazy.'

'I don't care,' I said.

'Neither do I.'

'I want you to kiss me.'

'I *want* to kiss you,' he said. 'I *will* kiss you. But not tonight.'

'Why not?'

'Because enough has happened tonight.'

I pulled back a few inches. If he wasn't going to kiss me, I wanted to see his eyes. 'You mean beating Texas or Ryan?'

He smiled, then cupped my face in his hands. 'Both,' he whispered, a current flowing between us, more intense than any kiss I'd ever known. 'But for now, just know that . . . your feelings aren't one-sided.'

'They aren't?' I said.

He shook his head.

'When did you know?' I said. 'When did you feel it?'

'There you go. Miss Reporter.'

I smiled. 'Tell me.'

'Oh, I don't know. I felt something during that Trivial Pursuit game at the lake. Then that first time you asked me a question at a press conference. That one about Reggie's fumble . . . You were so cute and nervous.'

'You hated that question.'

'I pretended to . . . And then the night we went running over at the track?'

I nodded, waiting.

'I had a hunch then, too. And the night you brought over Taco Bell.' He whistled and shook his head. 'I was definitely attracted to you all those times. I felt something . . . But as far as knowing for *sure*?' he said. 'Not until tonight.'

'When tonight?' I said, thinking that it made a difference. Was it when he came in to rescue me? Or was it only right now, in this quiet aftermath?

'After the game,' he said. 'After the press conference. After all the commotion and noise, when I was finally alone, at home. I sat down in my chair, picked up my phone, and saw all the texts and missed calls. Dozens and dozens of 'em . . . But I realized that there was only one person I wanted to call. Only one person I wanted to see.'

I smiled, feeling shy and unsteady, wondering if this was actually happening. It was surreal – and as sweet as a hundred undefeated regular seasons.

Coach smiled back at me and said, 'God, you're beautiful, Shea.'

I remembered to breathe, then told myself yes, this was finally, *really* happening.

35

By noon the next day, I was still in bed, and Ryan had already called me five times. His tone was erratic, sometimes even in the course of a single voice mail. First he was sad and sorry, then angry and accusatory, then calm and rational, then self-pitying, then so very sorry again. The only constant from message to message was the cold feeling that overcame me every time I heard his voice, even when he was telling me how much he cared for me. He sounded so convincing, so earnest, so *sorry,* but I had the chilling sense that he would say or do anything to get what he wanted.

From my hiding place under the covers, I deleted every message, every pleading text, every saccharine lie. It felt like a solid start, but after going to the bathroom and inspecting his purple fingerprints left on my arms, I knew that I had to do something more than passively erase voice mails. As much as I didn't want to see him, I knew I had to look him in the eye, hand him those diamond earrings, and tell him never to contact me again. I hated the idea of burning bridges, terminating a long-standing friendship, but I didn't see any other way.

Deep down, though, I found myself wondering if I would be so unwavering without Coach as my safety net. What if he hadn't come over last night and confided his feelings? Would I still be deleting Ryan's messages? Or would I be slowly caving, rationalizing, paving the way to give him one more chance, and maybe one after that? Would I be telling myself that we were still on that slippery slope? That everyone makes mistakes and deserves forgiveness? Would I be anointing myself as his savior, telling myself I could do what Blakeslee could not?

My phone rang again. I felt a wave of anger as I reached for it on the bed next to me, relieved to see that it was only Lucy. I wasn't ready to talk to her, but I answered, knowing that she deserved an update.

'Hey, sweetie,' she said. Her voice was so warm and nurturing that I went from not wanting to talk to feeling desperate to tell her everything. *Almost* everything.

'Where are you?' I said.

'In the car with Neil and Caroline. Where are you?'

'In bed.'

'Alone?'

'Yes, of *course* alone . . . Can you come over?' I said, before I lost my resolve to confide in her – at least all the parts about Ryan.

'Sure,' she said. 'I'll just drop them off first . . . Are you okay?'

'Yeah,' I said. 'I just need to talk . . .'

'Okay. I'll be right there.'

We hung up, and I took a deep breath. Then I called Coach, who answered on the first ring.

'Good morning,' I said, fleetingly worried that I had over-blown the best parts of last night.

But then he said, 'Yes, it *is* a good morning,' and, instantly, I felt better.

'Undefeated regular season,' I said.

'Yep. But it won't mean anything without one more win,' he said, as I realized that he had already turned the page, gone from celebration to preparation.

'Did you go to church?' I asked.

'Nope. Slept in. I think I dreamed about you . . . And I never dream. At least I never remember my dreams.'

'Oh?' I said. 'And what happened in your dream?'

'We sat on your sofa . . . I held your hand in mine . . . We talked.'

I smiled my first smile of the day. 'Did we kiss?'

He laughed and said, 'Almost. We came very close.'

I hugged my knees, curling up into a tighter ball under my blanket, listening to the silence crackle on the line. Then he cleared his throat and asked if I'd heard from Ryan.

'Yeah,' I said. 'But I haven't talked to him. He's just left a bunch of messages.'

'And what's he have to say for himself?' Coach said.

'About what you'd expect. That he's sorry . . . That it won't happen again.' I hesitated, then added, 'Oh. And that you grossly overreacted.'

'Ha. Right. He's lucky I'm so old.'

'I told you. You're not old,' I said as firmly as I could. We had our obstacles, but I was determined not to let age be among them.

'I'm a lot older than Ryan. And you.'

'I don't care about that,' I stated clearly for the record. 'And neither should you . . .'

'I don't really care about it,' he said. 'But we do need to talk about that . . . There are some long-term concerns there . . .'

I had a feeling he was referring to babies and motherhood, things I wasn't worried about, but I let it go for now. Instead, I addressed a far more pressing problem, and told him Lucy was on her way over.

'Oh, yeah?' he said.

'Yeah. I'm going to tell her about last night. I mean . . . Ryan coming over and everything . . . But I'm not going to tell her that you were here . . .'

He was so quiet that I thought we'd lost our connection.

'Are you there?' I said, feeling guilty for scheming, preparing to lie to Lucy.

'Yeah, I'm here . . . I heard you . . . and I think that's a good idea.'

'I feel bad. Keeping something so big from her, but . . .'

'Don't feel bad. It's just not the right time to tell her about us.'

I felt a burst of affection and excitement and hope. A thrill that there was an *us* to talk about. 'Right,' I said. 'We will. Eventually.'

'Definitely,' he said. 'When the time is right.'

A few minutes later, Lucy was at my door in one of her neat Jackie O frocks. 'So what's going on?' she asked, the light lavender of her perfume filling my apartment as she draped her trench coat over the back of a barstool and kicked off her heels. Her toes had been freshly painted, a beautiful lilac color that matched her scent.

'It's over with Ryan,' I said. The statement was dramatic, but I kept my delivery flat.

She stopped in her tracks and gave me a tragic look. 'Over?'

'Yes. Over. Done.' I made a slicing motion in the air.

She hugged me, but still said nothing, and I read in her silence a hope that it wasn't *completely, definitely* over and done.

'He needs to get help,' Lucy said.

'Yes,' I said, knowing where she was headed.

'You don't think there is any way you can forgive him? Work things out?'

'No way,' I said, rolling up the sleeves of my T-shirt and showing her the marks on one arm, then the other, a measure of irrational shame returning.

She winced, taking a closer look, running her finger along my skin. 'God, Shea. I'm so sorry.' She shook her head and said, 'I just can't *believe* this.'

'I know,' I said, letting my sleeves fall back again. I thought of all the women around the world who had to rely on long sleeves, turtlenecks, scarves, heavy makeup. And all those who couldn't so easily hide the evidence – who had to call in sick to work, lie to their families, fabricate accidents, laugh off their clumsiness, anything to hide the truth.

'There's more, though,' I said, as we both sat on my sofa, in the reverse spots that Coach and I were in last night.

'Oh, Lord,' Lucy said, her eyes wide. 'Is it bad?'

I nodded. 'Yeah. Ryan came over. After I left the bar. He just walked into my apartment while I was in the shower. Apparently I had forgotten to lock my door.'

'Holy shit. What happened?'

I made myself look in her eyes as I told her what happened, no sugarcoating. The way he had tried to kiss me, how he had pinned me to the bed, how he had scared me. Skipping over the rescue scene, I said, 'He finally left. I was lucky. It could have been worse.'

Lucy shook her head, staring back at me. 'God. I really thought he was a good guy. I really, *really* did.'

'Oh, I don't know, Luce. In some ways, he is,' I said, thinking that there was no point in demonizing Ryan James. It was over no matter what. It was over because I loved somebody else. 'He can be really sweet. To his friends. To his mother. To me. He's generous . . . He gives a lot of money to charity. He tips well . . .' I said. My list was factual, but felt anemic in light of everything else. So he gives valets twenties? So what?

'I know,' Lucy said, her wistful look returning. 'He can be so nice . . . and fun to be around ninety-nine percent of the time.'

Her estimate was both arbitrary and way too high, but I refrained from pointing out that even that one percent was too much.

'Do you think it's the culture of violence in pro football? . . . Daddy said three out of four NFL players own a handgun . . .'

'It's probably four out of four in Texas,' I said. 'And yes, it's a brutal, animalistic, savage sport. Hell, it's a *celebration* of violence. But I have to believe that most of those guys aren't roughing up their wives and girlfriends. Maybe they are. I don't know. Frankly, the whole psychology of the sport doesn't interest me at this moment . . .'

Lucy interrupted me and said, 'But *do* you think he can get help and . . . change?'

I shrugged and said, 'Well, Blakeslee doesn't think so, and she probably knows him better than anyone.'

'But you are different from Blakeslee. If anyone could help him, it's you.'

I fought back a pang of annoyance as I said, 'Maybe he can change. But I can't bank on that.'

'You don't love him enough to help him?' she asked. I could tell the question wasn't laced with judgment, but I still felt annoyed by her dogged focus on what *Ryan* needed. By her transparent attempt to hold on to what she saw as such a prize in my life.

'First of all, no. I do not love him enough to turn his violence into my cause,' I said, my voice firm. 'Second of all, I think that's a very dangerous game to play with your life. Sure, it *could* work out. But what if it doesn't? Not to be dramatic – and I don't think he'd ever go this far – but, theoretically speaking, that's how women end up dead.'

'Okay,' she said. 'I'm sorry. Don't be mad.'

I gave her a passive-aggressive shrug.

'I'm sorry,' she said again.

'It's okay, Luce,' I said, momentarily tempted to blurt out everything, the whole truth about my feelings for her father. But I tempered my reply, saying only 'Bottom line, I don't love him.'

'Because of this, though, right?' Lucy said, biting her lower lip. 'You don't love him because of this?'

'I'm not sure how that makes a difference. But no. I don't love him, period. I didn't love him before this. I cared about him,' I said, using the past tense. 'And I wanted to love him. Maybe I could have grown to love him. But those feelings just weren't there. I liked the *idea* of him. It was exciting. *He* was exciting.' I forced a smile and said, 'Too exciting.'

Lucy nodded as all dwindling hope in her was finally extinguished. 'So what next?'

'Well . . . I need to return the earrings,' I said. 'I need to tell him to stop calling me. I need to tell him face-to-face that it's over. I want him out of my life completely.'

'Are you scared?'

'No. But I should probably go with someone. Maybe you

and Neil?' I said, thinking that I didn't want to further embroil Coach.

'Sure,' she said. 'Of course. Whatever you need. You know I'm here for you.'

'I know, Luce. Thank you,' I said.

We sat in silence until I said, 'So this goes without saying, but don't say anything to anyone . . . except Neil.'

She gave me a somber nod. 'Of course. I would never.'

'I know . . . The worst thing in the world would be for the media to catch wind of this,' I said, imagining the horrible headlines, how it would be spun. Not as one man with a problem but as the dark, ugly side of Walker football.

36

Two days and more than twenty voice-mail messages from Ryan later, Lucy, Neil, and I met at Mi Cocina in Dallas, ready to execute my game plan. I had texted Ryan exactly once, simply asking him to come to the restaurant after the Cowboys' practice, which I knew ended at six thanks to the team schedule pinned to the fabric wall of Gordon's cube. Ryan had agreed, thanking me profusely, clearly under the impression that this was the opening he had been pleading for.

Little did he know I would have a protective posse in tow at the popular Mexican restaurant in Highland Park. I knew it was probably overkill to bring Lucy and Neil, and Coach and I were both a little worried that Ryan might mention Coach's involvement in our final fight, but we decided that it was better to be safe than sorry.

'Are you okay?' Lucy said to me as we walked into the restaurant. 'You look pale.'

'Just a little nervous,' I said, reaching into my purse now to rub the velvet box containing the earrings, as if for good luck or strength.

'Would a Mambo Taxi help? Or does that feel too celebratory?' Lucy said, referring to the famed frozen margarita with a swirl of sangria.

'Oh, hell. Why not? This *is* cause to celebrate.' I gave the queen's demure finger wave, then said, 'Buh-bye, Ryan.'

Neil and Lucy laughed, even though it really wasn't funny, as the waitress came to take our chips, guacamole, and drinks order.

'Are you ready for Christmas?' Lucy asked at one point after our drinks had arrived. She was obviously trying to distract me with idle chatter while intermittently eyeing the door.

I told her not even close, as she informed us that her shopping was pretty much completed, mostly executed online over her morning coffee.

'You really *are* your mother,' I said.

Lucy beamed; this was her favorite compliment.

'Seriously,' I said. 'How are you so efficient with a child *and* a business to run?'

She shrugged modestly as I told her that I hadn't even begun mine. I remembered the Cowboys gear that Ryan had given me for my family and made a mental note to drop it all off with the Community Partners of Dallas, a charity for abused children.

'So how excited are you for Pasadena?' Neil asked, referring to the venue for the BCS championship game. The question sounded stilted, and it occurred to me that, as the only guy in the group, he might have the most stressful assignment tonight, especially because he had clearly looked up to Ryan. We all had, really.

'Very,' I said flatly.

'Wait. I thought teams weren't picked until Selection Sunday? This weekend?' Lucy asked.

I nodded, proud of her for knowing this detail but explaining that it was only a technicality this year. There were only two undefeated teams left in the country, and we were one of them. We would definitely be deemed either number one or number two in the final BCS standings, along with Alabama, both teams earning their way to the championship game.

'I wish Mom could be there,' Lucy said, licking salt from the rim of her glass. 'She'd be so thrilled . . .'

Neil put his arm around her and said, 'This is all happening *because* of your mom, sweetie.'

'Do you really think that's true, Shea?' she asked, turning to me.

'Yes,' I said, running my hand over the cold glass and finally taking a long drink. 'Our guys are playing their hearts out for Coach. You can feel it in every win. And he is coaching for her. So . . . yeah. She has a lot to do with our success.'

Lucy swallowed, looking somber, and even more so as she switched gears and said, 'It's almost seven. Is there anything left to strategize?'

'No,' I said. 'It's going to be a very short conversation.'

'Well, get ready to have it,' Neil said. 'He just walked in.'

I braced myself but did not look toward the door, gathering strength by looking at Lucy's face as Ryan descended upon us, looming over our booth in baggy jeans, a crew-neck sweater, and a plain navy baseball cap that was lowered enough to hide his eyes from most anyone who might be watching us. From where I was sitting, though, I could see them, and could tell he was disappointed that I wasn't alone.

'Hey, y'all,' he said, his voice low.

Lucy and I said quiet hellos back as Neil stood, shook Ryan's hand, and said, 'Hey, Ryan. How ya doin', man?'

'Fine, man. Thanks,' Ryan said. He looked glum and ashamed. Or maybe it was an act, part of his strategy. I reminded myself that anything he said or did or felt was now irrelevant. My mind was made up.

As planned, Lucy stood, nudged Neil, and said that they would be at the bar. As soon as they were out of earshot, Ryan said, 'So? May I join you?'

'Yes,' I said, motioning toward the vacant side of the booth.

Ryan sat across from me and immediately reached for my hands, now clammy. I drew away and wiped my palms on my jeans.

'Shea,' he said, exhaling. 'Please. Please forgive me.'

'Okay,' I said, a flippant edge in my voice. 'I forgive you.'

Grossly misinterpreting my meaning, Ryan's face instantly relaxed, regaining some of its usual glory. 'Oh, *thank* you, babe. That will *never* happen again. That wasn't me . . . The next time, we'll both just take a moment . . . regroup . . . not let a silly misunderstanding escalate.'

I shook my head. 'No, Ryan. There isn't going to be a next time.' I took the velvet box out of my purse and extended my arm across the table, handing it to him. 'Here.'

He stared at the box and said, 'Are those your earrings?'

'Not anymore. I'm returning them.'

When he still wouldn't take the box, I put it between his forearms, resting on the table.

He pushed it back over to me. 'No. They were a gift.'

'I can't keep them.'

'Why?'

'You know why.'

'Because I got upset one night?'

My mind raced with strategic replies. I had prepared extensively for this, as I knew he wouldn't make it easy, but he was good. Clearly practiced.

'I don't want to discuss it, Ryan,' I said, pushing the box back toward his side of the table as if playing a contentious game of chess. 'It's over with us. And I don't want these earrings.'

He shook his head. 'No.'

'No?' I said, incredulous. 'What do you mean *no*?'

'Even if you never want to see me again, they're still yours.'

I drew a deep breath and audibly exhaled. 'Fine,' I said, scooping up the box and dropping it back in my purse as I caught Lucy glancing over her shoulder at us with a worried look. 'But just so you know, I'm going to sell them and give the proceeds to charity. There's a great organization that helps abused women and children.' I emphasized the word *abused* and stared him down.

He opened his mouth, too bewildered to reply.

'Listen,' I said, taking advantage of his silence. 'For the record, I think, I *know* you have a problem. I don't know if it has anything to do with your father . . . or the violence inherent in the game you play . . . or if there's any other psychological reason . . . but there is no question that you *do* have a problem.'

He stared at me, then shocked me by nodding, ever so slightly.

'And I think you should get help. I think your ex-girlfriends would all agree with me. And I'm worried about your future girlfriends, too.'

'I don't want anyone but you,' he said as our waitress returned, looking thrilled to see who was seated at one of her tables.

But Ryan quashed her mood by holding up his hand, announcing that he didn't want anything. Her smile instantly faded, as she nodded, then glanced at me.

'We're not staying for dinner,' I said, feeling Ryan's eyes on me. 'But you can bring me the check for the drinks and chips . . .'

'Actually,' Ryan said, skimming the menu, stalling, regrouping. 'I'll have a sparkling water and . . . the tacos al carbon. Medium rare.'

I rolled my eyes at his attempt to hold me hostage with a couple of beef tacos.

'So . . . umm . . . do you still want your check?' the waitress asked me, looking flustered, probably because she knew there was some kind of a disagreement in the works. And *this*, I thought, was how things ended up on TMZ.

'Yes,' I said, outmaneuvering him again. 'Thank you.'

When the waitress left, he said again, 'I don't want anyone but you.'

'You'll get over that quickly. You have lots of options. *Better* options,' I said pointedly.

'C'mon, Shea. That's not true, and you know it. We have something really special. Are you really going to throw that away?'

'Me?' I said. '*You* did this. You put us here.'

'I know. And I'll do whatever it takes to fix what I broke. Whatever it takes.'

'I'm sure you've said those words before.'

'No, I haven't.'

I thought of the promise I made Blakeslee and simply shrugged, opting to keep my word.

'Coach is full of *shit*,' he said, his face darkening for a few seconds.

'No, he isn't,' I said, though I was unclear how Coach fit into this part of the discussion.

'What did he tell you? Because this is the only time that anything like this has ever happened. I swear. With you, the other night . . . and it was an accident. A misunderstanding . . . I didn't mean to hurt you or scare you . . . You have to believe that. I love you, baby.'

'Don't say that,' I said, understanding with new clarity the expression *skin crawling*.

'But I do love you.' He cleared his throat, leaned toward me, his face as close to mine as the table would allow. Then he started talking, his voice intense, earnest. 'Shea, I'm so sorry I did this to you and put us here. I take full responsibility and will do absolutely anything to repair the damage. I can see in your eyes that you don't trust me, but I pray that there is some love left. Just a little. And if there is, we can rebuild upon it. I know we can. I love you so *much*. If you just give me one chance to prove that to you . . . *Please*.'

I said nothing, hating that I felt sorry for him. I didn't want to feel *anything* for him, indifference being the only route to true freedom.

'You have to understand how much that got into my head,' he continued. 'Everything with you and Miller . . .'

I started to reply, but he held up his hand. 'I'm not blaming any of this on Miller. And I know there is nothing to worry about with him . . . But when I didn't hear from you after you promised you'd call me . . . and it was the night before a big game . . . and I missed you so much . . . and then I had that disaster game . . . And then I let my dad – and everything – get in my head . . . And then Miller had your credit card, and you have to see how bad that looks . . . and I guess I just snapped. I'm so sorry. But you have to believe I didn't try to hurt you. Look in my eyes and tell me you know that.'

I felt myself questioning my own version of events, seeing his side of things, at least a little bit, but I managed to stare him down and say, 'You don't get to *snap* in a relationship,

Ryan. Not if that's what snapping looks like.' I glanced around the restaurant to make sure nobody was watching me, then showed him the bruise, now yellow, on my left arm, closest to the window.

A look of anguish crossed his face. 'Aw, Shea. I'm so sorry.'

'Look,' I said. 'I don't think you're a bad person. I think you're a guy with a problem. A big problem . . . And I do forgive you for what you did . . . But I don't feel right about this relationship. I just don't. I don't want to be in it anymore, Ryan. And you have to accept this as my final word. It's not going to change no matter what you say or do or promise.'

He stared at me, his jaw resting in his large hand, and for a second I thought he was finally hearing me, understanding that it really was over. But then he shook his head. 'I can't accept that.'

'You have to.'

He took a breath and blinked rapidly in the way that people blink when they're about to cry. Then he looked up at the ceiling and blinked some more until I could see that the rims of his eyes were turning watery, red. I told myself not to cave. It was pitiful – seeing someone that strong on the verge of tears.

'I'm sorry, Ryan. I care about you. I always will. And I want you to get help and change for *you*. But this relationship just isn't right for me. And in some ways it probably never was,' I said, feeling a little bit guilty for letting him think that this was all his fault. 'I'm not sure we were ever really right for each other . . . I'm really sorry.'

He nodded, then dropped his gaze from the ceiling to me and said, 'Will you at least keep the earrings? Please?'

I stared into his eyes for a long few seconds, then said, 'Okay. If it means that much to you—'

'It does. It really does.'

'Okay. I'll keep the earrings.'

'And you won't sell them? Or give them away? Promise me.'

'Okay,' I said again. 'I'll keep them. I promise. I do love them.'

'I wish you loved *me,* too,' he said. 'But at least you'll always have something from me. Something good.'

I gave him a small, genuine smile.

'I really am a good person, Shea.'

I nodded, believing that to be true – or, at the very least, believing that he *wanted* to be a good person.

'Get some help, Ryan. Will you?'

'I will, baby,' he said, looking into my eyes.

This time, I let him call me *baby,* but I stood up, put a twenty on the table, and said goodbye.

'Goodbye, Shea,' he said, stoic acceptance on his face.

37

Later that night, I made plans to visit Coach at his office, relieved to find the parking lot at the athletic complex virtually empty. As I entered the football wing, I glanced nervously over my shoulder, wondering how much longer we'd have to creep around and lie. It was still a necessity, but I didn't like it, and could feel myself starting to imagine a different reality.

'There she is,' Coach said when he opened his door, breaking into a dazzling smile. He took my hand and pulled me inside, nudging the door closed behind me.

I smiled back at him, both of us frozen for several seconds before he put his arms around me in a proper hug. I hugged him back, tentatively at first, then more tightly, deciding that if he didn't make a move soon, I was going to. I *had* to kiss him.

He pulled away just enough to be able to gaze down at me with an intense stare. It was the way he watched a play in progress, one that pleased him, one that was going exactly as planned. Sometimes when he had this look on his face, he'd say *yesss* with a couple of hard claps or a clenched fist pump. He didn't do that tonight, but I could tell he was feeling that way because I knew him that well, inside and out, all his tics and moods and expressions.

He cupped my cheeks in his hands, our faces at the perfect intimate distance. Feeling drugged and dizzy, I stared at the stubble on his jaw, his half-closed lids, the crescent shape of his top lip. He slid his hands back past my ears, lacing his fingers behind my head, tugging slightly on my hair. It was as if he were controlling me without trying to, making my lips part, my eyes close, my breathing shallow and rapid. I waited another few agonizing seconds, aching to be kissed. When he still didn't do it, I put my hands on his neck and made a little moaning sound, too overwhelmed to speak. Then, finally, his lips brushed against mine, lightly at first, then more urgently. It was like looking into a bright light that didn't hurt your eyes. Everything felt warm and right and complete until I stopped thinking altogether. I forgot where we were and what had happened to lead us to this moment and just focused on kissing him. I tasted him and touched him, feeling his close-cropped hair and his warm neck and the muscles in his shoulders and back straining through the thin material of his Dri-FIT shirt. I inhaled the scent of his skin and aftershave mixed with that familiar salty smell of practice. I listened to his breathing, could hear his excitement, mirroring my own.

We kissed and kissed until we finally separated, his hands still tangled up in my hair, our faces so close that his features were blurry.

'Damn,' he said, catching his breath.

'I know,' I said, staring into his eyes.

'Crazy,' he said. 'That was some *crazy* stuff right here.'

I laughed because it was so him to call a first kiss 'some crazy stuff,' and because I knew exactly what he meant. He laughed with me, then led me by the hand over to the leather sofa that I'd sat on for years. Only never like this. Never with my legs thrown across his, my arm around his neck. Never this relaxed, this close. I glanced around his office, taking in all his clippings and photos and plaques, as if seeing them for the first time. Everything seemed different now, elevated. My eyes rested on one framed quote hanging on the wall behind us that read:

A GOOD COACH MAKES HIS PLAYERS SEE WHAT THEY CAN BE, RATHER THAN WHAT THEY ARE.

The quote felt true for me, too, as I thought of how much he had changed *me* in the past few months, encouraging me to leave the Walker cocoon, begin a new career, end a relationship, then another. Now here we were, seemingly in the same spot, just where we had begun. Yet we weren't the same. Nothing was.

'I'm proud of you, girl,' he said, kissing my forehead.

'Why's that?' I asked, wondering if he could read my mind.

'For handling your business,' he said, his breath in my hair. 'For being strong.'

He was talking about Ryan now, so I said, 'I couldn't have been strong without you.'

'That's not true,' he said. 'You got us here.'

I smiled, accepting part of the credit, but thinking that a lot of things had had to happen, some of them really bad – like Ryan grabbing me and Connie *dying*. But I pushed those things away and said, 'You helped me. You've *always* helped me. You have no idea how much . . .'

He touched my cheek and smiled at me. 'I'd do anything for you, girl. You know that.'

I nodded – because I *did* know that – then I put my head on his shoulder, trying to place what made our first kiss different from all of my other first kisses. The answer was seemingly obvious – I was in love. Maybe for the first time; maybe just more than before. But there was something else, too. Something else that made our moment different, special. It meant more because we felt like a team. Not in a cheesy Go-Walker way but in the ultimate I-have-your-back way. There was none of the emotional negotiation that so often comes with a first kiss. No wondering what it meant, what would happen next, who had the upper hand. Instead, our kiss came from a sacred understanding of where we had been and where we were headed. We both wanted this. We both were committed to making it happen, and I felt certain that neither of us would enter into a situation so fraught with controversy and potential hurt feelings unless we were damn near *positive* that this was what we wanted. But we still had one major little blond obstacle.

'We have to tell Lucy,' I blurted out, breaking the tranquil spell. 'We have to tell her before she finds out. She deserves to know. It isn't right to keep a secret like this from her.'

'I know,' he said. 'When do we do that? . . . I gotta hit the road soon here.'

I knew he was talking about recruiting, that he only had two weeks until the next dead period, when coaches couldn't communicate with recruits. 'Where are you going?' I asked, avoiding the hard topic for a few seconds more.

'Chicago and Pittsburgh,' he said. 'Naperville and New Kensington, to be exact. Two quick trips to visit two quarterbacks. Up and back . . . And a couple day trips in Texas.'

'When do you leave?' I said.

'Chicago on Friday. Pittsburgh next week. In and out . . . Why? Do you want to join me?'

I smiled and said, 'I wish.' Then I remembered Lucy's tree-trimming invitation and asked him if he planned to be there.

'Yes. Why? You don't think we should tell her then, do you?'

'No. That will be emotional enough,' I said, knowing how much Lucy dreaded all the Christmas traditions without her mother. 'Maybe we should wait until after the holidays?'

'And after the game?'

'Yes,' I said, feeling a rush of cowardly relief. 'Maybe so. We just have to be really careful in the meantime.'

'I agree. Because this has to come from us.'

'*Both* of us,' I said, thinking that it wasn't fair to give him the task – and I wasn't sure I could handle it alone.

'Yes. When the time is right, we just have to do it,' he said in his intense, coaching voice. 'Man up and do it.'

38

Two nights later, I was at Lucy's house, doing everything I could to avoid eye contact with Coach while he did the same with me. We had not seen each other since the night in his office but had talked every few hours. I'd even fallen asleep the night before while talking to him on the phone.

'Oh, I love this one! It's Blitzen!' Lucy said now, holding up a frosted glass reindeer as we all assembled in her family room to decorate her tree.

'Dude,' Lawton said, as Lucy passed it off to him with a directive to hang it somewhere near the front. 'How the hell do you know that it's *Blitzen*? I'm getting a Prancer vibe.'

'It's not Rudolph,' Caroline sagely pointed out. 'See? No red nose.'

'Right,' Lawton said, addressing Caroline, while Coach kept his nose to the grindstone, supergluing a broken Bronco ornament. 'But it could be any one of them but Rudolph. How does she know that it's *Blitzen*?'

I had been wondering the same thing, figuring there was something I had missed in reindeer lore, as Lucy smiled faintly and said, 'Mom told me it was Blitzen. A long time ago.'

'Well, how did *she* know?' Lawton said.

'She knew her reindeer, Lawton,' Lucy said, rolling her eyes. 'Now get him up there . . . And take this one, too.' She handed him a wooden oar with LAKE LBJ painted on the side and told him it could go toward the back.

One at a time, Lucy unwrapped ornaments from the cardboard compartments nestled in large green plastic bins, then passed them off to Caroline, Lawton, Coach, and me, while

Neil, who had strung the tiny white lights earlier in the day, focused on careful placement of the generic gold and red balls. Lucy made it seem as if her ornament allocation was random, but I knew better, and quickly caught on that she gave the sturdiest and most garish ones to Caroline, so that they couldn't be broken and would be too low to see. She gave all those with a boyish theme (planes, trains, and automobiles; soldiers, elves, and masculine-looking snowmen and reindeer) to Lawton. And she gave anything Walker or football-related – which felt like every other ornament – to Coach and me. Additionally, Coach was in charge of all Santa Clauses, whether whimsical or dignified.

We took our assignments seriously, hoping that our branch selection would meet with her approval. For the most part, we didn't let her down, though she'd occasionally look up, frown, and point out an unpleasing concentration of one color or theme. 'Disperse those elves, would you, Lawton? They look too . . . *busy* all clumped together right there,' she'd say before returning her gaze to the bins, half of which came from her basement, the other half from her parents' attic, having given her father permission to forgo his own tree this year.

'It's looking good, y'all!' Lucy said at one point, and we all agreed that the tree was beautiful. That you couldn't even tell it was artificial, necessitated by Neil's evergreen allergy, unless you stopped to consider that no real trees were this full and symmetrical.

'Do you remember this one?' she said to Lawton, holding up a delicate painted ornament of a little girl pushing a cart full of toys. It looked Germanic and old, or at least old-fashioned, perhaps because the girl resembled Shirley Temple with her big eyes, ruby mouth, and fat sausage ringlets.

'Yep,' Lawton said. 'I always liked her . . . But I could never figure out why an angel would be bringing toys.'

'She's not an *angel*,' Lucy scoffed with faux indignation, as if Lawton had dubbed her a hooker. 'She's just a *girl*. And that's her *shopping cart*.'

'The *hell*,' Lawton said, pointing and peering through his long bangs in dire need of a cut. 'See that. It's called a *halo*.'

'You think *hell* and *halo* belong together?' I quipped, trying as hard as I could to be natural, light, festive, lest I give myself away. I had *still* not so much as glanced at Coach but was aware of his every move, and felt an electric current whenever he came near me.

Lawton laughed and said, 'Hell, yeah, they do.'

Lucy stared down at the girl-angel in disbelief. 'Well, son of a gun. You're *right*!' she said with a little laugh. 'But are you sure it's not a tiara?'

'It's a halo, dammit,' Lawton said.

Caroline giddily covered her mouth, thrilled with all the swearwords, as Lucy squinted further. 'Well. Now I love her even more. She's an angelic little shopper!'

'Just like you, Luce,' Coach Carr said, putting a hook on a snowman ornament. 'I bet there's some Channel and Vespucci buried somewhere in that cart.'

Everyone laughed at his joke, knowing that he was intentionally butchering Chanel and Versace, as I turned to Lucy and asked where the angel came from. I knew that she was eager to share any story related to her mother, and it was *my* job, I decided, to give her ample opportunity.

'Mom got it when she lived in Austria,' Lucy said. 'When she was a little girl. It was one of her favorites. Right, Dad?'

'That's right,' he said, although we all knew that Lucy was the authority on family heirlooms, and that he was likely just agreeing with her.

Caroline lunged for it while Lucy admonished her to be careful and said that she was going to hang this one because it was 'very breakable and very, very special.' She placed the angel near the top of the tree in the glow of a white light, then gave her cart a little push, watching it swing for a few seconds before returning to her bins.

And so it went, Lucy unveiling ornament after ornament, tweaking our placement, telling stories about her mother. I never would have predicted it, especially based on her mood around Thanksgiving, but she seemed to be genuinely happy, no trace of melancholy despite the intense sights, scents, and sounds of Christmases past pummeling us with the reminder that something – *someone* – was missing. Harry Connick, Jr., was crooning in the background. The aroma of snickerdoodles, Mrs Carr's specialty, wafted from the kitchen. It was even turning blustery outside, wind beating at the windowpanes, which Lucy mused her mother would have loved. In fact, her mood was so unexpectedly *stable* that I started to suspect her little white pills were involved, or at least an extra kick in her eggnog. Then again, maybe she had simply reached another small turning point in her grief. Maybe time really did heal all wounds.

Just a few minutes later, however, I landed upon another theory – that it was only a very convincing con job – when I heard Lucy say to Caroline, 'Honey, isn't this a magical night?'

Caroline said it was, taking another cookie from the snowflake plate while Lucy fired off a frantic few digital photos, close-ups of her daughter's profile, her own eyes glistening with a faraway sadness. Of *course* she wasn't feeling any better, not on the very first Christmas without her mother. She was simply doing her best to head-fake her daughter, put up a brave front, follow the advice her mother would have given her: *Make things perfect for your family, never mind your own feelings.* Her mood was as contrived as their fake tree, but still artful and beautiful in its own way. Later, when she and Neil were alone in their bedroom, I suspected that the tears would flow, but, for now, she had embraced her solemn duty to diligently construct and create memories for Caroline. I felt my heart fill with admiration for her and wondered if I could be so strong in her shoes. I didn't think so, but I suspected that motherhood has a way of bolstering your emotional reserves.

We all kept working until we neared the bottoms of the bins, where only the scruffy, trivial, recently acquired ornaments that Lucy humorously dubbed *nouveau accoutrements* remained.

'Time for the star. Neil, go get the stepladder.' She clapped twice as Caroline said, 'Chop! Chop!'

'*Wow.* Did you hear that, guys? Chop, *chop*? See how my wife's rubbing off on our child?' Neil announced to no one in particular. He clearly loved their mother-daughter sass, proud of the bossy women in his life, and he dutifully retrieved the ladder, setting it up as close to the tree as the branches would allow. He climbed three steps, then said, 'Caroline, would you like to do the honors?'

She nodded and eagerly scrambled up the ladder, then swiped the star from her father and fearlessly reached for the top of the nine-foot tree.

'Careful, careful,' Lucy commanded as Neil gripped Caroline's torso, lifted her slightly, and helped guide the star into place. We all oohed and aaahed and praised Caroline's tree-topping prowess. Then, as Caroline and Neil descended, Lucy stood, cleared her throat, and said, 'So *now* . . . Caroline has something to tell you . . . Caroline?'

Jumping and dancing and twirling about the room, Caroline screamed something about a sister, before falling to the ground in a dizzy heap. Lawton and Coach stared at her, confused, but I caught on instantly, my heart skipping a hopeful beat. *Lucy was pregnant!*

'Say it again, honey, slower,' Lucy said.

Caroline got up and tried again, forming her words more clearly. 'I'm going to be a *big* sister!'

This time, Coach and Lawton understood, both of them belting out their congratulations while I simply smiled in the background. I allowed myself to study Coach's face for the first time all evening, and could tell by his conflicted expression that he was thrilled by the news but also heartbroken that Connie wasn't here to share it. Or maybe he was just digging down, doing his best to rise to the occasion, give Lucy what she needed, say and do all the things that his wife would have so effortlessly said and done.

He took a deep breath, as if gathering himself, then stepped forward to shake Neil's hand and clap him on the back.

'Congratulations, son,' he said, beaming. Then he pulled Lucy into a big embrace, holding her for several seconds while I heard him say, 'Sweetheart. This is wonderful news. Just wonderful.'

'Thanks, Daddy,' Lucy said, giggling and blushing as they separated. 'We're really excited.'

Coach kissed Lucy's forehead, then chased after Caroline, who was still dancing around the room, and asked her if she wanted a brother or sister – a question as obvious as 'Do you want Walker to win it all?'

'A sister!' Caroline screamed at Lucy's stomach, as if volume could mandate gender, then allowed herself to be caught and scooped up by her grandfather.

'Do you know what it is?' Lawton asked, copying his dad's manly handshake and clap on the back for Neil, and big hug for his sister.

'No. We're still really early. I'm only eight weeks,' Lucy said. 'But I wanted you to know *now*. I thought tonight would be the perfect time to share our news.' She faltered a bit but remained calm, steady, purposefully joyful.

'Are you going to find out again? Like you did with this one?' Coach said, tweaking Caroline's nose before freeing her.

'No. Not this time. Mom will be the only one to know,' Lucy said, glancing up at the star before looking at me. 'What do you think, Shea?' she asked, as if making a point to fully include me in the family moment. Guilt-filled, I chose my words carefully, in a way I hadn't done nearly five years ago when I heard the news about Caroline.

'I think that's a wonderful plan. Be surprised this time,' I said and could feel myself getting choked up. 'I'm so happy for you, Luce.'

'I'm happy, too,' she said. 'I'm finally a *little* bit happy.'

I smiled, then inadvertently made eye contact with Coach, who was now standing just beyond Lucy. He gave me a look that seemed to say the same thing that I was thinking, *Thank goodness we didn't tell her yet.*

* * *

I wish I had left then, on a high note – the advice that Mrs Carr had always given us. Instead, I lingered, staying after Lawton departed, while Lucy and Neil went upstairs to put Caroline to bed, unable to resist Coach's magnetic pull.

'Another baby. Wow,' Coach said when we were alone, cleaning up the kitchen.

'I know. I didn't see that one coming . . . At all,' I said, though I wasn't sure why I was so surprised when I always knew that Neil and Lucy wanted more than one child.

'Me either,' he said, rinsing a cookie sheet, then putting it in the dishwasher while I wiped down the island.

'Do you think it's a boy?' I asked him.

'I do,' he said, turning to glance at me over his shoulder before returning his gaze to the sink. 'Which is weird because I never get feelings about this stuff. I'd love a grandson, but another girl would be great, too. And a little sister would be wonderful for Caroline.'

I nodded and studied Coach's back, as my mind selfishly raced with implications for our situation. Would Lucy's news make it easier or harder for us? There was no way to predict it, as babies had a way of making things better and worse at once. Lucy would have a distraction, but she would also have raging hormones stirring up her grief. And nothing, including holidays, would highlight the hole in her life like a newborn.

We could hear the clamor of bedtime antics upstairs, Neil and Lucy loudly negotiating with Caroline, and I knew that it would take them at least another thirty minutes to get her to bed. Coach must have been thinking that we were safe, too, because he bit his lower lip and took a few steps toward me. 'I need to kiss you again,' he whispered, glancing toward the front hallway. 'Everywhere.'

I shivered, then whispered, 'Let's go back to the family room. Safer.'

He nodded, leading me to the sofa, where we sat at a close but still strategically safe distance. We chatted about Lucy's baby for a few minutes more, before his face grew grave and he said, 'I need to talk to you about something important . . .'

'What?' I said, wondering if it had anything to do with the NCAA investigation.

He shook his head and said, 'Not now. Later.'

His expression concerned me, even more so when he touched my hand and said, 'Don't worry. It'll be okay.'

'Are you sure?' I said.

'Yes,' he said. 'I just need to . . . tell you something. That's all.'

I said okay, now thinking it had to do with Connie. Perhaps a confession that he still felt loyal to her. That he could move his wedding ring to his right hand but could not take it off altogether. He could kiss me, maybe even one day make love to me, but that he wasn't ready for a full commitment because he would always love her the most. My mind raced with other possibilities, all related to Mrs Carr, until he said, 'Stop worrying, honey.'

Then he wrapped my hand in his, brought it to his face, and tenderly kissed it. I felt myself melting, my vision blurring, my ears ringing, until everything froze and shattered with the sound of Lucy's voice behind us.

'Hi,' she said as Coach and I both jumped, then turned to look over our shoulders, in tandem.

'Hi,' I said, realizing that he was still holding my hand. I pulled it away. A clumsy, delayed reaction.

'Why did you just kiss Shea?' she said, her voice so sweet and innocent that she reminded me of Cindy Lou Who in *How the Grinch Stole Christmas!*

'I didn't,' Coach stammered.

'Yes, you did.'

'I kissed her hand. Not *her.*'

'Well, why did you kiss her *hand*?' Lucy said as Neil appeared next to her. She turned to him, crossed her arms, and announced, 'Dad just kissed Shea.'

No one spoke or moved for several seconds, until Lucy

circled around the sofa and sat on a chair across from us, the tree to her back. Neil joined her, sitting at her feet, looking completely discombobulated. I waited in agony, could feel my cheeks burning, sweat dripping down my sides.

'Is something going on between you two?' Lucy finally asked. She still didn't sound angry, but she was becoming less bewildered, more stern.

Neither of us replied, which was louder and clearer than any answer we could have given her.

'Oh. My. *God*,' Lucy said, looking at me, then her father, then me again.

I decided I had to speak since her gaze was now fixed on me.

'It's not like . . . *that*,' I said, although it was exactly like *that*. I reminded myself not to lie to my best friend. Not to make it worse than it already was.

'What is it, then? What *is* it like?'

Coach said, 'Luce. We're close friends. You know that.'

'I have never been kissed like that by a close friend. That's how Neil kisses me.'

Coach cleared his throat. 'It was only her hand.'

'Okay . . . well, have you *actually* kissed her, then?' Lucy asked with laser focus.

I looked at Coach, grateful that she was posing the questions to him, and I said a dreadful little prayer that he would lie, just a bit. But, once again, his silence spoke volumes about the truth.

'Oh, God, Neil,' she said, looking at her husband. 'They've *kissed*.'

'Just once,' I said. 'I swear.'

'When?'

'A few days ago,' Coach said.

'Where?'

'In my office,' he replied.

Lucy stared at the ceiling, then dropped her head in her hands, her voice coming back muffled. 'I can't . . . I can't handle this. I can't . . .' When she uncovered her face, she looked pleadingly at Neil and mumbled something I couldn't make out. Something like *Find out what's going on.*

Neil gave us a helpless, devastated look, then said, 'So you two . . . you have feelings for each other?'

Silence.

'Look. I think it's best if you tell us the truth . . . And then we'll handle it from there. Just tell Lucy the truth,' Neil said.

I heard Coach inhale just as I did, but while I held my breath, he exhaled and said, 'Yes. I have feelings for her.'

'As more than a friend?' Neil said, as I thought that he had never seemed quite this strong, in control. Not even through his mother-in-law's death – and he'd been great then.

'Yes,' Coach said. 'I really care about her.'

'And you, Shea?' Neil asked, turning to me.

I said yes, but my voice came out in a whisper.

'What?' Lucy said.

'Yes,' I repeated, more audibly.

Neil nodded, accepting the facts, then turned to Lucy, as if to ask her what else she wanted to know.

'When?' she fired off, her cheeks now as red as mine felt. 'When did you start feeling this way?'

'Not before . . .' I said, my voice trailing off.

'Not before *what*?' Lucy said. 'Not before Mom *died*? Good God, I should hope not. Or else . . . or else . . .'

She didn't finish her sentence, thank goodness, but I imagined that she was thinking *Or else you're both going to Hell.*

'Luce,' I said. 'This is all really new.'

'Like all of a sudden?' she snapped back at me.

'Well, yes . . . and no . . . It happened gradually . . . The feelings . . . But the kiss thing . . . just happened. All of a sudden, yes.'

I was babbling, my insides twisting, as I waited for the inquisition to continue. But instead of another question, Lucy said, 'You know what? I'm going to bed. I can't do this. I don't want to know. Just . . . do what you're going to do . . . and please leave me out of it.'

She rose as Coach tried to stop her, standing and reaching for her arm. He caught it, but she shook it off and said, 'I'm tired, Daddy. Good night.'

'Good night, Lucy . . . I'm . . . really sorry if this hurts you . . .'

'If?' she said, her eyes finally filling with tears.

'I'm sorry that it upsets you,' he said.

Lucy stared at her father, her eyes cold, remote. 'Don't,' she said. 'Don't say anything else. I just hope it's worth it to you both . . .'

'Lucy,' he said, his voice stronger, more urgent, with just a hint of authority. 'Wait.'

She shook her head, then walked out of the room, without so much as a glance my way.

39

'That was *brutal*,' Coach said when he called me from his cell just a few minutes after we had seen ourselves out of Lucy's house. In a mild state of shock, I gripped my steering wheel, trailing Coach in my car.

'She *hates* me,' I said, more to myself than to him. Without thinking, I passed the turnoff for my apartment, still following Coach in the direction of his house.

'She hates both of us,' he said, as if this were some kind of solace.

'You're her *father*. She can't hate you,' I said, realizing that that hadn't stopped me from hating my own dad for the longest time. In some ways, it was easier to hate someone in your family, the smallest betrayals magnified. But it was also far easier to write off a friend, without a bloodline holding you together.

'She *has* to forgive us,' he said. 'Eventually.'

I wondered what he meant by *eventually* – a couple of days, weeks, or years – and the thought that it could be the last, that it could be *never*, made me pull over to the side of the road.

Coach must have glanced in his rearview mirror, because he said, 'Where'd you go?'

'I stopped for a second,' I said, my hands shaking. I watched his taillights illuminate ahead of me as he pulled over, too.

'Are you all right?' he said.

'What if she never forgives us?' I said, thinking of all the grudges Lucy had held over the years. All the people she had written off for far smaller offenses.

'She will. Of *course* she will.'

'How do you know?'

'Because . . . we're the two most important people in her life after Caroline and Neil.'

'No,' I said, staring at his car. 'Her mother's far more important than we are. That's the point.'

'But . . . she's not here. This never would have happened if Connie were still with us.'

'Of course not,' I said, appalled at the mere idea that *anything*, even the most minor of flirtations, would have ever begun if Mrs Carr had been alive. I thought back to that dreadful time when she was really sick, and how I couldn't even look him in the eye. 'Do you think Lucy knows that?'

'Yes. She knows that. She knows *us* . . . Nobody cheated here. Nobody lied.'

'We sort of lied.'

'No. We just didn't tell her right away . . . This thing *just* happened . . . Nobody planned it . . . Lucy's just upset . . . She needs time to process it.'

'She'll never accept it,' I said.

'She has to.'

'She won't,' I said, wondering what in the world I'd been thinking. How did I *ever* think this could work?

'Yes. She *will*. Now c'mon. Follow me.'

I hesitated, then decided that where I went at this moment really wouldn't change anything. So I put my car back in drive and said okay.

A few minutes later, we were together in his kitchen, both of us checking our phones.

'Did she call you?' I asked.

'Nope. Did she call you?'

I shook my head.

'I'm sorry,' he said. 'I shouldn't have kissed you like that. I don't know what I was thinking.'

'I let you,' I said. 'I forgot where we were. You make me forget everything . . .'

He gave me a thoughtful look and said, 'Maybe it's for the

best that it came out now. There was never going to be a *good* time for that announcement.'

'Yes, but I feel like we ruined Lucy's news.'

'Nothing can ruin that news.'

'You know what I mean. Tonight was important. Really special to her. And we were reckless . . .'

'I know . . . But it's done. We can't change it now,' Coach said, always one to focus on the things he could control.

'But we have to fix it.'

'Time will fix it,' he said. 'Trust me. She'll come around.'

I studied his face, wanting desperately to believe that he was right but thinking it was a lot easier for him to be patient, wait her out. He didn't talk to Lucy three times a day. He didn't need her the way I needed her. I honestly couldn't fathom what I'd do if our friendship ended.

I sighed, then went to sit at the kitchen table, resting my chin in my hand. Coach followed, sitting across from me, as I remembered the last thing he had said to me in Lucy's family room. 'So what did you want to tell me?' I asked him.

He blinked a few times, his face blank, as if he had no idea what I was talking about.

'You said you had something to tell me,' I said. 'Right before Lucy came downstairs.'

'Oh. Yeah. Right.'

'Well?' I said. 'What was it?'

Coach looked tense as he took a deep breath.

'Is it Mrs Carr?' I made myself ask. 'Because I know how hard this must be. I mean, I understand that your loyalty will always be to her . . . which is the way it should be,' I finished awkwardly, wishing I hadn't brought her up.

Coach shook his head and said, 'No. It's not about Connie. I mean . . . I've had some pangs over the past few weeks. I feel guilty for being happy. For being excited . . . But I feel that way about football, too. After we win. Like how dare I be happy about a game when she's not here? Then I always come back to reason and remind myself that whatever you and I do or don't do isn't going to bring her back.'

I nodded, familiar with his rationale, but aware that he was evading my question. 'So what was it, then?' I said.

A few more seconds ticked by before he cleared his throat and said, 'It's about the past. Something that happened a long time ago.'

I froze, my mind flitting through the possibilities, praying that there hadn't been another woman while Mrs Carr was alive. Maybe he'd had an affair with a colleague. Or a random woman he met on the road. Or, most sickening of all, a ripe, bubbly coed. Maybe it was someone I knew, someone I had gone to school with. I couldn't bear the thought of any of these possibilities, but told myself it wouldn't change my feelings. Nothing could change the way I felt about him.

'*How* long ago?' I asked.

'Back when you and Ryan were in school.' He took a deep breath, exhaled, and said, 'Do you remember that gal Ryan dated in college? Before the one he married? Tish Termini?'

'Yes,' I said, my thoughts racing. *Surely* Coach hadn't been involved with Tish.

'Well . . . the night before we left town for the Cotton Bowl, I was in my office, doing some work, when she came to see me.'

I waited, bracing myself for the worst.

'She said she had to tell me something important and was very emotional. I told her to have a seat. So she sat down and told me this story . . . about the big blowout breakup fight she'd had with Ryan the night before . . . I think we can both picture that now.'

'Yes,' I said, my insides clenched as I mentally switched gears.

'Then she told me that Ryan had attacked her. I asked what she meant by *attacked*, and she spelled it out pretty clearly. She said that he pushed and shoved her . . . And then . . . Then she said he forced her to have sex.'

'He *raped* her?' I said, the word leaving a bitter taste in my mouth.

'Well, she didn't say that *exactly*. But yeah . . . That's what she alleged. That he had sex with her against her will. So yeah. That would be rape.'

I stared back at him, everything inside me deflating as I remembered how I'd felt on my bed the other night. How scared I had been even as I tried to tell myself that it was only Ryan. My boyfriend who would never *really* hurt me. Even with my own awful memories, I found it impossible to grasp what Coach was telling me now.

'So then what?' I said, feeling frantic. 'What did you say?'

'I said it was a really serious charge and she'd better be very sure about what she was saying.'

'And?'

'And she said she was sure.'

'Then what?' I pressed.

'I asked her why she hadn't gone to the police. She said she was scared and in shock and that she wanted to come to me first. She asked if I believed her, and I told her it really didn't matter what I believed. I told her that if she had been raped she needed to go down to the station. Or at least to the campus police.'

'Did you think she was lying?'

Coach stared at me for several seconds before answering. 'I didn't see any marks on her . . . There was no sign at all of a physical struggle . . .'

'But there doesn't have to be,' I said. 'Sometimes there aren't marks.'

'I know that,' he said. 'But I also knew that she had quite the reputation. My assistant coaches had been telling me for months that she was bad news. Bad for Ryan. Always out at the clubs. Drinking and smoking and carrying on . . . And I'd even heard she was up before the honor council for cheating on an exam . . . So she wasn't the most reliable girl . . . And Ryan was . . . well, he was *Ryan*. The golden boy. Heisman candidate. Good student. Squeaky-clean reputation.'

'So you didn't believe her?' I said, boiling it down to its essence. 'Did you?'

'No,' he said. 'I didn't believe her.'

'So you didn't do *anything*?' I said, my heart pounding in my ears.

'Shea . . . You have to understand . . . I didn't know what I now know . . . I only had the facts that I had at the time. And, based on those facts, it just didn't add up. I really thought she was manufacturing the whole thing . . . exacting some kind of revenge because Ryan had broken up with her. I thought she wanted me to bench him for the bowl game. Get even. Hurt him the worst way you can hurt a ballplayer . . . And, beyond that, beyond destroying a football career, I was aware that this type of accusation could ruin a young man's life. It's serious if it's true, of course, but it's serious if it's *not* true, too . . . And I didn't think it was true. Not a shred of me believed that girl.'

'Did you at least *talk* to Ryan?' I asked. 'Ask him about it?'

'Yes. Of course I did. Right after Tish left, I called him into my office and asked him what had happened. He told me a story that made more sense than hers. A story that I could . . . wrap my head around.'

'What did he tell you?' I said, knowing how convincing, down-right slick, he could be.

'He told me that he'd broken up with her and that she was very hurt. Very angry . . . He said she came after him pretty hard, and he just defended himself. Like this.' Coach held up his arms, blocking his face. 'He said he did push her out of his apartment, but only after she refused to leave. And he swore to me that he didn't hurt her . . . And that was it . . .'

Coach threw his hands up in the air and shook his head. 'It was a classic he-said, she-said, and, bottom line, I just didn't believe that girl. In my mind, she wasn't credible. He was. So yeah. I took his word over hers. A few days later, I did follow up with her.'

'And?'

'And she changed her tune . . . She changed her story. At least part of it. She maintained that he *had* roughed her up but said that the sex was "a little bit consensual" . . .'

'A *little* bit?'

'Exactly. It either was or it wasn't. Right?'

'Maybe she was scared. Maybe she knew you didn't believe her.'

'And maybe she had made that part up.'

'Maybe,' I said, acknowledging that this was definitely a possibility. 'So that was it?'

Coach nodded, avoiding my gaze.

'You didn't do *anything* else?' I asked, my heart sinking.

'You have to remember, Shea . . . There are rules now about this sort of thing. Rules that say coaches have to report all incidents to the university president or athletic director or police. Or all three. But back then . . . there was nothing in place. I had never dealt with anything like that before . . .'

'Did you tell Connie?' I asked, unsure of why this mattered to me.

'No.'

I stared at him, frozen, out of questions.

'Does this . . . change things?' he asked softly.

I started to say no, because I wanted it to be the truth. But then I thought of Tish. It had changed everything for Tish. It had also changed everything for Ryan. Maybe even for Blakeslee and me. Hell, it had changed the course of history. If Coach had believed Tish's story, at least enough to report it, the trajectory of Ryan's entire career would have been different. Even if ultimately cleared of the charges, he likely wouldn't have won the Heisman the following year, or gone nearly as high in the draft. It would have hurt Walker, too. Without Ryan on the field, we certainly wouldn't have won the Cotton Bowl; and, without that win, we might not have had the recruiting classes in the years that followed, success begetting success. Walker might not be on the brink of a championship this season, and Coach and I might not be sitting here tonight, in his kitchen.

Coach said my name, looking far more worried than he'd been in Lucy's living room.

'Yeah?' I said.

'If I could go back, I would change how I handled everything.

I would have done more. I really thought I was doing the right thing, but now I can see that I let that girl down.' He paused for a long beat, then cleared his throat. 'The other night, when I walked into your room and saw Ryan there on top of you . . . It was almost as if I were standing up for both of you . . .'

I nodded, as if I accepted this explanation, but couldn't help feeling that throwing a couple of punches in my living room couldn't fix the past, and I felt myself withdraw from him in a way that scared me.

'Talk to me, Shea,' he said. 'Tell me what you're thinking.'

'I don't know,' I said. 'This is a lot to digest . . .'

'Are you angry?'

'No,' I said, wishing that it were that simple, knowing that anger has a way of subsiding and passing more quickly than this brand of disappointment.

'Then what?' he said.

I opened my mouth, but couldn't find the words to describe the disoriented, disillusioned feeling I had. The feeling of questioning everything I had ever believed in. The NCAA investigation was one thing. But this was another matter, one I couldn't so easily dismiss or explain away.

'I'm really sorry, Shea,' he said.

'I know you are,' I said, thinking of Lucy, then Ryan, wondering if sometimes apologies were simply too little, too late.

'What are you thinking?' he said.

'I'm thinking I better head home now.'

As soon as the words were out, I changed my mind and hoped that he'd protest. I wanted him to say and do all the things that made him a great coach. I wanted him to make everything better the way he always had.

But he simply nodded and said okay. Then he walked me to the door, where he gave me a quick platonic hug, followed by an equally platonic kiss on the cheek, as if he, too, realized that something had shifted between us and was surrendering to a new status quo.

'So, you're going to Chicago tomorrow?' I said, stalling,

feigning normalcy. As if anything had been normal about this entire evening. Even decorating the tree had been a charade set to a Harry Connick, Jr., soundtrack.

'Yes,' he said, also pretending. 'I'll call you from the road.'

'Great.' I nodded as he reached beyond me for the storm door, propping it open with his outstretched arm. I stepped onto the porch, still stalling. Moths danced around the lanterns, and one collided with my cheek. I swiped at its soft, powdery wings, but kept staring at him, waiting for something more.

When he still didn't speak, I said his name. *Clive.* There was urgency in my voice, neediness.

'What is it, Shea?' he said softly, still holding the door open.

I didn't answer, and he pulled me back into the darkened foyer, letting the storm door snap closed. Then he pushed the front door shut, and put his arms around me, this time in a real embrace. 'Please don't go,' he said. 'Not yet. Not like this.'

I held on to him as tightly as I could and said, 'Why do I feel like we just lost?'

'Because we did,' he whispered into my hair. 'We lost because of poor coaching. Bad leadership. This is my fault. I take full responsibility.'

I didn't debate his statement, believing it to be true. I blamed him for where we were. I blamed him for not reporting the incident. Not doing more. But I still let him lean in and kiss me, softly, then more urgently. His whiskers were rough against my chin, but I kissed him back as hard and frantically as I could, holding on to his neck, clawing at his chest and back, slipping my hand down the back of his jeans. I tried to keep my mind as blank as I could, focusing only on the physical, the sound of his voice murmuring my name. And for a few seconds, it worked. His kisses erased every thought I had, until I heard myself say, 'I want you. *All* of you.'

He kept kissing me, his hands on my back and hips, stomach and breasts, as I made my request again, more clearly. 'Make love to me,' I said.

'Tonight?' he said, before moving on to my neck, his breath warm in my ear.

'Yes. Right now,' I said, pulling him from the foyer to the hallway.

We made it a few steps before he said, 'Shea . . . Wait. Slow down.'

'No. *Now*,' I said, still walking backwards, pulling him toward his bedroom, then changing my mind and guiding him toward the upstairs guest room.

'What's the rush?' he asked, grabbing my arms, stopping me.

'This might be our only chance.'

He stared into my eyes, then nodded, as if he got it. Because everyone who loves sports knows that sometimes you only have one shot. Sometimes you don't have the luxury to think or wait or plan. Sometimes you have to reach out and seize your moment. Your best, last, or only chance. And maybe this was ours. If I couldn't get over what happened years before. If Lucy couldn't get over what was happening now. This thing could be over before it ever really began.

I think he understood all of this, but he still shook his head and said no.

'Why not?' I asked, filled with a range of emotions. Disappointment and confusion and guilt. *Always* guilt. 'Because of Lucy?' I glanced down the hallway toward his bedroom. 'Or Connie?'

'No. Because of *you*. Because of *us*. Because we have some things to work through. We have to be disciplined. We have to be patient.'

'And what if we can't work through them?' I asked.

'We will,' he said.

'How do you know?' I searched for answers in his eyes and the lines around them. He was every bit as rugged and sexy as he always was, but he looked older than he usually did. He looked his age. *Too old for me*, I thought for the first time.

'I don't *know*. But I'm hopeful that we can.'

'Oh, you're *hopeful*?' I said, a caustic edge in my voice that scared me.

'Yes.'

'Well, I'm *angry*,' I said, finally acknowledging the emotion I'd been suppressing.

'At me?'

'Yes,' I said, shocked by the emotion, the very *notion* that I could be angry at Coach. 'You should have reported it. You should have at least *helped* her report it.'

'Yes . . . I should have . . . I know that now . . . But, Shea . . . I honest to God didn't think he raped her. I still don't.'

I looked at him, thinking this was the wrong response, feeling a fresh wave of indignation, this time on Tish's behalf. 'That's not the point,' I said. 'That wasn't up to you to decide.'

'I thought it was,' he said. 'So I decided.'

'What about Cedric's Escalade?' I said, now pacing along the runner in his hallway.

'What about it?'

'You know. The car that nobody in Cedric's life could possibly afford,' I said, shifting into full-on investigative reporter mode.

'Is that a question?' he said, adopting his prickly press conference voice. 'Or an accusation?'

'Did you really think that was okay? For Cedric to be given a *car*? Just because he was poor – and a good kid? That means you can break the rules? Or did you just want him to play for Walker that *badly*?'

He opened his mouth to respond, but I kept going. 'And what about Reggie? What do you *really* know about this current investigation? What are you covering up? Because I want to know the truth. I want to know what you'd do to win,' I said, pointing at him.

His eyes went from hurt to pissed, the hue of blue actually seeming to change, deepen. 'Well, I wouldn't let a girl get raped, if that's what you're getting at . . .'

'But you'd look the other way, wouldn't you?' I demanded, my voice shaking. I hated myself for asking these questions, but I'd hate myself more for not asking them.

'Look, Shea. If even one percent of me – even *half* a percent – believed that Ryan had hurt that girl, I would have reported it . . . And I sure as hell wouldn't have let you go out with him. Think about it.'

'I *am* thinking about it,' I said, staring at him, my arms crossed.

'And?' he said, raising his voice.

I took a deep breath, now on the verge of tears that I managed to blink back. 'From the time I was a little girl, watching that SMU death penalty press conference, I really thought you were different. I thought you were one of the good guys. Unlike the other coaches. Unlike my own father. You were one of the few who would *never* cheat. One of the few who didn't believe that winning was . . . *everything*. The *only* thing,' I said, quoting Vince Lombardi, his hero.

Coach shook his head and said, 'Wow. And you think making love would have fixed *this*?' He motioned in the space between us, our huddle of two.

'Just tell me,' I said.

'Tell you what? What do you want to know?'

'I want to know . . . is winning *everything* to you?'

'Do you think it is, Shea? Is that what you think?'

'Did you choose not to report the incident because of the Cotton Bowl? What if the season had been over? Or what if Ryan had been a redshirt? Or a benchwarmer? Would you have handled it differently? Would you have taken her more seriously?'

'I chose not to report the incident because I didn't *believe* that girl,' he said, now shouting and pointing back at me. 'Listen, Shea. I am the *head* coach of a major football program—'

'Which means you have a responsibility—' I jumped in, my voice as loud as his.

'Yes! A responsibility to *ninety* guys. If I had sat Ryan, I would have penalized eighty-nine other guys who had worked their asses off all year, some of them for *four* years. I would have penalized their families and friends. I would have punished my coaching staff and every Walker student and alum. Every man, woman, and child who gives to this program. Gives their blood, sweat, tears, dollars, time, hearts. I could have ruined Ryan's football career. Changed his entire future.'

'But if he *raped* her—'

'And what if he didn't! Can you really picture him doing that, Shea?'

I hesitated and then shook my head. 'No. I can't imagine him doing such a thing,' I said quietly. 'But I still would have reported it . . . Just to be on the safe side.'

'Well, good for you, Shea. Good for making that decision with fifteen years of hindsight and a whole lot more information than I had. Thank you for that classic bit of Monday morning quarterbacking. Just like those idiots who call in to my show.'

'This is different from questioning a play in a game . . .'

'I know that, Shea. And I also know that I made a mistake. A terrible mistake. I don't believe he raped her, but now . . . I do believe he did *something* to her . . . And I know I should have done more for her . . . And I'm manning up and admitting that to you. I would change it if I could. But I can't.'

'What about trying to fix what happened?' I said.

'How?'

'By apologizing to Tish?'

'I've already done that. Would you like to read the letter? It's back there on my desk. Go read it! Go on! Then tell me what else I should do. Turn myself in? Penalize my current team, which had nothing to do with this? Bring down the program, fifteen years later? Is that what you want? If *that's* what you want – go ahead and do it yourself. You're a reporter. Write the story. Write the damn story, Shea. Include what Ryan did to you. Write all of it! I'll give you a hell of a quote!'

I stared at him, speechless, more confused than ever.

Coach finally spoke. 'I'm not perfect, Shea. I never claimed to be perfect. The media did that. The media loves a black and white story . . . But guess what? It's never black and white. *Never.* I'm not the saint they made me out to be. And I'm not the demon they'd love to portray if they knew . . . *this.*'

'This what?' I said, because he was gesturing between us again.

'Well, for starters, if they knew that I'm involved with a girl I practically raised. My daughter's best friend. A reporter on *my* beat covering an NCAA probe into *my* program . . .'

'I'm going to resign,' I said. Although this was the first moment that such a thought had occurred to me, I was suddenly sure of the decision.

'You're doing no such thing,' he said. 'Because that's the least of it . . . That's a nothing little sidebar compared to this Paterno story we have going here. Forget the dubious rape allegation. There's still an assault and battery charge that I swept under the carpet on the eve of the Cotton Bowl.'

'This is nothing like Paterno and Penn State,' I said.

'They'll say that it is.'

'It's not true.'

'The truth doesn't matter.'

'You don't believe that. Of *course* it matters.'

'Well, then, you listen here, Shea. You listen good. Because I'd stake my life on what I'm about to tell you . . . That decision I made in my office fifteen years ago? . . . It was wrong . . . But it had *nothing* to do with winning a football game. It has *never* been about winning a football game.'

'What's it about?' I said, my voice cracking.

'It's about loyalty. It's about commitment to the people you love. Your wife. Your family. Your friends. Your *team*. It's about giving it your all and doing the very best you can with what you have, in every moment you're in. And that's what I did that night in my office. That's what I do on the football field. And that's what I'm doing right now as I defend myself to the woman I love.'

'You love me?' I said, my heart pounding in my ears.

'Yes, I love you. I'm *madly* in love with you. I want you more than anything. And a whole hell of a lot more than winning a football game. Even a national championship.'

'I believe you,' I finally whispered, my knees weak. 'I believe *in* you.'

'Well, that's a start,' he said. 'That's a really good start.'

40

The following morning, my mother called and demanded that I come over, right away, complaining of chest pains. So I raced to her house, finding her in her bathroom, wearing one of her many silk robes while putting on individual false eyelashes that she wore nearly every day, no special occasion needed.

'How could you do this?' she shouted when I walked in, spinning away from the counter to face me. I hoped that she was referring to my breakup with Ryan, which I had informed her of via email, but had the feeling that Lucy had spoken to her about last night.

'How could I do what?' I said, cursing myself for believing her wolf crying.

'Clive,' she said, shaking her head.

'So you don't have chest pains?'

'I have severe heartache, that's what I have. I honestly thought I raised you better than this.'

'Oh, *please,* Mom,' I said, steeling myself for the onslaught to come. 'Stop overreacting. You don't even know the facts here.'

'Don't play dumb with me, missy! Lucy called me. I know the whole story!' she said.

'What's the "whole story"?' I said, making air quotes.

'That you and Clive have a . . . *thing.*'

'A thing. Right,' I said, determined not to discuss any*thing* with my mother. This might be Lucy's business, but it wasn't hers.

'Lucy's your *best* friend, Shea. She's like your *sister,*' my mom said, using tweezers to pluck another lash out of the white plastic packet. It occurred to me that everything about her was contrived, one big stage direction after another, her anger quieting to a dead calm when she needed to get a lash in place. 'This is just wrong. Completely and totally *wrong*!'

'You're just jealous,' I mumbled – because part of me believed there was some truth to that. If someone was going to do a little widower rescuing, it should have been her. And talk about the ultimate in copycatting; if she had Clive, she could really *be* Connie.

'It is *so* wrong!'

'How is it wrong, Mom? Tell me how love can be *wrong*?'

I knew I sounded like a naïve, love-struck teenager, but it occurred to me that sometimes naïve, love-struck teenagers have it all figured it out, and their small-minded, judgmental mothers have it all wrong. Especially the kind who continue to apply false lashes during a supposed crisis.

'It's just . . . *wrong*,' she said again. 'Clive *is* like family to us. And Connie was my *best* friend. It is such a betrayal.'

'It's not a betrayal, Mom. Because Connie *died*.' I kept my voice and expression soft to mitigate the harshness of the words. It was the truth, though. Connie was gone; therefore I wasn't *taking* her husband from her. In fact, I deep-down believed that she would approve of us, maybe even root for us.

'Do you know how that sounds?' my mother said, looking stricken.

'Mom. C'mon. I just meant that this never would have happened if Connie hadn't died. That's all.'

'Well, I'm still here. And so is Lucy. And Neil. And Lawton. And Caroline. And it's not fair to any of us what you two are doing.'

'Caroline?' I said, crossing my arms. 'Really? And what about the fetus? Is it unfair to the fetus, too?'

'What fetus?'

'Lucy's pregnant,' I said. 'She called to tattle on me, but left out that bit of news?'

'Well, that should show you how hurt she is. And FYI, Shea, pregnant women are emotional . . . fragile . . . You simply can't do this to her while she's pregnant.' She paused, then got herself all riled up again, spinning to face me and point at me some more. 'You can't do this at *all*! Put yourself in her shoes. What if she were dating *your* father?'

'I'd tell her she deserves better.'

My mother was temporarily distracted from her mission by the satisfaction that came with any small paternal diss. 'Amen to that.' She turned back to the mirror, then said, 'He has a very small penis, you know. Your father.'

'*Mom.*'

'Well, he *does*.'

'Great. So I'd tell Luce that she deserves better – and a bigger penis . . . But if Dad and his tiny penis made her happy, I'd say go for it. I'd get over it.'

'I didn't say tiny. I said *very small* . . . And the point is, I don't think Lucy *can* get over it. It's just . . . *too* much.'

'She told you that? She told you that she *couldn't* get over it?'

'Yes. She told me that she could never accept this and that you had a choice to make.'

'A choice? You mean, like an ultimatum?' I said.

'Yes. A choice. And it's simple. You can date Clive,' she said, rolling her eyes. 'Or you can remain her friend. One or the other. Not both.' She raised her hands in the air, as if surrendering, and said, 'Hey. Don't shoot the messenger.'

'Mom, that expression only works when you're merely delivering a message – not taking sides.'

'I'm not on *her* side. I'm on the side of right. This isn't right. It can't work. You'd be Lucy's stepmother! Your children would be Lucy's half siblings!'

'Who said anything about having children? I don't think I even know if I want children,' I said.

'Don't be silly. Of *course* you want children,' she said. 'If you can't think of Lucy, think of yourself. Your own future.'

'Mom. I've been telling you virtually my whole life. I don't want the same things you want. I'm not *you*. Do you ever listen to me?' Then I hit her where it really hurt. 'Dad understands,' I said.

'You told him about *this*? When?'

'When he was down here. The day after Thanksgiving.'

'Oh, that's *rich*. And I'm sure he supported you one hundred percent, didn't he? I can just hear him. "Do whatever makes you happy – no matter how much it hurts anyone else!" Like father, like daughter, I guess.'

I felt slapped, stung by the comparison, but found myself wondering if it wasn't altogether unfair. Maybe my father and I were alike. Or maybe my mother was just a huge hypocrite. After all, hadn't she stolen my dad from Astrid and Bronwyn to begin with, rationalizing that it was over between them anyway? That she had nothing to do with their breakup? In the end, didn't everyone in the world at some point delude themselves in their own insular narrative?

'Well,' I said. 'At least Dad owns up to his mistakes . . . At least he sees clearly the choices he's made while you're still blaming him for what's wrong with your life. All these years later. Still stuck in the mid-eighties with your wounded damsel routine.'

She stared at me, her lips pursed, like an old Hollywood actress, probably a look she'd cultivated from watching too many TCM movies. 'You have a lot of nerve, Shea,' she said when she finally spoke. Her voice was flat, sad, and devoid of any melodrama. 'Your best friend lost her mother. And you go after her father before the one-year anniversary of her death?'

'I didn't *go after* him. It wasn't like that,' I said, staring at my feet, thinking of Coach and Ryan and Tish.

'It's disloyal, Shea. That's the bottom line. Even if you're madly in love with the man, it's still disloyal to Lucy. Especially after everything she and Connie did for you over the years. They gave you a happy childhood.' Her voice cracked. 'Do you realize that? Do you realize how much we both owe them?'

I didn't answer her question, just turned and walked out the door, a pit in my stomach. Because I knew she was right about that much. And because, of all the things in the world she could have said to me, calling me disloyal hurt the most.

When I got to work about an hour later, I bypassed my cubicle and headed straight to Smiley's office. 'Do you have a minute?' I asked him, popping my head in his half-opened door.

'I have exactly six,' he said, glancing at his watch. 'Unless you start to bore me. Then it's three.'

'Okay,' I said, thinking that my future, at least the professional part of it, was going to be decided in the next three to six minutes.

I walked the whole way into his office and closed the door, but didn't take a seat. 'I don't think I can work here anymore. At least not on this beat,' I said, forcing the words out before I changed my mind.

'What?' Smiley said. 'Is this a joke? Are you going to ESPN?'

'No. I just can't be objective,' I said, relieved to make the confession. I wasn't sure if I could sacrifice my best friend for love, but my job was another story. 'I can't be objective about this investigation. Which I think is a total bullshit fishing expedition, by the way. I can't be objective about Walker football. And I definitely can't be objective about Coach Carr.'

Smiley dropped his forehead to his palm, closed his eyes with exasperation, then, after taking a few seconds to gather himself, said, 'Because you attended the university?'

'Yes, sir. Because I went there. But also because I'm . . . sort of having a . . . relationship with Coach Carr.'

'A relationship?' He spit out the word, his face changing color.

'Yes, sir. I mean . . . sort of, yes.'

'Oh, hell, Rigsby. Don't *sir* me now. You're dating someone my age.'

I resisted the urge to tell him he was *much* older than Coach and instead said, 'I'm sorry I didn't tell you sooner.'

'Sooner?' he barked at me. 'How long has this been going on?'

'Not very long.'

Smiley stared at me, then mumbled something that sounded like *Well, fuck me drunk in the middle of a snowstorm.*

'I'm sorry. You took a chance on me and have been fair and good to me and you didn't deserve this. I told you I could be objective, and I can't. Because I really want *my* team to win. And that's how I will always think of them. As *my* team. And I hate the NCAA for tainting this season. Or trying to. And I would do anything in my power to protect our program because I believe it to be a really good, decent program led by a really good, decent man. So . . . how many minutes do we have left?'

'Just enough for me to fire your ass.'

'That's what I thought,' I said, turning toward the door. 'I'll clean out my desk.'

Smiley shook his head and said, 'Wait. Not so fast. I have something to say to you. In response to your lofty confession.'

I raised my eyebrows, waiting.

'There is no such thing as an objective sportswriter. Anyone in this business loves the game and was a fan first. And whether you're covering a team you love or a team you hate or a team you're indifferent to, you always have a bias because that team's performance always has an impact on *your* team, at least indirectly. And even when you watch a game that doesn't matter to you whatsoever, because there are zero implications for your team, you *still* care!' He slammed his open hand onto the desk, and I winced, both from the noise and because it had to hurt. 'You may say you don't care, but within seconds, you *do* care. You go with the underdog. Or the old quarterback making a comeback. Or the young point guard who got over a torn ACL. Or the coach whose wife just died of cancer! You somehow find yourself caring even when you don't give a bloody damn!'

Smiley was shouting now, and, as I glanced away, I caught Gordon and a half dozen colleagues staring at us through the glass wall.

Then, calming down a little, he said, 'Bottom line, every contest matters – and it should. Somebody is going to win and somebody is going to lose and that matters to the people playing the game so it should matter to us. It matters. Didn't you tell me this very thing when I first met you back at Bob's? That a good reporter will make you care about a random Russian Olympian?'

I stared at him, now thoroughly confused. 'Are you saying that *nobody* can really be deep-down objective?'

'Yes. That's exactly what I'm saying.'

'And that's okay?'

'Yes.'

'So I can keep my job?'

'No. You're definitely fired. Because *you,* Rigsby, can no longer even *pretend* to be an objective professional. The one thing I asked of you. I told you to keep your mouth shut in the press box and *pretend* to be objective.'

'I know,' I said, thinking that even if I didn't have feelings for Coach Carr, I was always one unbridled cheer away from losing my job.

Smiley looked at me and said, 'I heard you were dating Ryan James. That wasn't true?'

'Yes, sir. It *was* true,' I said. 'We were dating. But we're not anymore.'

'Jesus H. Christ,' he said. 'Burning a lot of journalistic bridges in the state of Texas, aren't you?'

'I guess so,' I said. It occurred to me to defend myself, explain that both relationships had unfolded naturally and not because I have a thing for famous sports figures, but I decided it wasn't really pertinent at the moment. Instead I said, 'I'll go clean out my desk now.'

Smiley said, 'Well, look on the bright side.'

'What's that?'

'You can put that awful teal bumper sticker back on your car.'

*   *   *

That evening, I considered all the constructive things I could do. I could start looking for a new job. I could clean my apartment. I could go work out. Instead I called Miller and asked him to meet me at the Third Rail for a beer. He immediately agreed, and, although I was grateful for his friendship, *any* friendship, it made me realize just how alone I was without Lucy. The loss was more than a void; it was a gaping hole in my heart and life.

'What happened?' he asked, after taking one look at me. 'You look like shit.'

'Why, thank you,' I said, thinking that if disheveled, un-showered Miller was telling me I looked like shit, it had to be pretty bad.

'Seriously. Have you been crying?'

'No. It's just the mascara,' I said. 'It always smears on me. I don't know why.'

'That's why you gotta go waterproof,' Miller said knowingly.

I laughed and said, 'How do you know about waterproof mascara?'

'Because I listen,' he said in his faux touchy-feely voice. 'Because, unlike a lot of guys, I care about women and their needs.'

I laughed again, thinking that I'd made the right phone call. Never mind that I really didn't have any other friends.

'How's Ryan?' he asked.

'We broke up. How's Hot-for-Teacher?'

'We broke up, too.' He raised his eyebrows and said, 'Wait. Are you hitting on me? Returning to the well?'

'No, Miller. I'm not returning to the well,' I said, rolling my eyes. 'I just needed to talk to someone . . . It's been a shit day. I'm in a fight with my mom. Lucy's not speaking to me. And I got fired.'

He whistled and said, 'You're making my life look pretty damn good. Thank you.'

'Anytime.'

'So why'd you get fired? Because you're bonin' Coach Carr?'

I looked at him, too startled to deny the charge. 'Why would you say that?'

'For one, I told you, I pay attention. I'm perceptive as hell.'

'And for another?'

'That night you left your credit card . . . I drove over to your place to return it . . . maybe get a little action . . . and there was his car. Right there in your lot. So to speak.'

'You haven't said anything to anyone, have you?'

'Nope. I'm sensitive *and* discreet.'

'Thanks, Miller. Seriously.'

He winked and said. 'So lemme guess . . . Lucy has a problem with you bonin' her old man?'

'Stop saying that.'

'*Bonin'* or *old man?*'

'Both. And we're not *boning*. But there are some feelings there . . . Anyway, Lucy told my mom – who is also really pissed off at me – that I had to choose. Him or her.'

'Easy choice.'

'You just hate Lucy.'

'True,' he said. 'But regardless. You gotta go with love.'

'You think?'

'Every time.' He hesitated and said, 'Unless the broad you love up and cold-blooded dumps you, and then you gotta limp away with whatever pride you have left.' He added a wink, in case I missed the point.

I shook my head and laughed. 'You got any more advice?'

'Take Walker and the points. Alabama won't cover.'

'I don't bet on Walker.'

Miller grinned. 'Oh, yeah, you do.'

41

Later that evening, after my Pabst Blue Ribbon buzz had worn off, I wrote Lucy a letter, in longhand, putting everything on paper as clearly as I could. But I knew her, and felt sure that she would return it unopened. I also knew that on some level it was cowardly not to face her, look her in the eyes, and talk to her. I had given *Ryan* that much. So I called her, pleading into her voice mail for her to talk to me, then calling back after I reached my maximum message length. On the follow-up call, Neil answered Lucy's cell in a whisper. 'Hold on,' he said.

I heard the sound of a door opening and closing, and then his voice again. 'Okay,' he said. 'In the garage now.'

'How bad is this?' I asked him.

'Oh . . . on a scale of one to ten? About ten *thousand*.'

'Shit,' I said.

'Yeah. It's not pretty around here, Shea. Throw in a little morning sickness? My life's hell.'

'I'm sorry, Neil . . . I really need to talk to her.'

'Yeah. Well. I don't think that's gonna happen anytime soon.'

'C'mon, Neil,' I pleaded. 'You have to help me out here. You can get her to talk to me.'

'I can't get her to do anything she doesn't want to do,' he said. 'You know that. But maybe if you just dropped by . . .'

'When? Now? What's she doing now?'

'She's in the bathtub . . . So that should mellow her a little.'

'So can I come now?'

'Okay. But don't you dare tell her I told you that. And I'm deleting this call from her log . . .'

'Okay. Thank you, Neil. So much.'

'You're welcome. But, Shea?'

'Yeah.'

'My advice? You can't do this to her . . . I mean, true love is one thing . . . But short of that, it just isn't worth it.'

Twenty minutes later, I knocked on Lucy's door. Neil answered, exaggerating his surprise. 'Well, hello, Shea,' he said, looking back over his shoulder, his voice stilted.

Lucy materialized beside him, her expression inscrutable but cold.

'Luce,' I said, looking past Neil. 'Can I please come in? We really need to talk. Please?'

She stared at me for an uncomfortably long few seconds before shrugging her permission, then stepping aside. Neil gave me a hopeful look as he ushered me in, both of us following her into their formal living room, the one they never used. She sat stiffly on her sofa, then pointed at the wingback chair across from her, where I took a seat, crossing, then uncrossing my legs. Meanwhile, Neil tried to make his escape, but Lucy called his name, as if she needed reinforcements, and he reluctantly returned, sitting beside her, staring at the floor.

'Thanks for seeing me, Lucy,' I began, marveling that I could be this nervous talking to the person I knew best in the world.

'You're welcome,' she said, her voice and gaze remote. She wasn't going to make this easy, that was for sure.

'How are you feeling?' I said, putting my hand on my stomach to indicate that I was asking about her pregnancy.

'Not quite as sick as last time.'

I gave her a small smile and said, 'Well, that's good.'

'Yes. They say girls make you sicker. So maybe this is a boy.' Her voice was prim and matter-of-fact, and I could hear her saying this same thing to a stranger in line at the grocery store, but it still felt like a good sign that she would share anything about her pregnancy.

I nodded and said, 'That's so exciting.'

'Yes,' she said. 'It is.'

Knowing that I couldn't delay the real reason for my visit any further, I took a deep breath, trying to remember what I'd written in my letter. 'Lucy, I'm so sorry that I've hurt you. And . . . I really do understand how you must feel.'

'Oh?' she said, crossing her arms. 'You know what it's like to lose your mother and have your best friend start hooking up with your father?'

'Well, no . . .' I said. 'Of course I don't know what that's like.'

She stared at me, waiting, as I remembered two of the lines I'd written, doing my best to recite them, verbatim. 'Losing your mother makes everything that much more difficult and complicated. And I'm sure you feel that we are betraying you, as well as her.'

'I *do* feel that way. Shea . . . This is a major betrayal.' Lucy's voice quivered as Neil reached for her hand but kept his eyes on the floor.

I took a deep breath, then another, and said, 'It's not something I'd do lightly. For the hell of it. I would never go down this road—'

'Go down this road? Is that what you call having a relationship with my father behind my back? Because let's cut to the chase here. You were sneaking around with my dad behind my back. How do you think that makes me feel?'

Neil slid closer to his wife, put his arm around her shoulder, and said, 'Luce. Let her talk, honey.'

She nodded, shockingly taking his advice. 'Fine. Go on. You were saying?'

'I just meant . . . that I would *never* . . . pursue any of this in any way if I didn't genuinely, deeply care about your dad.'

Lucy made a face and shook her head, but I kept going, doing my best to tell her the truth. 'At first it was just a silly crush, which was bad enough. Because you're not supposed to have a crush on your best friend's father. You're not supposed to have a crush on someone so much older than you. You're not supposed to have a crush on a man who just lost his wife. But a one-sided crush is far different from a relationship, and I *never* would have let those feelings come to light, or even fully acknowledged them to myself, if your mother were still here. I had the deepest respect for her and your parents' marriage, and would do absolutely anything in the world if I could bring her back and see them together and happy again.'

I stopped and looked at her – *really* looked at her – and saw something flicker in her eyes. She was really listening now. If not her blessing, at least I had her attention.

'I *love* your family, Luce. The family you grew up with. The one *I* grew up with. I loved your mom, and I love your dad and Lawton, too,' I said. 'It has always been and always will be the best family I know, and it has been my greatest privilege in life to be close to all of you. I honestly don't think I'd be the person I am today if it weren't for your family. You have given me my passion for Walker and football. You have given me role models for what it means to be good parents, siblings, spouses, friends. You have all supported me over the years and taught me so much about loyalty, honesty, integrity, and commitment. And I will remain forever grateful to you for all of these things and so much more.'

'Then please stop this,' Lucy whimpered, her hands clasped, prayer-style. 'Please don't do this. *Please.*'

'I would if I could,' I said. 'But I'm in—'

'Don't say it,' Lucy said, cutting me off, staring at me pleadingly. 'Don't say it, Shea. Please.'

I almost stopped. I almost gave in to her. But then I thought of him. The only person in the world I cared for more than Lucy. And I knew I had to keep going.

'But Lucy. I *am* in love with him,' I said, my heart thudding so hard I could hear it in my ears. 'It was there even when I didn't know it yet . . . And I can't help it or change it . . . I tried by keeping my distance. I tried by leaving Walker to take another job. I tried by dating Ryan James. Nothing has worked.

My feelings are strong and real and I think he feels the same way.'

'But you can get over it!' she said, her eyes filling with tears. 'You can both get over it. You have to. Please, Shea! Please just get over it.'

I put my head in my hands, my mind racing, wishing I could have a sidebar with Coach, trying desperately to channel him. I was pretty sure I knew what he would say. *Stick to your guns. Do what's right. Don't take the easy way out.*

With this advice swirling in my head, I opened my mouth and said, 'My mother said you want me to make a choice. I have to tell you that I don't think that's fair of you. But feelings aren't fair, and if you really want me to make a choice, then I will.'

'And?' she said, her face now streaked with tears that she didn't bother to wipe away.

I held my breath, ready to pull the trigger, ready to prove what I'd always believed to be true: that love conquers all. But looking into the eyes of my best friend, I wasn't so sure. I thought of everything we had been through, together. What I'd lost as a child to divorce. What she'd lost this year to cancer. And, in that moment, I decided that maybe I was wrong. Maybe the bonds of friendship were stronger than anything else in this world.

'We are on the same team and have been since we were babies,' I began, staring into her big, glassy eyes. 'And we will be together until we are both little old ladies in cute clothes – because of you . . . watching football on television – because of me . . .'

She gave me the smallest smile.

'So. I really hope you change your mind. I really hope you don't make me choose between the two things I care about the most. But if I have to pick one . . . then I choose you, Lucy. I choose you and our friendship. Now and always.'

She rose and walked slowly over to me as I stood to face her, waiting, praying for her to say it: *You don't have to choose.*

Instead, she gave me a hug and said, 'Thank you, Shea. I want to be a bigger person here. I really do. But I just can't . . . I can't.'

I hugged her numbly back, then said, 'Well, I'm glad we talked.'

'Me, too, Shea . . . Thank you.'

I nodded, the devastation slowly sinking in. It was the way I felt after Walker losses – only much, much worse. Because I had never lost this big before.

For a few minutes after that, we both sat again, and miraculously managed to change the subject, mustering small talk about her pregnancy, her next doctor's appointment, how she planned to decorate a nursery when she didn't know the gender of the baby. Then, when I couldn't stand it another second, I told her I should go and let her get some sleep. She nodded and walked me to the door, then gave me another hug. 'I love you, Shea.'

'I love you, too, Lucy,' I said, relieved to realize that I meant it, even if I hated her a little bit, too.

42

There was only one thing left to be done, and I was prepared to put it off for as long as possible, as if not telling Coach about my decision would somehow make it less real.

But right before I went to bed that night, there was a knock at my door. I went to look through the peephole and saw Coach staring back at me. My heart broke a little more as I answered the door and said, 'Aren't you supposed to be on the road?'

'I caught the last flight home tonight. I wanted to see you. I'd have called first,' he said, dropping his leather duffel at his feet and unbuttoning his navy overcoat. 'But my phone went dead and I forgot to pack my charger.'

'Rookie move.'

'Hey, now. Who you callin' a rookie, rook?'

'You,' I said, mustering a smile as my arms remained awkwardly at my sides. 'How did the visit go?'

'Great. Good kid. Nice family,' he said, still fumbling with his buttons.

'Do you think we'll get him?' I asked.

'Oh, depends on how much money we can scrape together to pay him under the table.'

I stared at him.

'It was a joke,' he said, leaning in to kiss me.

I turned my cheek slightly, his lips landing to the left of mine in no-man's-land.

'So . . . will we? Get him?' I asked again, stalling, pretending to focus only on the state of Walker recruiting.

'I think it'll come down to us or Ohio State. We'll have to see. How was your day? And why are you looking at me funny?'

'I'm not looking at you funny.'

'You are.' He stared at me. 'And now you're looking at me even funnier. I know you. I know your face.'

I swallowed, buying a few extra seconds with a lesser announcement. 'I got fired today.'

'You're kidding.'

'Nope.'

'Shit,' he said. 'You're not kidding?'

I shook my head. 'No. But it's okay. I was sort of resigning anyway. Smiley just beat me to the punch.'

'Shea. Honey. I'm sorry. Why?' He squinted for a second, then seemed to piece it together. 'Oh, *shit*. Did this happen because . . . of *us*?'

I shook my head, looking down at my feet.

He slid two fingers under my chin and lifted it until I was looking into his eyes again. 'Tell me the truth.'

'Well, yeah. I mean . . . kind of. It's just too much of a conflict,' I said, wishing that I'd talked to Lucy *before* I gave up my job.

'I feel terrible. Can I talk to Smiley? Surely there's some way . . .'

'No. Don't call him. It's okay. I'm sort of relieved. It really *was* a conflict . . .'

'What are you going to do? Get your old job back?'

'My old job's gone. J.J. already replaced me.'

'You can't be replaced,' he said, without missing a beat.

I tried to smile, hoping he meant that in all ways. 'I'll figure something out.'

'Okay . . .' he said, looking unconvinced and very worried. 'Let me know how I can help. Whatever you need. You know we can figure something out at Walker. There will always be a place for you here.'

'Thank you,' I said, thinking that my job was the least of my concerns tonight. 'I'll be all right.'

He put his hand out, as if asking me to slow-dance, his expression shifting from concern to one of pure affection. It melted my heart and made me want to take back everything

I'd promised Lucy. Instead, I led him over to my sofa and blurted it all out. Everything I'd told her. The choice I'd made.

'Well. There you have it,' he said with a long sigh.

'What do you think?' I asked, glancing at him while he stared straight ahead.

'What do I think?'

'Yes. Tell me.'

'I understand.'

'Do you agree with . . . my decision?' I said, wanting him to fight for me, tell me how foolish I'd been.

'Honestly? I don't know.'

'You *always* know,' I said, feeling frantic.

'I respect it. I respect you. I respect your friendship with Lucy.'

'So that's it?' I said, realizing just how much I'd been relying on him to save us, change my mind, find some of the gray area he was so fond of. But I was getting the terrible, desperate feeling that he actually agreed with me. That he believed that *not* being together was the right thing to do. That he might have known all along that this was our foregone conclusion.

Coach sighed and said, 'Listen. This isn't all on you. I had a talk with Lucy, too. Not as direct as yours, but a talk . . . And I think . . . I think she feels that I've abandoned her.'

'Abandoned her? *How?*'

'With her mother gone, she only has me . . . as far as parents go. And I think I've let her down. I know she feels that way.'

'But you're a wonderful father,' I said, comparing him to my own.

'But I'm a better football coach,' he said. 'In some ways, at least the ways you can observe and measure, I've always put football first. And I think she sees you as part of that . . . Because you and I share that love of the game. We have that bond. Lucy and I . . . don't. So I think being with you is just another example, in her mind, of me picking football over her. And I can't do it to her any more than you can . . . Maybe she'll come around. Maybe we'll have a chance later . . . Never say never, right? But in the meantime, you need to go live your life.'

I knew what he meant by living my life, and I shook my head. 'I'll never feel this way about anyone . . . ever again,' I said, crumbling inside but keeping it together.

'Yes, you will,' he said.

'No, I *won't*. Not even close,' I said, thinking that I could flirt in bars, go on dates, have sex. But that I was finished with love. Done.

He draped his arm on the back of the sofa, angling his body toward me, and said, 'Shea. I thought I could only love Connie . . . And then . . . *this* happened. And it's been scary and wonderful and so special. I guess I'm trying to say that . . . you just don't know what can happen in life. And you have to be open to things . . .'

'But I don't *want* to love anyone but you,' I said.

'And I didn't want to love anyone but Connie. Life is funny.'

'Life is *tragic*.'

'It can be . . . But you can't stop living. You can't give up.'

'But aren't we giving up now?'

'No,' he said. 'We're doing the right thing. There's a difference.'

I nodded, even though I wasn't so sure about that.

'You'll be all right, Shea. You could do better than an old football coach.'

'You're not old,' I muttered, envious of all the couples whose only barrier was a couple of decades.

'I'm not *young*. And let's be honest . . . you should probably be with someone younger . . . so you can have a family . . . children of your own . . . I'm probably too old for all of that . . .'

I caught his *probably*, fleetingly imagining having a baby with him, but then said, 'Why does everyone keep talking about that stuff? I'm not like other girls. I don't need all those things.'

'I know you're not. I know you don't. But you *might*. You might someday. You need to keep an open mind.'

I nodded, letting my head drop to my hands. 'I knew it,' I said, speaking mostly to myself.

'You knew what?'

'That last night would be our only chance to be together.'

'Yeah, you did call that one . . . But we'll always be friends,' he said – one of the saddest declarations in the world.

When I didn't reply, he said, 'And we'll always have football.'

'And you can call me "girl" again,' I said, trying to put on a brave face. 'You haven't done that in a while.'

'You got it, girl,' he said.

'We just can't touch,' I said, gazing up at him.

'Right,' he said, looking as sad as I felt.

'Or kiss,' I said, staring at his mouth, then back into his eyes.

He looked deep into my eyes and nodded.

'Because we made a decision and it would be wrong to go back on it,' I said, trying to convince myself.

He nodded again, as his face moved ever so close to mine. Close enough for me to catch a whiff of that damn aftershave.

'You're going to have to stop wearing that, though,' I said. 'When you're around me.'

'What?'

I shook my head and shuddered a little. 'That aftershave. It *kills* me.'

'So does your perfume,' he said. 'Please do something about that perfume.'

'Deal,' I said, his face moving closer still, our breathing growing deeper. 'But how 'bout . . . one more kiss?'

'You mean like this?' he said, his lips grazing mine.

'Yes. Just like that,' I said, as that familiar dizzy feeling overcame me. 'And then, after tonight . . . that really has to be it. Forever.'

'Unless Lucy changes her mind,' he said, kissing me more urgently, his hands entangled in my hair.

'She won't,' I breathed.

'I know,' he whispered. 'So let's make this count . . .'

43

For three days, I wallowed in self-pity and heartbreak, never leaving my apartment. I barely ate, slept at odd hours, and lived in my pajamas. Every time the phone rang, I jumped, hoping it would be him, telling me he couldn't do it. But that never happened, and, with every passing hour, I grew more depressed, until I eventually turned my phone off altogether. There was nobody I wanted to talk to.

On the fourth night, just as I was beginning to remind myself of my mother after her divorce, Lucy appeared at my door. I considered not answering it, but did. We stared at each other as if months had passed since our last conversation, until she asked if she could come in. I said yes and stepped aside, letting the door close with its own weight.

'Are you sick?' she said, taking in my pajamas and greasy hair.

'Just have a touch of something,' I said. 'You cut your bangs.'

She reached up to tug on them. 'Too short. When will I learn?'

I shrugged, hoping she realized how very little I cared about her hair.

'Are you angry with me?' she asked, eyeing my sofa, then opting to sit cross-legged on her favorite spot on my floor.

I told her no.

'Resentful?'

'No,' I lied again.

'Sad?'

'Lucy. Stop.'

But she couldn't stop; she could *never* stop. 'Did you tell my dad it was over?' she asked more softly, as if this changed the fact that she was pressing, digging.

'It never really began,' I said, joining her on the floor, both of us cross-legged in a way that reminded me of preschool. All that was missing were our little colored mats and thirty years.

'But you talked to him?'

'Yes.'

'And he's okay with everything?'

I took a deep breath, steadying myself. 'Yes,' I said, keeping my answer as simple as possible. 'We both agree that this is for the best.'

'And I heard you quit your job, too?' she asked, relentless.

I wondered how this news got to her. 'Or got fired. Hard to tell which. But yeah . . . I'm officially unemployed.'

Lucy leaned over to put her arms awkwardly around my shoulders and then burst into tears. I refused to hug her back, feeling a wave of rage, nearly telling her that she had no right to cry like this. She'd gotten her way; she didn't get to be the injured party, too.

But then she said, 'Shea . . . I started bleeding . . . two days ago . . . I'm not pregnant anymore.'

'Oh, *honey*,' I said, hugging her back. 'I'm so sorry, Lucy.'

She sniffed loudly, wiping her tears with her hand. 'I know . . . I guess it just wasn't meant to be this time . . . I'm sorry . . . I thought I was done crying.' Her face contorted in a failed attempt to smile.

'Do you think it was because . . .?' I started, then stopped.

'No,' she said, reading my mind. 'It had nothing to do with any of this.'

'It wasn't the . . . stress?' I was pretty certain miscarriages didn't work like that but wanted to gauge Lucy's feelings on any possible connection.

'No. The doctor said it just wasn't a viable pregnancy. We'll get pregnant again.'

'Of course you will,' I said.

'Or maybe we won't. Maybe Neil and I were just meant to have one child. You know, in a way, I'd be okay with that. Because I hate the idea of my mother never holding my baby.'

I looked into her sad eyes, relieved that I had made the decision I had, telling her again how very sorry I was.

'Were you really in *love* with my dad?' she asked, using the past tense, as if I had simply gotten over my feelings in a matter of days.

'Yes,' I said.

'But . . . *why*?'

I shrugged. 'Is there ever a why?'

She shook her head. 'God. I wish you weren't.'

'I know,' I replied. 'I wish . . . a lot of things.'

'Like what? What else do you wish?' she said. I couldn't tell if she was testing me or making conversation or something in between, but I answered her, choosing my words carefully.

'I wish your mother were still here,' I said, starting with the most important one. 'I wish you hadn't lost the baby. I wish Ryan weren't so messed up. I wish I could have been a better reporter. I wish . . . I wish that I were deeply, madly in love with Miller.'

Lucy cracked a smile and said, 'Miller? Oh, please don't wish that. He's worse than liking my dad.'

I smiled, realizing that I had forgotten an obvious one. The only one that would have been on my mind a few weeks before.

'But if we're talking realistic wishes?'

She nodded earnestly.

'I'd settle for one more Walker win this season,' I said.

She smiled. 'Me, too,' she said. 'You're going to the game, right?'

I hesitated, then shook my head. 'I don't think so.'

'What?' she said. 'Are you kidding? You've got to be kidding. You *have* to come. You're the one person in the world who absolutely needs to be there. I mean, other than the coaches and players. You can't miss this game!'

'I'm not going to miss the game. I'll be watching it on television.'

She stared at me, incredulous. 'Where?'

'I don't know. Right here, probably,' I said, pointing at my TV.

'But I want to watch it with my best friend. You have to be there.'

I shrugged, resisting the strong urge to tell her you can't always get what you want. 'We'll see,' I said. 'It's still a few weeks away.'

'What are you doing for Christmas?'

'Going to New York,' I lied, though the idea had crossed my mind. Anything was better than being with my mom this year.

'Oh,' she said. 'That will be fun.'

'Yeah,' I said, thinking that nothing in the world sounded like fun. Nothing seemed to matter at all.

'Well, if you change your mind . . . and don't go . . . will you spend the day with us?'

I knew exactly who *us* included and thought that there was zero chance of that. Less than zero.

'Sure, Luce,' I said. 'Thank you.'

'Of course,' she said. 'You're my *best* friend.'

'And you're mine,' I said.

'Promise?' she said, but I knew that wasn't really what she was asking. She was asking for my forgiveness. She was telling me that she knew how selfish and childish she was being. But that she just couldn't help it. Just as she couldn't bring back her mother or the baby she'd loved for only a few weeks.

So I looked at her and told her the truth. 'Yes,' I said, thinking that not only was she my best friend but she was really the only thing I had left. 'I promise.'

44

Because I had no other options, I decided to go to New York after all, booking the cheapest flight I could on Christmas Eve, the last one out of Dallas, and landing at LaGuardia so late that the airport had mostly cleared out. My father had said he was sending me a car, but there he stood at the bottom of the escalator leading to baggage claim, wearing a dark suit, holding a little white placard that read: MERRY CHRISTMAS, SHEA BUTTER STADIUM!

I laughed when I saw the pet name I'd almost completely forgotten about, feeling more touched than I could ever remember feeling when it came to my dad. This would be our first Christmas together since he'd left Texas, as my mother had put it in their divorce agreement that I couldn't go to New York until the twenty-sixth. In other words, she got Christmas with her daughter, just as he got Christmas with *his* daughter.

'Hi, Dad,' I said, grinning. 'Nice sign.'

He smiled, did a funny little at-your-service bow, and tucked the card into his breast pocket. 'Merry Christmas, honey.'

'Merry Christmas . . . You didn't have to come out here. I could have taken a taxi.'

'It got me out of mass,' he said, winking. Upon his third marriage, Astrid had made him convert to Catholicism, but his heart wasn't in it, any more than his heart was in being a college football fan or a Republican. They were just things he did, not *felt*.

'I'm sure she's thrilled with me,' I said as we walked toward baggage claim and the only active conveyor belt. 'Gotta be that one,' I said, pointing. 'Sorry. I had a carry-on, but they made me check it . . .'

'Yep. Carousel number three,' he said, slowing his stride and squinting up at the arrivals board. 'And stop worrying about Astrid. She's doing her thing. She's fine.'

'Still. It's Christmas Eve.'

'Oh, *stop* with that. I *wanted* to come. Did you decide how long you're staying? Because I want to get reservations and tickets.'

'Tickets to what?' I said, football still on my mind. I knew the Jets and the Giants were both off, so wondered if he might be talking about the Knicks. Basketball might be a nice change of pace, actually.

'To shows, plays, the Rockettes . . . anything you want.'

I smiled, then spotted my frayed roller bag, swooping in to grab it.

'Let me get that for you,' he said, as I wheeled it toward him. 'I'm your driver, remember?'

'Shea Butter Stadium,' I said, shaking my head and turning over my bag. 'I totally forgot about that.'

My dad laughed, clearly proud of himself. 'Nobody else calls you that?'

'Uh, no. Nobody's really thinking about the Mets in Texas.'

'What about butter? They think about butter in Texas.'

I laughed and said, 'What are you tryin' to say?'

'Y'all like your fried foods,' he said, doing a shitty Southern accent.

'Yes, we do.' I smiled, following him outside, the first few seconds of cold blasting my face and shocking me the way it always did. 'Damn,' I said, pulling my only scarf across my face.

'It's been really warm until today,' he said, which is what Yankees always say. Like we just happened to catch them in a rare moment of frigid discomfort.

'Right,' I said. 'What's warm? Thirty-five? Thirty-six?'

'No! Fifties,' he said, putting on his leather gloves as we walked. 'I swear!'

'Just tell me you got a good parking spot,' I said, struggling to breathe in another gust of wind.

'Always,' he said, pointing to his black Mercedes right in front of us.

He unlocked the passenger side, then tossed my bag in the backseat and went around to his side, whistling, as if he were strolling on a golf course on a balmy day. 'Twice in six weeks,' he said.

I smiled. 'Yep,' I said. 'Imagine that.'

'Now *that's* a Christmas gift.'

'So I can return the tie clip?'

My dad laughed. 'Yeah. Return it. I have plenty of those. Just not enough days with my little girl.'

We made small talk until we entered the orange fluorescence of the Midtown Tunnel. Then he cleared his throat and said, 'So. Your mother called me.'

I felt myself tense up, staring at the dirty-tiled wall streaking past us. 'When?'

'This morning.'

'Why?' I asked, glancing over at him. As if I didn't know.

He raised his eyebrows and looked at me for a beat longer than felt safe, as I reached over to put my hand on the steering wheel.

'She said you won't return her calls.'

'That is a fact.'

'Because she disapproved of Clive?'

'Because she was a *bitch* about the whole thing,' I said. 'She's so judgmental it's scary . . .'

'She can be.'

'But, listen, Dad, I really don't want to talk about all of that. I came here to escape it.'

'Oh? I thought it was to see your old man,' he said lightly.

I smiled. 'You're not my "old man." Somebody's "old man" uses a phone book to look up a number . . . drives thirty-five in a fifty . . . wears Velcro Hush Puppies. You're wearing Gucci loafers.'

'So that precludes me from being your old man?'

'Yes. It most definitely does. But it doesn't preclude you from being my dad,' I said, feeling unusually charitable and grateful toward him.

'Got it,' he said, smiling, as we exited the tunnel, spilling onto a strangely quiet Third Avenue.

'So I guess you heard I got shitcanned, too?'

He nodded. 'But you probably don't want to talk about that either?'

'Nope,' I said.

'Well, let me know if you change your mind . . . I have some ideas on that front.'

'Maybe later,' I said. 'Let's get through Christmas first.'

'Let's get *through* Christmas?' he said. 'Okay, Ebenezer.'

'Bah, humbug,' I said, only pretending to be joking.

Christmas Day was a surprisingly pleasant one, spent in the luxury of my dad and Astrid's Fifth Avenue pad. Bronwyn and Wiley were in St. Moritz skiing, so it was just the three of us, and Astrid was on her best behavior, a restrained, humble version of herself. She must have known a little of what was going on in my life, but kept her conversation general, avoiding her usual nosy questions, and not once bringing up my job or Walker. It was almost as if my father had warned or bribed her – or enrolled her in a crash course in discretion.

Right after dinner (which Astrid had catered), she gently raised the subject of Ryan, very tactfully addressing our breakup and asking how I was doing.

'I'm doing fine. Thanks, Astrid,' I said, feeling sincere.

'I'm sorry it didn't work out. But for what it's worth . . . I think that would have been really hard. Having such a famous husband. Women throwing themselves at him. And, you know . . . just living in the spotlight.'

I smiled and said, 'Oh, c'mon, Astrid! You know you thrive in the spotlight!'

'Okay. Okay. *I* think it would be *marvelous*! But I have the feeling that *you* would have hated it,' she said as my father refilled all of our wine glasses. I searched for the hidden dig, out of cynical habit, just as she added, 'I admire that about you. You like to keep things so . . . simple.'

I gave her a look.

'In a good way.'

'Authentic,' my dad chimed in.

'Yes, that's what I meant,' Astrid said, nodding effusively. 'Authentic, that's it.'

'Well, thanks, guys,' I said, taking a long sip of my wine, thinking of Ryan and the short email he had sent me a few days ago. There was no mention of wanting to get back together, only a few lines thanking me and telling me that he was seeing a therapist and working through his issues. I had written back that I was so happy to hear it, then wished him luck in the playoffs – and in life. Although I didn't believe that Ryan was capable of rape, I did believe the rest of Tish's story, and Blakeslee's, too, sure that he had been as rough with them as he had been with me. Yet I surprisingly felt no bitterness toward him, only relief that I was no longer with him, and hope that he really could change. I reached up now to touch my diamond earrings, the first time I had worn them since our breakup, and said, 'Ryan's not a bad guy. Just not for me.'

After that, Astrid changed the subject to Bronwyn's fertility treatments, explaining that she'd be heading to Cornell in February for her second round of in vitro. This was news to me, and I said how sorry I was to hear that she was having trouble. As Astrid prattled on about the process, I covertly checked my phone for the hundredth time that day, still hoping to hear something from Coach on Christmas. But there was nothing from him. Nothing from anyone in Walker, for that matter, except for Miller, who had sent me a text that said, *Merry Christmas to my favorite ho ho ho!* I had written back, *Why is a Christmas tree better than a man? Because it stays up, has cute balls, and looks good with the lights on!*

As the night wore on, I missed Coach more and more, and

tried to dull the pain with Barolo and cheesecake. The two-thousand-dollar check from Astrid and my dad helped, too, and I calculated that it would buy me a couple of months in my job hunt. Feeling slightly embarrassed, I went through the motions of saying it was too much, but Astrid reassured me that she had spent just as much on a handbag for Bronwyn, then kindly added, 'And I assume you'd want to select your own.' As if anyone in the room believed that I'd spend that kind of cash on a *purse*. It was absurd, but to each her own, so I smiled and said, 'Well, thank you. Really. This is so generous of you both, and I appreciate it. Especially this month.' It actually felt good to receive such a nice gift from my dad without the weight of the chip on my shoulder.

Then, after I gave them my gifts (earrings from Lucy's store for Astrid and plaid socks and a coffee table book on cigars for my dad), we opened another bottle of wine and hunkered down to watch *A Christmas Story*. It didn't seem like the sort of movie my dad would appreciate, but he cracked up over every single 'You'll shoot your eye out' and lost his mind during the tongue-on-the-flagpole scene. He told me that his brother, my only uncle, had done the same thing when he was little and that it really *does* stick. Then, right when Ralphie got his decoder ring in the mail, my phone finally rang, Lucy's home number appearing on the screen.

'Don't pause it. I'll be right back,' I said, scrambling for the safety of my lush guest suite before answering.

'Weren't you going to call?' she asked as soon as I said hello. She sounded wounded, which ticked me off a little. She had plenty of reason to be sad today, but no standing to be miffed at me.

'Sorry. The day just got away from me,' I said, a ridiculous statement given how slowly the minutes had dragged.

'I know. Ours, too,' she said. 'So how was your Christmas?'

'Lovely,' I said, a word I never use.

She called me on it. 'Lovely? You've been hanging out with Astrid too much.'

'She actually hasn't been too bad this time,' I said. 'It's like she got a personality lift with her last cosmetic surgery.'

Lucy laughed.

I hesitated, at a loss for a few seconds, before I came up with 'Was Santa good to Caroline?'

'Yes. Very,' she said.

'Good. Good,' I said, another awkward pause following. 'Tell her I love her.'

'I will,' she said. 'You want to talk to your mom? She came over a little bit ago . . .'

I started to say no, then made myself say yes, bristling when I heard her voice on the other end of the line.

'Hi, honey. Merry Christmas.'

'Merry Christmas, Mom.'

'This is the first one in your life that I haven't seen you. It doesn't even feel like Christmas.'

'Yeah. It's a little weird,' I said. 'But it's nice . . . being in New York and stuff . . .' I considered calling her out for talking to my dad but secretly liked the idea of the two of them becoming a united front on my behalf, completely unlike the tenor of my entire childhood. So I let it slide.

I heard Caroline's high-pitched voice in the background, then Coach's low laughter. My heart ached as my mother and I said goodbye, and she gave the phone back to Lucy.

'Hi,' Lucy said.

'Hi,' I said, straining to hear Coach again, both relieved and distraught that he had sounded so chipper.

'Are you sure you're okay?' she asked.

'Yeah. Why wouldn't I be?' I asked, trying not to sound as flippant as I felt.

Lucy mumbled something I couldn't make out, then said, 'Hey. My dad's here, too. Did you want to say hello?'

'Um, that's okay,' I said, my throat tightening. 'Just tell him I said Merry Christmas.'

'I definitely will,' she said.

'Okay. Well, I better get back to the movie . . .'

'Oh . . . okay. What are you watching?' she said, clearly not ready to hang up. *'It's a Wonderful Life?'*

I resisted the urge to tell her that was *her* father's favorite movie, not mine, and instead said, 'No. *A Christmas Story.* You know. "You'll shoot your eye out."'

'Ha. Yeah. Right . . . Well . . . enjoy the movie. And your night,' she said.

'You, too.'

'And what about the game? Have you decided about the game?'

'Not yet,' I said. 'I'll let you know.'

'Okay. We miss and love you. Merry Christmas, Shea.'

'Love you, too, Luce. Merry Christmas,' I said, hanging up and thinking, *Ain't nothin' merry about this Christmas. Nothing wonderful about this life.*

I was being dramatic, for sure. But then again, getting your heart broken at Christmastime *is* pretty fucking dramatic.

45

I ended up extending my trip and staying at my dad's through New Year's, filling my days and nights with classic New York distractions. I dined at fabulous restaurants, strolled through museums and art galleries, even went ice skating at Rockefeller Center. Meanwhile, I didn't watch *SportsCenter* or read the sports page or check a single bowl score for a whole week. A personal record.

It didn't begin to mend my broken heart – I still thought of Coach virtually nonstop – but at least it allowed me to more clearly analyze my life. Since Mrs Carr's funeral nearly a year ago, I had vowed to get out of my rut, shake things up. I had certainly done that. I had changed *everything*. Yet here I was, no better off, and quite possibly in the worst spot I'd ever been in. I told myself that there was nothing to regret. That sometimes you won – and sometimes you came up short. Or, in Coach Carr's words: *Sometimes you get the bear. Sometimes the bear gets you.*

On the third day of the new year, and the afternoon of my departure, my father and I went for a long walk in Central Park, just the two of us.

As we arrived at the boat pond, he cleared his throat and said, 'So. Shea. Can we please talk employment for a moment?'

'Mine or yours?' I joked, bracing myself.

He smiled. 'Yours.'

'Okay,' I said, telling myself to keep an open mind. I really couldn't afford another strategy.

'Do you think you'll go back to work at Walker? In the athletic department?'

I shook my head, adamant. 'No. That's the only thing I'm sure about. I can't make that my whole world anymore. As easy and tempting as it is . . . it would feel like going backwards.'

My dad nodded his agreement. 'Do you think you want to stay in journalism?'

'Honestly, I don't know,' I said. 'I don't know if I'm very good at it.'

'You're great at it,' my dad said. 'I'm so impressed with your stories, Shea.'

'Thank you . . . I think I'm pretty decent at it, too . . . I didn't get fired for my writing. I got fired because I couldn't be objective.'

'Okay. Right. But you could be objective in another town . . . covering another team. Right?'

I shrugged. 'Probably.'

'So let me throw this out there. I know you could find your own job, and I don't mean to imply that you can't, but I do have two pretty high-up connections. One at ESPN, the other with the *New York Post*. I'm not sure what the position or pay would be, but I'm pretty sure I could get you some interviews.'

'And so . . . I'd live here?' I said. 'In the city?'

'Well, for the *Post*,' he said. 'And in Connecticut for ESPN. If you want a little distance from Astrid. A.k.a. Ass Face.'

I looked at him, startled, and said, 'How . . .?'

'You let it slip once. A long time ago. Don't worry, I didn't tell her.'

I felt my neck grow itchy and hot. 'Sorry about that,' I said.

'Honestly, it's okay. It was funny – you must say it a lot not to have caught yourself . . . She can be an ass, but her heart's in the right place. Most of the time. She really likes you. Admires you, too.'

I wasn't sure I believed that she *admired* me, but I did have the sense that there was at least a modicum of respect there. 'I like her, too,' I made myself say, thinking that at least I didn't hate her anymore. It felt like a small miracle.

'So what do you think about the jobs? Do you want me to put in some calls?'

'Maybe so,' I said, shocked that I was even entertaining a thought of leaving not only Walker but the entire state of Texas, something I could never have imagined only a few weeks ago. 'I do need a job.'

'Well, I'm not worried about you finding one. And I'm sure you have plenty of contacts in Texas . . .'

'You'd be surprised,' I said. 'Very few that don't involve Coach Carr.'

'And that's another thing . . .' he said.

My stomach instantly knotted.

'Can we talk about him for a second?'

I shrugged, steeling myself. 'Sure.'

'Maybe I followed my heart a little too much along the way,' he said. 'And your heart can definitely get you into trouble . . . But, if I hadn't, then I wouldn't have you.'

This wasn't the angle I'd expected, and I felt confused as I said, 'Are you talking about Mom? *That* was following your heart?'

'Well, sure. Of course. What else would that have been?'

'What else? Well, it could have been a cheap affair with a woman you met on the road, then got knocked up before your wife divorced you . . . So you married her to do the right thing. And because Mom has a way of talking people into stuff.'

'Wow. That's quite a sordid spin on my life. And yours.'

'Well? Tell me I'm wrong.'

'You *are* wrong, actually. Believe it or not, I really loved your mom. Fell madly in love with her. But we just couldn't make it work. Oil and water. Square peg, round hole. So I gave up. And instead of starting over and potentially screwing up a *third* situation, I went back to take care of Bronwyn and Astrid. Tried to fix some of my scorched earth.'

It was the first time I'd seen the situation from his point of view, and also the first time I hadn't seen it as a head-to-head competition between the respective mother-daughter teams.

'So are you comparing Coach to Mom? Or Astrid?'

'Neither,' he said. 'I'm just saying . . . follow your heart. Even if it sometimes makes an absolute mess of your life . . . And, for God's sake, you *have* to go to this bowl game. This is the girl who started making road trips with the team in the third grade.'

'Second,' I said.

'Exactly. It'd be nuts for you to miss this game.'

I nodded, knowing he was right. 'Are you going?'

'If you want me to. If you need me to. But if not, I'll just watch it at home.'

'Not really the same as being there,' I said. 'The crowds . . . the noise . . . the energy. It's *electric*.'

'Aha. You see? Listen to yourself. You'll regret it if you don't go. Separate your feelings about Clive and Lucy and go support your team,' he said as we approached Wollman Rink.

I nodded but couldn't help thinking that Coach and Lucy *were* my team, at least they always had been, and, furthermore, it was absolutely impossible to separate my feelings for Coach from Walker and the biggest game of our lives. From *anything* in my life, really – which was the whole problem.

'Okay. I'll go,' I said, glancing around the ice rink, comforted by the thought that very few people in the crowd probably cared two licks about the Walker–Alabama game.

'Good. Great,' he said.

'But then I think I'll come back to the city and talk to your people,' I said. 'About those jobs.'

'Really?' my dad said, surprised.

'Yes. Really,' I said, thinking that this following-your-heart stuff was turning out to be pretty overrated – and that maybe it was time to try another approach.

46

It is 5:20 P.M. Pacific Time, ten minutes until kickoff inside the Rose Bowl. I am in the stands with Lucy, Lawton, my mother, and Miller, who came to Pasadena without a ticket. Up until two hours ago, he had been searching for one from scalpers, but at the last minute he inherited Neil's ticket when Caroline got a stomach bug and Lucy decided she couldn't be left in a hotel room with a random sitter. Lucy still made him beg for it.

'This ticket's worth all the groveling. So freakin' sweet!' Miller shouts over the din of two manic marching bands and ninety-two thousand frenzied fans, all wearing either red or teal.

I nod in agreement. Our seats *are* insane, what you'd expect for the head coach's family – right on the fifty-yard line, twenty-some rows back, with a sweeping view of the western hills rising above the stadium. Even the weather is scripted – warm with gentle breezes and clear skies. A perfect night for a national championship game.

Miller offers me a bite of his foot-long hot dog smothered with mustard and relish, and I shake my head, wondering how he could possibly eat at a time like this. Glancing around the stadium, I try to soak up the atmosphere, but am too gripped by fear to really appreciate the pageantry. My palms are sweaty, my stomach is queasy, and my heart is racing. Bottom line, I know that nothing about this game will be fun – and the best I can hope for is the absence of misery.

I feel Lucy tap me on the shoulder and turn to look at her in the row behind us, sandwiched between my mom and Lawton. 'Will you please talk to me? I'm bored.'

'I can't, Lucy,' I say, mystified by the mere notion of boredom with the countdown now at six minutes and twenty seconds.

'Are you getting sick, too?' she asks, adjusting the big loopy bow on her teal silk blouse. 'Maybe you picked it up from Caroline?'

'No. I'm not sick. It's just the game, Luce,' I say, trying to suppress a fresh wave of resentment, not the first since I arrived in Pasadena last night. It isn't only that she quashed a relationship before it ever really began but that she acts as if nothing *ever* happened.

'Oh, c'mon!' she says, slapping my arm. 'Have a little faith. We're going to win! I just know we are!'

'Yeah, I have a good feeling about this, too,' Lawton says. 'And would you believe it? Dad actually found a cricket out at some random park yesterday afternoon.'

I smile, picturing him with his Mason jar. 'Really?'

'True story,' Lawton says, holding his fingers up in a scout's pledge. 'I was with him.'

I nod, as if reassured, even though my usual pessimism has taken root. Fortunately, I'm not the coach, because I'd likely advise my team *not to lose,* rather than *to win,* always a recipe for defeat. I try to imagine what Coach is saying now in the locker room, and although I can conjure his words and the fire in them, I'm having trouble remembering the sound of his voice. I have not heard it since the night we ended things, which feels like a lifetime ago.

'You still look like you're going to throw up,' Lucy says to me.

'That's because I might,' I say, as I wave to a group of former Walker colleagues sitting one section over, many of whom I chatted with last night at the hotel lobby bar. They'd all heard about me getting fired, of course, and assumed that it was because I wouldn't write negative things about our program and the ongoing investigation.

Do you think the rumors are true? I was asked repeatedly. *Was an official notice of inquiry coming? Would we ultimately be slapped with sanctions?*

I said I didn't know, that it often took years for these things to be resolved. I am still clinging to the hope that we'll ultimately be cleared, at least of the big charges, and that Coach will be vindicated. I no longer hold him to mythic standards, and instead see him as a flawed man and a fallible leader. But, in an unexpected way, this only makes my faith and trust in him stronger.

'Tell Shea we're going to win,' Lucy instructs my mother now, as if any of our predictions actually matter.

'We're going to win!' my mother says, clapping along with our cheerleaders. She, too, has blithely ignored everything that happened before Christmas, not once mentioning Coach despite ample opportunity in our shared hotel room. The implication is that she is doing *me* a favor, instead of the other way around, which only intensifies my bitterness.

Miller informs us all that even Vegas has changed its mind, the line moving to one point in our favor after two injuries hit the Crimson Tide. You never want anyone to get seriously hurt, but well-timed minor injuries are another story, and I'm not-so-secretly grateful for the sprained wrist and hip contusion within the Alabama ranks. I'm even more grateful that I'm not up in the press box right now, pretending that this is just another day at the office.

'Did you bet on the game?' my mom asks Miller.

With a mouthful of hot dog, Miller says, 'Hell, yeah, I bet on the game. Five hundred bucks. Easy money!'

My mother says, 'Is it too late for me?'

'Nope.' Miller pulls his phone out of his pocket and says, 'I can call my guy!'

I can't keep myself from shouting, 'Enough! Both of you! Would you please shut up?'

'Jeezy-peasy, sorry!' my mom says. 'Forgot who we're dealing with. Miss Doom and Gloom.'

I roll my eyes and stare straight ahead, bracing myself for a painful few hours of college football. And that's if the game goes well.

★   ★   ★

But the first half goes anything but well. We come out flat and totally unprepared for Alabama's physical play, quickly trailing by ten. Obviously it's not an insurmountable deficit, but a hard gap to close against a team as good as Bama. While my mother and Lucy resort to Walker chants and cheers, and Miller and Lawton opt for cursing a blue streak at the refs, I pray and barter and promise, appealing to the football gods – and even God Himself. *If we can pull off a comeback, I will settle for a dozen utterly forgettable, lackluster seasons. I'll even take a few losing seasons, including humiliating losses to the Longhorns. I will never text Coach again. I will take a job in New York, leave Texas, and never look back.*

None of our strategies work, and as the sun begins to set over the hills of Pasadena, we head to the locker room down 23–7. Halftime is unbearable with the endless chants of *Roll, Tide, Roll,* giddy performances by both marching bands, and more optimistic banter among my mom, Lucy, Lawton, and Miller. Meanwhile, I try to stay calm and put all my faith in Coach. I remind myself that he does his best work on the ropes, and is back there now, regrouping, reconfiguring, and reinvigorating our troops. Telling them that it's now or never.

And then the second and final half of the college football season begins under a vibrant teal sky that I can't resist pointing out to Lucy. 'I know!' she says, staring up at it, her hand over her heart and the gold pin we are all wearing in memory of her mother. 'I was just thinking the same thing. It's *amazing* . . . I've never seen a sky like this before.'

One beat later, we nail a thirty-one-yard pass to the Bama forty-nine-yard line.

'Yeah! Fuck, *yeah*! That's more like it!' Miller yells, pumping his fist in the air, then high-fiving Lawton.

I clap for the first time all night, as we go deep once again, covering another twenty-five yards to our backup wide receiver. Coach definitely has the Tide off balance with his hurry-up offense, and I watch with satisfaction as they begin shuffling personnel to try to contain the sudden explosion. On the next play, they focus on our deep threat, but we mix things up, rushing to the line and calling an audible before Everclear takes the ball sixteen yards on a bootleg.

I turn and shout, 'Your dad's a friggin' genius!' at Lucy and Lawton.

On second down, Everclear fakes to Rhodes and connects with our tight end in the back of the end zone. There it is. *Touchdown!* In one minute and twelve seconds of flawless execution, we are back in the hunt. As Mike Green, our kicker, nails the extra point, I crack a small smile and high-five Miller.

On the ensuing possession, we load the box and blitz, looking much more confident on defense, too. Alabama is still able to convert a couple first downs, but the drive proves ultimately unfruitful as they punt from midfield, pinning us deep in our own territory. Coach plays it more conservatively from there, and the remainder of the third quarter becomes a battle for field position with an exchange of field goals.

'All right! All right, boys!' Miller shouts as we begin the fourth quarter with the ball on our twelve. 'We'll take it!'

I stare at the scoreboard, even though I have the 26–17 score emblazoned in my mind, telling myself it is entirely possible to erase a nine-point deficit in the final quarter of play. Over the next six and half minutes, we capitalize on a fatigued Bama defense by relentlessly attacking the line of scrimmage, only to be stopped short on the five-yard line. But Green nails another field goal, closing the gap to six with eight minutes and change remaining.

Alabama does us no favors on their next series, grinding out yards and ticking off seconds in a sustained drive that forces us to burn two time-outs. We manage to shut them down on a fourth and long, but by now they are on our fifteen, in easy field goal range for any kicker, let alone one who has been perfect on the night.

I drop my head to my hands, a gesture that alarms Lucy. 'What?' she demands, jabbing me in the back. 'Why are you doing that?'

I break it down for her. 'They're going to make this kick. Then we'll be down nine – which is a two-possession game. And we only have one time-out left.'

'Which means?' Lucy asks.

'Which means we don't have fucking time to win,' Miller says, finally exasperated with her, too.

'But he has to make the field goal first, right?' she asks.

'He hasn't missed yet,' Lawton says, as the players line up on the field.

I drop my face to my hands again, unable to watch the inevitable, but a few seconds later, Miller grabs my arm and starts yelling, 'He hooked it! He hooked it! He fuckin' hooked it!'

I look up to see the Walker offense taking the field. 'He missed it?' I say, with a shocked sputter of laughter.

'He fuckin' missed it!' Miller crows.

'Choke city!' Lawton chimes in.

'*Now* can we win?' Lucy yells over the din. She definitely has a mental block when it comes to basic football math.

'Now we have a *shot*!' I tell her, then break it down for her, explaining that all we have to do is cover eighty-five yards in one hundred and ninety seconds. It is plenty of time; it is almost *too* much time, because the last thing we want is for Alabama to have the final possession.

I turn my gaze back to the field as Coach begins to drain the clock with running plays and short passes, working his way to midfield while using up a minute and forty seconds. After that, we break into our two-minute offense, starting with a very long pass that Rhodes can't quite reach. Incompletion. On second down, Coach goes deep again, but this time it works, putting us on the Alabama thirty-two.

Miller and I stare at each other, wide-eyed, as the chains are moved and Everclear rushes the team to the line. I hold my breath as he goes with a surprise draw play for a gain of eight. The clock is still ticking, and my heart is in my throat, as he snaps the ball, keeps it, and picks up three more yards for another first down.

The next few plays are a blur that I can only watch in replay on the jumbo screen. Everclear throws it away to avoid a sack . . . A completion to the eighteen . . . First down at the ten . . . A loss of two with the clock still running . . . A mad scramble for a miracle gain of seven, safely out of bounds at the five, with four seconds left on the clock.

Suddenly, it all comes down to this. Our dream season – the whole awful, amazing year – whittled down to four measly seconds. We are one play and five yards away from a national championship.

Then, something bizarre happens inside of me. Something I never expected to feel, not in a thousand Walker games. A quiet sense of perspective washes over me. I know that whatever euphoric or devastating result follows will be indelibly inscribed, replayed in perpetuity in the hearts and minds of every Walker-loving man, woman, and child. But I also realize that it doesn't *really* matter what happens on this last snap. I still want to win, madly and deeply, but it's not the most I've ever wanted anything. Not even close.

The next four seconds unfold in slow motion. Everclear rolls out . . . dodges a defender . . . aims and fires, off balance . . . the ball spirals high into the end zone . . . Rhodes leaps with outstretched arms . . . so does an Alabama safety . . . the ball is tipped, disappearing into a heap of teal and red jerseys . . . A collective hush falls over the stadium as men are peeled off the pile, one by one, until the last remains. It is Rhodes, clutching the ball, then holding it up with an outstretched hand as the ref raises his arms high over his head, signaling a touch-down. One beat later, the kick is good, and Walker wins. Walker *wins*! *Oh my God, Walker wins!*

The stadium erupts with fans shouting and hugging and dancing and crying and snapping photos all around me. But I hold perfectly still, in utter disbelief, doing my best to memorize the moment, keeping my eyes fixed on just one man down on the field, tracing his every move, as he's embraced by his players, then doused with the customary cooler of Gatorade.

More pandemonium ensues, the stadium filling with teal streamers and confetti and the light from thousands of flashes as Miller never stops shouting in my ear, his voice hoarse and crazed. Something finally breaks my trance, and I start to hug Lucy, but she is hugging Lawton, so I settle for Miller, who reciprocates with a wet kiss on my mouth. I give him a startled look, and he retorts, 'Don't worry. I'm going to kiss your mother like that, too!' Then he does. I laugh as Lawton jumps onto Miller's back, toppling both my mother and me. Then Lucy piles on top of us as if re-creating the final play of the game, shouting how much she loves me.

'I love you, too,' I say, laughing and crying at once, then struggling to get up so I can watch Coach some more. Seconds later, J.J. appears, out of breath, with VIP all-access passes, telling Lucy and Lawton to come with him. They need to get down to the field for the trophy ceremony.

'Not without Shea,' Lucy says.

'Well, come on then! All three of you!' he yells.

I shake my head in protest, but I can tell right away that I have no choice in the matter. So I allow myself to be whisked down the rows of metal stands, hugging friends, acquaintances, and strangers along the way. Right as I'm about to step onto the field, I see a little boy, about ten years old, sobbing, the red *A*'s painted onto his cheeks now streaked by tears. I pause, kneel, and tell him that it's going to be okay.

'You'll get us next year,' I say.

He is inconsolable, but, in a strange way, I am happy for him. One day, the memory of this night will return to him, making the taste of victory all the sweeter.

We keep walking, in circles, until we find Coach. He is drenched from sweat and Gatorade, but I can tell that he's also been crying, the whites of his eyes pink. I watch him hug Lucy and hear him say, 'This is for her, Luce.'

'I know, Daddy,' she says, now sobbing. 'She'd be so proud of you. *I'm* so proud of you.'

Then it's Lawton's turn, and he starts crying like a baby,

too, and I can't help remembering his face at his mother's funeral. 'I wish she were here,' he tells his only parent. 'So much.'

'She *is* here,' Coach says, comforting his son, as I realize how much true grief can resemble pure joy.

I start to tremble, just as I feel Lucy's hand on my back. She is pushing me toward her father, right into his arms. I give her a confused look, thinking surely she doesn't mean for me to hug him, but she nods and says, 'I was wrong, Shea. Go to him. You belong with him.'

I stare at her, processing what she's told me, realizing that I've never heard her say those words before: *I was wrong.*

'*Go,*' she says, smiling through tears, pushing me again.

So I step forward. Coach grins at me.

'Congratulations!' I shout over the mayhem. Then I close my eyes and collapse against his broad chest, feeling his heart beat through his wet shirt, inhaling his salty skin. 'You did it, Coach,' I say, more quietly, directly into his ear.

'Yes, *we* did it, girl,' he whispers back, squeezing me tighter. 'We *finally* did it.'

I pull back and look into his eyes, and can tell that Lucy has talked to him. That he knew before the game what she has only just said to me. *I was wrong.*

Then, confirming my wishful thinking, he leans in and brushes his lips against mine. It is the quickest kiss ever, but very much a real kiss, right there in front of Lucy and the entire world. It is the sweetest moment of my life, yet I know there will be even better ones to come. And soon.

'I gotta go,' he says, beaming at me. 'But I'll see you later tonight, okay?'

Light-headed with elation, I smile and nod, then watch as he slips back into a mob of teal. For a moment, he is gone, but he soon reappears, hoisted high on the shoulders of a lucky few players, representatives of everyone who has ever put on a Walker jersey, Miller and Ryan among them. I stare up at Coach, against the backdrop of a black-velvet sky filled with a million stars, a planetarium above the most famous stadium in college football, and marvel that we can be this happy from winning a game.

Then again, I know it's not the win itself, but everything that went into the victory. The effort. The passion. The faith. The things that Coach Clive Carr has taught me to believe in. The things that endure in defeat, and even death. The things that make football like life – and life like a game of football.

ACKNOWLEDGEMENTS

This is my seventh novel – and every one has begun the same way: with an unformed idea followed by exhaustive discussion with my mother, sister, and best friend. Thank you, Mary Ann Elgin, Sarah Giffin, and Nancy LeCroy Mohler, for all of your support with this one, from beginning to end.

I am so grateful to Stephen Lee, the most loyal publicist in the world. I can't imagine this publishing journey without your friendship. Thanks, too, for the never-ending supply of peanut M&M's.

To my editor, Jennifer Hershey: thank you for believing in me and elevating this story the way you did. Your notes nearly killed me, but you were right, and I'm so glad I trusted you.

Many thanks to my entire A-plus team at Random House, including Gina Centrello, Libby McGuire, Kim Hovey, Theresa Zoro, Susan Corcoran, Jennifer Garza, Sanyu Dillon, Debbie Aroff, Melissa Milsten, Cynthia Lasky, Scott Shannon, Loren Noveck, Susan Brown, Kate Childs, Joey McGarvey, Matt Schwartz, and Paolo Pepe.

Deep appreciation to my brilliant agent, Theresa Park, for the unwavering guidance, wisdom, and thoughtfulness – and to everyone at Park Literary, especially Emily Sweet, Abby Koons, and Pete Knapp. Thank you to Mollie Smith for being the consummate behind-the-scenes pro, and Rich Green for all your work to bring my stories to the big screen.

A few words to my friends at St. Martin's Press, especially Jennifer Enderlin, John Murphy, and the late, great Matthew Shear: you remain in my heart, and I will forever be thankful for our decade and six books together.

I'm enormously grateful to three college coaches who are also among my dearest friends: Dave Odom, Jim Boeheim, and Billy Schmidt. I have loved your passionate, colorful, quirky world since I was a little girl, and although I changed basketball to football for this story, much of the dynamic is the same. Thank you for your generous insight into Coach Clive Carr. He had some big shoes to fill (but Coach O: he *still* walks around barefoot in his house).

Thank you to Jennifer New, Allyson Wenig Jacoutot, Doug Elgin, Lisa Ponder, Kate McDavid, Julie Portera, Jim Konrad, Kevin Garnett, Ralph Sampson, McGraw Milhaven, J.R. Moehringer, Michelle Fuller, Cameron Sherrill, Vahe Gregorian, and Bill and Kristina Giffin, for fielding various queries about this book or its cover.

Thanks also to Coach June Jones, Brad Sutton, and Herman Hudson for allowing me to soak up the atmosphere at SMU's spring practice. (Go Ponies!)

On the home front, I am indebted to Kate Hardie and Martha Arias for their daily support and kindness – and to Jeff MacFarland for keeping me physically and mentally strong enough to meet every deadline along the way.

To all other family and friends: while you may not have contributed in tangible ways to this novel, I thank you for your love, moral support, and uplifting emojis.

And, finally, I thank Buddy Blaha for wearing so many hats, including football consultant, proofreader, short-order cook, workout partner, carpool driver, homework checker, Little League coach, chicken caretaker, friend, husband, and father to our three beautiful children.

Edward, George, and Harriet: I love the chaos around here, most of it happy, none of it dull. Life with you sparkles.

ABOUT THE AUTHOR

EMILY GIFFIN is a graduate of Wake Forest University and the University of Virginia School of Law. After practicing litigation at a Manhattan firm for several years, she moved to London to write full-time. The author of six *New York Times* bestselling novels, *Something Borrowed, Something Blue, Baby Proof, Love the One You're With, Heart of the Matter,* and *Where We Belong,* she currently lives in Atlanta with her husband and three young children.

www.EmilyGiffin.com
Facebook.com/EmilyGiffinFans
@emilygiffin